1730\1038

D0569682

49530

HOO

Hooker, John

Standing orders

	DATE	
JUN 1 7 1987		
JUN 2 2 1987		
AUG 3 1 1988		
DEC. 2 6 1988		
JAN 4 1993		
JUN 2 4 1996		
JUL 0 9 1998		

© THE BAKER & TAYLOR CO.

STANDING ORDERS

By the same author

JACOB'S SEASON
THE BUSH SOLDIERS

John Hooker

STANDING ORDERS

ELISABETH SIFTON BOOKS

VIKING

ELISABETH SIFTON BOOKS • VIKING
Viking Penguin Inc.
40 West 23rd Street,
New York, New York 10010, U.S.A.

First American Edition
Published in 1987

Copyright © John Hooker, 1986
All rights reserved

LIBRARY OF CONGRESS CATALOGING IN PUBLICATION DATA
Hooker, John, 1932–
Standing orders.
"Elisabeth Sifton books."
1. Korean War, 1950–1953—Fiction.   I. Title.
PR9619.H64S7   1987   823   86-40276
ISBN 0-670-81339-7

Printed in the United States of America by
The Book Press, Brattleboro, Vermont
Set in Sabon

49530

For Jock Brookfield

*and thanks to B.H.H., his colleagues
and the Korean War Veterans*

There are two sets of standing orders
in my life: God's and the Army's.
Both bolt me together.

An Army Officer

And forgive us our trespasses,
As we forgive them that trespass against us.

The Lord's Prayer

AUTHOR'S NOTE

Although the military units mentioned
in this book fought in the Korean War,
all the characters are fictitious and bear
no relation to any person, living or
dead.

CONTENTS

STANDING ORDERS

1

Penshurst

The rain swept from the south across the plain, and water ran between the ancient rocks and buttresses. The sky was dark and the wind blew through the black, sculpted pines, across the dank sedge, and bent and bowed the bracken, fern, and gorse. Moss and lichen grew on the English oaks, the stockyard rails and bluestone barns; irrigation ditches overflowed; seagulls and kittiwakes wheeled and flew; and prime Friesians and Herefords stood in the drowned paddocks where the fences staggered and frogs croaked in the roadside ditches. Many trees had fallen and the rabbits ran through the scattered black timber. Dead sheep lay in the shallow, wet gullies; the ornamental hedges of the May trees were mossy, black, and bare, and the rotten, fragile twigs crumbled at a touch. It was late August but there was no sign of life in those brittle branches. Thunder echoed in the black ranges that rose from the plain. Rain clouds streamed from the grey hump of Mount Napier. Even the rabbiters were not at work this day.

Once, in this land, the mountains touched the clouds and fires sprang from their summits. The earth quaked and heaved, great stones were hurled down the mountainsides, followed by boiling streams of lava, and then the rivers flowed swiftly from the high lands and debouched in the Southern Ocean. As the centuries passed, fires wore away the mountain cones; the country was shaped by subterranean heat and by the movement of wind and water until the now familiar hills and plains emerged. The vast rich plains left from the lava flows stretched southwest towards the sea, and in the west the antediluvian mountains stood.

The ancient black people departed, driven away by sealers and whalers, then by Scottish farmers from the Lowlands and blue-eyed Germans from Bohemia. Trees were felled, the timber was dragged away by bullock teams, grasses were sown, and as the Europeans worked from dawn to dark, they grew wealthy on the sales of wool and beef. Bluestone mansions were built; with dozens of rooms, servants, towers, wide verandas, buttresses, expensive antiques from England and Italy and cellars stacked with French wine. The Scottish families prospered and bred well, their domains increased, they invested prudently, they owned thoroughbred racing stables, the men joined the Melbourne Club and sent their sons and daughters to be educated at exclusive schools in England and on the Continent. This vast, fertile, well-watered land belonged to them and they would do with it what they liked. Piles of volcanic stone stood in every paddock, pulled from the earth by bullocks and tractors: this was a place of endless husbandry.

David Andersen coughed and lay in his bed. Through the French windows David could see the wet leaves spinning and whirling across the rose garden and the pine tree that had fallen into the wire netting of the weedy asphalt tennis court. Thistles and convolvulus grew around the posts, the umpire's chair had collapsed, and smoke was rising from the tin chimney of the new rabbiter's house beyond the barns and corrugated iron outbuildings. He was reading *Sanders of the River*.

David's house was built of bluestone; it was large and turreted, with a tiled reception hall, arrow-slit windows, ice-cream-cone roofs and many rooms. It was set back from the main road and was approached through a tunnel of hawthorns, oaks and pepperinas. His mother always said that the blossom in the spring reminded her of the countryside in Gloucestershire, but there was no sign of it yet this spring.

Sheep huddled under the European trees, and then rose

14

the great blocks of basalt carved by unknown stonemasons; arches, roofs pitched and valleyed, ironwork, rounded pedestals, and ornamental bearers supporting the conical roof shaped like a pagoda. David used to play there on the flagstones in the pale spring sunshine; but the veranda faced west and took the full brunt of the sun in the long hot summers.

Cut into a block at the right of the steps an inscription read:

KILLARA
THIS STONE WAS
LAID
BY J. CLARKE SENr.
A.D. 1868

John Clarke was born in Meenveragh, County Cork, in 1793 but his grand house had, after his death, been taken over by Protestants. *Killara* lay in the richest and best fattening run in the district.

This winter, it seemed it had been raining forever. Every morning when David woke, the wind was gusting against the dormer windows; the worn sashes rattled, leaves and twigs banged on the glass and he could see the rain clouds, grey and bunching and bundling over Mount Rouse where the fire-spotter lived in the hut on stilts. He wasn't there now; but he lived there all summer when the fires started and the northerlies blew and the weather was so hot that they moved to the front part of the house, where the vacant dusty rooms were cooler, as they faced south and looked out on to the tangled garden. There was once a gardener, David remembered, an old man with Aboriginal blood, bent and stooped like an old black tree; but he had gone. Had he died or had his grandfather let him go? David had not been told. There was once a tribe of blacks right here at *Killara* but they had long since vanished. Mr Dickson at Sunday school said they had been a poor, benighted people, like the Afghan hawker who had once come to the door selling cheap frocks and bolts of grimy calico. David's mother shouted and closed the door in his face. David had watched as the Afghan drove away, down the winding path between the hawthorn trees, with his bony hack and little covered cart. Who would want to be an Afghan or Aboriginal in Australia? What, David wondered, did fire-spotters do in the winter? Rabbiters worked all year round. What was the new one like? He must ask his father. He'd have to be good to beat old Ben Hopkins.

Six summers ago, just before David's birthday, when the hot northerly winds blew for five days, the fires burned right up to the house. Every man at *Killara* was out with sacks and shovels beating at the flames, but most of the trees in the front garden were lost, including his mother's favourite silver birch. The fire was half a mile wide, and in the dark afternoon when the sun had disappeared, they watched from the end of the veranda and saw it roaring and crackling through the gully at Mr Schultz's farm on the other side of the main road. Trees exploded, fireballs streaked through the black sky, and it seemed that the whole world was on fire. Mr Schultz lost his old weatherboard house, his shearing shed, over a thousand sheep and five prize Herefords and now lived by himself in an old plywood caravan and annexe; Mrs Schultz was taken away to a mental home in Melbourne and never came back. For weeks, the district smelled of burnt flesh, the country echoed with rifle and shotgun fire as they killed the burnt animals, and huge pits were dug in the rocky ground to bury them. It was like a battle ground and the men moved over the black land like soldiers.

*   *   *

Mr and Mrs Schultz had thick accents and sometimes were hard to understand: they were born in Germany and were locked up during the Great War. After the war wool and meat prices were low, the seasons were bad, and Mr Schultz wanted to go back to Saxony, but he couldn't because he didn't like Herr Hitler and the Nazis. Another German neighbour, Mr Ubergang, always helped Mr Schultz with the shearing because the Lutherans always stuck together. His father said you had to admire them for that, and that they were God-fearing hard-working people.

The big problem all the farmers faced was rabbits. There were millions of them and they ate the pasture, not the weeds. The rabbiters shot them, poisoned them, trapped them and used dogs and ferrets. But the plague had settled all over Australia. The rabbits ate the best grass, uprooted the potatoes and ringbarked the exotic trees. Poor children made extra money in the trapping season, gathering and skinning the carcasses and hanging the skins on frames. They poisoned them with strychnine and chopped-up carrots and sometimes killed 300 a night. Then, it seemed, the whole place smelt of death. His father said that the new rabbiter would keep the farm clean: he was the best shooter in the district.

David thought Australia hadn't been kind to the Schultzes: the war, fires, floods and 1000 acres of rock. Not all the farmers were wealthy, and once a month on Sunday evenings, his father took out the battered leather-bound ledger from the bureau and did the figures; he always said that if you looked after the pennies, the pounds would look after themselves.

The late winter rain fell and beat on the slate roof, the chimneys and the weathercocks. *It rained and it rained and it rained.* David remembered Christopher Robin, opened his scrapbook and looked at his new pictures cut from the *London Illustrated News*: HMS *Hood* and the *Prince of Wales* with their depth charges, anti-submarine paravanes and sixteen-inch guns. They were the pride of the British Navy and looked invincible. He thumbed through his collection: a cut-away diagram of the *Ark Royal*, military drawings of the Bren carrier, the Bofors gun and the Vickers and photographs of the new Spitfire and the Hurricane. His

BSA .22 stood in the corner next to his tennis racquet; then he swore as his lungs rattled: he hadn't been out shooting for three months.

*　　*　　*

Killara was built on a basalt shelf of Mount Rouse where the knucklebones of red rock lay half lost in the bracken where Merino sheep browsed and wandered. Mount Rouse was an extinct volcano, and David had been down into the crater with his mother and father and old Ben Hopkins before he died. One of the first things he would do when he got better would be to climb Mount Rouse and make himself known to the new fire-spotter. They were lonely men. He remembered how quiet and eerie it was in the crater, pitted with rabbit burrows. When he was little, he had poked around the rocks and looked for steam from the inferno beneath, but there was none. Old Ben Hopkins used to say that rabbits were the lowest form of animal life. When they buried him in the Penshurst cemetery on the hill, they placed his old Winchester rifle in the grave beside the coffin. Apart from his six dogs, the Winchester was the only thing he owned. He had spent his whole life shooting and trapping rabbits. Did the new rabbiter have a horse?

David's lungs rattled, he wheezed and coughed and spat into his handkerchief. This was his second month in bed, but Doctor Jamieson said the worst was over and that he could start getting up for an hour a day next week. An hour out of bed. He laughed and wondered if his legs would carry him. He moved them under the sheets and candlewick; he was sure they would. He coughed again as his mother came into his room with the linctus. The doctor said that sulpha drugs had saved his life, but she said it was God. David thought it was all a bugger. She poured out a tea-spoon of Buckley's mixture and went to put it to his lips.

"I'll do it, if you don't mind," David said.

"There's no need to snap." Elizabeth Andersen put the

spoon back into the coronation mug, went to the window and looked out at the rain.

"There's a manor house in *Country Life* like ours," David said. He searched through the stack of old magazines in the rack beside his bed and found the issue.

"Is there?" She came back from the window. "Let me see." He turned the pages of "Country Properties – Hampshire" and she looked at the familiar Victorian towers, turrets and landscaped gardens. It was a large three-storeyed Victorian mansion by the Test with a mile of river frontage. She remembered the trout rising at dusk, her father fishing and the bats flying from the chestnuts and alders, the terraced green lawns and the comfortable gloom of the river. "It's in a little better condition, I should think."

"Yes, but it's like ours."

"Yes, dear."

"How's my horse?" David asked.

"Your horse is fine. Tom fed him this morning."

"Did you check?"

"Yes, I checked. I asked your father and he's supposed to be careful about everything, isn't he?" She straightened the eiderdown and ran her fingers through her long blonde hair. "You should do some school work today. 'History for Schools' is on the wireless at half past eleven. You should listen."

"I shall." He wished he was out riding with his father and Tom Quicksilver despite the weather.

"You do that, I shall ask you." His mother looked again at the manor house in Hampshire, then went to the fireplace and turned the log with the poker. The fire smouldered and she tried again. "What's *Sanders of the River* like?"

"Haven't you read it?"

"No, it wasn't meant for girls."

"It's good, but I'm getting a bit tired of Edgar Wallace. I've read ten. In fact I'm getting a bit tired of everything."

"Patience, David. One doesn't get over pneumonia in a hurry."

"I'll say."

"I'm going to the village in a moment," Elizabeth said. "Do you want anything?"

"No."

"No, what?"

"No thanks, Mother."

She picked up the linctus and the mug. "I shan't be long."

"Did you hear the possums last night?" David said.

"No dear." Last night she had slept by herself in one of the many cold bedrooms, facing south. She had not slept at all, and had listened to the rain and wind.

"They were over my room, I could have fixed them."

"I'm sure you could." Elizabeth bent and kissed her son, listened to his chest, shut the door and went into the cold, dark Victorian hall. Her shoe-plates echoed on the mosaic tiles and she wondered what her husband would do next.

*　　*　　*

"Lovely weather for ducks," his grandfather said.

"You can say that again."

His grandfather pulled off his gumboots, threw them down on the hearth and came over to the bed. His socks smelt, his hair and beard were wet, and his face was blue with the cold. He looked at the picture he had given David for his last birthday: *The Maxim Gun Detachment, King's Royal Rifles, 1895.* "A fine body of men. I bet they put the wind up the Zulus."

"If you don't dry yourself, Grandad," David said, "you'll end up like me."

"Pneumonia's nothing to do with the weather, it's a germ and you were unlucky enough to get it."

"The doctor says I can get up for an hour a day next week," David said, "but I think I'll make it two."

"Too right, stand up for your rights, old son." His

grandfather fished in his cardigan pocket, filled his pipe with Erinmore and struck the match. "What's on the programme today?"

"You know the answer, Grandad, as well as I do. Reading and lying around. I've read thirty-six books since it started, I've been keeping a score."

"There's nothing wrong with reading, old son, providing it's the right stuff. Give us the list."

"You know, Grandad, Edgar Wallace, John Buchan, Rider Haggard, *The Last of the Mohicans, Two Years Before the Mast.*"

"Have you read *The Call of the Wild?*"

"Of course I have, I've read it twice."

"Hold your horses, David," Alistair Andersen said, "don't get snotty with me."

"Sorry, Grandad."

"What about *Riddle of the Sands?*"

"I've not heard of that."

"What, you haven't heard of it? Disgraceful. I'll get it for you tonight."

"What's it about?"

"Espionage and sailing, and the buggers shot the author."

"What buggers?"

"The English, who else?"

"My mother's English," David said.

"I know that. It's just that we Scots don't care for Sassenachs. It runs deep."

"But you like my mother?"

"Of course I do, she's one of the family." Alistair got out his pocket knife and reamed his pipe. "Who made this miserable fire? It wouldn't keep a bandicoot alive."

"I don't know."

"There's nothing worse than a mean fire, you either have a good one, or you don't." Alistair got up, reached into the bucket, arranged the kindling, watched the flames flicker and tossed on the logs.

"Where's Father?" David said.

"Out with the sheep. We're going to lose the lot if this weather doesn't let up. It's the lambing season."

The old man thought: good years, bad years. The bank and the stock and station agents would be on their backs soon, the thieving bastards. His back was sore and cold and he went back to the fire and tossed on another log. There was only one thing worse than a mean fire, and that was a mean dram. He thought of the Glenfiddich.

"I've been reading about King Edward and Mrs Simpson," David said.

"Have you? You're wasting your time, bloody drones and oppressors."

"Why did King Edward give up the throne?"

"Him? He wanted to marry the woman he loved." Alistair pulled out his silver watch: it was almost eleven.

"Why couldn't he keep the throne *and* marry the woman he loved?"

"She was married twice before, I believe." Alistair probed at his pipe. "Mrs Simpson is divorced and divorce is a crime."

"Do you think Mallory and Irvine climbed Everest?" David said.

"It's very likely, but we shall never know." His grandfather picked up the *Times Atlas*. "Have you been tracing any maps lately?"

"No, I've given that up."

Alistair flicked through the greaseproof paper. "You've not done Asia."

"There's no sea in Asia."

"Yes there is, there's the sea between China and Korea."

"Where's Korea?"

"I don't know. Somewhere between Japan and China."

"I might do it tomorrow," David said, "but it will be the last." He laughed. "What's the new rabbiter like?"

"I don't know, I've hardly seen him. He's moved into the cottage with all his dogs and kids."

"How many dogs?"

"I haven't counted them. Half a dozen I should think."

"What's his name?"

"Bert Lawless, and from the look of him, Lawless by name and lawless by nature. He's a mean-looking bugger."

"That's an odd name."

"It's Irish, I think. Wasn't there a Lawless at Eureka Stockade? I can't remember."

"Do you really think there is a Loch Ness monster?" David said.

"Probably. Scotland's a strange place. All kinds of mysterious things have happened there." He thought of the stories of battle, blood and death in the glens and of the Celtic tombstones in the Hebrides.

"Have you seen these pictures of the *Repulse?*"

"Sorry, old son, I haven't got time. I'll look at them tonight. When the fire gets low, give Gladys a shout."

* * *

Grandfather pulled on his leaky gumboots, stuffed his pipe and pouch into his waistcoat pocket and left the room. Like his daughter-in-law, he stood for a moment in the cold hall. The water dribbled down the stained cornices and architraves and lay in pools on the mosaic tiles. The walls were streaked with the seepage of a hundred winters and countless nocturnal animals. Alistair Andersen put on his wet oilskins, opened the heavy, varnished front door and stood on the vast front porch, where the chairs and tables were upturned and the vases of flowers had long since been blown away. The starlings' nests perched in the rotting beams under the cracked slate roof. The south wind blew into his face; he crouched and went down the massive bluestone steps into the wild and neglected garden. The wind tasted of salt and the seagulls were far from home.

* * *

David wondered about his father and mother and watched the sparks fly up the grate to disappear in the chimney. His room smelt of gum leaves and burnt eucalyptus. Something had gone wrong; maybe it was the winter, his pneumonia and the bad season. Last summer, and the one before that, David had slept outdoors on the veranda in a bed beneath the lounge window. Sleeping out was very enjoyable and healthy for growing boys. *Mens sana in corpore sano*, his father said. Every morning, shafts of sun shone through the pine trees and woke him at half past five; he pulled on his clothes and sandals and ran down the steps and across the back garden to the stables to feed his horse. Dew was on the grass, the air was as sharp as his grandfather's knife, the dogs were barking and rattling their chains and the roosters were crowing.

Then, it seemed that *Killara* was open day and night with Vauxhalls, Austins and Studebakers parked in the gravel driveway by Mr Clarke's foundation stone. There was running and laughter in the trees, gentle screaming, the dogs barking, tennis balls lost, a glass broken and Gladys with the broom on the asphalt, somebody on the pianola, Peter Dawson on the gramophone, his father's rich baritone voice, barley water, tinned peaches and fresh dairy cream. And at nights on the veranda, the red summer moon shone, the Milky Way glittered with the stars in their constellations. What were the rings around Saturn?

*   *   *

Those summers, his mother, father and grandfather played endless games of bridge, five hundred, euchre, mah-jongg and whist. "Two, no trump," was the call, "open misère", "seven hearts", "watch the play", "sorry, partner". The mah-jongg tiles clicked and David heard the laughter as he drifted off to sleep on his camp bed, swathed in his mosquito netting as the stars in the heavens shone, listening to *Lily of Laguna* and *The Old Missouri Waltz*. But some summers were very hot: the temperature climbed to over 100° and every morning his grandfather wound his silver watch, tapped the glass in the hall and looked at the thermometer. For weeks the glass was high and fires broke out in the northern ranges. At night, they watched them burning from the dining room windows and his father and grandfather would go outside and stand on the veranda and David knew that the fire-spotter on Mount Rouse was also looking at the fires through his glasses. The nights were hot and dusty and the ash blew and drifted into every room, on to the window sills, architraves and mosaic tiles. During the day, hot dry winds from the Mallee, in the north, swept in over Penshurst, whirling and eddying on everything. The Mallee dust blew high in the sky, across thousands of miles and fell on the streets and houses of the coastal cities. It even flew over the Tasman Sea and fell on New Zealand. When it blew over Penshurst, Gladys ran around shutting all the doors and windows and gathering the washing off the line.

"Quick, quick, Mrs Andersen," she shouted, "it's a Mallee dust storm!" Those hot summers dragged on and on; the grass dried, the irrigation ditches ran dry; trucks carted water; chickens fell in their tracks; prime bulls staggered; cattle bellowed and wandered across the plain; old people died of heat strokes and the soldier-settlers left their farms and came south to Hamilton and Penshurst on the steam train, their belongings in old attaché cases and canvas bags, their wives and dirty children in tow. They had no work and no place to go. Father said the soldier-settlers were like Bedouins, always getting drunk, gambling their wages and belonging to no one anywhere. *Killara*, with its towers, outbuildings and strong fences was safe, so it seemed. The summers were hot, but the drought always broke; eventually the rain fell, the ditches filled and the rivers started to flow again toward the sea.

*   *   *

During the hot months, his mother rarely went outside; she sat in the drawing room reading copies of *Country Life* which her mother sent her by sea mail. Her two sisters in Gloucestershire also wrote to her, although the mail was irregular. She would walk down the drive under the May trees to collect it, and often there was nothing; then the box would contain parcels of newspapers – the *Daily Mail*, the *Sunday Express*, *Sphere* and *Champion* and *Hotspur*. For some reason, his grandmother kept sending *Sunny Stories*. She must have forgotten he had grown up. Sometimes David thought that his mother would prefer to live in England rather than in Australia.

Last summer it didn't rain for four months, the grass died, turned yellow then grey. The dust blew day and night, the moon was blood red, the fires burned in the ranges, the farmers began to move stock as the tanks and dams dried up and every day sheep and cattle buckled to their knees. Thunder rolled across the plain, but no rain fell and it seemed the barometer was stuck on high. Every morning his grandfather banged the water tanks with his walking stick, the level got lower and lower and the rings echoed hollowly. Then the cattlemen in the north decided to move their herds south.

Late one hot morning the drovers came. At *Killara* they saw the plumes of dust rising from the plain, and as the drovers got closer, heard the whistles, yells, hoofbeats and the profanities. The cattle bellowed, the horses sneezed, the grey dust rose and the axles of the carts and buggies creaked. They watched from the veranda. That summer, drovers were moving cattle and sheep all over Australia.

"Those buggers won't come here," Grandfather said. "They won't come here."

"How many are there?" his father said as he leant on the veranda rail.

"A dozen men and a thousand head, I'd say," Grandfather said.

"We'll keep the devils out."

26

"Maybe, Richard, but you'll need your shotgun." David watched his father stalk off the porch toward the kitchen.

"Come on, old son," his grandfather said, "let's saddle up and watch the fun."

David caught his horse and they rode out the back gate, past the tennis court into the back paddock and out on the Dunkeld road. All the farmers had put up notices warning drovers to keep off their properties. By law the property-owners were entitled to know if stock was coming across their boundaries, but as Grandfather said, these hard-bitten men from the north couldn't give a damn about that. They would go anywhere and do anything. The bony Herefords snorted and stamped, barging and breaking the fences, all one thousand of them, driving up the Dunkeld road. The drovers shouted, kicked at their horses, shouted and blasphemed; the bulls tried to mount the cows and the smell of fresh shit was on the air. The drovers rode with an ugly gait, loose in the saddle and with long stirrups. Their half-starved dogs ran around the mob, the women and children hung from the buggies and carts, and the flies swarmed in the thick, dusty air.

A drover rode out front to meet David's father and his grandfather. The stockman was tall, rawboned and filthy, with an old slouch hat and cold sores on his lips and chin. He tossed his cigarette end into the mob and wiped his face. His horse was covered with foam and sweat and he leaned on the pommel. David thought he looked a tough customer.

"Good day," the drover said. The hobble chains and pots and pans rattled in the carts as they stopped on the stony road.

"Good morning," Richard Andersen said, his Winchester in his lap. The dust and the Scotch thistles blew and the sun beat on their backs.

"We're going through to Hamilton," the drover said.

"Not down this road," Richard Andersen said. He saw the cattle breaking down his fences.

"It's public."

"That may be, but your cattle are breaking down my

fences. They're on my property." Richard Andersen sat upright on his thoroughbred mare. Its flanks gleamed in the sun.

"Come on, Mister." The drover rolled another cigarette, the dogs barked and ran and the cattle snorted and bellowed.

"Where are you from?" Richard Andersen said. He rode his horse up close to the drover and David was proud of him.

"Balranald. There's a drought on, haven't you heard?"

"I don't care where there's a drought, you're not coming through here breaking my fences."

Alistair rode alongside and scratched his beard. He took off his hat and ran his hands through his grey hair.

The drover looked at the three of them and said: "I see you've brought your bodyguard, Mister." He laughed as his mate rode alongside. "This joker says we can't use this road, Fred. What do you reckon?"

"It's public."

David sat on his horse and wondered what his father would do.

"We ain't got no option, Mister," the drover said.

"You thieving buggers aren't coming through here busting our fences," Grandfather said. "Your cattle are diseased. Go some other bloody way."

The flies were thick on their backs now, the north wind blew and David's horse was nervous. He hoped his father wouldn't give in.

"You're all the same," his grandfather shouted, "you're all bloody rogues, you drive your mangy cattle over anyone's property. Get off our land."

"We ain't on your land, grandpa," the drover said, "we're on a public road and you ain't going to stop us." The women in the carts and buggies started shouting and screaming and the children cried in the dust. The dogs barked and ran around and more fences fell. A horsefly bit David's horse, it reared and whipped around.

28

"Listen, Mister," the drover said. "I'm sick of all this fucking around. We're coming through."

Richard Andersen put up his shotgun, but the other drover laughed and spat and wrenched the gun away. It dropped on the road.

"Yah, yah, yah," the drovers shouted. They cracked their whips and rode through the mob. "Yah, yah, come on, boys." The Herefords and Shorthorns bellowed and surged around David and his horse, his father on the chestnut and his grandfather on the big grey waler. The bulls and stringy calves ran, the children shouted, the harnesses creaked, the hot wind blew; his grandfather shouted, cursed and blasphemed, his father grabbed the reins of David's horse and the three of them struggled to one side as the cattle, drovers, carts, buggies and dogs trampled down the fences and swept up the Dunkeld road.

"Jesus bloody Christ," Grandfather shouted, "Jesus bloody Christ." He shook his fist. But David's father swung off his horse, picked up the Winchester and said nothing.

*　　*　　*

"Those buggers won't get a penny for those cattle," Grandfather said, "they're only worth blood and bone." The big red sun was going down behind the hills and the mosquitoes swarmed.

"These are bad times," Alistair said. "Hawkers, trappers, amateur horse-breakers, swaggies, men who can't saw a log in half. We've got the lot."

Richard Andersen considered his bluestone house, the barns and sheds, from his veranda. "They won't work," he grumbled, "that's the trouble." David sat on his stretcher bed and listened. His father had lost. "Vagrants, loafers and drunkards," his father said. "These relief schemes, the only relief I'd give them is a quick kick up the arse. We've made this outfit, the country is going to the dogs." He walked over to the veranda rail. "Thieves and chicken-stealers, there's no moral fibre."

The night was hot, the distant fires burned in the ranges, the dishes clattered in the kitchen, his grandfather and father talked, his mother played a sad tune on the piano in the drawing room and David pulled the mosquito nets around him and went to sleep.

*   *   *

It seemed that there was always someone at the back door. Men were looking for work all over the country: shearers, fencers, splitters, sawyers, trappers and pale-faced men from the city who could do no farm work at all. David remembered one man who had been given the job of digging holes for fence posts; but the ground at Penshurst was hard and rocky, and at the end of the day the man's hands were raw and bloody and he was paid off. He said his wife and children were living in a tent made of hessian bags in the town domain. The Memorial Gardens had become a shanty town of old tents and lean-tos made of kerosene tins, and some men even slept out on the ground. Starving dogs and snotty-nosed children ran through the rubbish dumps and bottle heaps. His father said the place was a damned disgrace and that they should all be cleared out, but more men arrived every day and there was nowhere for them to go.

Swaggies and tramps were everywhere and it seemed they all came through Penshurst on their way southwest. What did they do when they reached the sea? A few of them got odd jobs with the Shire Council, working on the roads or trapping rabbits. Some of them worked on government relief schemes, but most filled in their days on sustenance and got food relief from the Police Station. There were appeals for old boots and blankets, charity concerts in the Shire Hall and an empty shop was turned into a soup kitchen. Strange men stole around in the night and, after several scares, David went back to sleeping inside. Then, it seemed, winter came on and people stopped coming to *Killara*: David caught pneumonia, there was no more laughing and shouting; the tennis parties stopped and no one played the pianola any more.

David lay in his bed, stretched his legs and wriggled his toes. He picked up *The Riddle of the Sands*, but let it fall to the floor. Drops of rain fizzled in the fireplace, the sheets were twisted and he felt uncomfortable. He had nothing to do and thought of the summer. Things had been good then, but his father hadn't kept out the invaders.

2

Rose Braddon

Richard Andersen stood amongst the rocks and cursed the wind and rain. So far he had found seven sheep down. That made forty-five so far this week. There was nothing he could do but leave the bodies for the crows. It offended him to leave dead animals lying on the property. It was an outward and visible sign of bad management. His torn oilskins flapped and the wind blew into his face as he turned toward the south. He mounted and the mare walked down the gully, picking her way between the stones and outcrops of rock. At least the Scotch thistles weren't blowing. Andersen squinted: it was hard to tell the sheep from the boulders. The rain drummed on his back and the dog ran along the fence line and over the crumbling stone walls. Andersen knew every stick and stone on the property; it was his thirty-ninth year at *Killara*, save the one he had been at the war. He wondered what David was doing this morning. The men o' war, the guns, the aircraft and books he had never read: the routine of sickness, rain and his father smelling of whisky as he read *Barrack Room Ballads* to his grandson. Richard thought as the rain trickled down his back: *You're a better man than I am, Gunga Din.*

Where was the new man, Lawless? For Christ's sake, if he could work in weather like this, so could the rabbiter. Maybe he was somewhere else; he would give him the benefit of the doubt this first time, but if he was no good, he would sack him. There were plenty of men looking for work. Andersen rode along the front fence, looked across the road to the Schultzes' place and saw the Vauxhall going down the drive through the May trees. It was Elizabeth. Where was she going and what was she going to do? Would she leave him? That was impossible. She loved David, and what would people say? What were they saying now? He sat on his horse like a statue, the water pouring down the brim of his hat and down his shoulders. He whistled the dog and rode east, to find more dead sheep, no doubt. Gulls from the sea, magpies and swallows flew from the pines, clouds streaked and streamed from Mount Napier and rain swept over the vast, grey plain. Richard Andersen saw none of this: he had been at *Killara* for thirty-nine years, and by Christ, he would still make it pay.

Tom Quicksilver was coming down the rise on his black gelding. He touched his hat to Richard Andersen and they sheltered under a pine tree by a stack of old fencing posts and coils of barbed wire. It was like a dug-out in France.

"I seen four," Tom Quicksilver said. "What about you, Mr Andersen?"

"Seven."

"Eleven ain't too bad, considering."

"They're all valuable."

"Yeah."

But as he stood in the darkness of the pines by the piles of wire, Andersen knew Tom didn't care much: it wasn't his property. What would the boy ever know about property? Tom was one of thirteen children and could barely read or write. He watched the lad roll a cigarette and flick the match away into the rocks. Tom's father, once a sharefarmer, was now a drunkard, living on sustenance and spending his waking hours in the Penshurst Hotel. Dan Quicksilver had fought at Messines and had been drinking on it ever since. The country was full of improvident Irish rabble. Lawless was no doubt the same. Tom smoked his cigarette and looked at Richard Andersen with his blank, blue eyes as the heavy drops fell from the branches. The dog ran back from the front fence line and they sat on their horses under the pine trees. Richard Andersen thought of

33

Elizabeth and David, and his father. What should he do? *Thou shalt not commit adultery.*

Andersen had once thought of teaching Tom Quicksilver to read and write properly, but what was the point? The boy was ineducable. Sooner or later, he would have to go and join his elder brothers and his father in the public bar of the Penshurst Hotel. Why was there no decent help these days? Where were the men and lads who would work hard and save to buy their own property? There was nobody who could apply himself. Application had built Australia. He looked at his land: it had once been a wilderness. The Lutherans could teach them all a thing or two. He must go and see Emil Schultz tomorrow. For the first time in many years, Andersen wanted an early drink, something stiff to keep the cold away. His father would have the Glenfiddich.

"Right, Tom," Richard Andersen said, "there's no point in freezing to death here. We'll go back to the house and get a hot drink."

"All right, Mr Andersen." The dirty, unshaven, fair-haired boy tossed the butt of his cigarette into the sodden pine-needles and spat on the stony ground. He turned his lean and bony black horse around and said: "Eleven ain't too bad, considering."

Andersen foraged around under the pine trees, thought of the dead sheep, his sick son and Elizabeth and saw that the fetlocks of Tom's horse were badly cut by the blackberry and barbed wire. The lad couldn't even look after his animal. He, too, turned his mare and said:

"Have you seen Mr Lawless?"

"Nah." Tom Quicksilver spat again. "Not a sight."

"If we can work in this, why can't he?"

There was no reply and they rode back through the rocks and piles of stone, past broken fences and collapsing timber sheds toward the house.

*   *   *

The three men, Richard Andersen, his father and Tom Quicksilver, sat in the cold kitchen as their boots steamed by the coal range. The fly door banged in the wind and the smoke and ash billowed from the fireplace. Socks, long-johns, collarless shirts and overalls lay draped over the fireguard. The kitchen smelt of bacon fat, onions, soup and old potatoes. Outside in the yard, the dogs were barking on their chains. The rain came down the chimney and fizzled on the hot plates of the stove.

"Whose dogs are those?" Richard Andersen asked. "Whose dogs are those?"

"They belong to Mr Lawless, I reckon," Tom Quicksilver said. He blew out the match and tossed it into the cast-iron bucket.

"Why can't he quiet them?" Andersen said.

"Aw, a new place." Tom poured the strong, sweet tea into the enamel mugs and they dunked their biscuits.

"Holy Jesus Christ," Alistair Andersen said as he scratched his beard and warmed his hands before the stove, "will it never let up?" The old bentwood chair creaked as he leaned and delved into the biscuit tin. "I missed you, Richard. How many this morning?"

"Eleven," Andersen said. "I found seven and Tom found four."

"That's not too bad."

"Every sheep we lose is bad." Richard looked at his father. "It's all profit."

Tom picked his nose and said: "How's the boy, Mr Andersen?"

"The doctor says he can get up for an hour a day next week."

"It's been a long time, he's been crook for ages."

"It's not been that long," Richard Andersen said. "He's getting over it, he's a strong lad." Outside in the rain, the dogs barked and pulled at their chains. Richard watched his father drink his tea at one gulp and sit at the stove with his hands on the knees of his moleskin trousers, sodden and grass-stained.

"I've forgotten something," his father said. "I won't be a moment." He went upstairs to his room to have a whisky. Tom Quicksilver sat close to the fire and rolled another cigarette, tossing the fine strands of spare tobacco into the grate. He was preparing to settle in for the morning.

"Right, Tom," Richard Andersen said, "I want you to go over to the back paddock to see how many more we've lost." He would make the young bastard work.

"All right, Mr Andersen."

The boy rose slowly, tossed his cigarette into the fireplace and pulled on his oilskins. "I'll see you tonight, then."

"You do that." He, too, got up from the fire and went to see David.

David put down his book and sat up straight as his father came into the room.

"And how are you this morning?" his father said.

"I'm all right. What's it like outside?"

"Dreadful, worse than yesterday."

"When are we going to get the tennis court mended?"

"We can't play tennis in this weather."

"It'll be summer again one day." David thought of the parties and the fun.

"The tennis court's the last on the list. This is a bad season, David." Richard Andersen looked at his son, the muddled blankets, the books and the boy's papers littered on the floor, the pitcher of water and the bottle of linctus. He didn't want to stay long: sickness depressed him. Sickness and poverty. The water seeped through the dormer windows and ran down the walls. He thought of the men hanging around the Shire Hall, the women with their children scavenging through the rubbish dump: he would never be like that.

"How's Mother?" David said.

"Mother? She's fine, it's you we're worrying about."

"I'm fine. She looks sad."

"Does she? I hadn't noticed. It's the weather, I expect. It's getting us all down."

36

"Not Grandfather."

Richard laughed. "Not him."

"What's Mr Lawless like? He'll have to be good to beat old Ben Hopkins."

"We'll see. They say he's one of the best rabbiters in the district." As long as the man was working: that was all he wanted. "I hope you're doing your school work," he said. He picked up the copy of *Country Life*. "You shouldn't be reading this, you should be studying."

David was going to show his father the picture of the English country mansion, but decided not. "I'm trying to, it's a bit hard in bed."

"Well, keep at it. You've lost two months. What are you doing now?"

David thought. "The Wars of the Roses."

"The Wars of the Roses. Who were the sides?"

"The House of Lancaster and . . . I forget."

"Look it up then, use the encyclopedias you've been given. You'll be at boarding school next year and the going will be tough."

"Yes, Father." David picked up the *Weekly Times*. "There's a letter here by a lady who wants to exchange duck eggs for used clothes. She must be poor."

"I expect she is." The wife of a soldier-settler, a no-hoper. "If I don't get back to work, we'll be in the same situation." Richard got up from the chair, went to kiss his son, but decided not. "Keep working, read the School Paper, not penny-dreadfuls and *Country Life*. I'll see you this evening." He gathered up his oilskins and made for the door.

"When will Mother be back?"

"She'll be back anytime, I expect. I'll see you this evening. Just keep at it."

Richard Andersen closed the door, went down the stairs, and like his father stood for a moment in the hall before going out into the rain.

David lay in bed, heard his father's boots creaking on the stairs and wondered what to do. There wasn't much.

37

He looked once more at the picture of the King's Rifles. What would it be like to fire a Maxim gun?

*   *   *

Elizabeth Andersen didn't shop much in Penshurst. She thought nothing was worth buying there. The town was mean and small: the bluestone Shire Hall, three churches, half a dozen shops and the Penshurst Hotel on the corner of the cross roads by the war memorial. She had never been inside and she wondered what the men did. They drank beer, she supposed, but what did they talk about? Sometimes they sat outside on the front porch, beer glasses in their hands, and watched the people go by. Once, when it was raining, she had walked past the door under the veranda. The door was open and she smelt sweat, beer and cigarettes and saw the men at the bar; they looked big and hunched, standing in the shadows. Was there a barmaid or a barman? She didn't know. If there was a barmaid, how did she cope with the men? What did she do when they swore and got drunk? What happened when they got violent? There were stories of unemployed men, drovers and trappers. Who lived upstairs in those rooms where the curtains were tied in knots? This was the town she had come to seventeen years ago and it was an unattractive place.

Some of the shops were failures, their window displays faded and flyblown, holes gaping in the fly doors. The lemonade signs were peeling, ginger cats slept in the windows and dogs slept in the dirt under the pepper trees. At the back of the small cottages, old American cars lay in the long grass, pigs rooted in the rubble, chickens picked and poked, horses stood by discarded wagonettes, and beyond, the vast plain of the Western District stretched north and south forever. There was no getting out, no place to go. But she knew that behind the rows of pines, oaks and ornamental hedges lay the mansions and landscaped gardens of the squatters, people who were seen only in the Members' Enclosure at the races or in their Buicks or French Panhards on the Hamilton Road. She had heard they spoke French at the dinner table, that their children went to preparatory schools, held magnificent balls and spent their holidays in Singapore and Ceylon. They sailed away on steamships, bought expensive furniture from Sotheby's and bespoke suits from Harrods. Those people had chamber-maids, servants and grooms. She and David had often glimpsed the mansions of the old families from the main road: they had seen the towers and minarets through the aspens and the pines. She wondered what they were like inside. They were like *Killara*, but the tiles weren't cracked, possums didn't live in the ceilings, there were no rats in the wainscot and the walls were not stained.

Before he was ill, she took David to church every Sunday. Elizabeth always took Holy Communion at eight o'clock and then went with David to Matins at eleven. She thought that St James's Church was small and mean, nothing like the churches in Gloucestershire, let alone the cathedral; but God was where the sacraments were. The vicar was Low Church and common, and the services not to her taste. She missed the red-cassocked choirboys, their young voices soaring to the vaulted rafters of the Lady Chapel; but there was nothing she could do about it. David would be confirmed next year and she hoped she would be there to see it. He already knew the Confession. *Almighty and most merciful Father; we have erred and strayed from Thy ways like lost sheep.*

*   *   *

Elizabeth Andersen stopped the car, struggled into her mackintosh and stood in the rain. She looked back at the timber houses, the tin chimneys and the washing dripping on the clothes lines. Mount Napier was lost in the mist. She climbed a small rise and stood under a pine tree. She hated this country and she hated the men in it. It was the cruellest place she had ever been in. The men who farmed this country had no sense of kinship with it, no real sense of belonging. To them, it was a breeding and killing ground. She had never felt so alone; all she had now was David. What should she do about Richard? Suffer in silence? She had written to her mother, but it would be weeks before she replied. The overseas mails often took two months, and what would her mother say? Would she tell her father and sisters? She had asked her not to. Who knew in Penshurst? Had the woman told anybody? She probably had. Should she see the woman? That was unthinkable. One thing was certain: she would no longer grant any favours to Richard whether the house knew or not. And what about Richard's father? What did he know? That drunken old man knew everything. And he was a bad influence on David, but she couldn't see what she could do. She was powerless. She would go to Holy Communion in Hamilton next Sunday and pray there. Her faith would see her through, she was sure of that. She took a step or two, saw a snake moving through the rocks and ran back to the car. She had forgotten to take her killing stick. David's tracing paper lay on the passenger seat; she had bought him some crayons, too. One day she would take him home; she would show him the cloisters at Bath, they would listen to the choir in the Abbey and watch the Morris dancers.

When she got back to *Killara*, Elizabeth stopped at the gate. The pines dripped and hundreds of rabbit skins hung, stretched on the frame by the stone pillars. The collector hadn't come and they were putrid. Her gorge rose, she held her breath and opened the lid of the mail box. There were several bills from the stock and station agents, but no mail from home. Then she saw a strange man coming across the home paddock through the pine trees, his dogs running before him, his gun on his shoulder and traps in his haversack. He was a rabbiter, another killer. The rain dripped off the man's greasy hat and she saw he was wearing a sheath knife under his belt and braces. His waistcoat was patched and open and black hair showed above the top of his collarless shirt. The rabbiter's dogs ran up, prowled around and growled at Elizabeth's brogues, their tongues lolling and their breath steaming in the winter air. She was afraid, but it was too late to get the stick. The man stood before her.

"What are you doing on my property?" Elizabeth said. "You can be fined for trespassing."

The man screwed up his eyes and the dogs growled and ran around. "I'm the new rabbiter, lady."

"What's your name?"

"Lawless."

"Good morning, Mr Lawless."

The man touched the brim of his hat, coughed once, whistled the dogs and moved on. Elizabeth watched him walk up the stony track, past the bare and dripping oaks, through the wild jonquils and disappear.

*　　*　　*

Richard Andersen opened the lid of the mahogany bureau and took out the ledger. The rain had eased, but the wind still blew and the room was cold. The wood was wet and the fire smoked and steamed. Elizabeth threw down her knitting and picked up *Home Beautiful*. The magazine rack was full and the papers spilled to the floor. She watched her husband and then the fire. A beetle crawled along a log, trying to avoid the flames. The wind gusted and the smoke billowed through the fireguard. The Persian carpet was pitted with ash and burns from sparks when the wood was dry, and the cat washed itself. Outside in the hall, she heard the dog scratching and padding up and down. Why didn't he go upstairs and sit with David? The beetle had disappeared. Richard turned the pages and looked at the columns of past debits and credits in his father's, and now, his own small handwriting. Three bad winters, one hot summer and another bad winter; lambing losses and last October's shearers' strike, the bastards. He wanted a drink, but decided not. A whisky perhaps? His father would be at the bottle as he listened to the wireless. The drawing room was quiet and he looked at Elizabeth reading her magazines. She knew. How had she found out? God knows. There was nothing to be done now: he would see it out. Time healed all wounds. He would slip away and see Rose tomorrow night; they had to end it now. He rose and got the bottle.

Richard Andersen owed Dalgetty's £556.7s 4d. for fertilizer, wire, sheep dip, petrol and tractor parts. The overdraft was £674. Unlike the soldier-settlers, they would not go bankrupt, but there seemed no end to it. He would never forget this season. He looked again at Elizabeth as she sat by the fire; the ash gusted and settled on the antique furniture and the newspapers rustled.

"You're not seeing her tonight, Richard?" Elizabeth said. The silence was bitter and he did not reply. "You're not seeing her?" she said. Again, there was no reply. "You're no doubt the talk of the town," she said. Again, there was no reply. "You must be the talk of the town." She laughed. "The talk of the town, or should I say township, settlement?" She watched her husband crouched over the ledger and hated him. "Does your father know? Of course he does, he knows everything."

Richard Andersen sat at the bureau, his broad shoulders hunched, his mouth dry, and drank the whisky. He looked at the clock over the mantelpiece: it was almost half past ten. When would she go to bed and leave him? The whisky warmed his innards and he looked at the rows of figures.

"There'll be no more favours," his wife said. "No more."

"I don't want your damned favours," he said. "I'm doing the books."

"There'll be no more favours," she said. She rose, gathered up her English newspapers, her knitting and left the room.

Her strange room was cold and the light bad. She pulled

on her nightdress and pulled the sheets and blankets around her. The possums scuttled in the roof and somewhere outside dogs barked and howled. She felt her body and shivered. What would she do? She thought about her mother and father. They had never liked him and had warned her against the handsome young Australian. Her father said he'd seen no action and couldn't be classed as a soldier. He'd not been blooded, her father said, not been blooded. At the time, she'd seen the men who had and was thankful. Those were the men who drank on the veranda of the Penshurst Hotel, with limbs missing, like Tom Quicksilver's father. She picked up *The Times* and turned to "London Properties". She had never liked London, it was smelly and noisy, but she had a great aunt living in S.W.1. Was it Vincent Street or Vincent Square? She remembered the gas lamps, the clatter of the horseshoes on the flagstones, the small back gardens, the fog and the smell of dung. She had been there with her mother and father during the summer for the Horse Guard's parade and the weather was hot and gritty. The small boys of Westminster School were playing cricket on the square and big marquees and rows of deckchairs stood on the grass. Her great aunt was very old, smelt of lavender and made her drink warm barley water in the stuffy front room full of books and bric-à-brac. In the evening, Mother and Father went to Shaftesbury Avenue to see *The Pirates of Penzance* and she was left alone with this strange old woman, her two ginger cats, the rows of old books and the sound of cabs and motor buses from Horseferry Road. She was given cold rice pudding and Horlicks for tea. She remembered a big cavalry sword by the fireplace and a Silver Jubilee photograph of Queen Victoria and the Royal Family on the wall, next to Lord Kitchener and Earl Haig. Her aunt showed her some medals from the Siege of Omdurman and a Chinese crossbow taken at the Boxer Rebellion. She belonged to a military family: her husband had been killed in the Boer War and her son had fallen at Mons. Her aunt was religious and believed that the angel had appeared at the battle there. She was quite small, but Elizabeth was frightened of her and couldn't finish her rice pudding. There was too much nutmeg and the Horlicks had a skin on top. Then after tea, her aunt read her poetry as the evening grew dark and the gas lamps were lit:

> Sceptre and Crown
> Must tumble down,
> And in the dust be laid
> With the poor, crooked scythe and spade.

Elizabeth put down her newspapers and drew the blankets around her head. She knew the woman and could sue for divorce, but that would mean evidence, a court case, disgrace for the family: that she could not cope with. All she could hope for was that the woman would go away. She was certain of one thing: she would never forgive her husband.

*   *   *

They stood apart in the small room and the rain dribbled down the plaster walls.

"Elizabeth's found out," Richard said.

"Oh my God. How?"

"I don't know, I didn't ask."

"What did she say?" She faced him, shaking and running her fingers through her hair.

"She said, 'You're not seeing her tonight?'"

"What did you say? Did you deny it? What did you do?"

"I didn't say anything."

"You didn't say anything?"

"I was doing the books."

"What books?"

"For God's sake, the accounts."

"Surely you said something."

"Maybe I said, 'Don't be silly' or something like that. But

she knows." He remembered the bitterness in Elizabeth's voice.

"Did she mention me by name?"

"No, but she knows who you are." He looked at her; he wanted her not to exist. Had he ever loved her? It was hard to believe he had.

"I wonder how she found out."

"God knows, it's not hard in a place like this. There's nothing to do. People talk, they see things."

"Does David know?"

"Of course not, he's too young, unless his mother's told him. But she wouldn't do that." He thought of David's questions about the tennis court and the parties.

"Is he back at school next term?"

"Yes. The doctor says he's doing well. He's up for an hour a day now."

"I wonder if anybody on the School Committee knows." She had always known it would come to this. It seemed that this kind of loving was impossible. She was cold and fearful now. "If they do, it means I'll have to go away."

"I'm afraid it does."

"Will you come with me?"

"Come with you? That's quite impossible." He turned away from her and looked out of the window. The whole country was black with the night and the rain.

"You've always said you loved me." She was crying now, sniffing and using her handkerchief.

"How can I go away with you?" he said. "I've got the property, a wife and a son. Where would we go?"

"If the School Committee know, I'll lose my job."

"They mightn't know. Can't you arrange a transfer?"

She blew her nose and wiped her eyes. "I don't know, it all takes time."

"Can't you plead ill-health?" She was standing next to him and he felt her cold hand clutching his. She smelt of old talcum powder. He sweated and wished she would go away; her thin fingers gripped and her hair touched his face.

"You've got to leave," he said, "you've got to leave."

"Where will I go?"

"Melbourne, Sydney."

"Sydney? I can't get a job there, it's in New South Wales."

"I know that, but you can't stay here, can you?" He pulled his hand away and walked around her small room. He wondered why on earth he'd done it: having an affair with David's school teacher, making love in this miserable little house. Her clothes were strewn on the threadbare sofa and her evening meal was half-eaten. He looked at a grey woollen dress and her chenille dressing gown. The kettle steamed and he took it off the coal range. The handle was hot and he cursed. He cursed her and he cursed himself. The rain kept falling on the iron roof and he listened to her crying. Her hair hung down and he hated her now.

"Richard, you're abandoning me."

"I'm not abandoning you. The whole thing's impossible. You can't stay here, for both our sakes."

"Will your wife tell anybody?"

"I shouldn't think so, not here. She's got no close friends. She might tell her mother, she's always writing to her. She might tell the vicar."

"The vicar?"

"You know, for God's sake, she's religious. She doesn't like the vicar, he's not high church enough, not of her class." He thought of her complaints about St James's, the building, the organ and the services. "But she might: a sort of confession."

She laughed through her tears. "If anyone should confess, Richard, it's us. We've committed the crime."

"It's hardly a crime, it's an unfortunate mess."

"Our love a mess? It's a crime, adultery. I could go to gaol." She felt herself condemned now.

"Don't shout, for Christ's sake." He wondered what she would do and was scared. Jesus, he thought, bloody

46

hysterical women: her and his wife. He wanted to see his father.

"Have you got any money?"

"Of course not, you know that."

"I could help." He thought of the overdraft, the unpaid bills, the dead stock and the rabbits eating the pasture.

"You mean you'll pay me to go away, pay me like some street woman, pay me for services rendered?"

"It's not like that at all. I just want to help."

"The only way you can help is to stand by me. You've always said that you loved me, that your wife didn't love you and that you wanted me."

Richard Andersen didn't want her now: he wished she were dead. "I still want you, but I can't have you."

"You don't want me at all, you just want to get rid of me." She turned upon him. "You're scared I'll ruin you, aren't you? What if *I* told people?"

"Who would you tell?" He felt cold and stood in front of the stove.

"I'm a Catholic."

"Lapsed."

"Once a Catholic, always a Catholic. I could go to the priest and confess."

"Priests don't tell anybody."

"How can you be sure? *They know.* Anyway, I know lots of people. I'd tell them that I'd been sleeping with Richard Andersen, upright grazier of the district and that he tried to pay me to go away."

He stepped toward her and raised his hand. "You bitch," he said, "you bitch."

"I was once your love." She blew her nose. "But now I'm a bitch."

"I didn't mean that." He tried to touch her. "It would ruin David."

"David? You don't care about David, all you care about is yourself and your property. All you care about is your reputation, joining the Melbourne Club. Respectable graz-

47

ier sleeps with local school teacher, his son's school teacher, and abandons her. Say I was pregnant, what would you do then?"

"You can't be."

"Why not? I might be, I'm due in two weeks and if that doesn't happen . . ."

"You can't be pregnant."

"I probably am, you've used me enough."

"Used you?"

"Slept with me."

"You wanted it, you enjoyed it."

"Did I? How do you know I did? I was just a bloody fool."

She sat down among her clothes and stared at him, her thin shoulders hunched, her stockings wrinkled, and brushed her hair away from her face. "If I'm a bitch, Richard Andersen, you're a bastard. I'll go when I want to. After all I've given you, you can't just chuck me out."

He wanted to get away. He looked at his watch. "I've got to go."

"All right, you go. Do you know who I feel sorry for? Your wife, married to a man like you. And your son. What a father he's got. You're gutless, a gutless wonder." He couldn't stay any longer, made for the door, and stepped out into the night and pouring rain.

Richard Andersen sat in the car and found his hands were trembling. He looked at the school house through the rain and saw the lights in the windows. She was moving around behind the blinds. He looked at his watch again: it was almost ten o'clock. Where could he say he'd been? It didn't seem to matter any more. He started the Vauxhall, shoved it into gear and drove down the narrow, rutted track. The windscreen wipers wouldn't work and he could hardly see a thing. A tree loomed through the rain, he cursed, swerved and stopped. He lit a cigarette and watched the fog cloud the windows. What should he do? And what would she do? He thought he saw a light moving through

48

the trees. Who would be out on a night like this? Then it was gone. Was he being watched? That was impossible. I'll go when I want to, she had said. What if she was pregnant? Jesus Christ, what a bloody mess. Should he tell his father? He'd had a few women in his day. He had to tell somebody. A trouble shared was a trouble halved. He'd have to wait. Maybe she'd see reason. There was nothing else he could do. He wished she were dead. He backed the car carefully on to the track and drove slowly home.

In the rain he saw the stone towers of *Killara*, the mail box and the rabbit skins hanging from the wire. He turned in and drove up the gravel driveway beneath the dripping hawthorn trees with the car windows fogged. How many sheep would be dead in the morning?

"You bitch," he said, "I hate you."

His father was sitting at the kitchen table; the whisky bottle was open. Richard slung his wet oilskins on the back of the chair and slumped down.

"Do you want a drink?" Alistair said. He looked at his son as he sat staring at the fireplace.

"Thanks."

"What's it like outside?" He slid the glass across the table.

"Wet."

The chairs creaked as they drank their whisky.

"I'm in trouble," Richard said.

"What kind of trouble?"

"A woman."

His father straightened up. "A woman? What do you mean, a woman?"

"I'm involved with a woman."

"Does Elizabeth know?"

"Yes."

"That calls for another dram." His father pulled the cork from the bottle.

"Your record wasn't exactly spotless, from what I've heard." Richard looked at his father.

Alistair smiled. "True, but I didn't take myself as seriously as you."

"Meaning what?"

"I wasn't concerned with my status."

"I'm not concerned with my status."

"Well, maybe. Who's the woman?"

"Rose Braddon."

"David's school teacher?"

"Yes."

"Jesus Christ." Alistair laughed. "That's close to home. A grave error, my son. How did Elizabeth find out?"

"I don't know, she must have seen me visiting, or something."

"David's school teacher, eh? And what does Elizabeth think?"

"Think? She's upset."

"Do you love the Braddon girl?"

"Of course not. I may have thought so, but not now."

"But she thinks you're a bastard, doesn't she?"

"Who?"

"The Braddon girl."

"I suppose they both do. So what do I do?"

"You stick it out, boy, you stick it out. You pay the girl off, you pay the bills and you run this place at a profit. Husbandry, that's what it's about." He waved his arm toward the window as the wind blew, the trees bent and the rain fell.

"This place is ours." Alistair coughed. "Do you want me to see the girl?"

"What for?"

"I could scare her off, pay her some money, get rid of her."

"What if she's pregnant?"

"If she's pregnant, it's her fault, not yours. She wanted the fun. They all say they're pregnant, it's their ultimate weapon." He laughed. "Jesus Christ."

"I can do my own work," Richard Andersen said. "I don't need you."

"Don't you? Well, see her off then, get rid of her. Get her out of town and we can all get back to running the place. Lawless is good."

"Who?"

"Lawless. He works hard, a good choice. He'll keep the rabbits down and keep the buggers out."

"What buggers?"

"The no-hopers, the bludgers, the vagrants and riff-raff, the girl. We'll keep them all out." Alistair Andersen rose from the table, slipped and clutched the bentwood chair. "I'll see you in the morning."

Richard sat at the table and looked at the whisky bottle; it was settled: he would pay her off.

*   *   *

Rose saw the car headlights gleaming through the rain and watched him go. She thought of opening the front door and calling after him, but did not. What was he thinking? She knew. There was no one she could turn to: she dare not tell her mother or father, or the parish priest; she hadn't been to confession for years. She thought of the children playing in the school yard, the poetry and the timetables, the running races on the sports ground, reading time, *The Tortoise and the Hare*, the little girls skipping. She loved them, but she would have to leave. She would never get another job. Did people starve these days? She had heard they did. She watched the lights of his car disappear and turned on the wireless. It was after ten and all the stations were closed down. The kettle steamed and her room smelt of ash and damp clothes. She moved into her bedroom: her few books, the *Ladies' Home Journal* and the *National Geographic*: journeys to Britain, America, China she would never take. She took her clothes off and stood, naked, before the mirror. What if she was pregnant? What if she was carrying his child? Say it was growing inside her? In a couple of weeks, she would know. How would she find out for certain? She would have to go to the town doctor and he would tell people. He wasn't a priest. She had seen ads for pregnancy tests in weekend magazines. *Your reply under plain wrapper.* She felt her belly; he was inside her and she couldn't get him out. There was nothing she could do to get rid of him. He was in her womb, and there he would stay. Where could she have the baby? Nuns knew about these things. No one could help her now. Holy Mother of Christ, she knelt and prayed, let me not be pregnant. I have sinned, let me not be pregnant. I will do anything you ask. She could sin forever and have an abortion, but how did you find an abortionist?

Rose picked up her purse from the bed and opened it: a ten-shilling note, neatly folded, her bank book, a lipstick, her library card, her grandmother's wedding ring, a railway ticket and the red dust from last summer. There wasn't much: she hardly existed at all. She pulled on her nightdress and lay on the bed. The night was cold: she crawled under the blankets, wiped her face and eyes and, at last, went to sleep.

*   *   *

"What do you intend to do?" Elizabeth asked her husband. They stood in the rose garden as the trees dripped and the watery sun shone.

"About what?"

"You know very well what I'm talking about. The girl."

"Nothing. It's all over now."

"So you admit it?"

He faced his inquisitor. "Yes, you'll have to forgive me. It was most unfortunate."

"I shall never forgive you."

"Jesus Christ, what makes you so high and mighty?"

"Not only do you fornicate, you also blaspheme. I feel sorry for her. Where did you do it? In that shabby little school house? Has she told anybody? Do you intend to leave me for the love of your life?"

"I don't know."

"You don't know?"

"If she's told anybody."

"Have you told anybody?"

"Of course not."

"Not even your father?"

"No."

Elizabeth saw a single daffodil in bloom under a May tree. "I wouldn't even pray for you."

"I don't want your prayers." He wanted to leave and find some work to do, but she was standing in his way. "Look, Elizabeth, I'm very sorry. It won't happen again."

"How do I know? How do I know you won't take your pleasure with any little tart that comes along? What if the girl's pregnant? Have you thought of that? If she's pregnant, you'll be the father of an illegitimate child, David will have a step-brother. How will you explain that to him?"

It was starting to spit with rain and he wanted to get away. "I've got work to do."

"I'm sure you've got work to do. You're like your father, you're a fornicating pig."

"Don't you talk about my father."

"Everyone knows about your father. He had his way with every girl that worked on the place, and he's a drunkard."

"Don't you talk about my father."

"I'll talk about whomever I like. If she's pregnant, you'd better get something done to her. When was the last time you did it?"

"Would you please move? I've got work to do."

She came up close and slapped him across the face. "You're like your father, Richard, you're a vile, adulterous man."

He hit her in the mouth and she fell on the sodden ground; then he went to help her up, but she turned her face away and lay there, sobbing. He looked up at the house

53

and thought he saw David's face at the window, but he couldn't be sure. The rain fell and he strode away up the path.

*   *   *

A month later, one fine and breathless morning, Rose Braddon did not appear as the children laughed and skylarked in the classroom. When it got to half past nine, David and two little girls went over the yard to the school house, but found the door locked and the blinds drawn. They called her name several times and waited at the door. The crows and chaffinches perched on the roof and sounds of laughter came from the classroom. When the caretaker broke in, they found Rose Braddon lying face down on the bed. Her dressing gown was soaked with blood, her legs were open and her breasts were bare. The two girls screamed, the flies crawled and David was sick on the wooden floor. They took her to the District Hospital, but by the time they got there, Rose Braddon was dead. That night, in his room in the tower, David wept.

3

Grammar

Richard Andersen looked at the front page of the morning newspaper, then turned to the back for the cricket scores. The carriages rattled and cinders flew into the bracken; the day was hot and the compartment stuffy. David's suitcase sat in the rack above their heads; his school uniform was new and uncomfortable. He hoped that the train would break down, that there might be a cow on the line or a bush fire, but the wheels clattered on the rails and the dry countryside slipped by. Maybe there would be a summer storm? But the sky was cloudless.

"This war's not going to last long," his father said. "I give it six months at the outside; the Huns will never get past the Maginot Line."

His mother did not reply and gazed out at the dead trees, the piggeries, the wheat silos and the unpainted cottages. It was the start of another hot summer and she was dreading it. What would she do without David? There was nothing to look forward to. This country had no meaning for her.

Richard put the paper down and looked at them both. "It's just another European show, nothing to do with us. God damn the Germans. I expect wool prices will rise."

David thought of *Tom Brown's Schooldays*. "What will they do on the first day?" he said.

"Who?"

"The senior boys."

"What senior boys?" his father said.

"The senior boys at Grammar. Will there be initiations?"

"Initiations? I should think not, those days are past.

There might be some innocent fun, not much else. I had to go through it and it didn't do me any harm."

"Did you put in your catechism?" his mother asked.

"Yes."

"You're sure?"

"Yes."

"It's Evangelical, isn't it?" she said to her husband. Ashes were in her fair hair.

"What?"

"Grammar."

"I'm not quite sure."

"Of course not."

The cinders flew and the three of them sat in the compartment and watched the parched landscape roll by. Tom Quicksilver had left to join up the day before. Good riddance, Richard thought, he'd never been any good and God knows why he'd kept him on so long. If wool prices *did* rise, they'd get out of the financial doldrums. At last David was going to a decent school, then he remembered Rose Braddon.

"Did you put in your toilet gear, David?" his father said.

"*I* saw to that." His mother took out her knitting and wondered what was happening at home; it was winter there now. Would there be rationing? That was unthinkable.

"I think Bradman will go on and make a double century," his father said. "What do you think, David?"

"I hope so."

"The Melbourne Cricket Ground is quite close to Grammar. They might take you."

"Do you think so?"

"They might. Cricket's compulsory."

"I think I might do some running."

His father laughed. "Well, you're built for it."

"How long will it be now?" David said.

Richard looked at his watch; the train trip was interminable, but at least there would be a drink or two at the Club while Elizabeth went shopping. He'd given her £10 to keep her quiet.

"Another two hours."

Richard looked at Elizabeth who had gone to sleep in the corner. She was getting thin and unattractive. He took up the paper again. There was a rumour that the Germans would invade Norway. If they did, it would be a big mistake; the British Navy would see to that.

"Shouldn't' we send soldiers to help the Mother Country?" David said.

"We did that last time and look where that got us. Hitler's at the end of his rope. Did you hear what the Prime Minister said: 'Business as usual,' and that's what it will be."

His mother slept in the corner of the compartment as the train rolled north across the yellow plains.

*   *   *

"You look after yourself, old son," his grandfather had said as they stood on the flagstone veranda.

"What will it be like?" David said.

"Hard work, but fun. English, history, mathematics, Greek, Latin and lots of sport. Things I never had. After a week or two, you'll love it and never want to come home."

David looked at his mother's rose garden, the tennis court and the bluestone steps worn down by countless hobnail boots. "I think I will."

"What?"

"Want to come home."

"Never."

"I shall miss you, Grandad." Crumbs were stuck in his grandfather's beard, and holes were burnt in his waistcoat.

"No you won't, not for long, you'll soon be in the swim."

"What about the war?"

"What war?"

"Hitler."

"How on earth is the war going to affect your going to boarding school?"

"There could be air raids."

"Air raids? Who's going to bomb us?" Alistair Andersen stuck his thumbs in his braces.

"Someone might."

"Rubbish. What you've got to do is to study hard and go to university. Do you want to go to university?"

"I'm not sure."

"What do you want to do then? Have you any idea?"

"I might become a soldier."

"A soldier?" Alistair laughed. "That's a turn-up for the troops. I think you'd better get your schooling done and think about that later."

"Rudyard Kipling liked soldiers," David said. "He admired them."

"Did he?"

"You *know* he did."

"Have you packed your suitcase yet?" his grandfather said.

"I'm going to do it this evening. Mother will help me."

"Are you taking anything special?"

"Yes."

"What?"

"My picture of the King's Royal Rifles."

"Good on you."

"What will happen to Mr Schultz now?"

"Emil Schultz? What should happen?"

"We're fighting the Germans."

"Mr Schultz isn't a German any more, he's lived here for over thirty years. The war's got nothing to do with him. Look, David, you'd better go upstairs and help your mother pack. You're off first thing in the morning."

"I know," David said. "Will they have a wireless at Grammar?"

"Of course they will, but you might not be able to listen."

"Then how will I know what the Germans are doing?"

58

"Look, old son, don't worry about the bloody Germans, you've got six years of school ahead of you." Alistair Andersen stood up from the veranda rail. "I've got to go and help your father, I'll give you a game of cribbage tonight." He walked through the garden and out into the yard toward the sheds. How could David ever become a soldier?

David hung about on the veranda and watched his grandfather striding over the gravel. His hat was old and stained. There would be no more games of cribbage, no more Robert W. Service and no more Kipling. He wondered if he could pretend illness, but everybody would see through it. The garden with its flower beds and tunnels of May trees stretched down to the road and he thought he might walk down there. Rifle fire echoed in the still afternoon heat: that would be Mr Lawless. He went down the worn steps toward the trees.

"There you are, David," his mother said. She was standing in the front doorway, her hands shading her face from the sun. "Have you got your list? You should start packing."

"It's upstairs in my room."

"Off you go then, there's a good boy."

He went back into the cool, tiled hall and climbed the stairs.

David looked out of the window; the tennis court had never been repaired and sheep browsed on it now; the wire netting had been torn down for Mr Lawless's chicken coop and the umpire's chair chopped up for kindling. What was the fire-spotter on Mount Rouse doing today? The fire season had started once again. He thought of the drovers and the thirsty cattle on the Dunkeld road, the flames leaping from tree to tree and the men beating with sacks and shovels all through the summer nights. His mother had never replanted her silver birch. He started to take down the pictures of the *Hood* and the *Ramilies*, the *Hindenburg* and Amelia Earhart: the room looked bare already. He leafed through the issues of *Country Life* and the *Illustrated London News*: the manor house in Hampshire, King Edward and Mrs Simpson, the Loch Ness Monster and diagrams of the Maginot Line. David rummaged and found yellowed copies of *Beano*, *Film Fun*, *Champion* and *Hotspur*. His grandmother in England was dead and his aunts in Gloucestershire wrote to his mother, but sent him nothing. The hot north wind blew and rattled the casements as he looked at the school list and packed his suitcase. The coronation mug sat on the top shelf and he remembered the linctus, the cod-liver oil, the tracing paper, the rain and her sickness. He found his school atlas and a half-finished map of China and Korea. He had got as far as the Imjin River and the Yellow Sea. His room was hot and the fireplace empty. The first holidays were in May and that seemed ages away.

His mother appeared at the door and looked around the room.

"What a mess," she said, "and you haven't even started to pack yet. Have you got the list?"

"It's on the bed."

"Let's get on with it." She picked up the piles of *Country Life*. "You won't want these."

"I was going to save them."

"What's the point? You won't read them any more."

"*You* might, Mother."

"I don't think so, David." Elizabeth tossed the familiar magazines into a heap.

"I was just thinking of Miss Braddon," he said.

She straightened up and looked at her son. "Why?"

"She was my teacher for a long time and I remember the day we found her. I wonder why she died? She looked healthy enough."

Elizabeth felt cold and said: "Where are your new school shirts?"

"I suppose people *do* drop dead," David said, "but I liked Miss Braddon." He looked at his old school journals

60

and exercise books. "She was much better than Miss Giles, I loved Miss Braddon. She was the best teacher I had."

"Look, David," Elizabeth said. "You're going off to boarding school tomorrow. For God's sake, start getting ready."

"How's it all going?" Richard Andersen said as he stood at the door. He was sweating and his boots were covered in dust; his broad shoulders were hunched and his face was red.

"We're doing quite well, thank you," his mother said. She looked, and still hated him.

"Don't forget your sandshoes," Richard said.

"We've seen to that." She gave him the pile of comics and magazines. "Would you take these? They can go in the incinerator."

He looked at her cold, blue eyes and shut the door.

That night, David beat his grandfather at cribbage and was sent to bed early. It was twilight and the western sun shone in shafts through the windows. This time tomorrow night he would be in a strange bed in a dormitory with boys he didn't know. What would they be like, and what would they talk about? What would the teachers be like? He listened for the sound of possums in the ceiling, but they were silent. Where had they gone? They had been his friends for many years. He lay in his bed and could not sleep. At tea, his father had said that Tom Quicksilver had left to join up. He was going to be a soldier. After a while, he got up to open the window, and thought he heard raised voices as he returned to bed. He thought his father was shouting, but couldn't be sure. Then as the owls called and the frogs croaked in the streams and drains, David went to sleep.

*   *   *

The school was built of bluestone with a clock tower, minarets, slate roof and double chimneys. Oak trees and aspens grew; gas lights lined the drive and flocks of seagulls were gathered on the green playing fields. "Well, here we are," his father said as they stood in the quadrangle of the Junior Boarding School. The afternoon was fine and hot and the wind blew the gravel and dust in the yard. David held his suitcase and looked at all the boys: they were standing with their parents and no one seemed to know anybody. Then a master, wearing a gown, and a senior boy appeared and considered the newcomers. The boy was wearing a prefect's badge and holding a clip-board, he was tanned and looked big and strong. The parents began kissing their children goodbye and walking down the drive toward the main road. Pigeons fluttered and flew around the stone towers and battlements.

"It's time to say goodbye, David," his mother said as she bent and kissed him on the cheek.

His father took his hand and shook it firmly. "Work hard and play hard," he said. "It's the finest school in Melbourne and you're one of the privileged. Don't forget that."

His mother was weeping and David turned away. "Write once a week," she said.

"Yes, Mother."

"Goodbye then," his father said, and David watched them walk away toward St Kilda Road where the trams rattled and the cars ran. More prefects appeared and began calling their names from lists; David listened carefully in case he misheard. His hands were sweating and he put the suitcase down on the gravel; his new black shoes were hurting and he wanted to go to the lavatory. Then his name was called and he was put into a group of other boys: they all wore blank stares and no one spoke. The summer wind gusted and blew grit and sand into their faces.

"Right, you lot," the prefect said, "follow me and I'll show you your dorm." They straggled down the path, behind the prefect, lugging their suitcases. "You're in Mac-Arthur House," the prefect said to them. "It's the best house in the school and don't you forget it. You call me sir, and don't forget that either."

They climbed four flights of wooden stairs to the dormitory; the building smelt of carbolic and their shoes echoed on the linoleum. The prefect assigned them their beds and lockers and showed them the showers and lavatories.

"Right," he said, "unpack your gear, put your personal stuff on the shelves and the rest in your locker. And keep it neat. If you don't . . ." He ran his hand across his throat. "The housemaster's name is Mr Bainbridge. Tea's at six in the main boarding school, so you've got two hours. Any skylarking or mucking about and you're in deep trouble. As I said, MacArthur House is the best in the Junior School, and you little runts will soon find out why."

He left the dormitory as the dusty western sun shone through the narrow windows.

The boy next to David was short and thickset. He threw his old suitcase on his bed and stuck out his hand. "Hello," he said, "my name's Gage, Jack Gage."

"Andersen, David Andersen."

They sat on the beds as the other boys unpacked.

"So far, so good," Jack Gage said and grinned, "but you wouldn't want to get on the wrong side of that prefect, would you?"

"I suppose not." David started to unpack and placed his clothes neatly on the shelves. He left the picture of the King's Royal Rifles in the suitcase: there seemed nowhere to put it.

"Where are you from?" Jack Gage said. He tested the mattress.

"Penshurst."

"I knew it, I'm from Colac." He bounced up and down and the bed creaked. "Is your father a farmer?"

"Yes."

"What's the place called?"

"*Killara.*"

A bell rang, but no one took any notice.

"My father," Jack said, "is a dentist. He's not the most popular man in town." Finally he opened his case and threw his stuff on to the shelf. "Do you play football?"

"No."

"Really?"

"Only in the school yard." David was hopeless at it, but didn't want to say.

Jack Gage shoved his empty suitcase under the bed with his foot. "Well, you soon will. It's compulsory here, along with a lot of other things."

"What other things?"

"Didn't they tell you? Boxing, cricket, cadets, you name it. It makes a man out of you, so they say."

"Boxing?" David wondered.

"Oh, I suppose they'll make us bash each other up. They'll have trouble hitting you, won't they?"

"Why?"

"Never mind." Jack got up and shadow-sparred. "What do you say we have a scout around until tea?"

They walked across the quadrangle and down the drive. Some new boys were still coming in with their parents. One of them was crying.

"That's no way to start, is it?" Jack Gage said. "Poor little bugger. What do you think about the war?"

"My father," David said, "thinks it will all be over before Christmas."

"Does he? My dad doesn't. He says Hitler's a clever devil, but the Spitfire's better than the Messerschmitt 105."

"Do you think so?"

"Yeah, more manoeuvrable. I make a study of aircraft. I'm going to be a pilot. What are you going to do?"

David thought about becoming a soldier. "I'm not sure. We've got six years ahead of us, haven't we?"

Jack Gage groaned and kicked at the gravel with his new school shoes. "We sure have. Never mind, I'm going to play football, train hard and get into the first eighteen when the time comes. They won't keep me out, and then I'll be a pilot and travel the world. Do you read *Biggles*?"

"I used to."

"Used to? I still do, great stuff. What do you read?"

"Robert W. Service, Kipling, all kinds of things."

"Have you read *Kim*?"

"Yes, it's my favourite."

"Are you a Scout?"

"There was no troop in Penshurst."

"There was in Colac. I could have become a troop leader, but I had to come here." Jack Gage stopped on the path: he was squarely built with close-cropped, curly hair. "What do you think you're best at?"

"Running," David said. "I can run, I'm going to win the school mile."

"Are you? That will take some doing."

"I will, you'll see."

The seagulls rose and fluttered across the green turf, and somewhere from the bluestone buildings a bell rang. The trams banged on St Kilda road, and the church spires and the Victorian buildings of the city rose in the dusty sky. It was the first time David had seen Melbourne and it seemed strange and dark.

*   *   *

The bell rang at 7.00. They stumbled on the linoleum and went to the showers as the crows called from the oaks and the pines. The sun shone across Port Phillip Bay: it was going to be another hot morning. Rolls were called, bells rang, prefects shouted; they had breakfast, dashed to the main school, consulted the notice board, ran up and down the stairs, got lost in the corridors, found their form room at last and stood behind their desks.

The master's hair was turning grey; he was square-shouldered with a moustache. "You may sit down," the master said. "My name is Livingstone, Captain Harold

65

Livingstone. My nickname is Stanley and I'm an officer in His Majesty's Militia. Apart from mathematics six periods a week, you've got the pleasure of my company as your form master and on the parade ground." He placed his cane on the top of the desk. "The rules here are very simple: if you play the game, *I* play the game." He coughed. "If you don't play the game . . ." He brought the cane down on the desk and the dust flew. "You'll have one hour's maths prep three nights a week, and if that's not done to my satisfaction . . ." He brought the cane down again.

They all sat, fearful, watching Captain Livingstone, and David wondered how many canes he went through in a year. The blowflies buzzed at the windows; the room was hot and as silent as the grave.

"I shall now call the roll," Captain Livingstone said, "and on hearing his name, each boy shall rise in his place. Keep standing as I want to commit your visages to memory and see what gifts Providence has granted me in 1940 *anno domini*. Adams, Andersen, Baker, Christian, Donald . . ."

They rose to their feet. A desk lid banged, but Captain Livingstone appeared not to hear it, and when he had finished, thirty-two boys were standing.

"The next boy who bangs his desk lid," Captain Livingstone said, "gets it."

The master walked down the aisles of desks, his black gown trailing. He stopped in front of David.

"Andersen?" he said. "Tell me, why is your name spelt with an 'e'?"

"I'm not quite sure, sir."

"You're not quite sure? Here's a boy who's not quite sure why his name is spelt in an unusual way."

"I think some of my family were Norwegian, sir."

"You *think*? You should *know*. One's antecedents are of prime importance. The breeding determines the physique and strength of character."

Captain Livingstone gazed at David's bony frame, the fair hair and pale blue eyes, and passed on. His black boots squeaked. He coughed and walked up and down the rows.

Was this like being in the army? David thought. They had Captain Livingstone for a whole year, but maybe his bark was worse than his bite. He looked at Gage, but he was staring out of the window. The inspection over, Captain Livingstone stepped up behind his desk.

"Most of you," he said, "are dressed like savages and Hottentots. That, I will not tolerate. Ties are to be firmly knotted, shoes polished, all buttons secured." He touched his moustache and leaned over his desk. "You will all perform to the best of your abilities and you will not waste time. I will see to that. Every year I have the best form in the Junior School and every year I have the best company in the cadets. You will not fail me. Who was Demosthenes?"

Not one hand was raised and the blowflies buzzed. David dared not turn his head and kept his hands under the desk.

"Your ignorance is abysmal," Captain Livingstone said, "but that doesn't surprise me. He was a Greek philosopher, one of the greatest, my young, ignorant friends, who was aware of the impending catastrophe." He pointed at Jack Gage. "What is a catastrophe?"

"Something dangerous, sir."

"Something dangerous. I suppose that will have to do. Mr Hitler is a catastrophe, the whole German race is a catastrophe. Demosthenes warned the men of Athens against apathy, he warned them against being undermined. If you study hard, if you play sport hard, if you drill hard, you will not be undermined. And I shall see to it that you are not. And remember, my young friends, that there are two enemies: one without and one within. I shall make certain that both are kept at bay. Remember that while the enemy may scale the walls, ash may be in the bread." Captain Livingstone opened the textbook, pulled out his blackboard ruler and drew. "This is a rectangle."

At recess, David missed Jack Gage in the crush. He chose the most private place he could find and watched the boys milling around the quadrangle. It seemed now that many

67

knew each other, but he did not. He looked at his school diary: history, English, Latin, Greek, geography, mathematics, French and physical education. How would he get on? He didn't know a soul. Ash in the bread?

"There you are," Jack said. He was eating chocolate. "Do you want some?"

"Thanks."

"What do you think of Stanley?"

"Stanley?"

"Livingstone."

"Oh, he's all right. A bit strict, I should think."

"I think he got gassed in the last war. That's why he coughs."

"My father fought there," David said.

"Did he? Where?"

"I don't think he saw much fighting. I think he went there to marry my mother."

"I've decided to train for boxing," Jack said.

"Have you?" David was going to ask him if he was scared of getting hurt, but decided not.

"I'm going to be Grammar's Joe Louis." Jack laughed. "Well, I'll try. I'll tell you what: I'll be the school boxing champion and you win the mile."

David felt cheered: maybe life at Grammar wouldn't be so bad after all. "I'll give it my best."

"You sound like old Stanley," Jack said.

They both laughed as the bell rang and they ran for the next lesson.

They stood in the gymnasium; it smelt of sweat and liniment. David looked at the battered equipment: the vaulting horses, the parallel bars and the Roman rings.

"Right, you lot," the gym master said, "I want you three times round the gym and the three last have to clean the place out at the end of the period. Wait for it."

He dropped his hand and they ran, their sandshoes skidding on the teak floor. Around they went, jostling and shoving, sweating and pushing; David ran like a rabbit and came in first. He thought the gym master might say something to him, but he didn't.

"Healthy bodies, healthy minds," the gym master said. He laughed. "That's what they say. You, and you: get those mattresses out. Right, I've got you five periods a week for my sins, and I'm going to have you leap-frogging, vaulting, tumbling, climbing and running around the oval until your hearts give out. We'll see who're the sheep and who're the goats." He stood in his white shorts and singlet. "God, you're a scrawny lot. Never mind, Rome wasn't built in a day."

David wondered if the teachers said the same thing at the beginning of each year; they probably did. He wasn't sure about the gym, but he thought he liked the gym master.

"Everything here is compulsory," the gym master said. "God knows why, but it is. If you have any trouble doing anything, let me know, and if you're frightened, tell me. There's nothing to be ashamed of, there's nothing wrong with good old-fashioned fear. It's doing what you can do best that counts."

They spent an hour, tumbling, running on the spot and doing exercises. At the end of it, David was tired and pleased: he liked the gym.

"All right then," the gym master said, "into the showers. And I forgot to tell you, my name's Fairweather. You don't call me sir, you call me Mr Fairweather. Have you got that?"

"Yes, sir."

When they were under the showers, Jack Gage said: "What do you think of Mr Fairweather?"

"He's tops. I hope he lets me run."

"I think he will," Jack said.

*　　*　　*

The senior boys came into the dorm at about 9.15 before lights-out. They looked big and hairy and stood at the head

69

of the room by the door. One of them stepped forward. "Okay, you little squirts," he said, "you're going to be examined: it's the rules and if you fail, you're in for a beating."

They stood by their beds and quaked; the senior boys moved into the dorm. What were they going to do? Where was Mr Bainbridge? One of them began to sniffle and the senior boy laughed. "Lost your dummy?" he said.

The senior boys moved down the aisle, then between the beds, and began tearing things off the shelves: clothes, books, tooth mugs and toilet gear. David's catechism fell under the bed, but he did nothing. Jack Gage started to move forward and David held his arm.

"This dorm is disgusting," one senior boy said, "I think you little buggers will have to clean it up."

David thought of the drovers on the Dunkeld Road and hoped Mr Fairweather might appear at the door.

"Okay, you little bastards," the leader said, "pin your dirty ears back and listen. Here's the rules, and I'll only say them once. There's ten of us and there's twenty of you, so we'll examine you in twos tomorrow night. Okay? And if any of you doesn't turn up, you'll wish you were dead."

The boy sniffled, David didn't know his name. Was it the one he'd seen with his parents on the driveway?

"Here's the list," the big boy said. "You've got to tell us the names of the prefects, the probationers, and the words of the school song by this time tomorrow night. You be at the East Dorm by nine tomorrow night."

"We'll tell Mr Bainbridge," Jack Gage said.

"Listen, you tubby little shit, you just try."

They left the dormitory.

"Isn't there something we can do?" Jack said.

"Yes," David said as he picked up his catechism. "Just learn the words. We can beat them."

The following night, David was examined by the senior boys; he was word-perfect, appeared unafraid and they could find no excuse to beat him.

"That's a tough little bugger, isn't it?" he heard one of the boys say as he closed the door and stood shaking in the corridor.

"How did you get on?" David said to Jack as they undressed for bed. The other boys were quiet and two were crying.

"I couldn't remember the last verse of the school song, so the devils beat me."

"Very hard?"

"No, not really." Jack grinned. "I've got lots of padding. How about you?"

"I got through."

"Without a mistake?"

"Yes."

"Cripes, you're a hard worker, aren't you?"

"Yes," David said, "I suppose I am."

"Were you scared?"

"Yes, I was."

"What happened to Greene?"

"He failed, so they beat him."

*　　*　　*

One of the boys' parents sent him a war map and they pinned it up on the dormitory wall next to the picture of the King and Queen and the two princesses. Each night after prep they followed the progress of the war until lights out. From what they could gather, not a lot seemed to be happening. Jack Gage knew all about the war and pointed out the Rhineland, and the Siegfried and Maginot lines; he was following the Russian invasion of Finland. He said his father said the Russians were treacherous and no one should trust them. Another boy had a cigarette card collection of British aircraft: Lysanders, Beauforts, Hurricanes and Spitfires, but Jack said that the German Stuka was the best dive-bomber in the world. They all wondered how long it would be before Mr Menzies would send an Australian

71

Imperial Force to help England. But despite the war map, it all seemed very far away and by the time they had done their prep, they were dog-tired and wanted to sleep. Only Jack stayed awake and listened to the nine o'clock news on his crystal set. Sometimes he lent it to David who listened to the chimes of Big Ben through the static and wondered about his aunts living in Gloucestershire. He thought Mr Chamberlain had the situation under control and there wasn't much to worry about; the school chaplain was optimistic and said that God was at work in this turmoil to bring a good issue out of it. He said that God had allowed a Second World War to draw all nations to the paths of righteousness. He made them pray for the success of British arms.

The summer of 1940 was fine and hot; that season Donald Bradman scored his ninetieth century; two large military marches took place with bronzed young soldiers marching down Swanston Street and along St Kilda Road past the school; the summer racing carnival was held at Flemington; one night the temperature didn't drop below 85°, and during the day they sweated in their uniforms as they ran through the corridors from room to room. Some of the boys were caned for not attending roll calls or failing to finish prep, but David escaped punishment. Every morning, the headmaster said prayers at assembly and gave instructions and notices they couldn't understand; they sang songs from the school songbook. Every evening they practised cricket in the heat of the dusty sun, ran around the oval, and ate stringy cold mutton and potatoes for tea in the dining room. On Sundays, David went to Holy Communion at nine and all the boarders went to the chapel in the evening. At the end of a hard week, they enjoyed chapel: it was a place to sing *Jerusalem, Jesu, Joy of Man's Desiring* and *O, Valiant Hearts.* The senior boys left them alone now, but bells always seemed to be ringing, rolls were called, prefects kept shouting and masters threatening. Their minds were cluttered with Latin declensions, French

72

verbs, chemical formulae, algebraic equations, chapters from Brett's *Colonial History*, and passages from *The Merchant of Venice*.

Outside the school, the militia drilled in the bush and on the roadsides, air-raid shelters were dug in parks, wardens were issued with gas masks and women knitted socks and balaclavas for the soldiers. Those people with shortwave radios listened to the BBC for the war news, but since the invasion and the scuttling of the *Graf Spee*, nothing much seemed to be doing. In the papers there was a report that Hitler was suffering from cancer and had only eighteen months to live. In March, Finland capitulated to the Russians and there were reports of more Japanese atrocities in China and Korea. David wrote to his mother and father once a week: she said they were sweltering in the heat and that the plants in her garden had died; his father said that wool prices were getting better; and his grandfather said he was feeling fine and that Emil Schultz had suddenly sold his farm and gone away. It seemed a lot of things were happening in Penshurst and David longed to be home, riding his pony up the winding road to the top of Mount Rouse where the wind blew through the grass and the spindly pines and gorse ran wild.

*   *   *

"Well, Andersen," Mr Bainbridge said, "we've got you for the junior school mile. Okay?"

"Yes, sir, I'll do my best."

"You've got to win for MacArthur House, right?"

"Yes, sir."

"Why do you like running?"

"Because I'm on my own."

"You like being on your own?"

"Yes, sir, I do."

"You've been training hard?"

"Yes, sir."

The housemaster looked at the thin, brown body and the fair hair. "I think you have."

They stood on the edge of the oval as the hot north wind blew, smelling of salt and exhaust. The factory chimneys smoked and the Victorian churches and buildings stood against the dusty sky; the trams and motor cars ran down St Kilda Road and the seagulls flew in from the bay. Somewhere a hooter blew: he wished they would allow him out to see the city. Boys were running around the track, dust spinning from their sandshoes. Others were cheering their teams home, stamping and screaming on the sideline. The masters strolled in their gowns, and flags flew from the school tower.

"If you win the junior mile, Andersen," Mr Bainbridge said, "it'll be a great thing for the house. Competition is the essence of life, that's why we're all here." Mr Bainbridge was red-faced and sweating in his gown and Harris tweed jacket, and David stood before him in his white shorts and singlet as the boys in the 880 yards dashed by. He tried to see who was in front, but Mr Bainbridge was standing in the way.

"I know, sir."

The housemaster looked at his watch. "It starts in half an hour, so come back here in twenty minutes."

David wandered around and watched the events, his feet sweating in his sandshoes. He was going to be no good at football, so the mile was his chance. The senior boys, wearing blazers and straw boaters, paraded around the edge of the barren ground, and David wished his grandfather were here to watch him run, even if he lost the mile. He looked up at the clock tower: ten minutes to go. Jack Gage was putting the shot and David watched him for a minute or two, then wandered around the track. *There's nothing wrong with good, old-fashioned fear.* MacArthur came third in the hop, step and jump; and a boy he didn't know had sprained his ankle on the hurdles. It was all a bit disappointing so far, so no wonder Mr Bainbridge had given him a talking-to. The sun seemed hotter now and he wriggled his feet in his sandshoes. David looked at the clock again, saw the time, and ran back for the start of the mile as the dust blew over the track. He would do his best: he could do no more than that. He stood with the other boys on the starting line and at last heard the crack of the pistol.

* * *

David lay on his bed and wrote carefully with his fountain pen.

Dear Mother, Father and Grandfather,

I thought you might like to know that this afternoon I won the junior school mile for MacArthur House. I ran it in 5 minutes 40 seconds which is only 8 seconds outside the school record.

All the boys of MacArthur House clapped and cheered when I won and Mr Bainbridge was very pleased. The House came second in the competition and it was a very exciting day.

The weather here is very hot. Tired but happy, I remain,

Yours sincerely,

David Kinross Andersen

He folded the letter, licked the envelope and put it on the shelf behind his bed.

"Well, Hero of the House," Jack Gage said, "how do you feel?"

"My feet hurt."

"You *will* win the senior mile when the time comes, and you'll be made a prefect."

"Do you think so?"

"I'm sure, you try very hard. Are you going home for the Easter break?"

"Yes."

"We could travel on the train together."

"Come on, you blokes," came Mr Bainbridge's voice. "I know we won the mile today, but there's no need to overdo it. Lights out."

They lay under the sheets and Jack fiddled with his crystal set. "What do you think the Germans will do?"

"I don't know," David said, "I'm too tired to think."

Jack said: "How are you liking Grammar?"

"It's better now."

"Since you won the mile?"

"Yes."

"We've got Mr Searle for chemistry first period in the morning. You know what he's like. Have you done your prep? If we're not prepared, he'll cane us."

There was no reply: David was asleep. That night, he dreamed of Rose Braddon and Mr Lawless, something happened on the slopes of Mount Napier, but in the morning he couldn't remember what.

*   *   *

David spent the Easter recess at Penshurst. The trip with Jack Gage was dusty and long. The train was packed with young soldiers and militia men. The engine broke down three times; they read all their comics and ate a whole bag of Minties. David wondered where Emil Schultz had gone, thought about his homework programme and studied Jack's book of aircraft silhouettes. When he got home, he rode his pony to the top of Mount Rouse and along the narrow road by the racecourse, past the ornamental hedges and old trucks resting in the grass. His mother took him to Holy Communion at St James's Church, and he played cribbage with his grandfather. His father bought a prize ram at the Hamilton sales and his mother had the local women in the front room to discuss the plan for the Soldiers' Comfort Fund. It was good to be home.

There wasn't a great deal to do at *Killara*, and in the

evenings David mucked about in his room. He fossicked through old copies of the *Illustrated London News, Champion* and *Boy's Own*. His mother and father sat in the dining room as he did the books and she read her magazines from England. David studied chemistry, French, geography, the poems of Alfred, Lord Tennyson, and Latin past participles. It seemed that the house was deathly quiet. On Easter Monday, his grandfather stayed in his room all day and didn't appear for tea. Mr Lawless and his dogs prowled about the property; poison was laid; and rabbit skins were stretched on the frame at the front gate. On Easter Tuesday, David and his mother went for a drive in the Vauxhall and looked at the mysterious mansions beyond the rows of oaks and pines. The streams and drains had dried up and the frogs were silent. A fire burned on Mount Napier and the summit was hidden by smoke; Tom Quicksilver's father had died and Richard Andersen said that Tom had gone to Egypt with the Imperial Force. He asked his mother and father where Miss Braddon was buried, but they said they didn't know.

On Thursday, David's mother, father and grandfather waved him goodbye at Penshurst station and Jack Gage got on at Colac. The Germans invaded Norway and Denmark and more young men joined up. David was confirmed in the school chapel. In the dorm, someone had pinned up pictures of Lord Mountbatten and Winston Churchill. It was good to be back at school.

4

The Enemy Within

The lighthouse stood, red and white, above the stone walls
and embattlements of the river. The summer sun shone,
the gulls wheeled, the children laughed and climbed the
bluestone breakwater where the old rocks lay, tumbled.
The thick, green kelp streamed and heaved away to the
south toward Tasmania and the Antarctic. A big, gaff-
rigged yacht was sailing down the river, only its masts and
rigging to be seen above the walls and rocks. David sat
up on the sand, watched the canvas sails flapping, and
remembered pictures he had seen of land-locked freighters
steaming south through the Suez Canal. He thought of
Joshua Slocum, of Nordhoff and Hall, of four-masted brigan-
tines battling through the Straits of Magellan: Punta Arenas,
Tierra del Fuego, South Georgia, remote places of courage
and hardship he might never see. Sandpipers chatted and
crowed on the sandbanks, rye-billed terns landed, picked
and poked in the flotsam and debris and flew away, black
and white in flocks, south to Water Tower beach, then east
and then north beyond the Norfolk pines and the spires of
the small country churches.

His mother opened the wicker picnic basket and handed
him a corned-beef sandwich and a glass of barley water.

"You should cover up, David," she said as she passed
the beach towel, "or you'll get burnt."

A schooner sailed, close-hauled, across the bay; and the
sea curled and broke upon the reef where the silver whiting
and the mullet flashed and swam.

"Cover up, David."

He didn't reply, but draped the towel over his head. His

father had walked off down the beach and was talking to two young girls; they ran back to the dunes and his father strolled on. He saw his mother watching.

"Has the cat got your tongue?" she said.

"No, Mother." David, too, thought about walking up the beach: he might meet somebody.

"Will they make you a prefect next year?"

"It's possible."

"They should, seeing how well you've done. You've been top of your form for the last three years and already won the senior mile. You've never been in any trouble. What more can you do?"

"I'm not much good at football," David said. "It's the first eighteen that counts."

"It's a brutal game of violence."

"That's not the way the school sees it." He stood up and tossed the towel on the sand. "If you don't mind, I'm going for a walk."

"Don't forget your hat." She handed him the topee.

"I'm not wearing that thing."

"Well, take your father's panama then."

David stuck it on his head and moved off toward the breakwater.

He walked toward the sea wall, sprang to the top, and when he was out of sight, took off his father's panama and carried it. He stood uncertainly on the wall, and wondered what Jack Gage was doing. He was lucky: he had brothers and sisters. His grandfather had disappeared, but David knew where he was: in the pub chatting to the locals. He smiled. What would life at home be without that old man? Tonight they would play cribbage in the hotel lounge. He moved through the trees toward the cannons and gun emplacements, built when they thought the Czar and the Russians might come. Through the scrub and trees, he could see the flagstaff and the Union Jack flying. The good old red, white and blue: next year he would be the regimental sergeant major. He thought of the quarter guard competitions, the endless practising and the passing-out parade, the regular army officer had been proud and nodded for a job well done. David had been told that Mr Livingstone said he was the best senior cadet he could remember. Sometimes Jack Gage laughed at the drilling, the swords, the spit and polish and the Sam Browne belt, but when they won the competition, even he took it seriously. David thought of Mr Livingstone and the first lesson at school: *the enemy within* and his fears. Those days were over now, and next year he would command the whole battalion. He was sure he would be house captain at least.

David moved silently through the tea-trees and the brush. Not a twig snapped under his sandshoes. Then he saw the couple in the hollow under the blanket: their bodies were moving, the girl was laughing and the man was clutching her hair. He stopped and crouched in the shadows and watched them. The girl laughed again and the man mounted her, his body thrusting beneath the rug; she screamed, laughed and David saw her bare, brown legs; the man fell back and looked at the summer sky. They talked and the man kissed her as she lay: he covered her, looked up and saw David, watching.

"Jesus Christ," the man said, "Jesus fucking Christ."

David saw the slouch hat and the uniform and ran. He ran down the slope, past the guns and the flagstaff, along the breakwater and faced the open sea.

*   *   *

"Well," his grandfather said, "who's for a game of crib?" He drank his whisky and produced a pack of cards; he pulled the scoring board from his Harris tweed and broke the matches.

"Are we going fishing tomorrow?" David asked.

"We are indeed, we are indeed," Alistair said. "It's two days before Christmas and I can think of nothing better." He laughed and the table shook. "Well, almost nothing better." He shuffled the cards and looked at the young men and women at the house bar. "Now, who's for a game?" David saw a woman with her dress hitched above her knees, her hands between her boyfriend's legs. The barman was pouring the drinks and polishing the glasses.

"I wouldn't mind a game or two," Richard Andersen said. Elizabeth considered the people at the house bar. "If you're going fishing in the morning, David, you should have an early night."

"It's my shout," Alistair said as he drained his glass, "then we'll see if we can beat the boy." He got up and felt for his wallet. "Christmas comes but once a year." His mother looked again at the couples at the bar, her husband, her father-in-law and her son. "It's two games at the most, David, then I want you in bed."

David watched the man and the girl: he was strongly built and wearing sports clothes. Were they the couple he had seen? The door opened. More people came in and the wind blew from the sea.

"Would you like a beer, me young sarn't major?" his grandfather said. "I can get you one."

"He's under age," Elizabeth said.

"That may be, but he's going to be a soldier."

"What's that got to do with it?"

"It's being a man, Elizabeth, it's being a man."

Alistair flourished the ten-shilling note. "Do you want a beer, David, or not?"

"Yes, I do."

"Good on you." Alistair smiled and left the table.

"Just two games," his mother said, "then off to bed."

"I shan't be long," Richard said as she got up from the table.

"Stay as long as you like. There might be some young girls you could talk to. It's David I'm concerned about." His father shrugged and turned back to his drink, but David watched the girl at the bar. She had thrown off one shoe and was lighting a cigarette. She looked about eighteen, only a year older than he. Suddenly she looked his way, and he shuffled the cards.

"There's a bit of it around," his grandfather said as he put the drinks on the table.

"A bit of what?" Richard said.

"Skirt. I'm too old now, but it's still good to watch it."

David lost the first two games. The lounge was crowded with sunburnt holiday-makers and men in uniform; the noise from the public bar grew louder and somebody was playing a banjo. His grandfather sucked at his pipe and stuck the matches in the scoring board.

"A good time in the old town tonight," he said. "Thanks to God, there's no six o'clock closing here." He turned to David. "I'd watch the cards if I were you, old son, not that piece at the bar." He stretched his legs and scratched his beard. "Not that I blame you."

"The police will come," his father said. He drained his glass and wished he was at the bar. "I think you'd better go up to bed, David."

"Aw for Christ's sake," Alistair said, "the boy's seventeen, he's been in bloody boarding school for six years, let him see how the world lives. Anyhow, we're staying here, they've got nothing on us." He coughed. "The war's ended, the Germans are on trial, and that calls for a drink."

"What will you do next year?" his father asked.

"English, history, maths, physics and chemistry."

"And you'll be the regimental sergeant major?"

"Yes."

"And then what?"

"I've told you, Dad: I'm going to the Royal Military College."

"Is that what you want?"

"Yes."

His father leaned across the table, took his hand, shook it and said: "David, I'm proud of you."

"And," said Alistair, "so am I. That *does* call for a drink." He grabbed the tin tray and marched over to the

82

bar. David was embarrassed and fiddled with the playing cards; he cut the pack and turned up the Queen of Spades.

The lounge seemed packed now: people were laughing and shouting, the banjo played and some couples were dancing; the air smelt of steak and onions, boiled vegetables, cigarette smoke and beer. The barmen turned the spiggots, served the whisky, rum and gin; the people sang *Roll Out the Barrel*, *It's a Long Way to Tipperary* and *The White Cliffs of Dover*; the soldiers pushed and shoved at the bar, the girls laughed, the babies cried and the wind from the sea blew under the door as the music played. Grandfather had disappeared in the crush.

"I take it this is the first time you've been in a pub?" his father asked. "They're pretty rough places, hardly your mother's style, but you can't blame them now the war's over."

"Will they hang Goering?" David said.

"You bet, I hope they hang the bloody lot."

"Good day," the girl said. "Can I sit here? I've just had a row with me boyfriend."

David stood up, but he couldn't think of anything to say; he looked for his grandfather, but there was no sign of him.

She sat down on his grandfather's chair; her hair was tangled, her blouse half-open and her lipstick smudged. She grinned at David. "It's nice to see some people have still got manners."

She looked like Rose Braddon and Richard sat as still as a stone. Then he said: "That chair's taken."

"It doesn't matter," David said, "it belongs to my grandfather. When he comes back we can get another."

"Me boyfriend's a soldier," the girl said. "They all think they can get away with anything, but not with me, you can't." She was thin, her stockings were crooked and she was wearing pearl earrings. Richard sweated. What if Elizabeth came back?

"A bit of a hectic night," the girl said, "but it's Christmas, isn't it?"

"My name's Mr Andersen," Richard said, "and this is my son, David."

"Pleased to meet you. Any port in a storm." She shifted on the chair. "Playing cards, eh?"

"Cribbage," David said. Was it the girl he'd seen on the beach?

"Crib? Haven't played that for years, used to play it with me grandma." She got out her cigarettes. "The name's Joan."

"It's getting late," Richard said. "We'd better go."

"Where are you staying?" Joan said.

"Here," David said. She smelt of tobacco and scent. "Are you?"

"Nah, can't afford it. But one day, maybe. What do you do?"

"I'm at school."

"At school! You look too old for that."

"Come on, David," his father said.

"Shouldn't we wait for Grandfather?"

"He can look after himself, he's old enough. Excuse us, Miss." Richard stood up: she was a young tart.

"I think I'll stay a bit, Dad."

"You will not, it's after hours and you're under age."

"We're all under age," Joan said, "but seeing David's staying here, he's okay." She giggled. "I'll look after him."

"David," his father said, "I'm telling you to come up-stairs."

"I'm staying, I can look after myself."

Richard said nothing, turned on his heel and made for the door.

"Do you want a beer?" Joan said.

"I'll get them," David said, "can you mind that seat?"

"Don't worry, I'll keep it warm for you." She crossed her legs. "Don't be long."

David pushed through the crush: it was the first time this had happened to him. At last, he got served, paid the barman and found his hands were shaking.

"Don't forget your change, son," the barman said, and winked. David looked about for his grandfather: he didn't want to see him now.

"Whoopee," Joan said as he came back. "Two glasses of ice-cold, there's nothing better, well almost. I can't believe you're still at school. I left when I was fifteen. Do you smoke?"

David shook his head and wondered what he should talk about, but it didn't seem to worry the girl. He drank his beer quickly and felt it cold in his gut. Then he felt her legs touching his under the table.

"Are you staying here long?" Joan asked.

"A couple of days." David lifted his glass again. "We're going home for Christmas."

"Where's home?"

"Penshurst."

"Is your dad a farmer?"

"Yes."

"You're a lucky bugger, aren't you? One day you'll get the lot." She pressed her legs against him. "What are you doing tomorrow?"

"Going fishing."

"That's a bit boring, isn't it?" She put her glass down. "Do you want another?"

David got up and felt his head swimming; someone pushed his arm as he tried to find his way across the room. What if his father came back to see what was happening? He turned around and saw Joan sitting at the table; she waved and blew him a kiss. Somehow he got the beer and then wondered where her soldier boyfriend was. If he saw them together, he'd be killed: now all he wanted was to get out, but he couldn't just leave her at the table. He'd have this beer and make excuses. Wait until he saw Jack Gage; but would he tell him?

"You're a good-looking joker, Dave," Joan said, "better than those uncouth soldiers. They're only after one thing: you know how to treat a lady. I bet you've got loads of girlfriends." The beer ran down her chin and she wiped it with her hand. She scraped her chair on the floorboards and sat close. "What say we go outside after this one? I could do with a breath of fresh air." She ground her butt out in the ashtray. "We could go for a walk along the pier."

"All right then." David swallowed the beer down and got to his feet.

"Not so fast," Joan said. "Christ, you're keen, I thought you were going to be a gentleman." She delved in her purse, produced her compact and lipstick. "I've got to repair meself." She dabbed at her face and straightened her dress as his stomach heaved and his heart thudded.

The sea air hit them like a hammer and they stumbled down the street. Men were drinking under lamp-posts and in the doorways; they whistled as they saw them go. Joan dropped her purse, David went to pick it up, almost fell, grabbed her arm and felt the salt breeze on his face.

"Are you all right?" she said.

"Yes, I'm fine."

"Good, we can look at the fairy lights."

She held his arm and, somewhere, David heard the big sea running.

They stopped under a pine tree as the summer moon shone and the lights from the pier gleamed. Cars passed and there was the sound of a bottle smashing somewhere; a ship's siren sounded and a diesel engine pumped as a fishing boat went down the river. Joan drew him close and put her arms around his shoulders.

"Give us a kiss, Dave."

He felt her tongue against his teeth and her hands between his legs; she felt his crotch as he fumbled with the buttons at her breasts. A cyclist went past, the headlamp flickering.

"Jesus, Dave."

She undid her buttons and groped for his belt; David felt her breasts beneath her bra and petticoat; he tasted her lipstick and breathed her perfume.

86

"Jesus, Dave." Her hands went for him.

David's gorge rose. "I'm sorry," he said. But it was too late and he was sick down her dress.

"Jesus Christ," she hit him on the mouth and he fell under the pine tree. "Jesus Christ," she shouted as she ran, "fucking schoolboys."

* * *

The houses around the school were large and turreted. Tudor and Italianate, built by sea merchants, stockbrokers and millionaires from the gold rushes, with old English maples and aspens and ornamental gardens, where sprinklers played on the rockeries and flower beds where the gardeners worked. David had never been inside any of the mansions, nor strolled beneath the exotic trees, but he had come to like this place: its richness and peace, its grand castles and Victorian towers rising above the smoke from the brick factory chimneys of the city.

Each afternoon in the summer, David and Jack ran along the tan track that encircled the Botanic Gardens. They ran over two miles beneath the imported trees, over the wrought-iron bridge, along the bank of the river and back down the boulevard. It was hard, satisfying work: the fours and the eights trained on the water; anglers sat on the banks and the air was fresh as the southerly drifted in from the bay. David was determined to win the mile a second time and Jack was going for the boxing championship. They both knew all the rules at Grammar and it was good to be back.

"Do you realize we can go into town this year?" Jack said as they ran, "and that means girls."

"The place is full of tarts and soldiers." David wondered if he should tell Jack about the girl at the pub. It would make quite a good story. Or would it?

"I wasn't thinking of tarts, the Yanks can have those. I was thinking of wholesome specimens like us."

87

"I suppose we're wholesome," David said, "but the dancing lessons have been a bloody disaster."

"I don't know: we can do the foxtrot, the waltz and the palais glide, and there's at least one girl who fancies me."

David thought of the girl groping for him in the dark. "I'm going to run the last mile very hard. Do you mind?"

"No," Jack said, "not at all. I'll see you back at school."

David took off under the oak trees and left Jack Gage far behind.

"Cheerio, sergeant major," Jack shouted as his friend disappeared through the trees. But David didn't hear.

*   *   *

They crouched in the bush in the drizzle. David thought they looked a scruffy lot. The corporal had lost one of his eye-teeth; their battle dress was patched and ill-fitting and their webbing frayed and stained. He looked at his watch: it was 16.35, with less than two hours daylight left. He had worked them hard all day through the ugly, broken country and they were tired and hungry. One of them stood up to ease his back.

"The next time you stand up against the skyline, whatever your name is, you're up on a charge. Do you understand?" David said.

"Yes, sir."

"How many times do I have to say that we should see, but not be seen?"

"I forgot, sir."

"The next time you forget, the enemy will put a bullet through your thick skull." David turned to the corporal and produced the ordnance map. "Right, Cooper, where are we?"

The cadet squinted at the contours and co-ordinates. "I'm not sure, sir."

The others listened and hated him. "You're not sure?"

"No, sir."

"Why are you not sure?"

"I'm just not sure, sir."

"You've got two stripes and been on map-reading courses?"

"Yes, sir."

"But you've got no idea, is that what you're saying?"

"I think I've got some idea, sir."

"What state are we in?"

"Victoria, sir."

"Well that's a start, isn't it?"

Cooper tried to grin. "Yes, sir."

"You think you've got some idea. Let's have the benefit of your limited knowledge."

One of the boys laid his Lee Enfield on the ground and fished in the pocket of his tunic.

"What do you think you're doing?" David said.

"Who me, sir?"

"Yes, you."

"I'm not doing anything, sir."

"What are you not doing?"

"I can't understand you, sir."

"Give me that rifle."

"Yes, sir."

"Right," David said, "when you're crouching, you hold the rifle like this. You don't chuck it on the ground so you can stuff chewing gum in your mouth." He threw the Lee back hard and the boy dropped it. "That better be spotless in the morning," David said. "Well, Cooper, where do you *think* we are?"

"I think that's the creek and the ridge there, sir."

"Well, you're wrong, disastrously wrong. Does anybody know where we are?"

There was no reply and the drizzle was becoming rain.

"Shouldn't we go back soon, sir?"

"Go back where?"

"To the camp."

"How can we go back," David said, "if we don't know where we are?"

"But you know, sir."

"Yes, I know, but you don't, and you've got to find out. That's the point of the exercise." David looked at his watch again. "There's less than two hours left to sunset. If you don't use what passes for a brain, we'll be out here all night."

"It's only a game, sir."

"What?"

"It's only a game."

"One day, God help us, some of you will be doing this for real," David said. "What would happen if one of you was wounded and you had to give a grid reference of your whereabouts?" David tossed over his compass. "Now start working." He turned his back on them as they clustered around the map.

"There's a creek, and I reckon that's the one," someone said.

They were bloody hopeless, David thought. He couldn't keep them out all night, but he'd scare them. He looked at the weather: it was coming down and the night would be cold and uncomfortable. He remembered his grandfather when they were fishing on the river. *It doesn't matter how cold and tired you are, be patient and wait.*

"Excuse me, sir," Cooper said, "we've tried, but no one's sure where we are, we've really tried but it's got us beaten. Shouldn't we be starting back now?"

David faced them with his Sten gun; his uniform was neat despite the hard day. "You're all bloody hopeless; there's no bigger crime than to get lost on patrol. Not only do you endanger your own lives, but the lives of the entire battalion; you'll go out tomorrow and the day after until you get it right."

"For Christ's sake, Andersen, this is all bullshit. Get us out of here or you'll be in the soup with the rest of us."

"Who said that?"

"I did." The boy was big and strong and his rifle was lying in the grass.

"Pick up your rifle," David said. "I'll remember you for the rest of the year. You're now the leading scout and I'll be right behind you, telling your thick head where to go. Right," he said to the rest of the section, "follow me and I'll get you home to your warm little beds."

They moved off through the bush as the rain fell.

They were happier now they were on their way home and some of them were laughing and talking. The rain fell and their greatcoats were heavy and sodden. Then David saw the shell in the earth near some burnt stumps and shattered trees.

"Freeze," David said to the boy in front, but he walked on. David lunged and dragged him down by his webbing.

"I said freeze, you stupid bugger."

The ragged column stopped and the boys collided, their rifles tangled.

"What's happening now?" someone said.

"Don't any of you move," Dave said.

"Aw Christ, Andersen."

"If you look over by those stumps," David said, "you'll see an unexploded eighteen-pound shell and even the vibrations of your clod-hopping feet could set the thing off."

"You're kidding."

"I am not. This is an old artillery range."

The boy in front collapsed and lay on the ground; the others lay prone in the bush and already someone was sobbing.

"Right," David said. "I want you all out of here now, and I'll be the last to go."

Not a body moved and David kicked at them and poked with his Sten. "Move, you stupid buggers, move."

They got up and ran like rats through the brush, and when they had gone, David walked slowly and joined them. He double-marched them home and no one said a word.

*   *   *

"Where the hell have you been, Andersen?" Mr Livingstone said. "We've been waiting here for over an hour."

The rain was falling steadily now, the tents were sagging and the trees dripping. Cooper and the section stood, dirty and wet, in their over-sized greatcoats; some were still white-faced and shaking. The mess chimneys smoked and the hurricane lamps gleamed. In one of the tents the boys were laughing and playing cards. Mr Livingstone stood like a ramrod in his officer's uniform. David was as tall as he.

"A spot of bother, sir," David said.

"Bother? What bother?"

"We ran into an unexpected shell, sir."

"Did you?" Mr Livingstone stared. "I assume you've got the map reference?"

"I have, sir."

The section looked on and watched David and the teacher.

"Let me have it."

David pulled out the map and said: "It's there, sir."

"Right, we'll phone the engineers and they'll look after it."

Mr Livingstone turned. "You lads can cut away and get some food, and then get your heads down. Okay?"

"Yes, sir."

They moved off silently through the wet.

"You take nine men out and bring nine men back," Mr Livingstone said.

"I've done that, sir."

"I can see you have. Well done. I assume nothing else happened?"

"No, sir."

"How did the section go?"

"Not well at all, I'm afraid, sir."

"How was the map-reading exercise?"

"Dreadful, sir. They need more training, I'll send them out all day tomorrow until they get it right."

"And you'll supervise?" Mr Livingstone looked at the

fair hair, the blue eyes and the square shoulders and remembered their first meeting when he had quoted Demosthenes and the ash in the bread. Andersen had come a long way since then.

"I will, sir."

"You do that. Well done again, Andersen, now get some food and sleep."

"Yes, sir."

"You're still going to the Royal Military College, aren't you? The country's desperately short of good officers."

"Yes, I am, sir."

"We'll have that thing exploded in the morning, and they can see what could have happened."

The next morning, earth flew and the bush caught fire as the battalion watched from the hill. None of the cadets argued with David after that.

*   *   *

That year, David and Jack always had lunch in the orderly room and went into town once a week. David bought a new suit. They ran along the tan track every afternoon and studied hard in their room beneath the clock tower. David played centre-forward in the first hockey eleven, Jack won the school boxing championship and was captain of MacArthur House. David won the mile a second time, gained exhibitions in English literature, mathematics, chemistry and physics and was awarded the unit prize for the most outstanding cadet of the school. He won the inter-school rifle shooting trophy and commanded the quarter guard at the passing-out parade. The boys in the lower school feared and respected them. It seemed they could make no mistake.

That night at the end-of-the-year school dance, the band played *Tuxedo Junction, In the Mood* and *American Patrol*, the girls were stunning in their long dresses, and the evening was balmy. David was described as the dashing young hero, had many dances, smelled the perfume, danced expertly, drank lemonade and thought about the routine orders in the morning. The band played: they danced the foxtrot and the waltz; couples kissed and hugged in the passage-ways and walked across the oval. David was immaculate and the girls adored him; but he thought of Joan in the pub, her legs crossed and her hands groping. *Fucking schoolboys.*

The following February, David said goodbye to his mother, father and grandfather; he climbed aboard the train at Penshurst with his baggage, his books, his trophies and his school reports and travelled north to the Royal Military College at Duntroon.

5

The Apple Orchard

David Andersen rode in the US Army jeep along the road and munched an apple, his Sten gun on his knees and his greatcoat wrapped around him. He wiped his face with his grimy woollen gloves and looked at Hart and Cash; they were all filthy and hungry and hadn't washed for over a week. It was autumn and the mist lay below in the steep unfamiliar valleys. As he rode up the dirt road, David shivered and considered the two brown farm eggs in his steel helmet. He would have them for tea tonight when the show was over.

The mountains to the north were saw-toothed and barren with great outcrops of yellow rock, and the deserted paddy fields smelt of dung. The bunds were collapsing, the rice stalks black, and the farmhouses gutted. No peasants worked in these fields where the silty river ran and rows of poplars grew. Their yellow and brown leaves were falling and thick on the ground.

The Shermans rumbled, their tracks squealing and throwing up clouds of yellow dust; the air was filled with blue smoke and the smell of stagnant oil. The Shermans were big powerful machines, their pennants flew in the cold breeze, and the commanders stood confidently in the man-holes, surveying the country with their binoculars. Back down the column, David heard the GMC trucks backfiring: the Negro drivers were trying to scare the locals, but no one seemed to be about. He turned around and saw the drivers laughing. Surely the enemy could hear them coming for miles. David tossed the apple core into one of the big ditches that lined the road. They had gone without breakfast. David was hungry and thought about another apple.

At last, the battalion had been given a job to do: to make contact with a company of American paratroopers surrounded on a ridge. Everyone was looking forward to it. Earlier that month, the Americans had thrust north to Pyongyang and beyond. It was a wild, exciting affair, with the 8th Army crossing the 38th Parallel and dashing up a narrow valley into thickly wooded, mountainous country. The narrow road wound through gorges and rocky buttresses where fir, brush and bracken grew. As they retreated, the enemy started fires in the bush: this was dangerous terrain where enfilades and ambushes were easy. A well-placed heavy machine gun or a mortar battery could hold up the advance through the mountains. But it was a push-over: there was slight resistance and the main road north was packed with tanks, guns, jeeps and trucks full of eager, laughing young troops. After the breakout at Pusan and the landings at Inchon, the enemy had disappeared. The North Koreans were on the run; the dust rose from the tyres and tank tracks and the flags flew as the US Cavalry hammered to the Yalu behind a hail of napalm, shells and rockets. The autumn weather was brilliant, the sky clear and blue, the US 8th Army was on the move and it was invincible.

*　　*　　*

The jeep jolted in the pot-holes and the eggs rolled in the steel helmet. David picked it up, turned to the back and said, "Take these, Paul, we don't want them broken."

Jesus Christ, Cash thought, we're going into our first show and Andersen's worrying about two bloody eggs. David looked at his watch. It was 07.30. Paul Cash looked a bit white around the gills and David wondered if he was fingering his rosary. After all the weeks of travelling in all kinds of cracked-up transport, the boredom, bad food, the

96

dust and the flies, the battalion had been asked to do something positive. The men were very eager: so far they had seen no real action and it seemed they had arrived too late. David's back was stiff: last night it had rained yet again and he had slept upright, sitting on his helmet against a tree; but it was a change from digging in and this time the pork and beans were hot and tasted good. Of all things, he most missed sitting on a chair and remembered the winter evenings at *Killara*, the sofa, his grandfather with his Glenfiddich and his father listening to Richard Tauber on the gramophone. After the worst of days, when the tired horses were stabled and fed, when the washing up was done in the cold and steamy kitchen, they could sit on the sofa and the old armchairs, watch the fire and listen to Elgar and Gilbert and Sullivan and hear the bells of Big Ben chime on the wireless at nine. There was no Elgar or Gilbert and Sullivan in this country; here there were the refugees, the howitzers, the Brens, the rockets and the napalm. No crops grew in the muddy fields and no strawberries and tomatoes flourished in the broken glasshouses. This was a sad and remote land.

David wiped his face again, watched the tank commander with his scarf and binoculars, the antenna bending like a bow and the turret traversing. The diesel fumes pumped from the exhaust, the tracks rattled on the stony road, and Sergeant Hart changed gears as they topped the rise. He turned and looked at Cash who was sitting, dusty and white-faced, the steel helmet with the eggs jammed between his muddy boots. The countryside slid by like a silent film; because of the noise of the big diesels and the GMCs, he could hear nothing. He reached into his tunic pocket; the bakelite buttons were broken and missing and the pouch of the Webley was hard against his chest; he got out the map. The nearest village was a place called Yongyu and apple orchards grew there. It seemed they were everywhere in this part of North Korea. His empty stomach rumbled and he watched Sergeant Hart roll and light a cigarette as he drove. Old Ben Hopkins could do that while going full tilt on his station hack as he rode across the plains of Penshurst where a million rabbits ran. That seemed a long time ago. Sometimes David wished he smoked. It was something to do and steadied the nerves. He studied the map again and pulled out the chinagraph pencil; he considered the co-ordinates. This was uncharted territory: hills, mountains, farms and apple orchards. Someone had told him that the traditional tribute of the Koreans to the Chinese was apples. The jeep lurched and jolted behind the Sherman; the windshield was down to prevent sun flashes, and there was nothing to protect them. He felt the enemy were watching from those bald and rocky hills, as this noisy column barged down the narrow road. Hart tossed the cigarette butt from his strong and bony fingers and drove like a veteran. He looked at David Andersen and grinned. Hart had done all this before; he *was* a veteran.

No one quite knew where the Americans were: somewhere to the north on a ridge beyond the orchards. They passed a few more mud-brick houses, some oxen and two-wheeled carts. A Korean peasant, dressed in white and wearing an old panama hat, raised his stick as they rumbled by. The trooper on the Sherman set his machine gun sight on the peasant and watched for enemy movement in the shabby, broken buildings. No one else was around. What was the old man doing by himself?

David hoped that Cash would come up to standard. Hart would: he'd fought in New Britain and Rabaul and didn't think much of fresh, young subalterns from the Royal Military College. The battalion was a bit makeshift and thrown together; it was poorly equipped and half the wireless sets didn't work, but David was sure they'd make up for that with their enthusiasm and all would be right on the day. He remembered his father telling him about the Battle of the Marne. It wouldn't be like that. He also recalled his instructor at the College: *If you take thirty men to capture a hill, you try and get thirty back.* Hart drove the jeep close behind the tanks.

When they heard the sound of rifle and machine gun fire at the head of the column, the Shermans stopped short and the truck behind ran into the jeep. Hart cursed and shouted and the captain ran up and told them to assemble in the ditch at the side of the road. They all jumped down with their haversacks and Sten guns. The firing clattered and echoed across the grey hills, then stopped: the tanks had taken the enemy out. The ditch was deep, they couldn't see what was happening and David started to sweat in his greatcoat. He saw Hart, rawboned, freckled, and red-haired, grinning and watching him. The clay was yellow and dry, the concrete culverts cracked and crumbling and the iron mesh protruded like old bones. More firing started and the Shermans started up again, pumping shots into the hills ahead. David looked at the men in his platoon: many of them were farm boys, some were delinquents from the orphanage and had not been in the army very long, but no one looked anxious. They were grimy but open-faced and cheerful, like the boys who rode the buck-jumpers and bulls in the country rodeos on the showgrounds at Penshurst and Hamilton. He remembered the Country and Western music, the beer drinking, the caravans and the little boys in ten-gallon hats climbing the stock rails and opening the gates as the bulls and horses charged across the dusty, pitted turf. They lived in caravans and the women had dirt ground into the lines in their faces. Those people were gypsies: they had no home. They had not been to a public school, read *Country Life*, and lived in a house with mosaic tiles and a tennis court.

Suddenly, a mortar bomb came over and dirt and gravel landed in the ditch. Smoke drifted from fires burning in the brush. They heard the sound of the Shermans grinding on the road and the Brownings firing. Another bomb landed very close and they all ducked in the ditch.

"Christ," Sergeant Hart said, as he tossed away his cigarette, "them bastards are not bad, are they?"

"Fucking gooks," Cash said, "they'll be the death of us."

That's why we're here, David thought, to be the death of them. Make the enemy die for his country, not you.

Sergeant Hart was from Maitland in New South Wales and looked after the men. The colonel was from the country too, and knew what he was doing. David stood with his men in the ditch and thought of his quarter-horse and the dog running across the stony plains of Penshurst. He heard more firing, looked up and saw a buzzard wheeling in the bright morning sky. They were ugly birds, fearless, and lacking the grace of the eagles he knew so well. Cash was delving into his tunic pocket for a Lucky Strike, but the packet was empty. Then the captain came up and told them to move up the ditch, cross the road under the covering fire of the Shermans and assault the enemy in the apple orchard on the other side of the ridge. Then, he said, it was their job to find the Americans. He looked at David and said it wouldn't be too difficult as long as they kept their heads down and got the map reference right.

David and his platoon moved up the ditch under the covering fire of the Sherman 75s. The noise was deafening and the ground shook; they splashed through the puddles, heaved themselves out of the ditch and ran across the road into the apple trees on the hill. The trees were old and well spaced, the grass was wet and long. The apples hung down, and gleamed deep red as David and his men ran through the gnarled trees, their Sten guns raised and their greatcoats flapping. They topped the rise and ran down the other side. Suddenly, gunfire cracked and chattered through the trees and echoed in the early morning. It seemed that the enemy was firing everywhere. The North Korean soldiers were dressed in white smocks like peasants, looked like angels; some of them started up and ran from the pits where apples were piled, threw their arms up and surrendered; others sniped and fired rifles, burp guns and pistols. They were in their hundreds and it looked like a full regiment. But the attackers had taken them in the rear by surprise, and the Australians shot them down as they ran through the trees; they fell like puppets and lay still in the grass. Men were shouting and a soldier in white raised a rifle at David; he shot him in the chest and then shot two more as they ran away to his right. His mouth was dry, he turned, took out a fresh magazine and saw Sergeant Hart running everywhere, firing his Sten gun at the North Koreans who ran, surrendered, crouched, fell and ran down the spur toward the valley and the paddy fields. Hart was grinning and then shouted something at David. Someone threw a grenade, David ducked and fell, got up, saw Cash firing through the trees, was hit through his greatcoat, got up and ran up the spur and looked at the valley below. Had Hart not shouted, David thought, he wouldn't be seeing this valley, the orchard, the men. It would be Hart he had to thank for his life. Why not someone gentle like Cash?

The captain had told him to get his men through to the Americans. But where were they? In the orchard, the men were searching the North Koreans, taking their weapons and herding them into groups. The prisoners would need watching, David thought, and what was happening behind them? He felt the ragged hole in his greatcoat, and then considered the dry paddy fields, the stooks of rice, the small haystacks and the long stretch of road to the next ridge. The enemy would be hiding there in the open country that lay between them and the Americans on the next ridge. Then Hart, Cash and the other men joined him, and to the sound of shouts, rifle-fire, burp guns and grenades, they ran down the hill.

"Your hand's bleeding, sir," Cash said as they ran down the road.

David looked at his left hand and the blood seeped from the veins. "It doesn't matter, Paul," he said. He wiped his hand on his mouth and tasted the blood. "Just keep going."

A horse and cart lay across the road. The horse had been

wounded in the throat by shrapnel and two of its legs were broken, the cart was upturned and apples lay everywhere. The horse was still conscious, its ears flat and eyes cloudy. Its bony flanks rose and fell, and bloody spume dribbled from its mouth. Bullets banged into the cart and the road, but none of David's men was hurt. They crouched by the cart beneath the fire from the paddy field.

"Jesus Christ," Hart said, "those bastards are making it hot for us."

"Right," David said, "one of you shoot the horse. We've got to clear the road before the transport gets here."

A young soldier called Brownlee, whom David knew was an enlisted man, took his Lee Enfield and shot the animal between the eyes as the fire from the paddy field cracked around them, and they heaved the tangled mass into the ditch. High in the sky, birds were flying south. They looked like geese.

Cash said, "There's more blokes coming, sir. There's more coming."

"Right," David said, "let's get on with it."

And they ran off down the road, dust rising from their boots and up the spur toward the American Airborne. The sounds of battle still came from the orchard, and as he ran, his lungs bursting, David looked at his watch. It was just past twelve noon, and he was still alive.

The spur was a bloody shambles. The Americans were on a narrow ridge and had not dug themselves in. Bodies of dead men and discarded expensive equipment lay everywhere: boxes of ammunition, entrenching tools, machine guns, clothing and rations. A top-sergeant lay stiff under a ground sheet; he had been shot through the head and his skull was shattered; medics were running everywhere giving aid and David couldn't work out who was in command. Some Americans were crying, but rose to their feet, threw down their weapons and hugged the Australians. David was embarrassed and tried to shake hands, but Sergeant Hart shrugged his shoulders and turned away. Men lay dying, and one told David that twelve of them had been killed three nights ago by North Koreans as they slept in a church in the valley. David had never seen men dying before, and he remembered his childhood prayers. *Gentle Jesus, meek and mild.*

Hart poked around among the discarded equipment and said: "Serves the stupid bastards right, anyone who sleeps in a church and trusts the fucking gooks deserves to get it. Christ, if we had all this gear, we'd win the war before Christmas."

The smoke from the wood fires spiralled in the hills, the Americans cheered and shouted, the Australian medical team arrived and David searched through the brush for casualties. He went down the spur through the fir trees and brambles, keeping an eye out for snipers and heard the transport arriving at the top of the hill. Somewhere to the south, heavy machine guns rattled and mortars thumped.

David came across freshly dug earth: someone had tried to dig himself in. That was one lesson the instructors always drummed into them. *It doesn't matter how bloody tired you are, always dig yourselves in.*

"Can you get me out of here?" the American soldier said. David pushed through the thick brush and saw the man lying in a narrow pit. There was another soldier dead beside him. Unfamiliar wild flowers were growing and the American had a thick accent that David could hardly understand. He was from one of the southern states, he thought.

"Yes, I can," he said. The American was big, maybe over six feet, blond, hit in both legs and the flies buzzed and crawled. He had put a towel over the wounds to keep them off.

"You're an Aussie?" the American said. "I been here two days."

"I beg your pardon?" David said. He crouched over the American, took out his water bottle and gave him a drink. "Can you get me out of here?"

"Oh, yes," David said, "we've got a medical team on the spur."

"How's that?" The American moved a little and gave David his empty water bottle. He was about nineteen and looked like a country boy that David had seen in the film of *The Grapes of Wrath*.

"I'll give you a hand," David said. "You come with me."

"I'm a quarter-back, maybe I won't play no more."

David got the young American on to his back. He was badly hit, by a mortar it looked, and the blood was black and the wounds festering. David saw that both his legs had been taken away below the knee. Oh, Lord Jesus, he thought, let me never suffer that. He wondered if he should call for help, but decided against it. Somehow David picked up the carbine as well and staggered up the slope. It seemed like a long haul and the American smelled of shit and blood.

"Thanks, buddy," he said, "thanks, buddy. I been in that hole two days."

The flies clung to them both, but David couldn't brush them away. Then he heard the drone of motors: it was the MASH helicopters coming in. At least the Americans had got that right, David thought, they knew how to evacuate their casualties. He stumbled and tripped over some gear and at last got the paratrooper on to a stretcher.

"Thanks, friend," the American said.

"It was the least I could do."

"How's that?"

"I said it was the least I could do."

The boy looked puzzled. He was carried to the helicopter pod and David turned away.

*   *   *

"What have you been doing, Andersen?" the captain said as he looked at David's bloodied, filthy uniform.

"I've just picked up a wounded American, sir."

"I don't care if you've picked up Betty Grable, you're an

infantryman, not a bloody nurse. I want you and your chaps down in that paddy field. Go in and clear it out. The CO's under fire and we can't have that."

Sergeant Hart got the men together and they moved off down the hill. The Americans were still cheering and shouting and two more big helicopters were flying in. An American windcheater was lying in the brush. David picked it up and stuffed it under his battledress. It was now three o'clock and getting cold. This was difficult country: what would the winter be like?

They ran back through the battle into the paddy fields. The afternoon air was filled with the crack and rattle of small-arms fire as the enemy shot at them from rice stooks and from behind the bunds. The men shouted and fired their Stens as the Koreans ran across the open stubble and splashed through the stagnant pools. Again they fell like puppets at a shooting gallery, and some crawled along the earth only to be shot once more. David's blood raced and he, too, fired his Sten at the Koreans. He didn't pause to look at the bodies: it was like hunting game, it was like coming home with a full bag. The mist drifted down from the mountains and still the soldiers fired, ran and chased the enemy. The killing was easy and the bodies lay on the ground, their white smocks bloodied.

Sergeant Hart ran and jumped over the canals and bunds; he dug the Koreans out of the stooks with his bayonet, shouted and ran back and forth across the paddies as the enemy hid and scuttled. It seemed that every quarry was his and he never missed his target. The enemy went down like nine-pins. Those who didn't surrender were shot; when it was over, there must have been seventy bodies lying on the rice stubble and in the canals, and the prisoners were herded away.

David stood in the paddy and counted his men: there were no casualties. It was a successful day. Hart came bounding up and said: "We got the bastards, sir, we got the bastards, a turkey shoot."

David looked at Hart and the other men as they came up through the rice stalks, their guns on their shoulders; they were laughing and chatting, their faces grinning and covered with mud.

"Yes," David said, "yes, it was."

After the battle was over, they felt tired and dusty and wanted a good meal. They had eaten nothing hot for forty-eight hours. The western sun grew low and the clouds drifted, grey and purple. The paddies seemed quiet now. The mechanics fiddled with the engines and the drivers started their trucks. Two jeeps came up the road on the ridge, the dust and stones spinning. David felt suddenly weary and longed to sit down with a cup of tea; he looked at the bodies spreadeagled in the paddies, as the buzzards and crows flapped and swooped in the chilly sky.

But the captain ordered them back into the paddies to count and search the bodies, and they walked down the slope beneath the apple trees. Some of the North Koreans lay in the concrete apple pits, others lay alone under the trees and some lay in groups near the rice stooks. The bodies lay at all angles in the grass; their blood was congealing, and even though it was getting cold in the late afternoon, the flies were gathering in their wounds and crawling over their open eyes. It was the first time they had seen the enemy close up. A light wind with drizzling rain was starting to drift in from the mountains as they counted and searched the bodies. There wasn't much to find: the North Koreans travelled light. Under their white peasant smocks they wore cheap brown padded uniforms and canvas boots: there were no signs of rank, this was the People's Army, and they were defeated. They carried brown rice in thin cotton rolls, wrapped around their bodies; their black hair was close-cropped, their faces were like marble and they all looked the same. Some wore quilted pyjamas and lay in the mud, their boots split and laces untied. They found the usual burp guns, Russian-made light machine guns, some old US Second World War carbines, cheap grenades and some Czech army pistols. They piled the weapons up in the paddies and fossicked for mementoes, something to take home to show their wives and girlfriends. David walked under the apple trees and down to the paddies. It seemed ordinary. The vultures, crows and buzzards waited patiently on the branches; and the seagulls flew high in the gloomy sky toward the coastal estuaries.

Paul Cash walked through the long wet grass, past the apple pits, the fallen branches and the white-smocked bodies lying in the rice stubble. There was blood on the ground, empty shells, a heavy machine gun with its tripod broken, and ammunition belts lying in the grass. He moved carefully, trying at first not to touch anything. He wanted to cross himself, but someone might be watching. Shouldn't the *padre* be here? The wind drifted through the trees and down the slope, and Paul Cash saw Andersen and Sergeant Hart moving over the stubble searching and counting. There was no one to turn to now. He walked on down the slope. He wished he was back home.

On the first body, Cash saw the beads of a rosary. He knelt and carefully extracted it from the tunic of the dead man, and in doing so, found the missal. He opened the tiny leatherbound book, and read the familiar Latin words. He ran his fingers over the beads of the rosary and felt the crucifix, the tiny nails in Christ's hands. Cash didn't know that some North Koreans were Catholics: he thought they were all Communists. He looked around the paddy field. The other men were about fifty yards away, bending over the bodies and pushing them over with their rifle butts. No one was watching him, so Cash stuffed the prayer book and the rosary into his greatcoat pocket. Nobody would ever know. He picked up his rifle and walked forward over the wet ground, his boots trampling the broken rice stalks.

Hart went through the bodies roughly, kicking them and prodding them with his Sten gun. Bits of rice paper flew about in the breeze, fluttering around like large white butterflies. David stooped and picked one up. He looked at the fine, elegant script. What did the signs mean? He felt far away. He folded the rice paper and put it in his pocket book. Then he saw a photograph and picked it up from the stubble: it was of a young Korean woman in her wedding dress, standing on the church steps. She was very beautiful.

"Not bad, sir, eh?" Hart said as he looked over David's shoulder.

"I suppose so." David dropped the photograph and ground it into the mud with his boot. He turned away from the big sergeant and shouted: "I hope you blokes aren't missing anything, we'll want it all for the de-briefing."

"No, sir." The men laughed, smoked their cigarettes, shouted and stalked about in their grubby uniforms, pushing and poking at the bodies.

The light was failing now and the sun was going down behind the pine forests on the mountains. The thunder cracked and boomed in the hills and David felt very tired. He was hungry, sick of counting and searching and wanted a cup of tea: he wanted to go to sleep. What was the time in Australia? He saw Cash coming up, carrying his Lee Enfield in his left hand, not looking at all like a soldier.

"Well, Cash," David said, "what have you found?"

"Nothing, sir."

"Keep looking and don't muck about. Maps, papers, anything. I've got to be at BHQ by 1800 hours."

"Yes, sir."

David watched Cash walk down the paddy to some distant rice stooks. He wondered how many they had killed. Three or four hundred perhaps? It had been a good day.

* * *

It was now early evening, and they stood around Battalion Headquarters. The body count was over seven hundred and the senior officers laughed and talked and drank their tea. Cranes' nests perched in the trees and the last of the American helicopters swung away with their dead. To the south, the North Korean prisoners were being herded into groups; those who looked like officers were separated from the men for interrogation, and the men were pushed on to the trucks. Without their weapons, they all looked like harmless peasants now.

David stood apart from the other officers and wondered how soon de-briefing would be: he was numb and wanted to stretch out somewhere and go to sleep. He thought about the day and didn't want to talk to anyone. He hoped he had done well; it seemed to him that he had; there were no cock-ups and his men had fought well. He thought of the American paratrooper with his legs missing: it was the first time he had seen a man wounded in combat and he hoped to God it would never happen to him.

"David Andersen," the colonel said, "that was a very good show."

David turned and saluted, and saw two other officers standing under the trees. One was an English brigadier and the other a young subaltern. The colonel introduced him to them both. "This is David Andersen," he said, "one of our rising stars."

"A fine effort, Mr Andersen," the brigadier said. "Thank God we have Australians in the Commonwealth Brigade." David was pleased. "Thank you, sir."

"You'll pass on my congratulations to your men, won't you?" the brigadier said.

"I will indeed, sir."

"Good. It's been a great pleasure meeting you; it's been one of the best shows I've seen. I can't tell you where you'll be next. They say the war will be over by Christmas, but you never can tell, can you?"

"No, sir."

"If you want to look around, Tom," the brigadier said to the subaltern, "you do so. We leave at 19.00."

"Right you are, sir," the young officer said.

David and the young English officer both saluted the brigadier, and the colonel left and strolled up the slope through the trees.

"Do you smoke?" the English officer said as he held out the packet of John Players. He was wearing a black beret; he was carefully groomed, with neatly parted hair; he had a hawkish nose and wore a moustache. He looked like a thoroughbred racehorse and leant on his walking stick.

"No thanks, I don't," David said. "I'm sorry, I didn't catch your name."

"Tom Fleetwood, the 1st 28th Gloucesters. I'm the brigadier's intelligence man." Fleetwood lit his cigarette and blew the smoke out through his nostrils. "The brigadier meant what he said, you know."

David didn't know what to say, fiddled with his webbing, and gazed down the slopes at the trucks moving away along the narrow road. Where would they be next? He hoped they would see more action.

"Your first show?" Fleetwood said.

"Yes, it is."

"You've got one up on me then. I must say I admired your men."

"Did you?"

"Yes, I did." Fleetwood tossed his cigarette butt away into the bushes. "I'm in the advance guard. The Gloucesters are coming in from Hong Kong."

"The battle of Alexandria," David said.

Fleetwood grinned. "So you know about us?"

"Yes, the Glorious Gloucesters. We've been told about you."

"Well," Fleetwood said, "that's a start, isn't it? We don't want the Royal Australian Regiment stealing our thunder all the time, do we?"

"No," David said, and he, too, smiled. "I suppose you don't."

"They're not bad fighters, are they?"

"Who?" David said.

"The North Koreans."

"We routed them today."

"You did, but they're tricky and strong. They'll take

some beating. It's not all over by a long chalk. How did you find the Americans?"

"In a mess." David thought of the tears, the shouting, and the screaming.

"They rely too much on their equipment," Fleetwood said. "They think firepower and armour is the answer, but it's not. From the little I've seen, this is bloody awful country for transport. There's hardly a decent road anywhere; it's a foot soldier's war, and they're long and bloody. Had they dug themselves in?"

"No, they hadn't."

"I thought not. Forgotten their spades, had they? The first principle of infantry fighting overlooked."

"When do the Gloucesters arrive?" David said.

"In about a fortnight. We've been all over the shop since the war: Berlin, Bermuda, Jamaica. Nice work if you can get it, but something tells me that this show won't be nice." Fleetwood looked at the thin, fair Australian: he was built like a greyhound and his uniform hung on his thin body. He was obviously a cut above the rest, remote and intelligent. "You're a Duntroon man?"

"Yes, I am."

"My father used to have a friend there, Colonel Hawkins. He was killed at Monte Cassino."

David was so tired now he could barely stand. "If you don't mind," he said, "I'd better get back to my men."

"Of course. One of these days, come over and see the Gloucesters if you can wangle it. You'd be most welcome."

"Thanks, I might do that."

"Good luck then."

They shook hands and Fleetwood strode up the slope, his buckles gleaming. He was out of the top drawer, David thought, no doubt about that. He remembered the photographs of society weddings in *Country Life* and smiled. His mother would certainly approve of Mr Fleetwood.

* * *

III

They lay under the trees and the tea tasted hot and sweet. The night was clear and cold and the stars shone.

"A great day, a fucking great day," Sergeant Hart said. "Seven hundred of the bastards, it was like shooting rabbits, and they ran like bunnies, didn't they? What do you think, Brownlee?"

"It was good, Sarge."

"Good? It was fucking marvellous, much better than the jungle. At least here you can see what you're doing."

"I suppose so, Sarge."

"Suppose so? I fucking know."

"That's right, Sarge."

"What's that you've got there, Cashie?" Hart peered in the half-light. "Are you playing with yourself, or something?"

"No, Sarge."

"What is it? You haven't been pilfering, have you? If you have it's curtains for you." Hart leaned over Cash. "All you orphanage blokes are the same, you can't be trusted, and if you smoke on the piquet tonight, I'll have your balls for paperweights whether you're Mr Andersen's batman or not. What have you got there?" Cash held up the rosary. "My rosary, Sarge."

"Jesus Christ, you're always playing with that bloody thing. Why don't you pull yourself off like the rest of us? What are you? A fucking nun or something?"

The other men watched, silent; the trouble was that Hart knew his job and they couldn't do without him; he had fought before and knew the tricks of the trade.

"What's this then?" David said as he came up.

"Nothing, sir," Cash said, "we were just talking." The other men of the section sat in the shadows.

"Is there any hot tucker, sir?" one of them said.

"I'm afraid not. There's tea and apples."

"Your eggs got broken, sir," Cash said.

"Never mind, the colonel and the English brigadier both

112

send you their congratulations. They said it was a fine show."

"Was the Pommy brigadier here, sir?" someone said.

"He was, he saw the whole thing, and he said, 'Thank God for the Australians'." He turned to Hart and said, "Thank you for your help, Sergeant."

There was no reply and they gathered their greatcoats around them. David looked at the sky and tried to recall the solar system: which was closer to the Earth – Mars or Saturn? He couldn't remember. Where was the Milky Way? Then the company sergeant major appeared and said: "A good effort, you blokes, the colonel's pleased. Two Poms were there and we showed them. We've got you on the 04.00 piquet, sir."

"The what?" David felt the ragged hole in his greatcoat.

"The 04.00 piquet, sir."

"Oh, that's fine."

"Hadn't you better get some sleep, sir?"

"Yes, I suppose I had."

"Goodnight," the company sergeant major said and walked away. Then he turned. "Hart, would you make sure everything's shipshape?"

Hart grinned. "Yes, sir."

Paul Cash made another brew of tea, but when he carried the steaming mug over, David was fast asleep. He did not see the planets, or the Milky Way.

6

The Sniper

David and Paul Cash squatted in the foxhole as the cold wind blew. It was almost 2300 hours; the weather had become warmer during the day and now it was starting to snow. Black clouds blew in from the north. Snowflakes spun and settled on their tunics, helmets and weapons. Neither of them had seen snow before; in Australia it fell only in the high country, where they had never been. A full, early winter moon shone through the flurries, and the steep hills loomed in the dark. David shivered and quaked and thought of the Christmas cards sent by his grandmother in England. He thought of Santa Claus, empty pillow cases and stockings on the fireguard by the chimney.

A fire was burning. Was it a farmhouse or an army vehicle? All was dark, save its distant glow. It was a beacon in the night. He thought of a poem he had learned at school: *Tyger, Tyger, burning bright*. He fiddled with the breech of his Sten and stretched his toes in his hob-nailed boots. The metal of his submachine gun was hard and cold, his hair in his balaclava was starting to freeze, and there was nothing to eat or drink: it was all turning to ice. He wanted to blow his nose, but could not. He watched the fire: it was burning on the mud-flats by the frozen river. By day, the river was ugly, meandering and shingly as it stretched east toward the Yellow Sea. Was the fire built by refugees, or the enemy? David rubbed the bristles on his chin: it was too cold to shave in this weather. Yesterday, at dawn, one of the men cut away his upper lip using a cut-throat.

His empty belly rumbled. Now the moon disappeared

behind the snow clouds, and the night was fathomless. There was no sound. David knew that Hart and Kershaw were sitting hunched on the other side of the observation post a hundred yards away, and the other men lay sleeping in their pits, covered with blankets, greatcoats and straw. The snowflakes blew and spun through the night. He knew that Hart and Kershaw were awake and covering his position; they would see the enemy if they came across the rocky ground. Then he thought he heard something moving in the brush and flipped off the safety catch of his Sten. His armpits itched. Was it lice? He thought he heard the sound again and dared not move. He shifted in his greatcoat, wanted to have a piss, felt the itching and gripped the cold metal of the Sten. His feet were aching inside his boots, the snow was heavier now, and he pulled his balaclava over his face. He thought of the log fires at home, the starched dinner napkins, silver salt-cellars, roast lamb and mint sauce and the smell of burnt toast from the kitchen. Where were the dogs barking?

* * *

Word had come through last month to the battalion that the Chinese had entered the war, but no one seemed worried about it. The destruction of the North Korean armies would be decisive, General Douglas MacArthur said: the Chinese had no air force and were badly equipped and only about 50,000 men could cross the Yalu River. But David thought a lot more could come if it froze over.

About a fortnight earlier, the Australians had found a combat diary on a dead North Korean officer saying that the Communist armies were in a bad position and that a new propaganda plan was being established. To the Australians it looked at the time as if they might be home for Christmas and the war would be over. After the success at the apple orchard, David wasn't sure whether he wanted the war to end quickly or not. Combat life was much harder than he expected, but he was getting to know his men now and they were getting to know him. Even Hart, he hoped, was starting to show him some respect. David felt young and strong and wanted to succeed. When he returned home after this strange battle he wanted his senior officers and his mother and father to be proud of him. Makeshift the battalion might be, but the men were tough and there was plenty of *esprit de corps*. It was an adventure, and David was glad he had come.

Then, the campaign changed for the worse. The US 8th Cavalry was badly mauled by Chinese regulars at Unsan, and the retreat was disastrous: massive jams of half-tracks, jeeps, tanks and howitzers on the narrow dirt roads; and an ambush at night in the freezing weather with the Reds trapping the convoy and firing point-blank into the struggling cavalrymen and stalled trucks. Vehicles were stacked bumper to bumper on an ancient road that for years had borne only draught animals and handcarts. The enemy sprang, screaming and shouting with whistles and bugles blowing, out of the darkness on either side of the road and poured automatic fire and grenades into the packed trucks. The slaughter was terrible. Enemy troops were everywhere; the front of the column was hit hard and burning trucks and jeeps blocked the road. There was no detour and the Reds fired straight into the Americans. The troopers abandoned their tanks and plunged into the undergrowth and tried to fight hand to hand. Most of them were killed or captured, and many of them were burned to death in their tanks and trucks. The 8th Cavalry lost 1000 men, many trucks and artillery pieces. Rumour had it that some American soldiers turned tail and ran and that some officers were involved in the panic, but David's officers said that it was a one-off defeat, that it couldn't happen again, and that the UN forces would win the war easily with their superior equipment and firepower. All the same, the Chinese were obviously tough and cunning fighters, and knew the country well. They had little transport apart from mules and their own feet, but in this country maybe that was a good thing.

After the disaster at Unsan, there was a confusing lull; the Chinese didn't seem to want to take up their gains and instead disappeared back into the northern hills while the Arctic winter set in. The UN forces were all unprepared for the cold, the Australians most of all. The clothing issue was hopeless, most of it from the Pacific War. Everything froze: beer in bottles, water-carts, eggs in their shells, petrol in drums, graphite on Brens, and some men on guard duty had to be chiselled from their rifles. The yellow dust of the Korean summer had turned into a hard glaze and the rice stalks in the paddy fields were now spears of ice. The fields were like torture pits and no one dared enter them. Many of the older men who had served in the last war had kidney trouble, lumbago and rheumatism. A lot of them had cheated on their age to get back into a war, and now they were feeling it. The tidal river to the north was now a gleaming field of ice. No seagulls and cormorants flew. Then the British arrived: the Northumberland Fusiliers, the Gloucesters, the Argylls, the Ulsters and the Hussars with their Centurion tanks. It was good to have the Brits alongside: they were the Empire; they were the stuff of Omdurman, Ladysmith, Arras and Loos. Most Australians felt that the British were tougher and more reliable than the Americans. David knew all about the Gloucesters and their famous back-badges and the battle in Egypt. They dug into the stony hills at Pakchon and waited as the Arctic winter progressed.

David had never been so cold. He was reading the Royal Australian Regiment news-sheet during the afternoon, but gave up when the night came down. The Chinese were reported to have invaded Tibet, and both the Americans and the Russians now had the atomic bomb. What would President Truman do? What was happening in Berlin to the air-lift? The Communists were taking over everywhere. It all seemed a bit risky, but there wasn't much anyone could do. There was nothing he could compare this cold with. Nothing in Australia, he supposed. He thought of the clear, crisp winter mornings at *Killara*, the dew on the fence posts and the grass. He remembered walking to school and smashing the ice in the puddles with his Wellington boots.

On the piquet a couple of nights ago, Kershaw and Brownlee both said they heard voices. It was hard to tell, but nobody could believe that the Chinese would be patrolling in this weather. They had all sat still for about an hour, their teeth chattering and limbs aching, but nothing happened and in the morning there was no sign. Nothing, not even a twig, it seemed, was disturbed. But Kershaw and Brownlee had sworn they heard something, even though no Australian patrol was out that night. They were both country lads and knew the signs. The watching and waiting was starting to get at everybody. Hart said that piquets and patrolling sorted the men from the boys as much as combat; he said again that the apple orchard had been a turkey shoot. The battalion was well dug in and life was tense and boring. Some nights, a North Korean biplane made of canvas and wood flew very low down the valley; the pilot dropped a bomb or a hand grenade, but nobody was killed or wounded. They called the plane Bed-check Charlie, and it just made things more difficult. One week they heard a bugle playing the *Last Post* from the opposite ridge.

They worked by night and rested by day, sitting about in the wintry sun, trying to get some shelter from the north wind. All the men learned the value of sleep and if you couldn't sleep in the daytime hours, there wasn't much to do. There wasn't much to think about either, except surviving the weather and the enemy. David tried to write home every other day and had read all his books twice. *A Tale of Two Cities* was falling to pieces. A lot of the men traded comics until they disintegrated. Some of the men read a book called *Fanny Hill*. One thing they all knew: if they dozed on the piquet or fell asleep on patrol, they might never wake again. Three men died that way.

Where were the Chinese? It was said that they were cleaning and oiling their weapons and eating their cabbage soup in bunkers carved into the hills. What were *they* thinking about? The only reminder of the enemy now was the distant drumming of the American artillery and fire-flashes in the mountains. How did the Chinese survive the cold?

*　　*　　*

Where was that stand of firs? David knew the gully was reasonably open, with rocky outcrops and sparse brush. The enemy could be anywhere. He rubbed his eyes and watched like a fox. Watching for what? In the afternoon they had seen the fishtraps standing fragile, disused and frozen into the lake, where the mountains rose, reflected. David shifted the Mills grenades on his belt and thought of Scott's *Last Expedition*, which he had read at school, and of the final march to One Ton Camp: Scott in his tent as the four-day blizzard blew, composing his last letters home. "*You must understand that it is too cold to write much.*" David had not written home for two weeks. The ink had frozen. They would be worrying about him, especially his mother and grandfather. He shifted his body around the pit, saw Cash was asleep and prodded him in the ribs. Jesus Christ. Cash straightened up. "Sorry, sir."

He bet Cash was dying for a cigarette. Poor little bugger. Sometimes David wished he smoked like most of the men. It was something to do during the day. He never thought that a soldier's life could be so idle. Maybe nothing would happen after the apple orchard? Maybe they would sit in the hills all the winter and the summer too, until the politicians sorted the thing out? Soldiers were powerless. He thought of Hart in the pit 100 yards away. He was awake, no doubt about that. Hart seemed to hate everything and everybody: he certainly hated subalterns from military college. But he was a resourceful soldier and had saved

David's life at the apple orchard, almost casually, it seemed. Maybe he was keeping him for later? Hart had fought in New Guinea and the Solomons. David remembered the drover on the Dunkeld Road, his father on the mare, and the Winchester falling. "*Yah, yah, come, on boys.*" That was Hart. He hadn't read *Tom Brown's Schooldays*; he hadn't been to Melbourne Grammar or eaten at the Melbourne Club as his father's guest. There was no Sword of Honour for Hart.

It was bitter now: the cold was reaching into his entrails; he wheezed and shifted his body again.

"Cash," David said, "are you awake?"

"Yes, sir."

"You'd better be."

"I am, sir."

"Well, stay that way. If I catch you asleep again, you're in big trouble."

"Yes, sir."

"You watch. There's half an hour to go."

"Yes, sir."

Cash was a natural coward, but David liked him. He was an orphan, a country lad, raised in a Catholic institution in Portland, Victoria. His fingernails were bitten to the quick and his face was blotched with freckles. He couldn't survive outside the Christian Brothers or the army.

*   *   *

Two months earlier, in October, the battalion had travelled by train from Pusan to Taegu. The rolling stock was decrepit, the carriages foul and bone-breaking and the trip seemed endless. They stopped time after time for the coolies to gather wood for the steam engine and to clear rubble off the line. No one knew exactly where they were going, except that the Argylls and the Middlesex would be there. The mountains rose, bare and steep, from a broad alluvial valley where the poplars and willows were skeletons reflected in the still, black water of the lakes and paddy fields. The countryside smelt of piss and shit, and nobody was working it any more.

Taegu was flattened, smashed, broken and derelict; hardly a house was standing and the smoke from the fires choked and drifted. The road leading out of it was full of peasants, bicycles and handcarts as refugees streamed to the south. Children's bodies lay on the roadside and in the ditches, and old Korean men and women with faces like wood pushed carts, pulled the tethers of donkeys, and carried babies on their backs. The younger men, with bodies as thin as sticks, carried A-frame packs on their backs along the narrow roads, past the broken bunds and deserted paddy fields. When the Australians had been in Japan, they were told that the Koreans were a strange, cruel people; but aggression was aggression: the North had invaded the South. David had met an American journalist in the officer's mess in Japan who told him he saw Koreans beating a dog to death in a sack to make the meat tender. He said they had a strange sense of humour and that it was hard to tell what the Koreans meant by a laugh. But now, as they saw the Koreans who trudged the roads, they looked pitiful and harmless enough.

The air smelled of dead animals and shit, and David saw dogs gnawing at torsoes and human heads. The children were in rags, bare-arsed and crying. It was a sad, ruined place: David had never seen such a primitive people, such a poor country. It was like being in the Dark Ages. He thought of Goths, Vandals, and Huns, and the stories he had read at school of Genghis Khan and the cruelty, pillage and rape. There was no comfort at Taegu.

They were told there were no Reds at Taegu, but they had to comb the area out for guerrillas and stragglers: for enemy who were left in the hills with burp guns and grenades. It was easy terrain to lay an ambush, and they had to be wary from the moment they rose from their blankets and drank their early morning tea. They laboured and sweated up and down the steep grey ridges with their Stens and Lee Enfields. The peasants lived in straw-covered shacks with mud-brick stables, bars and small silos. They ate dried squid, locusts and chillis. The lower slopes were terraced to the last inch, but the land had been ruined by battle and there were no livestock, no farmers, and nothing growing. The enemy was not to be seen. All they found were smashed pots, broken bicycles, trinkets, wooden ploughs and worn oxen yokes. What roads there were meandered into the hills and mountains, became brambly tracks, and disappeared into the brush. They moved carefully day after day, and the work was tense and exhausting. It seemed that even the birds had deserted the mountains of South Korea. The cranes would not return to their nests in the poplars and oaks. Every morning, the mist lay on the water of the lakes and paddies and the dew was wet on the ground. Then late one rainy afternoon, when they were all very tired, an officer whom David barely knew was killed when his driver strayed into an unmarked minefield. It was the battalion's first casualty, and it shocked them all. Korea was going to be a tricky, deadly place: the people all looked the same and you couldn't tell the northerners from the southerners. The only good gook is a dead gook, a lot of the men said, but David wasn't so sure. There had to be right and wrong. And they were on the right side; there was no doubt about that. When they were leaving Taegu for Seoul one of the men picked up a North Korean propaganda leaflet lying in the rubble. It read: *Don't forget the forty degrees of frost which are waiting for you. Why not move over to our side?* Moving sides wouldn't change the temperature, David thought.

*   *   *

At Pakchon, the weather grew warmer: it stopped snowing. The skies were grey and the river was still frozen. The colonel decided they should send out patrols and David's platoon was chosen. On Monday afternoon, the patrol master gave David his orders: he was to choose six men for a reconnaissance patrol in the hills on the other side of the river. It would take three days and the patrol could be put under the command of Sergeant Hart, but David decided to go himself. The patrol master said he didn't have to, but David wanted to lead the men.

"All right, Andersen," the patrol master said, as he looked up from the maps on the card table, "it's your show. Don't bugger it up. You take six men out and you bring six men back."

"Yes, sir."

"And if any of your men falls asleep or runs or fucks the show up, it's the high-jump, right?"

"Yes, sir."

"You probably won't see anything, but who knows with these tricky bastards." The patrol master gave David the map references and co-ordinates. "Christ knows if the map's accurate," he said and laughed. "It's a Japanese survey made in the thirties. It shouldn't be too difficult, just uncomfortable. There's you and Hart and Kershaw and the best three men you can find. Check your wirelesses, the equipment's a load of shit. And mind the Middlesex, they're putting men out and we've told them about you." He looked at David hard in the eye. "I'll see you on Thursday night, and bring them all back. Right?"

All day David and his men worked through the brush in twos, each pair covering the other. The snow had melted and the ground was sodden underfoot; this made the going tough, but silent. They kept to the high ground: the spurs, ridges and saddles. The work was dirty, thirsty and un-comfortable and nothing was to be seen; it seemed that they were the only people on the earth. The silence was complete, too: maybe the world had ended and they were the last survivors? All the time, they looked for signs: scraps of food, cigarette butts, faeces, or cut timber. Their hearts pounded as they went forward, covering each other. The enemy was lying in wait and they must not be ambushed. David could not remember ever being so tired or fearful. Every four hours they netted in on the wireless: they had nothing to report. Hart was by far the strongest, despite his age; he moved quickly and quietly and never let up. But he was like a character in *We Were the Rats*, foul-mouthed and heavy-drinking, who blew his nose in the dirt and belched when he ate. David's father would have hated him, but would have employed him, no doubt. Hart was an experienced soldier, the best in the patrol, and they couldn't do without him. He moved like a tiger across the country. It was exhausting work, and at the slightest sound their backs rose with fear.

At 1500 hours they stopped for a breather and crouched on the ground, their bodies aching and feet sore. Cash and Brownlee stood on the piquet, covering them, while David consulted the map. Thank God, he still knew where they were: he was certain of that. The men squatted and scratched at themselves, their eyes blinking and their faces grey beneath their balaclavas.

"What time do we net in?" Hart said as he swallowed his hard chocolate and dredged his gums with his finger.

"1600 hours," David said.

"There's no fucking thing to report," Hart said.

"Yes, there is."

"What, sir?"

"We're where we're supposed to be and there are no casualties."

"Jesus."

David thought: keep to the high ground, don't be ambushed. He pointed to a saddle on the map, about four hours away. "That's where we'll bivouac."

"Okay by me, sir," Hart said and got up ready to go.

"Watch yourself, Sergeant," David said.

"What?"

"I said, watch yourself."

"Why?"

124

"You're standing against the skyline."

Hart grinned, crouched and said nothing. Clever young bastard. He proffered the broken chocolate in his large, knotty hand. "Do you want some, sir?"

"No thanks. Let's get moving."

They climbed toward the saddle in pairs, taking turns to scout ahead. The place was noiseless and unnerving; the fir trees dripped and the track was uncertain. They watched for signs of the enemy: birds fluttering, voices, cigarette smoke, garlic. But not a twig snapped, not a leaf moved. They were alone in this inhospitable country. David looked at the sky: there was no sign of snow, and for that they should be grateful.

They heard the voices at 16.35. They stopped and froze, crouching in the brush, filthy and sweating despite the cold. David thanked God they had been so careful. The voices were sharp and strange: it wasn't the Middlesex, it was the Chinese. They weren't being very careful, so they must be out in strength. The enemy seemed to be on a track beneath them, moving southeast toward the Australian lines. What was Hart thinking? David saw him crouching behind a tree fifty yards away. Should they ambush them? Their first blood, the first patrol of the battalion, his first chance. He decided to wait and see how many there were. He watched, waited and tried to count the enemy as they moved through the trees. His skin prickled and his hands shook: it was the first time he had seen them close up. Twenty of them went past. They were wearing forage caps and quilted jackets, and carrying burp guns; two were carrying light machine guns with tripods. There was no sign of wireless; they used whistles and bugles. Hart was signalling and David supposed he wanted to engage the enemy but knew that simply wasn't on. The last thing he wanted to do was fire: it would give them away. Let the Chinese move on and then they could report their position on the net. He held his breath. The Chinese disappeared down the ridge and David reported on the wireless.

"Roger," said a strange voice. "See you on Thursday night. Good luck. Over and out."

David made them wait half an hour before they continued up the ridge toward the saddle. As they changed the lead, David saw Kershaw and Brownlee were white-faced and quaking. Hart was not. David remembered the advice given him by an old warrant officer: *You've got to fight again tomorrow.*

It was 19.15 when they reached the saddle. David hoped to God his map-reading was correct; he was sure it was. He chose a spot on the south slope in the lee of the north wind. There was no point in freezing to death. The C-rations were opened and they sat on the ground in the dark, legs and backs aching. The trees dripped on their heads and shoulders. They sat on the cold earth, the four of them: David, Hart, Jones and Kershaw. Cash and Brownlee stood piquet.

"We could of had them bastards," Hart said munching.

"I think not," David said. "Did you feint the tracks?" he asked Jones.

"Yes, sir."

"We were right on top of them," Hart said. "Jesus Christ, what are we bloody here for?"

"We're here to complete the patrol," David said.

"We're here to kill the buggers." He turned to Jones. "What do you think? You don't say a fucking word. Are you scared shitless or something?"

"No, Sarge."

"Well, fucking say something."

"I reckon there were too many of them."

"Balls." Hart spat. "We haven't knocked off a bloody Chink since Yongyu. Jesus, that was good. Those bastards in the haystacks."

David thought of Hart's saving his life, but said, "Shut up, Hart."

"Yes, sir." Bloody little poofter. Hart moved away and sat watching in the dark. He didn't need the sleep. He would show these young buggers; he had fought before and knew all the rules. Be aggressive and kill. As for young Andersen, he couldn't pull the skin off a rice pudding. Fucking graziers, fucking public schoolboys. The night closed in with wind and cloud and Hart sat in the brush, his Sten between his knees. If Cash was asleep, he'd kill him. What was he doing here with these bloody kids? At home, a piss-up in the mess and then off to the night-trots. He listened in the dark. He thought about the Chinese patrol they'd let go. You could never tell: they could be back.

The wind got up during the night, driving and gusting through the pine trees, and it was safe to talk.

"Well, Kershaw?" David said.

"Well what, sir?"

"About that Chinese patrol?"

"You're in command, sir."

"Never take on something you can't handle," David said. "We couldn't have got them all, and then where would we be?"

"Up shit creek, I suppose. They'd know we're out here."

"They would. How did you feel?"

"When, sir?"

"When you saw the Chinese patrol."

"A bit scared."

"So was I. Join the club." David didn't know Kershaw very well but was starting to like him. He was a regular army NCO, thickset and built like a front-row forward. One of his eye-teeth was missing; it looked like a football injury. "What school did you go to?" David asked.

"The State School, Bathurst. There were seven of us so I left when I was fourteen to help me Dad."

There wasn't much else to say and they both sat in the hole, their greatcoats draped around them. It was starting to snow again and David hoped to God it wouldn't go on too long. If it did, they'd leave tracks everywhere. He remembered Pooh and Piglet tramping around the spinney.

He thought of Penshurst Primary School and Miss Braddon found dead in her room. That was sixteen years ago. No one ever found out what happened. Why was he thinking of her now? Then he remembered Tom Quicksilver and his father and older brothers sitting outside the Penshurst pub by the war memorial. Tom was killed at Tobruk, his name added to the list on the plaque. *In Memoriam*. He hoped his name wouldn't be there. Kershaw crouched in the pit; he was glad he wasn't leading the patrol. Too much responsibility. He picked at his teeth and scratched himself. Leave it to the private schoolboys: they were born to rule, or so they thought. He thought Andersen was a bit of a prick, a rules man, but most of the Military College blokes were like that. Like Cash, Kershaw was desperate for a cigarette; it was a long, bitter night and there was nothing to warm them.

*　　*　　*

Next day at 16.05, they came across the hut. This small, solid mud-brick building stood in a clearing, high in the hills. All the other farm buildings, the barns and some out-houses, had been flattened, and only rubble remained. Millet was growing in a small enclosure. There was no sign of life: no animals, no birds, nothing. As they considered the building from the edge of the brush they smelt charcoal. The tree stumps stood like gravestones, the timber lay black and rotting and they crouched uncertainly. The wind was very cold now; they could shelter in the hut, have their rations and brew a cup of tea maybe? It was a place to doss down for an hour at least. David looked at the sky: it was threatening to snow once more.

"What's the smell, sir?" Cash said.

"Charcoal," David said. "It's a charcoal burner's hut."

Cash wasn't sure what charcoal was used for, but said nothing.

"I think we should give the hut a miss," David said.

"Give it a miss, sir?" Kershaw said.

"There could be someone inside." Their teeth chattered and they looked at the clear field of fire around the building. It was all open ground.

"What do you think, Hart?"

"You're asking me, sir?"

"I'm asking you."

Hart looked at the building, the clear ground and the ruined outbuildings. Nothing had been moved for some time. It looked safe to him. These bastards weren't as cunning as the Japs, and he, too, wanted a cigarette and a brew of tea. Andersen could show his leadership now, it was nothing to do with him. The wind swept the leaves and twigs: to the north the clouds bunched big and black; it was going to rain very soon and they would be in the open. "A pound to a peanut there's nobody there," Hart said.

David thought of Taegu and the landmine, of foolish risks and false comforts. They were safer in the brush. People sheltered in buildings, and the ground was open. There was no cover. What to do? It was getting colder and they could shelter there for an hour or two. "All right," he said, "Hart, Cash and I will dash for that charcoal pit and the rest of you stay here."

Dash for the charcoal pit? Jesus Christ, Kershaw thought, Andersen's on manoeuvres at the Military College. All this bullshit; all he wanted was a rest, a cigarette and to put his legs up under cover.

As they ran for the charcoal pit, three quick shots rang out.

"Jesus Christ," Hart said as they dropped to the pit, "there *is* some bastard in there. He's got a fucking carbine."

"Are you all right, Cash?" David asked.

"Yes, sir."

But David could feel him shaking. He wondered what the men in the brush were going to do. There was no point in using Stens and rifles against the mud brick. He cursed himself and he cursed Kershaw: this was a bloody mess.

The sniper had their range now and they couldn't get back without taking an appalling risk. One of them was bound to be hit. Why hadn't he insisted that they bypass the building? What on earth was a rifleman doing in there in this wilderness? And how many were there? The pit was black with charcoal and half filled with water. How long could they stay there?

"I could chuck a grenade, sir," Hart said.

"If you want to lose your arm, Hart, you try. I've got the feeling he's pretty good."

Another shot rang out and nobody knew what the sniper had in reserve. The three of them crouched in the pit and watched the hut, the fallen fences, the piles of split tiles, the walls and the ruined barn beyond. The wind blew through the millet. David wondered what to do. He could order Hart, order any of them to dash to the building. But that was unthinkable. They would never respect him again. Did they respect him now? He doubted it: they were all working class. *You take six men out and you bring six men back*. It was starting to rain and if they stayed where they were for long, they'd freeze to death. The ground was clear all round and the sniper seemed to be on the west side of the hut, to the right. Cash was white and shaking and smelt of piss, and Hart was chewing gum; he looked ready to go when ordered. Hart chewed and spat out the gum.

Cash farted and said, "Sorry, sir."

Hart looked at Cash, but said nothing. Then he looked at David and said: "What do we do now, sir?"

David saw Hart grinning, drew out his Webley, cocked it and said: "I'm going. Cover me." He leapt from the pit and ran like a hare across the flat ground, the leaves and ash spinning from his boots; he sprinted, heart pumping, his mouth sucking in the cold air, the Webley heavy in his right hand, listening for the crack of the sniper. His heart felt it would burst. *I shall be dead, I shall be dead*. He kept running toward the hut. *I shall be dead*. But he was not. He reached the door, terrified and shaking. There was one wooden step. His mouth was dry, he was giddy, his legs shook and his vision was impaired. He couldn't see anything. Where was the pit? Where were Kershaw and the other men? Where was the brush? He stood by the door with the Webley. It felt heavy and useless, like a piece of scrap iron, like a brick. The chamber held six shots, and he remembered the practice on the firing range. Always hold the butt with both hands, they kicked like mules; aim low and you'll get your target in the chest. He kicked open the door and leapt inside: the room was empty. Broken rice bowls and cartridge cases lay on the floor. There was another door. Two rooms; the sniper must be in there; he had heard. David stood stock still. He couldn't go back now. He ran through the second door and then saw the sniper in the corner by the window. It was a Chinese boy, younger than he, about eighteen. He was struggling with some bandages on his arm and the shoulder strap of his carbine, gasping and tangled. David held the Webley in both hands and fired. The Chinese coughed and struggled with the bandages and the shoulder strap as the shot missed. It was a Russian carbine. He backed into a corner; he was very thin, almost skeletal, wearing a fur hat and quilted jacket; his mouth was open like a dog's and spittle dribbled down his chin. His beard was thin and boy-like. David fired again and hit him in the groin. The Chinese grunted and clutched himself, the blood was thick and red and dark and ran through his fingers and down his trousers; he clutched at himself, smelt of shit, and David fired again, hitting him in the chest and neck and the boy slid down the wall and died. The small room reeked of shit and cordite, and already the flies appeared and swarmed. David shook, vomited and messed himself, his thighs foul and C-ration beans dribbling down his tunic. He threw the Webley down and went to the young Chinese, thrusting his scarf into the wounds and mucus, trying to save him. But he was dead. *Forgive me, O Lord*. He sobbed.

Then Sergeant Hart was standing in the room. He

prodded the dead Chinese with his Sten and looked at David, the vomit congealing on his tunic.

"Christ, sir, you're in a mess." He took up the Russian carbine. "Ugly bastards, aren't they?"

David stepped outside for fresh air, but it too smelled of wood and urine. He walked back to the pit, Hart following him with the carbine. Cash stood up, covered with soot and ash.

"Good on you, sir," he said.

David noticed that he, too, was shaking. The rest of the men, led by Kershaw, came out of the brush and stood around.

"A good show, sir," someone said.

"Have you got a drink, Cash?" David said.

"A drink, sir?"

"Liquor."

"No, sir."

"I think you have."

Cash bent and fished in his rucksack. He proffered the small bottle and David drank down the cheap Australian whisky; he retched and threw the bottle in the pit.

*   *   *

They sat on the ground in the dark, eating their cold rations. Hart was talking, his flat voice grinding in the still air. "North Koreans, South Koreans, Japs, Chinks, they're all the same to me. They're all vermin. Half the yellow bastards we're defending worked for the Nips in the last war. Jesus Christ, the Koreans were the fucking worst, evil bastards who raped our women, ran Changi and the camps on the Burma railway. Fucked if I know why we're here. Let the bastards kill each other, I say." He drained the cold tea from his mug and threw the slops into the brush.

"It's a job, Sarge," Brownlee said. "We're here because we're here. It ain't that bad, something to do. Better than the abattoirs."

"It's all the fucking same," Hart said. He cleared his

132

throat and spat. "Do you know why you're a soldier, son? You're a soldier because you can't do any fucking thing else. Being shot at is all you're good for."

David listened and said nothing. He'd tried to wash himself with a dixie of water, but he still smelled and his underwear was foul. He wondered about the young Chinese. What did the Chinese believe in? Confucius? He wasn't sure.

"Why do they all stink?" Hart was saying. "Why do the bastards all stink? I'd rather fuck a tin of PX beans than one of them Korean bitches. They all stuff garlic up their rings and they've got no tits." He laughed and turned to Cash. "Not that'd you know, eh Cashie?" He laughed again. "Have you got any more of that cheap plonk you gave Mr Andersen? Stashing away, are you? Keeping it from your mates? You sly little bugger."

David sat in the trench and listened to Hart. The moon was rising in the inky sky and the light gleamed on the small lake. Somewhere, artillery rumbled and lights flashed. It sounded like American Long Toms; he was learning all the different sounds now. A flare shone and dropped beyond the hills; he thought of Guy Fawkes Day at *Killara*, the bonfires of rubber tyres burning, the rockets and the sparklers, the jumping jacks fizzing beneath his feet. Then he saw star shell and tracers of orange, green, red and blue.

"Christ, you should have seen Cashie in the pit," Hart was saying. "He was shitting himself."

"Shut up, Hart," David said, "bloody shut up. God knows where the enemy is, we've had enough for one day."

Hart thought of David standing with the Webley before the sniper with the vomit on his shirt, and said nothing.

"Any more talking tonight, you blokes," came David's voice, "and you're all up on a charge."

He slept badly that night and thought he might die tomorrow.

They all got back on Thursday night and the patrol master was pleased. When he learned about the sniper, he said he'd put David up for a mention in dispatches.

133

7

The Retreat

Now it was winter, the wind blew from the north; through the morning fog, the trees looked like skeletons in rows along the frozen rivers and streams. The mud on the road had turned to yellow rock and the apple trees, oaks and aspens were dead: they were torn to shreds by mortar and artillery fire. The paddies were filled with black ice, the walls and bunds had collapsed, the temples and shrines were reduced to rubble. The people were suffering from malaria and tuberculosis; every last dog, cat and rat had been eaten. Some of them looked like the inmates at Belsen and Auschwitz. Even the leaves and bark were stripped from the trees. It was the coldest winter for forty years.

A thousand men and vehicles were on the road: infantry men, half-tracks, two-ton trucks, jeeps, motor bikes and tents. They were jammed up with field guns, ambulances, flame-throwers, drums of napalm and chemicals, mortars, supply wagons and howitzers – all the baggage and impedimenta of war. The drivers, hunched, goggled and swathed in scarves, leaned on the horns, but nobody could get through. The foot soldiers marched along the side of the road, some in line and some straggling and trying to help the wounded. The ice splintered and broke beneath the tank tracks; the exhaust from the smoke stacks pumped into the freezing air. The refugees pushed through the crush with their handcarts, bicycles, A-frames and bundles on their backs. Some were carrying firewood, cooking pots and furniture, and the women had babies strapped to their backs. The old men wore filthy white coats, panama hats, and sandals stuffed with straw. The children clutched

134

strings of dried chillis, branches, and leaves, and bunches of rags. The corpses lay in the ditches and the babies lay on the ice like small wooden dolls. There were no dogs alive to eat them.

The mountains were as high as steeples, the north wind blew at their backs and into the marrow of their bones; the road was winding, narrow and treacherous. It was too narrow for more than one tank or half-track, and if one broke down, the column stopped, the men shouted, and their blasphemies echoed in the air. David marched with his men, avoiding the pitfalls, wrecked vehicles and corpses. His legs ached and it seemed his boots were made of iron. He remembered the rules of the training manual: *Avoid jams – safety lies in dispersion.* On this road, any place was a place for an ambush. He remembered the fate of the US 8th Cavalry, the enfilade and the men crushed to death under the tank tracks. They had to get out: only God could deliver them safely now. *Good Lord, deliver us.*

Many dead men were lying on the rocks, in the ditches and in the brush on the slopes. Some had lost their legs and arms and stomachs. Their frozen eyes shone like marbles and they had tried to cover their wounds with rags and straw for some kind of decency. The blood from their bodies was as hard and black as rock: they looked like fallen statues and smashed masonry, their legs broken, their skulls open, their brains congealed and turned to ice. They lay crumpled beneath the tracks of burnt-out tanks, blackened by gasoline and phosphorus, their mouths open and uniforms pockmarked by shrapnel and machine-gun fire. Fires burned in the steep hills; the ice turned to dust as the tanks slithered and spun, their pennants frozen, their turrets jammed and their commanders cursing and shouting. The men on foot staggered under the weight of their mortars, bazookas, wireless sets and their frozen greatcoats. David thought of the retreat from Kabul, of the Afghans following the British column and cutting them down at nightfall, of the slaughter, and of one man surviving, his naked body swathed in the British flag. Mortars lay in the rocks, the caps and strikers removed: howitzers and gun tractors lay upturned and petrol drums discarded; the men cursed and groaned, vehicles collided and smashed; the refugees wandered and dropped in their tracks. Someone had blundered.

David and his men stopped at 1800 hours, opened the C-rations, and put their dixies on the back of a trailer. The men were dirty, frozen and dog-tired; they were fearful and the beans smelt foul, like frozen pig food. David thought of the rancid rabbit carcasses lying in the pits in the winter at Penshurst. Some of the men went to piss in the brush, but could not open their trousers, their bodies hunched and bent like old cripples. Some crouched to pee like bitches. Cans of hot water were put out for them to warm their spoons; otherwise their lips would be torn off by the metal. But the beans were half-frozen and the water stone cold within seconds. David had never seen the men so reduced. There were no wisecracks that evening, the men were unshaven and silent. David reached for the salt and pepper to spice his beans. He raised the spoon to his mouth carefully. *I am not an animal*, he kept saying to himself, *I am not an animal.*

They tried to settle down behind the trailer and the stalled trucks. There was no point in standing piquets now as none of them would sleep. The trucks and tanks continued to grind along the road, their headlights gleaming and faltering in the night; there seemed no end to it. The column would go on forever. David sat behind a gutted Bedford truck with Cash, Kershaw and Jones and tried to remember the rules of contract bridge but was too cold to recall them. He thought of the tennis court, his grandfather in the umpire's chair, his dog, the laughter, the plates of lamb chops, the hot summers when the sea was as still as glass and the drovers moved the cattle through the dust on the Dunkeld road.

*   *   *

The Chinese attacked at 2300 hours and Kershaw fell first, hit in the chest, his blood spraying and frosting over David's face. A star shell lit up the darkness, Kershaw looked surprised, fainted and collapsed against David, his body crumpled, his blood already freezing, his lungs punctured and cold breath wheezing. David reached for his Sten and tried to push Kershaw's body away, but he couldn't shift it. Men cursed and shrieked in the night; more star shells fell, whistles blew and bugles sounded. Kershaw's blood was caked on David's face and frozen in his eyes. Then Jones got up, knelt to fire at the machine gun, his rifle at his shoulder; he was struck in the torso, his lungs bursting from his back, his uniform shredded. A flare exploded and fell through the night and a man David didn't know knelt to shoot, but the Chinese machine gunner hit him in the mouth, and the man turned and looked at David in the half-light, his lower jaw smashed and teeth and gums dribbling down his throat: his brains squirted like offal, running down David's greatcoat.

On the road, a Sherman caught fire and blew up, with the men struggling and screaming in their manholes, their clothes on fire.

"Fucking Jesus Christ," came Hart's voice through the night. "Fucking Jesus Christ."

The battle lasted a long time: all through the night.

* * *

In the morning, after the Chinese had gone, Kershaw was still alive, wheezing, his lungs rattling and blood dribbling. He lay in the oil under the Bedford truck, his blanket soaked solid. The medics hadn't come yet, so all they could do was to cover him up and make him feel warm. He snorted and coughed: he was taking a long time to die. It seemed to David that Kershaw's face was made of wax or plaster-of-Paris; they dared not examine the wounds. It was a little warmer now and started to rain, but the rain could not wash the blood away. The drivers and the mechanics were trying to start the trucks and tanks, but the diesel fuel and lubricating oil were frozen and the gun tractors couldn't haul the wrecks away. Many vehicles were still smoking and burning and men were ransacking the wrecked PX trucks, trying to find something to eat. If the Chinese attack again, David thought, it will be curtains for all of us. They must be watching from the tops of the ridges. Why didn't they consolidate their gains? They were a puzzling and cunning enemy. Then, through the mist, American helicopters appeared and hovered above the ground. The casualties were put into pods on each side of the aircraft and flown back to the mobile surgical hospitals. Then the Starfighters and Corsairs came in, flying down the valley, and they knew they were safe for the time being.

David heaved Jones's body over, trying to avoid the icy, clotted wounds. He couldn't undo the buttons on Jones's uniform, got out his pocket knife and cut the stiff material away. In the wallet were two one-pound notes, his driver's licence, a library card and a snapshot of his wife and children. It looked like a family scene at the beach: two little girls in print frocks smiling, Jones's young wife with bare legs and sandals, a rug on the sand and a fox terrier. There was nothing else: the photograph was enough. David put Jones's wallet carefully in his inside pocket next to his and cut off the dog tag. *There but for the grace of God. . . .*

"We're on our own," Hart said. He stood over David, Sten in one hand and rolling a cigarette in the other.

"What?" David asked. He put the dog tag in his tunic pocket.

"There's no sign of BHQ," Hart said, "or any of the company. It's a fucking shambles, sir."

"I'm aware of that, Hart," David said. "Who's here?"

"Brownlee, Cash and us."

"And Kershaw."

"And Kershaw. He won't make it."

"He probably won't, but he's here, isn't he?"

138

"Yes, sir."

"Well, get a fire going, we'll have a brew and march with the Argylls." David got up and looked at Hart. "We're all going to the same place. Where's Cash?" Hart coughed. "Asleep, sir."

"Wake him up and tell him to put on some tea."

"We haven't got any, sir, as far as I know."

"Well, for God's sake, tell Cash to scrounge some. Jesus Christ, Hart, I want some tea. Get it and look after Kershaw while I try to find the Argylls."

"Kershaw's had it, sir."

"Say a prayer for him, then. Do you know any prayers?"

"Yes, sir.'

"Say one, and I want hot tea when I get back. Okay?" David walked down the slope toward the column as the helicopters swung away to the south and the fires burned. He would see Mrs Jones when he returned home. He didn't seem so cold now, but he still reeked of blood. He couldn't find the Argylls and would have to go out again. The column was in chaos, and he was confused.

* * *

David sat on the rocks with Hart, Cash and Brownlee and they drank their tea as they watched Kershaw die. An American medic came up and asked if he could help, but David thanked him and said: "No, it's all right, he hasn't got long to go now. Look after those you can save. He's with his mates."

The medic looked at Kershaw and said: "You're right, sir, he won't last long. Are you guys okay?"

"Yes," David said, "we're fine."

Kershaw, his eyes open, watched them all, snorted and wheezed as the blood flowed. He didn't say anything. He didn't seem to be in any pain, but it was hard to tell. David thought about the Chinese sniper in the slab hut: he was getting used to death now. He looked at Cash as he

139

crouched by the Bedford, his hands reaching for his last Lucky Strike. Cash could not bear to look at Kershaw and kept squinting at the soldiers and the smashed trucks, the paddies and the mountains on the other side of the valley.

David thought of saying: Look, Paul, look at the dying man, your dying mate. Look at his bones and lungs, listen to the sound of his breathing. You joined the army and you must have known this would happen. This is what soldiers have to do to each other. Kershaw's dying for a principle; he's on the right side; if you don't stop the Reds here, the Free World will be in danger. He's dying so that those left will be free. But David said nothing to Cash because he knew it wasn't true. Kershaw's dying was tragic and obscene, and he would never forget it. Someone had covered Jones's body with a blanket and he was made decent: he was simply a corpse, a carcass that would be taken away. Jones hadn't felt a thing: there was a prefabricated stone cross waiting for him, he was out of the way. But a man dying slowly was another thing: a living human being butchered, some of his organs still working, his arteries cut and the blood flowing and freezing black upon the ice. Military killing was a horrifying puzzle: something David had not counted on. Now he had killed and asked for forgiveness, and now Kershaw still bled through his bandages and greatcoat and his uniform, now as he wheezed, his mouth gaping speechless and his eyes of glass gazing at the dark sky. Maybe he should have given Kershaw to the American medic, maybe Kershaw would recover, but he knew that was not possible. They listened to his wheezing and rattling and drank their tea. After a while, David got up and went to find the Argylls.

A bony red-headed major said he would be delighted if they could march with them. He looked in his mid-thirties and carried a walking stick. He said he had fought with the Australians in Tunisia in the Second World War. His accent was very thick and hard to follow and David wondered if he should tell the major that his second name was Kinross, but he wasn't sure about Scottish clans and loyalties and it didn't seem quite the time. His grandfather would have known.

Kershaw died at 05.45. David took particular note of it. Hart said: "Poor bastard, he took a while. I hope I don't croak like that."

Cash crossed himself and no one else said anything. Brownlee took out Kershaw's wallet, removed the dog tag and gave it to David. He didn't look inside the wallet this time and shoved it inside his pocket next to Jones's. David didn't know if Kershaw was married or not; he would find out when they got to Chasan.

"Right, you blokes," he said. "We're marching with the Argylls. They're leaving at 06.00."

*   *   *

The Argylls were a cheerful, hardbitten lot in fur caps with thin weatherbeaten faces, a mixture of regulars and National Servicemen with accents so broad that David couldn't understand them half the time. They marched with the men of A Company in single file with the pipers leading. The music was stirring and comforting and it didn't matter about the noise. The Chinese knew where they were and were probably outflanking them. They played *Cock o' the North* and tunes of the '45, the pipes echoing over the hills. The tanks and trucks still jerked and crashed down the road, bumper to bumper, carrying the alive, the wounded, and the dead. No one waved or cheered at the foot soldiers: it looked as though the Americans wanted to leave the scene as fast as possible. The soldiers looked fearful, beaten and demoralized, and it seemed that the whole US 8th Army was in retreat. General MacArthur was wrong, and maybe the war would go on for years. The artillery boomed in the hills and now and again, as they marched, they saw flashes and puffs of smoke. There was no counter-fire, so maybe the Chinese had gone? Maybe they weren't to the north but to the south, and they would meet them again before they got to Chasan? Maybe Chasan had fallen? But that didn't bear thinking about. Meanwhile, the pipers played and David and his men marched with the Argylls. The wind blew with flurries of snow, and the clouds were too low for the Corsairs to give them air cover. Once again, David thought of Robert Scott and the march to One Ton Depot. His toes were aching and numb inside his boots: he hoped it wasn't frostbite. That would mean losing his toes and not being able to ride again. The traffic banged and rumbled on the road and the Argylls marched, sprayed with chips of frozen mud and ice as the pipers played. They were being outflanked by the Chinese moving silently in the hills. Every soldier knew that.

They stopped at 1200 hours for food and a brew of tea. The Argylls were a resourceful bunch: as there was no wood, they pulled down telegraph poles, splintered them and lit fires in the ice. The tea was hot, black and sweet, and they sat in the shallow ditches and watched the trucks, tanks and gun tractors grind past. The young American soldiers clung to the sides of the two-tonners, their heads lolling and helmets dangling. They looked helpless and shell-shocked; their comrades' bodies, covered with groundsheets, lay in the bottom of the trucks, their arms and booted feet sticking out and David was reminded of the young Americans on the ridge in the apple orchard, weeping, the top sergeant with his brains blown out, and the boy from Atlanta with his legs missing who would never play quarter-back again. It wasn't a retreat now. It was a rout. What was happening at Chasan? Nobody knew.

A watery sun shone. Brownlee gave Cash a cigarette. He dragged the smoke down deep, expelling it through his nose and mouth into the cold air. Cash looked hunched and old, his face creased and lined and his hands shaking. He coughed and dragged at the cigarette, crouched in the muddy ice and stared at his boots.

"How are your feet, Paul?" David asked.

"Freezing, sir." Cash looked at the ground. "It's the hobnails, I reckon."

"Take your boots off and have a look. You could have frostbite."

"What's the point, sir?"

Cash was right: there was no point and David stood up as Hart came across with his mug of tea, a roll-your-own stuck to his lip. He looked hard and gaunt, with no sign of fatigue, his slouch hat on the side of his head and his Sten slung across his back. He looked as though he could survive anything: the scarecrow in the back paddock of an outback farm who remained standing, season after bad season. Hart poked his finger at the Argylls. "Not a bad bunch of bastards?"

"They'll see us through," David said. He thought of his grandfather, the rain dripping from his beard, looking forward to the Glenfiddich. There was something special about the Scots.

"They're bigger than I thought they'd be," Hart said.

"Who?" David squinted at the hills and the outcrops.

"The Poms. I thought they were all runts compared to us. Some of them are big buggers." Hart looked at Cash crouched on the ground. "How are you, Cashie?" He spat out the cigarette butt. "Feeling it, eh?"

David wished Hart would go away. He stood there, rolling another cigarette. He wanted to give Hart a job but couldn't think of one.

"What time do you reckon we'll be on the road again?" Hart asked. "The fucking Chinks could be anywhere."

"I don't know," David said. "It all depends on the Argylls. Why don't you go and find out?"

Hart looked at David. "All right, I'll see the RSM."

The pipers were tuning up and the droning sounds drifted, melancholy, down the valley. They sat and watched the column. Each of them felt far away and longed to be home, in Australia.

"You haven't got another fag, have you?" Cash said to Brownlee.

"All right, you scrounging little bugger." Brownlee grinned and fished in his tunic pocket. "It's your bloody last, there's no more after this."

But they all knew there would be more and Cash lit his cigarette from Brownlee's lighter.

"I've been thinking of Kershaw, sir," Cash said.

"What have you been thinking?"

"That he didn't die in vain."

David didn't reply. Another American truck was stalled in front of them and the drivers were shouting and screaming. The men in the back were too weary to get out: they looked like cattle going to the slaughterhouse. They smelled and looked like cattle going to the slaughterhouse. David thought of Kershaw's smashed chest, his wheezing, his wounds frozen and pitted with dirt and shreds of uniform. He suddenly considered: why did everybody refer to soldiers killed in battle as the "fallen"? They might have fallen, but they were cut to pieces and dismembered by bullets and shrapnel, or incinerated by flame-throwers. They were mutilated and dead. They weren't the glorious dead: they were the disfigured, ugly dead. They looked worse than the carcasses at the local abattoirs: at least after all the head-smashing on the killing chain, the meat there was neatly carved up, ready for the butcher and then for the table. David wondered if he would stop eating meat; somehow it was becoming obscene. When this war was over, David thought, there would be military cemeteries like those in France: rows of cheap marble crosses in a field far away, with no one to lay wreaths and grieve for the dead. What was the point of that? Then Hart came back, striding over the ice and said: "We're on the move in five minutes, sir."

"Right-oh, you chaps," David said, "we're off." *And God be our protector.*

When they got to the top of the rise, David could see the column stretching away to the south and little was moving, except the infantry and the refugees. He hadn't realized how huge the retreat was until then. When they got to a bridge spanning a frozen river, David consulted the map but didn't know which river it was: he was disoriented now. The snow clouds bundled from the north, from China and Mongolia and the Arctic Circle, where many brave explorers were dead beneath the ice. Strange names sounded in his head: Darien, the Aleutian Islands, Novaya Zemlya, his childhood geography.

They looked down at the river from the steep banks: it looked like some weird and horrible graveyard. Heads and arms protruded from the ice; the long barrel of a howitzer stuck up like a factory chimney and a Centurion tank lay immobile and upturned like some antediluvian animal, trapped forever in the Ice Age. What would happen, David wondered, if the spring never came? What if the ice did not melt and tiny streams did not flow? What if the oaks, aspens and maples never produced green buds and leaves? What if there were no spring flowers on the hills? What if the sap did not rise? Would the bodies of the soldiers, the guns and the tanks lie there entombed? The bodies of the soldiers would not decay, but be perfectly preserved forever.

The column was stopped once again and the men sat around, chatting and drinking their tea. Some drank whisky and brandy, but it seemed to David that they hadn't seen the bodies in the river. They hadn't seen what he had seen. Why was that? He couldn't ask Cash, he couldn't ask Brownlee or Hart. He couldn't ask anyone. The Argylls laughed and swore and cut more wood, and the fires burned on the ice where the frozen leaves lay.

*   *   *

It seemed that Brownlee was hit by a single shot in the left eye. The bullet came out through the back of his skull and burst into fragments; he died before anyone could reach him. He lay in the ice on the embankment of the frozen

145

river. David and the men of the section threw themselves flat on the ground, but most of the soldiers stood around drinking their tea as though nothing had happened. They hadn't heard the shot and chatted and smoked their cigarettes. Brownlee looked quite neat as he lay face down on the ice, his legs together and his arms by his side. He was a good soldier. No one returned the fire because there was nothing to shoot at: only the rocks, the brush, the fir trees and the hills. Yet a man up there with a rifle had killed Brownlee quite at random; he was living and breathing and Brownlee was not. What was the point of that? It was starting to rain and David lay on the ground and waited for the sound of carbines, mortars and machine-gun fire as the Argylls stood around and the trucks stalled and backfired on the bridge. He was about to shout out and say they were being fired on, but what was the use? Then an Argyll got up and said, "Jesus, laddie, what was that? Your mate's bought it."

For the third time, David knelt over the body of a friend, took out the wallet and removed the dog tag.

"Jesus Christ, laddie," the Argyll said as he looked towards the hills, "the fucking bastards."

"I'm sorry," David found himself saying as though it was his fault, as though he had disturbed some social function, "it's what we've all got to expect." Three of his men were dead now. Maybe it *was* his fault.

Hart got up and grabbed his Sten, his eyes gleaming. "It was a fucking refugee that got Brownlee, I'll get the bastard."

David looked at the ragged civilians trudging across the bridge between the trucks and tanks. It was said that many of them were Chinese or North Koreans with pistols and burp guns concealed under their clothes to shoot the Allied soldiers and disorganize their retreat. They needn't have bothered: the weather and roads were doing that. He knocked the barrel of Hart's Sten down. "There's no need for that, Hart," he said. "You'll get your chance."

146

"One of the Aussies bought it," David heard the Argyll saying and a couple of the men turned around.

"Dead?" one them said.

"As a doornail."

But nobody seemed very interested: death was now commonplace.

David looked around for Cash and saw him crouching behind an abandoned Oxford carrier. "For Christ's sake, Paul, get up," he said.

"Poor bloody Brownlee," Cash said, "poor bloody Brownlee. He only gave me a fag an hour ago." He looked at David. "Can I get his cigarettes, sir?"

"You take them, Paul," David said. "You take them." He picked up Brownlee's Sten; it would be serviced and re-issued. The Australian battalion threw nothing away. They shouldered their gear and marched across the bridge with the Argylls.

*   *   *

It became apparent by the end of the day that the Americans had given up even the pretence of trying to control the traffic; there was no spare transport to be had and the route was now becoming impassable. Late in the afternoon, the Australians passed an American artillery battery deployed to the west of the road. The snow, turning to sleet, hammered at their backs while howitzers blasted away from the river flats. They looked for some pattern of fire, but there was none: the big guns were firing north, east, west and south.

Hart stood on the side of the road and said: "Jesus Christ, am I right or wrong? These stupid buggers are firing south and that's where we're supposed to be going. They're firing on their own lines."

David watched with Hart. "You're right, they're firing south. I don't like the look of this. It's an absolute bloody shambles."

The retreat was turning into a death march. Who on earth was in charge? When the darkness came, they settled as best they could in the lee of a broken-down Chaffee tank. David wondered if they could spend the night inside. He climbed up and dropped down the hatch. In the pitch black he hit his head on something, probably the breech of the gun, drew blood and cursed. The Chaffee was like an ice chamber and he realized what kind of life the troopers led: to get caught inside one of these things by a mortar or a grenade must be horrifying. He thought of the few troopers he'd met; there was something special and desperate about them. Now he understood as he crouched in the bottom of the ruined Chaffee. The deflector was full of shell cases and something smelled badly in the cabin. It was a burnt body and he hoped he wouldn't touch it. The tank, he thought, must be the ugliest military machine of them all. He heaved himself back up the hatch into the wind and sleet; it was warmer outside than in. Cash scrounged some wood from the Argylls; they got a fire going, ate some beans and dossed down for yet another night in the open.

*   *   *

Just before dawn, the darkness was lit up by flares; soldiers and vehicles stood out brilliantly against the snow. As they went to grab their weapons, mortar fire and machine-gun bullets burst from the hills. Men cursed and shouted and milled around among the trucks and half-tracks. The Shermans and Chaffees that were moving slid out of control on the ice, and two were directly hit by mortars, caught fire, and slid down the embankment, their turrets immobile and their guns silent. In the glare of the tracers and flares, David saw men struggling out of the hatches, their clothes on fire, dropping to the steel decks and burning to death. Heavy mortar bombs came over like claps of thunder and the earth shook. David, Cash and Hart crouched by the Chaffee, white-faced and shaking. Hart's face was drawn and his

148

mouth slack: he knew all about mortars and couldn't forget; he knew what to expect.

"Fucking Christ," he said, "this is worse than the last time."

Cash tried to crawl beneath the Chaffee and felt for his rosary beads as the bombs fell and the flares lit up the dawn. One Sherman lumbered and ground through the ice and managed to get into the paddy field, pumped off half a dozen rounds in the wrong direction and sank into the mud; it was hit by a mortar at the turret, exploded, glowed bright red and slid down into the melting ice. As it burned in the dawn light, hissing and steaming, its diesel fuel ignited, reeking in the frozen air. David thought of being trapped inside the Chaffee, looked at the hills and rocks in the on-coming light, but there was nothing he could see to fire at. He went to pick up his Sten, but his mittens were in shreds and the skin of his fingers was torn off on the freezing gun metal. The Chinese mortars and machine-gunners were well hidden and this time there were no whistles and bugles. The attack was accurate and deadly, each tank singled out by the mortars in the rocks and behind the outcrops.

Only the Argylls were organized: they set up their Brens and fired carefully at the hills and the mortar flashes; they also fired at the bunds on the paddy fields for they knew the Chinese were there. The Argylls knew what to do under mortar fire and David admired them.

The attack lasted four hours and at about 0700 hours, the Chinese mortars ceased, but the carbines, machine guns and snipers were still there. Now it was death at random. Who would be the first to move? Who would be the first to run across the open ground to get to the wounded and dying? Who could not resist the cries of their dying mates? Men were bellowing and crying in the brush, in the ditches and in the rocks as the snow and sleet fell. The tanks still burned and glowed, and the black smoke rose in the grey and windy sky. This, David thought, was a bloody awful place: the butchered trees would never grow, the ice in the

149

streams would never melt and spring was gone forever. He thought of the frozen river and the guns entombed in the ice. No fish could swim or spawn in these cold waters.

The Argylls moved carefully from their positions to help the wounded and pick up their dead. There were no pipers playing now; no sounds of *Cock o' the North*, but the deadly rattle of occasional fire from the bunds. Two Argylls dropped as they went out for the wounded; they could be held up for ages. Hart ground his teeth and knelt by the Chaffee. It was starting to snow again and they were bone-weary and uncomfortable. This was as nerve-racking as the mortar assault; no one was safe. The column was spread for miles down the road and once again the starters of the GMC's whined and the engines fired to avoid the freeze-up. It seemed as if they had been on this road for all their lives and there was no end to it.

"Bloody Christ," Hart said, "bloody Christ." He squinted. "I think I know where those bastards are and I want a cup of tea without a bullet up me arse." He put up his Sten. "It's my turn now, sir." He crawled around the back of the tank and disappeared.

David thought he saw Hart dashing for the bunds, but he couldn't be sure. He was too tired to watch. "Well, Paul," he said, "if we lose Sergeant Hart, we're down to two. What do you make of it?"

"Make of it, sir?" Cash's flesh was crawling and he was dying to piss; his mouth was full of saliva, but he could not swallow.

"Make of all this?"

"I don't make anything of it, sir. I suppose it's what we were trained to do. It's our job. I'll try and not let you down, sir."

Lord, help us, David thought, I'm sure you won't.

What was Hart going into? Why didn't the Argylls send men out? Maybe they had. Jesus, David found himself blaspheming, all he wanted now was for this to end. He wanted to get back to BHQ, the men of the battalion and organized army life. Organized army life? He laughed to himself, looked at Cash and wanted a cup of tea. That wasn't too much to ask. More shots were fired, echoing through the hills; the rifles and light machine guns sounded like the start of the duck season on the small lakes and swamps of the Western District. Some soldiers were lighting a fire in a ditch for their breakfast, out of harm's way. Somewhere, bacon was frying. Maybe he and Cash could go and join them? But they had to wait for Hart. Where was the fighter support, where were the Corsairs and Starfighters? He looked up at the grey sky but not even a bird was flying. Life in the army, one instructor had said, was boring, dirty and dangerous. He thought of talking some more to Cash, but couldn't think of anything to say. The trucks backfired and the howitzers fired aimlessly.

Hart appeared from the paddy field with two men. He was carrying two burp guns and a light machine gun. They walked slowly up from the paddy and on the road through the light snow. One Chinese soldier was wearing a black Russian greatcoat and boots with no laces, the other was wearing a ragged quilted jacket and pants. Hart walked easily across the ice and said, "I got the bastards."

What did one do with two Chinese prisoners on a retreat? To whom would he deliver them, David wondered, and why had Hart taken them prisoner? Hart threw the burp guns down in the snow by the Chaffee and looked at David and Cash. "Here's the bastards," he said. The Chinese stood quite straight in their threadbare uniforms. They were both young, and one of them had a large wart on his neck. Hart pushed them with his Sten against the side of the tank, where they stood in the falling snow. Several Argylls came up, coughing in the cold, joking and rolling cigarettes. The trucks rumbled and jerked on the road and the small petrol fires smoked. Hart said: "We don't take no prisoners, do we, sir?"

The two young Chinese stood by the armoured plate of the tank. David thought of Jones, Kershaw, Brownlee and the troopers burning to death in the Shermans and Chaffees. "No," he said. "We don't." He found himself shouting at the Chinese: "You bastards! You bastards!" He flourished his Webley. Hart raised his Sten and machine-gunned them both. The brains of one man came out of his nose and he made a snoring sound and looked at them with his black eyes until they finished him off. The other's legs were cut off: he cried for a short time and Hart killed him, too. They had their tea and reached Chasan fourteen hours later.

8

Imjin

Nothing moved along the battalion front for three weeks. A ground mist hung over the Imjin; the ice on the river had melted and now the river, broad and silty, flowed slowly toward the Yellow Sea. Seagulls soared and wheeled above the sandbanks and mud flats. It was spring and the air was dry and cold; the earth and wind smelt fresh and the sap was rising in the trees. Despite past battles, cranes' nests still perched in the oak trees and poplars. The willows and aspens were now a light, fragile green and on the steep hills the azaleas were blooming, pink and purple. Several old peasants, carrying walking sticks, were walking along the bunds where the muddy water flowed. The roads and tracks were winding and dusty; fires were burning in the hills and sunken barges lay in the mud of the river. The nights were cold, the days blue and cloudless and to the east the girders of the Imjin River bridge lay, twisted and broken.

To the south the country was leached, steep-sided, eroded and stony with little natural cover. This was bad terrain for tanks and transport: gun tractors could not be used and most of the mortars and supplies had to be man-handled by the men and the Korean porters. It was heavy work, but the Gloucesters were well dug into high ground south of the river, with listening posts along the flats and in the valleys. Mortars, Vickers and Brens were placed about the hills and outcrops. Men with wirelesses and headsets looked, listened, and waited. Gulls, kites and magpies flew in the clear sky and on patrol some men saw deer, pheasant and ground squirrels. There was talk of a mountain tiger. Some of the men stripped and tried to tan in the warm sun; spring on the Imjin made life bearable in this barren, inhospitable land and as the oaks and poplars turned green, many men thought of home. But everyone knew that, sooner or later, the Chinese army would come.

* * *

David Andersen and Tom Fleetwood stood on Castle Hill by the Land Rover, surveyed the countryside and ate their frankfurters. They watched the men moving across the river flats and paddies.

"There's nothing much to tell you chaps by way of action," Fleetwood said as he took out his Players. He proffered the packet. "Do you want one?"

"No thanks." David turned and watched a buzzard disappear south over the hump of Kamak-San. He swallowed his strong, sweet tea and leant over the front of the Land Rover. The metal was pockmarked, hard and cold.

"Sorry," Fleetwood said. "I forgot the first time I offered you one. It's a filthy and stupid habit." He blew the smoke from his nostrils. "The brigadier sends his regards. He still talks about the show at the apple orchard." David was pleased and said nothing. "Do you want some more tea? Then we'd better get going."

"Yes, thanks."

The Englishman poured the black brew into David's mug. "There's quite a lot to see. When do you go back to your outfit?"

"Monday."

"Do you want to go out with the Centurions? There's a squadron of Hussars pushing off at 11.00."

"Yes, I would."

"Right then. Do you play Brag?"

"No."

"Never mind, it's not hard. We'll have a game tonight." Andersen was well turned out, he thought, especially for an Australian. He considered the thin, white face, the fair

154

hair and the spare body and then studied the orders. "Andersen?" he asked, "with an 'e'?"

"There's Norwegian in the family somewhere," David said, "and my grandfather is a Scot. Alistair Kinross Andersen."

"Scotland," Fleetwood said, "my God how I love that place. Do you fish?"

"Yes, but there are few rivers where I come from," David said.

"That's a pity. A country's no country without rivers, even the Imjin."

Fleetwood thought again of the trout rising and looked across the river at the purple flowers on the northern hills. "My mother would like the azaleas. She's a great gardener." He put his mug down on the front of the Land Rover, turned and got the ordnance map from the front seat. The dust rose from his boots. "I'll show you the situation, then we'll go and have a look."

The two soldiers looked at the map as the spring sun shone on their backs.

"I don't know what's happening at Kapyong," Fleetwood said, "but it's a bit tense here. We think there's a Chinese army corps out there, thirty thousand of the devils, but no sign of them. We're patrolling every day from dawn to dusk, we're using Harvard spotters, but not a bloody thing. They're clever buggers. They know how to fight. And *they* must be patrolling too."

"I was on the road to Chasan," David said.

Fleetwood looked up. "Were you? A shambles, I heard."

"It was."

"Tough?"

"Very."

"That's soldiering, isn't it?" Fleetwood said, "that's what we're about. That's our vocation, I should know, I'm from a long line." He thought of his father on the beach at Dunkirk, where something dreadful had happened and his father would never talk about it. He lit another Players.

155

"We're a bit light on the ground, but we've done our best."

David studied the placement of the four companies of the Gloucesters and noted the ambush platoon by the crossing on the south side of the river.

"The Chows have got to use the crossing," Fleetwood said. "It's the best fordable place." But everybody knew the river was very low this spring and there could well be other crossing places.

On the right of the Gloucesters were the Northumberland Fusiliers; on the right of them, and further back in the hills, were the Hussars; and across the Imjin to the north were the Belgians; the Royal Ulster Rifles, badly hit in the January fighting, lay in reserve; three miles southeast lay the 25-pounders of the 45th Field Regiment. It all looked well planned.

"We're going to lose the Hussars tomorrow," Fleetwood said, "they've got fuel problems." He folded the map. "This is a bugger of a place for supply. We've got to get the petrol in on the coolies' backs."

"What are the Belgians like?" David said.

"God knows. They put up a bit of a show in 1941, I seem to remember." Fleetwood laughed. "This is the United Nations, all kinds of odd bods: Puerto Ricans and Filipinos, Canadians, the Frogs, Dutch, the New Zealanders, the Americans who think they run the show, but don't. We're making history: refugees who can't be trusted, talk of the atom bomb and germ warfare, it's not quite what I expected, not what we were taught at Sandhurst." He ground his cigarette against the heel of his boot. "I'll take you down to Chokson and BHQ, then we'll visit the river."

Visit the river, David thought, it sounded like some picnic. They might see Toad and Mole. They got into the Land Rover and drove down towards the Imjin.

The fragile poplars stood in lines, their delicate thin branches curved, reaching for the sky. On the north side, the Centurions rumbled, pennants flying and dust billowing from their tracks. Cormorants and gulls squatted on the sandbanks and lone clouds flew high. A cable ferry was sunk at its moorings and row boats with high, painted prows were stranded in the mud. The shallow river ran, silently, twisting and curving through the barren valley. Fleetwood looked at the water. No trout spawned in these muddy waters: no water weeds streamed, no deep pools, nor overhanging branches where the big trout slept. There was no waxed trout line curving here, no nineteenth-century houses, ornamental gardens and pretty girls sitting at tables on the lawn. He thought of fishing on the Test at dusk, his trout line flicking and the bats flying from the alders and the pines.

"It looks quiet to me," David said as they strolled east over the shingle banks of the river. He watched the Centurions racing away to the north. The enemy was not to be seen.

"They'll come," Fleetwood said. "The Chinese have two armies in those hills: the 63rd and the 65th. We know that. I went out with the Hussars two days ago, eight miles or more, but there was no sign of the Chinks. They're past masters of the old disappearing act. Thirty thousand Asian Houdinis."

David thought of the adventure stories he read when he was young: *Rorke's Drift* and *Waiting for the Zulus* and *The Siege of Ladysmith*. The rattle of spears on leather shields and the chant of death.

"This has got all the signs of a classic battle," Fleetwood said. "It could be another back-badge show."

David remembered reading about the Gloucesters at the battle of Alexandria in 1801 and watched Fleetwood as he strode down to the water's edge, the badges on his black beret gleaming. *Honi soit qui mal y pense.* He poked at the rocks with his walking stick; then he came back and said: "Oh, to be England, now that April's there." He laughed. He was a strong-boned, elegant man. "I'll take you round so you can see how the battalion's dug in. We'll give the Chows a run for their money."

David wondered if the Chinese had transport. Did they

have tanks? They had no aircraft, but they must have scouts. Was the battalion being watched? He was sure it was.

* * *

The Centurions lay, turrets down, below the brow of the hill. The Rolls Royce engines thudded and the major opened his case and worked out his co-ordinates on the map. He was very good-looking, with a black moustache; he wore Erwin Rommel goggles that pushed up his beret, a hunting knife, a white silk scarf; and he smoked Kent cigarettes. David noticed the hand grenades and the Bren in the turret.

"Have you been in one of these before?" the major said.

"No, Chaffees and Crusaders."

The major wrinkled his nose. "Centurions are streets ahead, but this is bloody awful country for armour. You've probably heard you can't get the tankers in and we've got to refuel by hand. We burn five gallons to the mile and we're going back this evening, so the Gloucesters will be on their own for a bit."

"So I've been told," David said.

"There's not much else we can do. We've been patrolling for three weeks and haven't seen a bloody thing, but the bastards are here all right. We'll go out about ten miles to the northeast and sweep around to the west. Plug in your RT so you can hear the other chaps."

The Centurions moved out of the lay-by, gears grinding, tracks squealing and dust rising. The spring air reeked with smoke and exhaust. The terrain undulated toward the foothills of the mountains in the north and the Centurions kept to the low ground, their turrets traversing and thundering across the open spaces. As David squinted from the turret, it was hard to spot the machines against the dull landscape, and the countryside slid past silently, any noise covered by the roar of the engines.

"As far as we know," the major said on the intercom,

158

"they've got no armour, but you never can tell. We're going to a spot we haven't looked at for several days. When we get there, I'll tell you, and keep your head down."

He grinned and pulled his mittens down his fingers. The voices of the troopers crackled and sounded thin on the radios, and David looked down at the driver, his hand on the gear lever and his left foot working the clutch. The gears ground and crashed: it was very hard work. He wondered what they might see as the turret swung and the grey land slid by.

About half an hour later, they saw the vehicle sitting at the base of the gully.

The squadron stopped and the major looked through his field glasses. "It's a Soviet T34," he said. "What the fuck is it doing out here?" He kept looking. "They must have seen us. Why don't they scarper? Maybe they *have* got armour. I hope to Christ not."

The major considered the Soviet tank, and spoke to the gunner on the intercom, and the Centurion shook as the 20-pounder pumped off a couple of rounds. The gunner heaved another shell into the breach, and they waited and watched the smoke drift around the T34.

"It's derelict." The major told the other commanders to stand to and they crept down the slope. They stopped about 500 yards from the Soviet tank and the trooper crouched behind the Browning machine gun. The major stared from the turret, his silk scarf drifting in the wind. David looked at his watch: it was almost 1500 hours.

"I think I'll take a look," the major said, "they're not bad tanks. I haven't had much excitement lately."

He spoke to the trooper as the engine idled. "Cover me, Frank, if you will. I'm going to have a butcher's."

"Right you are, sir."

The major swung up out of the hatch and dropped down by the side of the Centurion, his revolver in his hand. The machine-trooper signalled and David crawled across the deck toward the Browning.

"The major's a cool bastard, isn't he?" the trooper said.

"What?" David asked as he watched the Englishman run toward the T34. It was newly painted and bore no signs of recent battle.

"I said, he's a cool bastard. You're an Aussie?"

"Yes." David looked at the trooper. He was a big man with a Cockney accent, his two front teeth were missing and he had a strange tattoo at the base of his throat. It said: *Cut here*. "That tank could be booby-trapped," David said.

"Maybe," the trooper said, "but the major knows what he's about." He picked his nose. "He's a Sandhurst man. They're all the fucking same, toffee-nosed but great in a scrap. What's Aussie like? I've always wanted to go there. I've heard it's great for filthy lucre."

Jesus Christ, David thought, is this mad trooper watching the major or not? But the major was waving his arms and they clambered down and ran across the dry, stony ground. It was getting colder now. The major was crouching by the tank tracks, holding a dip-stick. "They've picked up some wire and they're out of fuel," he said. "Some fun, eh?"

"The tank could be booby-trapped, Major," David said.

The English major smiled. "I'm quite aware of that, Mr Andersen." He tossed the dip-stick on the ground. "But if you don't mind, I'm going to have a look inside. I'll look out for wires and things and make sure nothing's attached."

He clambered up the side of the T34, ran over the deck, climbed carefully over the turret and dropped through the hatch. David thought of the Chaffees and Shermans burning and steaming in the ice on the road to Chasan. They heard the major moving around inside the tank and waited; then he appeared, smiling from the turret, holding two burp guns and a pair of Russian binoculars. He polished the lenses with his white silk scarf and threw them down to David. "There you are, Lieutenant Andersen, a gift to Australia from the 8th Hussars. Present them to your grand-children."

They stood around the T34 and examined the booty.

"Being a cavalryman is sometimes like being a pirate of the Spanish Main," the major said. "We can move fast and there's loads of dash." He looked at David. "With no offence to the infantry, Mr Andersen." He slid his mittens up his fingers and lit a Kent cigarette.

"Do you want some tea, sir?" the broken-toothed trooper asked.

"Yes, Frank, I do."

David hung the Russian binoculars around his neck and walked around the Russian tank. It was an ugly machine and yards of wire were enmeshed in its tracks. Where was the crew? He looked at the brush. Nothing moved. They stood around in the afternoon sun and the trooper walked over with a thermos flask and mugs of tea. A machine gun fired and the big trooper fell, the mugs of tea spilling and his chest cut open. David and the major ran into the lee of the T34 and crouched. "Bloody hell," the major said, "bloody fucking hell."

The firing stopped and from where they were, they could see the trooper's body, the blood, and the smashed thermos. He was dead.

"This bloody place is lethal," the major said, "much worse than the last show. You're never safe: even at BHQ there's a feeling that a gook porter will put a bullet in your back. I've seen men killed while having a shit. Now I've lost a good trooper, and I hate losing men."

David thought of Kershaw dying in the ice and oil under the Bedford truck, and Brownlee spreadeagled on the snow. "We all do," he said.

"Here's comes Charlie," the major said. "He'll blast the buggers to kingdom come. I hope he sets fire to the whole fucking valley. Why couldn't the bastards have given themselves up? They must have seen the squadron. I'll never understand these people."

As the Centurion drew close, two North Korean soldiers came out from the brush with their hands up. The gunner fired the flame-thrower, the North Koreans ran about and burned to death.

"That's that," the major said.

They put the trooper's body in the Centurion and travelled west. No more enemy were seen that day. On the way back, David thought: T34s had a crew of three. Where was the third man? What if the Chinese knew the Hussars were leaving that evening?"

*   *   *

Tom Fleetwood was popular with the men of his platoon, and he laughed and joked with them. His game was obviously cricket, not football. He was carefully groomed and benevolent and they sat around the gun pits drinking Japanese beer and rum and cocoa. The birds were asleep and the moon rose over the serrated land and shone on the waters of the river. The hurricane lamps gleamed and the smell of kerosene hung in the still air. Some men were singing to a banjo. The soldiers played Crown and Anchor and Lying Dice and ate tinned steak-and-kidney pudding. It was hard to believe there was a Chinese army waiting somewhere. The breeze was gentle but chilly, and spots of light glowed in the mountains. A platoon of Gloucesters was watching the Imjin, where the seagulls and cormorants were asleep.

"Do you want a gin, David?" Tom Fleetwood said. "I've got a bottle of Gordon's in the Land Rover. I'm afraid there's no tonic or ice, but I've got some bitters."

David laughed. "The beer's fine." He hoped the rules of Brag weren't too difficult; he was only good at the card games he used to play with his grandfather, and, like his father, hated to lose money.

"So your grandfather's a Scot?"

"From Skye."

"Ah, that marvellous island where the wind and whisky are the best in the world. And your mother?"

"She's English, from Gloucestershire."

"Gloucestershire? Good Lord. Which part?"

"A village called Uley. I've never been there."

"Uley? I know it well. God moves in mysterious ways. How was the recce with the Hussars?"

David told Tom Fleetwood about the abandoned T34 and the British trooper.

"*C'est la guerre*," Fleetwood said, "*c'est la guerre*. The major was a little slap-happy, don't you think?"

"I don't think it was anyone's fault, just one of those things."

Fleetwood looked at the river and said: "So your grandfather's a Scot and your mother's from Gloucestershire? Celtic blood flows in your veins?"

"Yes, I suppose it does."

"What school did you go to?"

David thought he should be getting tired of Fleetwood's questions, but he wasn't. He liked this tall, English subaltern; he was as lean and as dark as a thoroughbred and he looked as though blue blood flowed through *his* veins. Why did they all carry walking sticks?

"Melbourne Grammar," he said.

"Public, of course?"

"We call them private. And you?"

"Wellington, called after the Duke, the best school in England."

"And then to Sandhurst?"

"Indeed. And you went to Duntroon?"

"Yes."

"Well," Tom Fleetwood said as he poured himself another rum, "that clears that away. Do you want to play Brag?"

"If you don't mind," David said, "I don't."

"All right then, there's a film on, *In Which We Serve*. Have you seen it?"

David remembered Noel Coward and the sailors struggling in the oily water. "Yes I have," he said, "but I wouldn't mind seeing it again."

"All right," Tom Fleetwood said. "We shall, as our American friends say, go to the movies."

The Gloucesters sat in the gun pits, drank their beer and laughed and chatted. The Hussars and the Centurions had gone home. The battalion was on its own now.

*   *   *

The Gloucesters' chaplain set up an altar in a ruined Korean temple in a village overlooking the river. Sunday morning was crisp and the sky was cloudless as they knelt and took the Host. After the service, the men and officers stood around in the broken building, boots crunching in the stones and rubble. Fleetwood introduced David to the chaplain, who shook his hand and said: "It's a pleasure to have you with us. I trust you're impressed."

"I am indeed, sir."

"God knows what we're facing," the chaplain said, "but we'll do our best. You'll tell your chaps that?"

"I think they know it already, sir." David liked the chaplain: he looked tough and able as he stood in his surplice.

"Where are you from?" the chaplain said.

"Melbourne."

"Ah, the city of parks and churches. I've a colleague there who's sub-dean at St Paul's. You know it?"

"I do, sir." David thought of the Sunday services on the cold winter mornings, the walk back to school as the trams rattled along St Kilda Road and the wind blew oak leaves into their faces. Why did it always seem to be winter? Maybe it was the war.

"Melbourne is one of the great Victorian cities, I believe," the chaplain said.

"I don't know it well, sir," David said. "I went to boarding school and we didn't get out much." He thought of the

164

early morning runs along the tan track and watched the chaplain pack the chalice away in his case.

"I hope Mr Fleetwood's looking after you properly," the chaplain said, "and offering you the hospitality of the battalion?"

Tom Fleetwood leaned on his walking stick. David was reminded of the men in the Maxim Gun detachment in the King's Royal Rifles. "I'm doing my best, sir," Fleetwood said.

"I'm sure you are." The chaplain laughed. "Mr Fleetwood's the only officer in the entire battalion with an inexhaustible supply of Gordon's. No one knows quite how he does it."

"Loaves and fishes, sir," Fleetwood said.

The chaplain looked at the river and the ambush platoon, and then at the hills beyond. "We may need your loaves-and-fishes talent in other directions, Lieutenant, before this show's finished." He turned toward David. "When do you return to your outfit?"

"Tomorrow night, sir."

"Well, God speed, Mr Andersen." He proffered his hand. "Tell your people that the Gloucesters control the Imjin."

"I will, sir."

"I've just remembered," Fleetwood said, as they walked through the ruined village. "The chaplain's from Uley. He probably knows your mother's family." David stopped and turned to go back to the chaplain, but he had gone.

* * *

At about 14.00, they were told that a Gloucester patrol had made contact with a Chinese platoon, and had killed them all. There was no sign of reinforcements, and the front was empty. David wondered if he should contact his captain and get permission to return to Kapyong that evening. Now that the Hussars were gone he didn't want to get stuck on the Imjin with the Gloucesters. He and Fleetwood went

165

over to CHQ to call the battalion, but reception was bad and they couldn't raise them.

"I should think you'll get back tomorrow," Fleetwood said. "There's still a bit to do if you want to put in a thorough report."

David agreed and thought: if he were to get through to the battalion and get permission to go back to Kapyong tonight, it would mean altering the time of the helicopter pick-up with the Americans and that would involve endless mucking about. It seemed a bit unnecessary.

"Do you want a cup of tea?" Fleetwood said, "I spy a B Company stove going."

"So your father's a soldier?" David asked as they drank, their feet in the trenches.

"And my grandfather and great-grandfather. The Fleetwoods go back to the Peninsular War. My great-great-grandfather served under the Iron Duke himself. They were all in the Royal Artillery. I'm the first foot-soldier. That almost broke my father's heart."

"Why?"

"The family tradition is that one always stays in the artillery. But I had a favourite uncle in the Gloucesters, so in I went."

"Did your father serve in the last war?"

"He did, with the BEF in France under Lord Gort, a most unhappy time. After Dunkirk, he was given a desk job down at Camberley. We don't see each other much. I spend most of my weekends in town, seducing debs. And you?"

"What?" David hoped Fleetwood wasn't going to ask him about girls.

"Where do you go on leave?"

"Home sometimes, to a country town called Penshurst. There's a great deal of travelling. It's seven hundred miles from Duntroon."

"Good Lord." Fleetwood tossed the tea slops into the dust. "Do you like being a soldier?"

"Yes, I do. Why do you ask?"

"I just wondered."

David barely knew this young Englishman. What should he tell him? Should he tell him about the Korean sniper? "Chasan was unpleasant."

"So you said."

"It wasn't a retreat, it was a rout."

"The Americans behaved badly, I've heard."

"They may have, but this is an unusual war."

"Unusual? But every war's a soldier's war."

David was about to reply, but the sound of rifle and machine-gun fire echoed from the river.

"Jesus Christ, sir," one of the men said to Fleetwood, "that's A Company."

The men were ordered to stand to. It was dark now and hard to see down the moonlit slopes. They ran to the Land Rover, grabbed their Stens and stuffed spare magazines under their webbing. The firing became intense, and tracers streaked, yellow and green, through the night. Bugles and whistles sounded and David knew the Chinese were there in strength. They must be wading the ford. It appeared to Fleetwood as he looked through his night glasses that it wouldn't be long before A Company was surrounded. From the heights, they heard the firing, saw the flashes, heard the bugles, but could not see the men as they fell. As the battle went on deep into the night, the officers and men of B Company crouched in their gun pits and watched the flanks. It was the west that concerned them; that was where the river crossing was, where the Chinese could be wading through the shingly river.

"It's unfortunate about the Hussars," Fleetwood said, "we could have done with them. I'm sure we can stop them at the river and you'll be back at Kapyong tomorrow night."

God speed, the chaplain had said. David crouched and listened to the sounds of battle.

*   *   *

167

When they were fired on from the western flank shortly before midnight, they knew the Chinese were coming up the valley and trying to get behind them. The enemy fired from the rocks, from the fir trees and from the outcrops. Several men fell and the dying started. A Land Rover was hit by a mortar and burned like a ghastly beacon, exposing the slit trenches and gun positions. Once again the men cursed and groaned at the mortar bombs: it was the same deadly litany, and the medics could not move to find the wounded and the dead until first light.

"I'm sorry for this, David," Fleetwood said, "it looks as though it might be difficult to get you back to Kapyong." He laughed. "At least you've chosen a propitious time: tomorrow is St George's Day."

David looked at the flashes of gunfire to the west and at their backs. The Chinese were moving very quickly in this dark and bloody night. He too laughed and said: "Where better than to be with the Gloucesters on St George's Day?" But he remembered Hart's words to Jones: *Being shot at is all you're good for.*

It seemed that the Chinese came head on, shouting and screaming from the hidden ground of the gullies and shadows of the rocks and the trees. They were ghosts in the night; they attacked in the moonlight like the Tartars and the hordes of Genghis Khan, and when they fell the men behind them used the bodies as sandbags. The slaughter seemed endless, and it was clear from the radio reports from A Company that an army corps had fallen upon the Gloucesters. The Chinese were crossing the river in thousands; the noise of mortars, machine guns, small arms, bugles and whistles was deafening and the enemy came shouting and screaming up the ravines on all three sides. David knew then that he might not see the Australian battalion again. The Vickers guns fired at the Chinese until the cooling jackets boiled over and they seized up; the Brens, Stens and rifles became too hot to handle and the men threw grenades, beer bottles and rocks from the foxholes and gun emplacements; but the Chinese came on over the spurs through the howitzer fire and shells of the 45th Artillery regiment behind the southern hills. The news from all the companies was bad: it now seemed that two army corps had crossed the Imjin and fallen on the Gloucesters. David fired his Sten at the enemy in the dark, threw down the empty magazines, fired again, heard the screams, fired and thought: somewhere there is a cross for me. But at last the dawn came, and there was not.

At first light the fighting eased and the men crawled from their gun pits to try and help the wounded and bring in the dead; but the Chinese snipers picked them off in ones and twos from the ridges and no one was safe. David's mouth was dry, his limbs ached and shook and he wished he was with his own men. What was happening at Kapyong? Had the Chinese attacked there? What was happening to Paul Cash? Was he still clutching his rosary, and was Hart still persecuting him? Could the Chinese be to the southeast, too? That was impossible. The trees, brush and vehicles were still burning and somewhere, close by, a man lay crying. The bearers went out, some bent double, some crawling to try to get them in.

*   *   *

Fleetwood opened a tin of C-rations and they ate their cold breakfast in the slit trench. Two Oxford carriers rumbled down the road toward the river to extricate the survivors of A Company. David watched the vehicles, the dust spuming from their tracks, and wondered what the men would be like when they were brought back. Chests would be punctured and bloody and arms and legs would be missing. Sooner or later, it would be his turn: he would lose an eye, an arm, a leg, or surgeons would expertly place a metal plate in his skull; his face would be reconstructed; and he would live out his days on a military pension.

169

Half of A Company were dead and the survivors were haggard and exhausted from the night's battle. Ammunition was running low, and they were under machine-gun fire from the Chinese dug in on the peak overlooking the valley. The colonel asked BHQ for reinforcements, but there were none, and they were told to stay where they were. Fires burned in the hills and the Chinese kept coming across the river. There seemed no end to them, and they worked their way through the rocks and gullies to outflank the battalion.

Then in the afternoon B and C Companies were attacked; the numbers were overwhelming, and when the grenades ran out, the men were reduced to throwing entrenching tools and beer bottles. By the end of the day, it was obvious that the companies and platoons were cut off from each other and the Gloucesters' colonel decided to call all his men into one perimeter on a hill called 235.

In the last light of the day, David and Tom and the survivors of B Company staggered into BHQ; machine-gun fire and mortars swept the hill; the battalion now numbered less than 300, and the winding road to the south was cut. The Gloucesters were on their own. The cold night came down and Fleetwood did his best to see that his men were fed and settled in. There was no hot food and they all ate cold C-rations; they lit the stoves and made porridge with hard biscuits and had tots of rum. The medics patched up the wounded, gave them morphine and arranged the dead for burial in the morning. All had lost friends and it seemed now there was little chance of getting off the hill. At least they were all together: the riflemen, the pioneers, cooks, signalmen, machine-gunners and medics, and this gave them comfort.

"Well, David?" Tom Fleetwood said as they sat down in the dark and listened to the shocked and wounded men crying.

"I think I've drawn the short straw."

"I think we all may have done that." Fleetwood sat on a rock, his walking stick between his knees. "Getting off this hill is not going to be easy."

"What are our chances?" David said. He never dreamt he would die in the mountains of Korea, in the company of strangers. He longed for the familiar accents and conversations of home. It was getting cold and his body shook.

"Do you want a greatcoat?" Fleetwood said. "I can scrounge one."

"No thanks, I'm all right." David sipped the rum and it warmed his innards. It was autumn in Australia now and the leaves of the oaks and hawthorns at *Killara* would be falling. What would his family be doing? He knew: no burp guns and mortars *there*, no white-faced, shocked and dismembered men, no landscape torn to pieces by 25-pound shells and burnt by napalm, but the southern moon rising and the crickets singing in the dewy grass and the frogs croaking in the drains and weedy pools.

"The American boxcars are coming over in the morning," Fleetwood said, "to drop supplies and evacuate the wounded. While there's life there's hope." He stretched his legs and unlaced his boots. "You were an athlete of sorts?"

"Yes, I was." David remembered the school mile.

"What distance?"

David looked up. "The mile. I was good at that."

"I'm sure you were. You run like a hare."

"I haven't got much weight to carry."

Fleetwood laughed. "And neither have I. You *won* the mile, I take it?"

"Three times."

"A record?"

"I think it was done twice before."

"Why did you join the army?"

"Because," David said, "I wanted to."

"I had no choice," Tom said. "Tradition and paternal pressure. Do you know, you're the first Australian I've ever had a long conversation with?"

"We aren't all that different." But, David thought, *Terra Australis Incognita*. He wondered about Cash: would he ever see him again? Some medics passed, carrying a dead

171

soldier on a stretcher; he had lost both legs and was covered up with a grey blanket. Firing echoed in the dark hills, a mortar bomb burst and tracers lit up the darkness. Somewhere, bugles and whistles sounded and a man screamed. The stragglers were still coming in, heavy-laden with Brens, bazookas and field wirelesses. They looked tired and collapsed on the ground. The air was dry and the flies swarmed upon the wounds.

"Do you want another rum?" Tom said.

"No thanks."

The dead and the dying came in all through the night.

At dawn, the men dug graves in the hard and rocky ground and the chaplain buried the dead, while the wounded lay on stretchers, some unconscious, others staring at the blue spring sky. The 25-pounders from the Field Regiment in the south hammered at the slopes below the Gloucesters' hill, the Chinese pressed on, and everyone knew that the artillery support could not last for more than a day or two: the 45th would have to withdraw in case it, too, became surrounded.

*　　*　　*

The flying boxcars appeared from the southern hills, but the fog and mist prevented them from dropping supplies and, rotors drumming, they flew away. They watched the helicopters leaving the fire zone and heard the bugles blowing in the gullies. Then the Starfighters came in and dropped bombs and napalm on the Chinese; many men were killed and burnt to death, the valleys reeked of gasoline, cordite, gunsmoke and flesh burning but it made no difference. The entire Imjin valley was on fire, but the Chinese kept coming. They ran, crawled, stood and fired from the shoulder and the hip; they jumped from rock to rock, from pit to pit and could not be stopped. David, too, ran from trench to trench, with his Sten; he fired at the enemy alongside Fleetwood. They tossed the empty magazines into the brush, shouting

172

and blaspheming, they ran back and forth across the stony ground, covered each other, stumbled, fell and cursed as around them men fell. The noise was intolerable and David clapped his hands to his ears to keep it away. God knows how many men he killed that spring morning, but it made no difference. All food and water was gone and the ammunition and wireless batteries were exhausted.

*   *   *

To the west, the Northumberlands, the Ulsters and the Fusiliers were attacked and the brigadier decided to withdraw the brigade for fear of encirclement. The message came through over the wireless: hold on where you are. The Hussars tried to get down the defile, but they were ambushed by the Chinese in the rocks and mountain passes. The leading tank was hit by mortar fire, the Centurions faltered and stopped and the Chinese tossed their grenades into the hatches and clambered on the armour plates, slippery with blood. The Hussars could not get through.

*   *   *

The next morning, the colonel assembled the remaining officers and told them that all hope of the Gloucesters carrying on as a unit had gone. The battalion was surrounded and the road south was cut. David listened to the colonel as the ground shook, the fires burned and the men shouted. It was Anzac Day. At Penshurst and in every town in Australia, the bands would be playing, the veterans marching and wreaths would be being laid on bluestone and marble monuments. He thought of the Boer War veterans, the limbless men from the Somme and Pozières, the Last Post and the dawn parade when he was a child. His father would be marching behind the fire brigade band. He and Tom stood among the burning vehicles and listened to the colonel tell them that each company should try and break out independently. They could break out at will, he said; there was no more relief, no more air strikes and no more artillery support. Every man should do what he thought best. He gave them God speed and his best wishes.

"This is it," Tom said, "we've done our best." They and the remaining men of the section grabbed what spare magazines and grenades they could and ran down the southern slopes of the hill as the enemy machine guns fired.

* * *

They scrambled through rocks, slit trenches and bomb craters. Broken and burnt bodies lay everywhere; some were piled like sandbags, their heads and limbs missing. Flies swarmed over the bodies and maggots crawled in the gun pits. Were some men still alive that bloody spring morning? They ran and fell over the wreckage and could not tell. Smoke hung over the valley of the Imjin.

* * *

It was Tom who first saw the Chinese on the rise. There were about a dozen of them, brandishing their burp guns and shouting. More appeared, dressed in yellow quilted jackets and forage caps. They were small, nut-brown men, agile and wearing bandoliers. Some were grimacing and others were smiling. One face was badly burned by napalm. Shots were still being fired, but this was the end of the battle. The valley grew quiet as the sump oil burnt from the trucks and carriers and the smoke drifted toward the pines. Men groaned and cried in the debris and already the seagulls were returning to the mudflats on the river.

The silence was stunning as Tom grabbed David's shoulder and shouted to his men. "We're cold turkey, chaps."

David held his Sten and wondered what to do. He wasn't

sure if there were any rounds left or not. There was still the Webley; he hadn't fired that and he wasn't sure he wanted to. Should he drop his weapons on the ground and raise his hands above his head? He thought of the Germans in the war films shouting, *Kammerad, Kammerad*. He wasn't sure and felt a sense of shame; his feet were sore and blistered, his socks filthy and his body ached; his hair was matted, his face unshaven, his fingernails were split and black, and he was sure his breath was foul. It seemed there was shit everywhere, paper fluttered and the wrecked latrines reeked. Some of the Chinese were still smiling. This was the first time he had seen the enemy. The Chinese were everywhere, running like rabbits down the slopes, rummaging in the foxholes, searching for booty and rounding up the men. They seemed good-natured and inquisitive. One found a Swiss army knife, another a pair of spectacles and they laughed. David watched the Chinese approach and looked at Tom, his proud, grimy face, the black beret and the back-badge; his tunic was torn and his boots were dirty.

"They've got us cold, David," Fleetwood said, "you'd better put your Sten down. And your Webley, if you don't mind. I want to see this thing through."

The Chinese walked over and shook hands. They smelt of cabbage, chilli and garlic and looked very fit. Their hands were as hard as wood, and they were wearing cloth ammunition pouches and fur-lined boots. A most formidable enemy. Their automatic weapons were new; they wore no insignia of any kind and there seemed to be no rank. This was the People's Army of Mao Tse Tung; they travelled on their feet, transported their guns and supplies on mules, and lived on rice. They looked invincible.

David gave a Chinese his Sten, his Webley, and the Russian binoculars, and the soldier smiled and bowed. They seemed friendly and gathered around.

Tom Fleetwood fished out his lighter and lit a Players. "We have many wounded men on the slope." He waved his arm. "Up there." His voice was loud in the spring air. But the Chinese smiled and squatted on the earth; they examined the Sten guns and looked at Fleetwood's lighter.

"We have many wounded men," he repeated. "They need help."

But nothing was understood and they were taken farther down the slope as the men in the foxholes and on the slopes, in the sun, lay dying

The river valley was bright with sunlight; the gulls swooped, the rooks croaked and the flowers were still on the hills. Lines of mules and horses were being watered, and David looked for some kind of headquarters, some senior officers, but there were none. The Gloucesters stood around in groups and lit up cigarettes as the Chinese searched them. They took away watches, binoculars, penknives and lighters. David saw the colonel trying to explain about the wounded on the hill, but there was no response. There was much uncertainty; it was hot in the sun and after a while they were moved into a shadowy ravine where pine trees grew; it was cool and pleasant but it all seemed very confused. No one said very much. David sat next to Tom, who said nothing. A crane flew south, its long legs dangling. Then they learned that the entire battalion was surrounded by the Chinese, and they could not take the wounded out. The chaplain, the adjutant and the colonel argued, but it was no use. David thought, this is not like fighting the Germans. A man like Sergeant Hart would understand. Fleetwood was talking to the colonel. What were they talking about? But David knew: it was the wounded, the dying and the dead. *If I should die in some foreign field.* Gulls and gannets were fishing for herring in the river, water spinning from their feathers. Some of the Gloucesters greeted their mates as they came in from the hill, but there was no one David knew. Tom was the only friend he had now. He wished he would stop talking to the colonel. The sun shone in the ravine in shafts, as through high cathedral windows. He wished he was with his grandfather.

"You're an Australian, sir?" a Gloucester said as he squatted on the ground.

"Yes," David said, "I'm a liaison officer."

The English soldier rolled a cigarette. "It looks as though the Chinks have won, don't it?"

"Yes, I suppose they have, for the time being."

"Well, sir, we've got to escape at the earliest opportunity, haven't we?"

"Yes," David said, "I suppose we have."

"Luck not running your way, sir?" the soldier said. "You could be back with the Aussies."

"I could well be."

David remembered the advice: *When captured, a soldier's first duty is to escape.* The Chinese were not prepared for such a victory and didn't know what to do with the men or where to take them. The Gloucester officers continued to argue about the wounded on the hill; at last they were given permission to take the stretchers up and get them out. Tom came back and said: "I've got permission to escape whenever I like and many of the chaps are going to give it a try." He looked at the soldiers and the Chinese guards milling around. "With all this going on, it shouldn't be too difficult. I normally like to travel alone, but when I go, do you want to come?" He laughed. "We can both run like hares and you're a country lad."

David considered the mountains: it wasn't exactly like the country he was used to. "Whenever you go," he said, "count me in." Then he said, "I might go first."

The Chinese laid their dead neatly by the roadside while others washed in a creek. Then the Gloucesters were finally marched down the road to the old BHQ by the ford. It was looted: papers, newspapers and clothes were scattered about, and dead mules and ponies lay on the ground. Chinese soldiers slept in small holes carved into the banks while others passed by on old English bicycles; still others kept looking up at the sky; they feared an air attack. Everybody was tense. The prisoners sat around in the rubble of the village and waited for darkness; it was now obvious that the Chinese would move them off the river at night only, in case there was an air attack. At the end of the day they were given rice and pickled vegetables. The afternoon became cloudy as the reserves marched past to the front. The guards watched over them, bayonets fixed to their Russian rifles; some looked young – no more than teenagers.

"What do you think, David?" Tom Fleetwood said.

"I can see why they won. You don't want tanks in this country, you want mules; and you don't want trucks, you want bicycles."

"And numbers."

"They help. But they know this place and we don't."

He had heard about the Long March and now he knew why the Reds had succeeded. Try to avoid fighting the enemy on his home ground.

"They'll take us north," Fleetwood said, "God knows how far; they must have camps up there."

David wondered if they would be ill-treated. Would they be tortured? Were the Chinese signatories to the Geneva Convention? He couldn't remember. Fear and unease began to steal over him. It would have been better to have been captured by Germans: he thought of the *Wooden Horse* and *Stalag Luft 3*. The Germans had a military code and were Europeans: they had common rules of war, but these people didn't. He knew little about the Chinese: only the Boxer Rebellion and the Forbidden City, but now that Communism had come, all that must have changed. Maybe they would take them into China and make them work on communal farms. Maybe he would never see Australia again. He wondered what Tom was thinking. "What do you know about China?" he asked. "Maybe they'll take us there?"

"No, they won't. We're getting out at the first opportunity. I'm not repairing the Great Wall or working as a slave for Chairman Mao, or whatever they do."

"But what do you know about China?"

"Bugger all, I've never really thought about it." Tom stuck his boots in the dirt. "Teeming millions, opium dens and Charlie Chan, and lots of Russians now they've gone Commo. Not my style. I'm getting back to dear old England and a pink gin or two in the Naval and Military." He spread his hands. "They must have *some* rules; they could have shot us out of hand. How far do you think it is back to our lines?"

"About four miles, but that means going back through the Chinese front."

"And you don't like that?"

"I think we should try and go down the river, southeast to Seoul. It may be a longer way, but it's safer."

"How do you know it's safer?"

"They've got two armies up here, so the southeast should be more lightly occupied and I don't like the idea of buggering around a crowded battle front. We would be shot by our own men or the South Koreans."

"Can you manage this country?"

"Probably, I've done a great deal of fieldcraft, and as you said, I'm a country lad."

"I didn't mean to be rude."

"No offence, and I've still got my map and compass. They haven't found them."

"Have you? That settles it."

They waited for the night.

* * *

The road to the Imjin was packed with troops, mules, porters and bicycles; and the Gloucesters carried their wounded on stretchers. Chinese reserves went by in thousands, the coolies carrying shells on bamboo poles. The night was cool and cloudy and the long column stumbled down the winding track to the canals and paddies, splashing through, and then to the mudflats and the river crossing.

Guards moved up and down the column, and David and Tom watched them carefully. David hoped to God that the Englishman was a strong swimmer. Many other officers and men were planning to escape too and he wondered how many would try and leave the column at the river. A light breeze blew and David tried to keep near Fleetwood as the water came up to their knees. The guards shouted, and somewhere in the hills an artillery battery rumbled; lights flickered in the dark and the soldiers cursed as the men groaned on the stretchers. Now the water came up to their waists; the nearest guard raised his rifle above his head and stumbled. David touched Fleetwood on the shoulder, and they both took a deep breath and disappeared into the muddy waters of the Imjin. No one saw them go and they swam south in the strong current.

9

On the Run

Part I

David gasped as the deep water hit him: after the shallows at the crossing, the Imjin was very cold from the winter snows. His boots were like lead and dragged him down; the current was swift, and he stayed under as long as he could, his lungs bursting and his body like ice. When he surfaced, he looked back at the crossing for Fleetwood, but the night was black and there was no sign. The river took him east along the deep channel between the sandbanks and levees where the seagulls and cormorants slept. When he surfaced a second time, he saw the river was full of timber and a half-sunken rowboat drifted by; he swam toward it, almost went under and at last grabbed its gunwales. He grazed his hands on some barnacles but kept holding on, choking and spitting out water. There was no feeling in his hands, but he kept gripping and praying: *God help me now, please help me now.* The banks drifted by and he kept looking out for Fleetwood: what if he had drowned and now he would have to go it alone? The rowboat passed an island and David looked to see if it might afford a safe landing. What if he got cramps and couldn't swim to shore? The pale moon shone as he prayed. Where was Tom? Ages seemed to pass and there was no place safe to go ashore. He might be found dead in the estuary on the mudbanks of the Yellow Sea. The current was much stronger than he expected and he could not even see the river banks.

At last the channel narrowed and he saw willows with overhanging branches: this was his first and last chance. He pushed off from the boat and swam slowly toward the trees, but the current was against him, dragging him back into the deep channel. The boat disappeared and it seemed nothing could save him now. He swam as hard as he could, thrashing and heaving in the water, and the branches neared; he grabbed for one and missed, he grabbed again, the branch bent and held as the current swept around his body. He held on and rested: he knew he was safe now. Then, letting the branch go, he grabbed some reeds and hauled himself through the mud and on to the bank. Dear God, he thought, you have saved me. He would live to fight another day.

After a while, David unlaced his boots and tipped out the water; he took off his socks and tunic, wrung them out and laid them on the reeds. He pulled out the ordnance map together with Jones's and Kershaw's wallets and put them carefully on the ground to dry. He hoped his hand compass was still working, but it was too dark to see. Where to Christ was Fleetwood? Which side of the river was *he* on? If it was the north side, it would mean another swim tomorrow night and a day would be wasted. David stood up in his string vest and sodden trousers and looked down the bank, but nothing moved. He would wait for Fleetwood until the morning, then he was alone after that. He lay down in the reeds.

He must have been dozing despite the wet and cold: then he awoke to hear somebody moving through the trees and brush. David rolled over and lay prone; he listened to the leaves rustling and boots splashing in the boggy ground. He looked for some kind of weapon, a stone, a branch, but nothing was at hand. It might be a night patrol, and he listened to the boots. The noise stopped for a second or two, then came closer, as he tried to hide himself in the reeds and brush. When he saw the figure was too tall for a Chinese, he got up suddenly and shouted, "Halt".

"It's me, it's only me," Fleetwood said. "It's the first time I've swum fully clothed and it's not easy, whatever they say. Have I found Moses in the bullrushes?" They both grinned and shook hands. "You've come a long way," Fleetwood said. "I've walked bloody miles, hoping to Christ I'd find you. What side of the river are we on?" His teeth chattered as he flopped down.

"I'm not sure, we'll have to wait until it's light."

"How did you get this far?"

"I hung on to a boat."

"A boat? God looks after his own, doesn't he?"

"A half-sunken boat."

"A boat, nevertheless. All I had was a piece of timber, a broken cartwheel or something."

"Are you all right?" David asked.

"I'm fine, just rather damp. And you?"

David squatted on the ground. "The same. I wonder if they've missed us yet?"

"Our chaps will have, but not the Chows. They can't tell one European from the other." Fleetwood, too, dragged off his boots and tipped out the water. "Christ, I could do with a fag, even that dreadful toasted muck. Are you hungry?"

"I could eat a horse."

"How far do you think Seoul is?"

"Your guess is as good as mine." David rubbed his feet and toes. "A fortnight's march."

"We've got to get some food soon, and that means contact with the locals." Fleetwood took off his black beret and ran his fingers through his wet hair.

"They can't all be treacherous," David said, "there must be someone we can trust."

"We'll see about trust. This is a hostile place, and we don't know the lingo. There are no rules here."

*   *   *

183

After the battle, the defeat and the shouts of the Chinese soldiers, all seemed as still as the grave. The northern hemisphere stars were shining brightly now, and the broad river ran. Small animals crept through the brush, locusts sounded and frogs croaked; herring flopped in the water and night birds flew. A salty breeze drifted in from the Yellow Sea. They sat on the grass and waited for the dawn. Light glowed over the eastern hills, but it was the false dawn and David guessed it must be about 04.00. His stomach ached and he was very hungry: he longed for a cup of cocoa and a tot of rum, for an idle conversation with his men in the gun pits. David realized he had not spoken to any Korean, except to shout at porters. He knew lots about the French and the Germans, but nothing about Asiatics at all.

"It will be light in a couple of hours," he said. They lay in the bracken in their heavy, wet uniforms, limbs shaking. Fleetwood wondered why he had thrown in his lot with the Australian: he could have asked one of a dozen men. It was partly the apple orchard, partly because Andersen looked reliable and partly because Australians intrigued him. From all accounts, they were tough and resourceful and knew what they were about. His father had a high opinion of them; he said they had fought well in the Great War. He remembered his father talking about an Australian general called Monash. He thought of his father, drinking pink gins in the morning at Camberley while his colleagues were away in the Western Desert. It was spring in England now and he listened to the river moving quietly over the shingle and the stones, remembered the Test: the cherry trees, the alders, the wild cherries and the roe deer, the squirrels and the poplars: the belts of Victorian forest planted to keep the sound of the steam engines and carriages away. He longed for the English countryside: it was peaceful and friendly there. The false dawn faded and the night was black, once more. He listened to Andersen's breathing, raised himself to his feet, walked to the water's edge and

184

pissed in the river. The rocks and pebbles were hard beneath his feet.

They found they were indeed on the south side and the country was deserted. Seagulls were sitting in rows on the tops of the levees and the morning sun shone on the water. David looked at the sodden map.

"I think we're about here, and if we are, there's a ferry crossing and this village, Tuju-ri within three miles."

"They're both to be avoided, I should think," Fleetwood said.

"Absolutely. If the ferry's operating, it'll be packed with Chinese troops and so will the village. We'll have to bypass the village through these hills to the south, but there's a lot of open ground. It looks like paddies, I suppose we can go down the river-side of the levees."

"We can be seen from the north side."

"We can, but not clearly enough to be identified, I hope."

"I wish we had some kind of weapon."

"So do I. We might pick something up. It's a pity they took your stick."

"It is. My father gave it to me." Fleetwood stood up. "Christ, I'm cold. How long can you go without food?"

"I've never thought about it until now. I've never gone without. A week, not much more."

"And the objective is Munsan and the railway?"

"Yes, if that's okay with you."

"Right," Fleetwood said, "I'm ready when you are."

They rose to their feet and walked along the river to the southeast.

The going was easy on the shingle and they warmed up a little. After a couple of hours they saw their first human being of the day: a man standing on a retaining wall, his back toward them. He was wearing a black Russian greatcoat and was carrying a rifle and bayonet. They dropped down behind a bank and considered.

"He's North Korean, the *Imnun-Gun*, the People's Army," Fleetwood said.

185

"Are you any good at hand-to-hand or judo?"

"I boxed at school and I was hopeless. What about you?"

"Not me. Bowling fast-mediums was more my style."

Now David was glad he didn't have his Webley: he didn't want to kill close-up again. He wished the soldier would go away, but he stood there on the retaining wall as the last of the mist cleared from the river.

"If I stroll along the beach," David said, "there's a good chance he won't shoot me, he'll jump off the wall and you can belt him on the head with a rock."

"A bit *Boy's Own*, don't you think?"

"I can't think of anything better, and we could do with the rifle and his greatcoat."

"And if he's got any friends?"

"We'll just have to chance that."

"All right then."

David rose from the bank and, heart thudding, walked along the beach. Fleetwood unlaced his boots, placed them on the gravel, picked up a stone and waited, standing in his socks. He remembered his commando training. It was easy to strangle a sentry: you wait on the path until he passes, leap and seize him by the edges of his helmet and pull it toward you; the strap throttles his jugular vein and stops him from crying out; then the knife at his kidneys goes in quite easily. He had never done that, and anyway, the man was standing on a wall and he had no knife. He gripped the stone hard; it weighed about two pounds and was round and flat, worn smooth by the waters of the river.

David walked casually toward the wall as if he were a local. His flesh crept and his boots crunched on the gravel; the seagulls cried and swooped for herring as he walked with his hands in his pockets. He got to the edge of the wall: surely the Korean would turn around and see him now? He started to shake in his damp battledress, but kept walking and hoped to God that Tom was reliable. A pelican was swimming on the river, ducking tail-end up for fish.

186

David kicked at a pebble and it splashed into the water. The man on the wall shouted and David turned.

"Good morning," he said, "good morning."

The soldier raised his rifle to his shoulder, shouted again and jumped from the wall. David smiled, walked toward the Korean and said:

"Is this river good for fishing? I've heard it is."

The Korean was small and nuggety and looked very strong; he kept the rifle up to his shoulder and the bayonet looked long. The seagulls swam on the water and the soldier came forward, his cheap canvas boots squelching on the shingle.

"I'm a fisherman," David said, "and I've been told the Imjin is very good. Do you live around here?"

It all seemed idiotic. He glanced around for other men, but there were none. Then he saw Tom creeping up in his socks; the Korean spoke again to David, Tom came up close behind, raised the stone, cracked the man on the top of the head and he went down. The soldier's red forage cap fell and he lay on the beach. David ran to the Korean, hoping he was not dead. The man lay, blood in his black hair and running down his neck.

"Well done, David," Tom said. "What did you say to him?"

"I asked if the Imjin was good for fishing."

"Good Lord." Tom bent over the body and searched the black greatcoat pockets; he found three balls of cold rice wrapped in paper. "Food," he said, "it's not much, but it's better than nothing."

The rice reeked of garlic and they swallowed it as they squatted by the river; it tasted good and they tossed the paper into the water.

"Is he dead?" David said.

"I gave him a fair whack." Tom picked up the bloodied stone. "But I doubt it." He examined the Korean soldier. "They're strong little men, aren't they?"

David watched for the flies and buzzards, but none came

187

and he felt easier. He turned the body over, searched the pockets and found rice paper inside a quilted tunic: the Korean script was fine and elegant and the paper fragile and delicate. He folded the rice paper carefully and put it next to Jones's and Kershaw's wallets. If he got through, he would show it to his mother. Tom picked up the rifle.

"They're ugly weapons, aren't they?"

David thought of Hart, the slab hut and the vomit and said nothing. Then he said, "What do you want? The rifle or the greatcoat?"

Tom looked up. "If it's all right by you, I'll take the rifle."

"I'll take the greatcoat and the bayonet."

"What else do we want?" Tom said as he fossicked. He found ten rounds of ammunition and put them in his pocket. "Do you want to swap his trousers?"

David looked at the Korean. "No, I don't, he's much too short anyway."

"Well, I'll take his boots off in case he wakes up. You never can tell with these little buggers. They've got more lives than a cat."

Tom removed the canvas boots and tossed them into the Imjin, retrieved his, pulled them on and they walked on up the beach.

*   *   *

They walked separately down a wide, flat valley where poplars grew by the levees and the ruined gardens. The apple trees seemed wild and neglected and tattered flags flew by the small shrines. Greenhouses were smashed, haystacks brown and rotten, the paddies stinking of shit, and the bodies of animals lay in the black water. They walked behind the levees, crouching and spying out the country ahead.

After four hours, they saw smoke. They guessed it must be the village and sat down in the brambles to look at the map. It was Tuju-ri and lay in the middle of paddies and open ground.

"That's where the crossing is," David said. "The Chinese are sure to be using it."

Tom crouched on the ground, the rifle between his knees. "All right then, we'll have to go south and get into that broken country." He looked up at the sun. "It's coming to mid-day and we'll have to get some food before dark. We should drink what we can now, there may be no water where we're going." They went down to the river, lay upon the rocks and drank the muddy water, then moved south toward the hills.

In the Korean gardens, small shrines stood at the corners of the paddies, the ornamental bridges were broken; in the orchards, where the trees were about to blossom and the green shoots grew from the black rice stumps, the sap was rising in the pruned black trees; snow and ice were melting in the mountains; but they saw no peasants there to cultivate the land. The low-slung houses were tiled and thatched, with young maize and corn growing at the front doors but there were no living things, save the birds flying south from the mountainous country to the north where the Chinese were massing with their mules, ponies and ancient field guns. Tom remembered reading about the Hundred Years' War at school: the universal ruin, the pillaging and the mercenaries. He thought of the Crusaders and Richard Lion Heart. They were all mercenaries now.

David ran ahead across the open ground, through the muddy fields and paddies; Tom covered him with the rifle, as David only had the bayonet. They moved as they had been taught as soldiers: David through the Australian bush and Tom through the open spaces and hedgerows of Camberley Plain. David ran the school mile at every step and did not falter. They were hungry and getting tired; they sweated and were filthy, and the mud clung to their boots as they crouched and ran and waited for each other. They splashed through canals, climbed crumbling levees, and rested behind rotting haystacks. The foothills rose before them and dead mules and oxen lay reeking in the mud. When the sun shone from the west and they both guessed it was mid-afternoon, the smudge fires burned and they knew that people were still living in the village. David, sweating, waited for Tom in the lee of a small temple: he had never felt so alone. He sat in the excrement of animals with smashed and scattered masonry around him and listened for the crack of a carbine, but there was no sound. Tom reached him, smiling but shaking with tiredness. Rats and mice ran through the millet stalks, mosquitoes swarmed and they slapped at their faces and bodies.

"In an hour or two," David said, "we shall be in those hills and we shall be safe." He hoped that were so.

*   *   *

Much later they came to a house in the middle of a field. Corn was growing in the doorways and wild potatoes sprouted from the earth. Its walls were made of mud, the roof was thatched, and the small windows were vacant. It was starting to rain and mist blew in from the river. They considered the building carefully and David thought of the house in the clearing at Pakchon and the sniper.

"What do you think?" he said. "I've been in this situation before and there was a sniper inside."

"Where?"

"In the hills at Pakchon." David kept looking at the windows. "We were on patrol."

"Did you lose anybody?"

"No."

Tom handed David the rifle. "Cover me and I'll have a look. There could be food. Who knows?"

Tom pulled his black beret down hard over his head, rose and ran toward the house; he ran across the flat ground. David saw him stop by the door, open it slowly and disappear inside. The sun-shower was stopping and two crows on a pile of broken tiles sat watching them. One of them squawked, took off, and flew north toward the village. What was Tom doing inside the house? David waited for a sound, but none came; his legs ached as he crouched in the dirt and millet stalks. Then he saw Tom appear and raise his arm at the door. He ran across to him, carrying the rifle. The house smelt of rotting grain and old vegetables, and the interior was dark and unwelcoming. Something moved within and David raised the rifle.

"Rats," Tom said, "lots of them. But that's all, no snipers."

"Is there any food?"

"There is, but it's not much. Some seed potatoes."

"Are they worth taking?"

"Anything's worth taking, I should think. We can't ask for dinner at the Café Royal." Fleetwood turned and went back inside. "Let's not hang about here too long. These places give me the creeps." He fossicked around the dark house and prodded with the bayonet. "We're in the Dark Ages. I wouldn't be surprised if Tamerlane turned up at the front door." He turned around. "Maybe you'd better stay there in case someone calls."

David stood at the door as Tom poked and searched and filled his pockets with potatoes. The house smelt of smudge fires, rats and death. Then he saw someone moving behind the bunds and into the millet. The figure seemed small. Was it an animal? But there were no animals left in Korea. David watched from the door and raised and uncocked the rifle as Fleetwood moved around in the darkness of the house. He heard his rummaging. The shape moved again between the bunds and ran toward the stack of broken tiles, then came into the open. David watched and held the rifle. It was a child, and it came up to the door.

The little girl stood impassive, holding a string of locusts in her hand. Her apron was filthy and her eyes wide. David put the rifle down, placed his hand to his mouth and chewed, but she didn't seem to understand. He guessed she was about seven years old. What to do? She stood at the door with the locusts dangling from the string. Tom appeared, his pockets stuffed with potatoes.

"Aha," he said, "a visitor?" He looked at the Korean child. "Do you think she'll tell anybody?"

"Who can tell? She'll certainly know we're not one of them."

"Then we'd best be on our way?"

"It looks like it. Goodbye," David said to the child. They cut away across the paddies and the Korean girl watched them go.

* * *

At dusk, they saw a line of soldiers walking along the top of a bund ahead.

"This is awkward," Fleetwood said. "We'll have to double back. Do you think it was our little visitor?"

"Probably." David had never thought he would be betrayed by a child. He looked north and thought he saw more men in the paddies, but he couldn't be sure. "Let's go back. With any luck we can lie doggo until it gets dark."

"Right you are."

As they ran back through the mud and rice stalks; they seemed very exposed, and both wondered how long they could keep it up. Seoul seemed a thousand miles away, and Tom wondered how his men were getting on. Maybe he should have stayed with them? Then they saw more soldiers walking along a levee to the north of them: there was no place to go. Their shadows were tall in the failing light. The evening mist drifted and they crouched in a paddy, then heard the sound of dogs barking.

"Jesus Christ," Fleetwood said, "they're not using bloodhounds, are they?" He thought of the hunt, the dogs and the bloodied fox and made up his mind never to ride again. David didn't reply and watched the soldiers jump off the levee and advance through the paddies; their voices could be heard now.

"The best we can do," David said, "is to stay put and hope they pass. What do you think?" He saw Tom cocking the rifle. "I shouldn't think there's much point in that. Shouldn't we plan to fight another day?"

Fleetwood put the rifle down and they watched and waited. They hoped for darkness but there was light, and they hoped for rain but the late afternoon sky was clear. Their mouths were dry as the soldiers came close. The dogs barked, and it was hopeless: the Chinese saw them, stood over them, and they rose to their feet from the hollow in the paddy. Fleetwood threw down the Russian rifle, and they raised their hands. The Chinese laughed and talked, seized their arms and tied them behind their backs with telephone cable. The dogs snapped at their heels and trotted after them.

*　　*　　*

The North Korean officer was a handsome man wearing blue riding breeches and black boots, a white shirt and a civilian jacket. He needed a shave; he had green eyes and was friendly and apologetic. His English was fluent. He spoke to the soldiers who undid the telephone cable. They rubbed their hands and stood in the centre of the room. It was getting dark and the hurricane lamp shone on the small table. The room smelt of smoke and kerosene and the Korean lit a cigarette.

"My name is Kim." He laughed. "We are all called that. I am a major in the North Korean People's Army. I regret the use of the telephone cable, but it is necessary." He blew the smoke from his nostrils. "These are difficult times." David and Tom gazed at the major and said nothing. Where had he learnt his English? "It is well you are both in military uniform," he said, "or you would have been shot as spies. We follow the military conventions." He smoked his cigarette and looked at Fleetwood. "You smoke, Lieutenant?"

"I do."

"Ah, we smokers can always tell, cannot we?" He spoke to David. "And you do not?"

"No, I don't."

"It soothes the nerves, do you not think?"

"I don't care for the habit."

"Maybe you have no nerves? You are an Australian?"

There was a bench in the corner of the room and David looked at it, but the North Korean kept them standing.

"Yes, I am."

"The 1st Battalion, 3rd Royal Australian Regiment. I have some Australian friends. Sydney has a large bridge, I believe. Notice that I say *have*; this war is not the Australians' fault; it is the fault of the warmongers of Wall Street. You have both made a grave mistake in coming to Korea. This is not your war."

"We're professional soldiers, Major," Fleetwood said.

"You *were* professional soldiers. Now you are mercenaries, the worst possible kind of soldier. You are at the beck and call of the imperialists. You should know better; you, Lieutenant, would be better employed supervising the changing of the guard at Buckingham Palace or drilling your men at Aldershot. I know all about these things, I am not a peasant. Would you care to sit down while we talk? We three are gentlemen." He spoke to the soldiers and they carried the bench over. "You say you are professional soldiers," Major Kim said, "but I am not. None of us is. This is a people's army. When the war is won, I shall go back to teaching the truth to people less fortunate than I. I am, as you might say, a rare bird in Korea. Your names and serial numbers?" He drew a piece of paper from his jacket and noted them down with his pencil. "And what were you doing on *Imnun-Gun* territory?"

"We were escaping, Major," Fleetwood said, "our first duty as prisoners."

"I know what your duties are, you have no need to

lecture me." He coughed. "Fleetwood and Andersen," Kim said. "Fleetwood, a very English name, it reminds me of the hunt and the foxes. You are well-bred, and your father was a soldier too, was he not? I know all these things, I shall go to England one day when the imperialists have been driven out of my country. I shall drink Guinness and watch the tennis at Wimbledon. I know all these things. I shall go to the palace at Hampton Court."

The room was dark now. Outside the house the smudge fires burned, and the kerosene lamp smoked in its cracked glass. The room was becoming stuffy, and Major Kim yawned.

"That greatcoat," he said to David, "is the property of the *Imnun-Gun*. You are a thief. We should have it back for our gallant soldiers; stealing military equipment is a capital crime." He turned to Tom. "As for you, Lieutenant, the stealing of weapons is an even greater crime, if there can be one where death is involved." He smiled, rubbed his chin and leaned over the table. "But because you are both the tools of the American imperialists, you will be forgiven. You have fallen into the hands of an educated man. What are you doing with the Gloucesters, Mr Andersen, when the 3rd RAR is at Kapyong?"

"I am not obliged to say," David said. He was tired and drowsy now. Dogs barked outside and he wondered what Tom was thinking. His armpits itched, but he dared not scratch himself. Rats rustled in the roof; it was getting cold, and somewhere he smelt food cooking. How long would Major Kim keep them? Would he question them again?

"Would you care for a cigarette, Mr Fleetwood?" Kim said. "We smokers must keep together. It is bad for the lungs, so they say. But I say a short, happy life is preferable to an unhappy long one."

He proffered the pack and Fleetwood took one. The Korean tossed over the matchbox. "They are not Senior Service, but needs must when the devil drives. This is a poor country, there is no Beaujolais and steak and kidney pudding here." He watched Fleetwood smoking. "Alas, there is no food at all. It has gone to our fighting men and I can offer you nothing." He turned the Russian greatcoat upside down and the seed potatoes rolled across the wooden floor. "Aha, stealing food, too? But I shall forgive you." He raised his nicotined fingers. "That is three forgivenesses. What is the word? Absolution? Our Roman Catholic friends. Again, I regret the lack of sustenance." He stretched his legs behind the table. "The living quarters are not exactly like the officers' rooms at Aldershot, but you are unexpected guests and we shall do our best." He looked at Fleetwood. "I expect that you British will celebrate Imjin in the years to come as a gallant defeat, like Dunkirk; that is your way. We shall celebrate it as a great victory. People's armies always win, the French are learning that." Kim ground the butt of his cigarette beneath his riding boots. "I shall see you quite early in the morning, if that does not inconvenience you." He smiled and got up from the table. "If you have any complaints about your accommodation, please do not hesitate to tell the management." He laughed and left the room.

*　　*　　*

An unconscious man lay on the cold stone floor of the cell. He was badly cut about the face and head; the blood was clotted on his skull. A blowfly buzzed around the hurricane lamp outside, then flew in and settled on the man's head.

David brushed it away and said: "He's an ROK."

"It looks like it. They're not too kind to their own. As our educated friend Kim said, this is a people's war."

"I wonder where he learnt English."

"God knows. Hong Kong possibly, that's about the only place. He's an odd cove. Trust our luck, I thought the Beaujolais and steak and kidney pudding was a nice touch; he's worked in a British club or something. I only hope he was treated decently or he'll take it out on us."

"There's nothing we can do for this man," David said as he crouched and listened. "He's still breathing."

"The gooks have got heads like four-shilling iron pots," Fleetwood said. "He'll survive. More importantly, what do *we* do?"

"Seeing we're officers, I should think Kim will send us on somewhere. He's only a major and their top brass may want to interrogate us." He was apprehensive, but hoped his face wasn't showing it. "I wonder why he didn't ask us any military questions."

David thought of the few war films he had seen and of torture at the hands of the Gestapo. Would he be as brave as Leslie Howard?

"Maybe there was no need," Fleetwood said, "he seemed to know everything. He knows the Australians are at Kapyong. Maybe he was sizing us up? Inscrutable Orientals. Christ, I'm hungry. Do you think he's going to try to starve us out?"

"I'm not sure, I'm not sure what he's going to do." David's legs started to shake and he sat down on the stone floor, his back against the wall. He hoped to God he would be strong enough to face the new day. The cell was bare except for a chamber pot in the corner and the fly buzzed in the gloom. The place stank of stale urine and there was no one to help them, no company of men, no organization, and no standing orders. He thought of the Gloucesters' *padre* and taking communion in the ruined temple.

"What's Uley like?" he said.

"A small English village with a fine parish church and a manor house, rolling country. It's not far from Edge."

"Edge?"

"The Vale of the Severn. You can see the Welsh hills," Tom said. "I used to fly kites there during the holidays; it's ideal, the wind takes them out over the Vale and they hang there like birds. Lovely country." Tom shifted his body on the floor. "Have you got a batman?"

"Yes."

"He'll be missing you?"

197

"Yes, he will."

"Is he good?"

"Good?"

"At his job. Does he look after you properly? A good batman's essential, don't you think?"

"He tries," David said, "he tries, but he's a natural coward." He laughed. "Paul's always first in the trench when the mortars come over. A devout Catholic. I don't know what he'd do without his rosary. And yours?"

"A man called Walters, an ex-groomsman, ever reliable and excellent at polishing brass. It shone like the sun on a summer's day. An honourable fellow."

"Why wasn't he with you at Imjin?"

"He's dead, he got hit in the winter show by a bloody sniper. He was getting my breakfast at the time. The bastards. I wonder what our friend Kim is doing?"

"No one knows where we are," David said.

"No they don't, it may be some time before we can write home."

"They've got to pass us along to a camp."

"I expect so." But Tom was starting to feel defenceless now and was wishing he had never left the column.

"If you don't mind," came David's voice through the gloom, "I shall try and get some sleep now."

"Right you are."

It was hard to see the body of the ROK soldier now and the building was as still as death. Then something scuttled across the floor. Was it a rat? Fleetwood couldn't see. What would Kim ask him tomorrow? I am Thomas Reginald Fleetwood, 2nd Lieutenant in the 1st 28th Gloucesters, he said to himself. I am Thomas Reginald Fleetwood. That was all he had to say. He watched the moths and insects burning themselves to death against the kerosene lamp and went to sleep.

*   *   *

198

In the morning they turned the body of the ROK soldier over and found him dead. The wounds on his head were already fly-blown. They looked at each other and stood by the bars of the cell, but nobody was about.

"Jesus Christ," Fleetwood said, "this is too much. We're being starved to death and sharing a filthy cell with a dead man. We're in the hands of savages; this is a country with no standards whatsoever." He banged at the bars with his boots and shouted. "Come here, you bastards, come here, a man's dead, you fucking gooks." He banged at the bars. "Come and take your dead away and give us some food. We're officers of the King's army."

David wondered if he looked as bad as Tom: unshaven, ragged and gaunt. They were losing their dignity: he had lost it once before on the retreat to Chasan. "Be quiet, Tom," he found himself saying. "Someone will come."

Tom stood by the bars. "They'd damned well better."

A North Korean soldier appeared, cocked his burp gun and shouted. Another man came up, they unlocked the door and dragged the ROK soldier away. The door banged shut and they waited, stomachs groaning and rumbling and limbs shaking in the cold dawn. People went by outside, laughing and talking, and the sun shone through the small window. The old men and children were going to the fields. The shafts of light became brighter: it was another day: the now familiar smell of the Korean countryside drifted through the small window and the smudge fires burned. Men stamped on the stone courtyard outside, a rifle cracked, and a cart rumbled by.

"What the fuck is going on?" Tom said. "What the fuck is happening?"

"Just keep quiet and wait," David said. "They'll bring us something." He opened his fly and pissed into the chamber pot; he listened to the activity outside and thought of the azaleas blooming on the hillsides and the fish running in the Imjin. There was nothing to be done. Major Kim would see them this morning and they had to be ready for that.

After half an hour another North Korean soldier appeared and pushed two bowls of watery soup through the bars of the door. It was lukewarm, with chicken fat congealing and floating on the surface, but they swallowed it down and sat on the cold floor.

"I suppose while there's life there's hope," Tom said as he licked his fingers. "You're lucky you don't smoke. I could do with one."

"Maybe Major Kim will oblige."

"Maybe he will, but it's a chink in the old armour, isn't it?"

"I don't know." He thought of Walters polishing Fleetwood's brass as bright as the sun on a summer's day. It was like poetry and he tried to remember a sonnet he once learned at school. The morning sun shifted and the cell was becoming dark again. He sat down against the wall and prayed: *God, who hast kept me through the night, keep me through the day.*

"What's Penshurst like?" Tom Fleetwood said.

David thought of the arrow-slit windows and the turrets of the house, the deserted plains and ranges to the north, St James's Church, and the fire brigade band playing by the war memorial as the crows screeched from the pine trees.

"Small, about seven hundred people."

"And how big is the estate?"

"What?"

"The farm."

"Six and a half thousand acres."

"Good Lord."

"Most of it's rock, not exactly the green fields of England."

"Rock like the Pennines?"

"I don't know the Pennines. It's a volcanic plain, and there are large palaces and landscaped gardens, sometimes fifty miles apart. We're mostly Scots, and some Germans."

"Germans?"

"German settlers from Saxony, frugal, hard-working people."

David thought of Mrs Schultz, with her black bread and blond plaits, of the floods and bushfires. "It's where I belong." He stopped and said: "It's what's dear to me."

"More than the army?"

"I'm not sure. I can't get anything clear. The landscape here doesn't mean anything to me. It's unfriendly, not like *Coral Island*." David laughed. "Maybe you and I are like Ralph and Peterkin."

"Ralph and Peterkin?" Tom laughed. "Ralph and Peterkin alone, prisoners in a gaol in Tuju-ri, Korea. What would they do to get out? What would Ralph and Peterkin do? They'd dig a tunnel under the floor and escape, like the men in *The Wooden Horse*. They were resourceful boys, if I recall."

"They were," David said. "They made rafts out of drift-wood and shelters out of saplings, but there are no saplings here. Only Major Kim, and he's waiting for us."

"What was on the farm?" Fleetwood said.

"Six thousand sheep, two house cows, chickens, a dozen dogs and my family."

"A dozen dogs?"

"Maybe more. The rabbiter had at least six."

"The rabbiter?"

"A man called Bert Lawless. As my grandfather used to say: Lawless by name and lawless by nature."

"And what do rabbiters do?"

"They kill rabbits."

"And your father employs this man Lawless to kill rabbits?"

"He does."

"Why?"

David laughed. "Because there are about a million rabbits; they eat everything, they're a plague. They overrun the land: it's like the locusts in the Old Testament, I can't remember the story."

Rats ran and whispered in the ceiling of the gaol, but Tom appeared not to hear them. "And what does your man, Lawless, do?"

"He shoots them, traps them, poisons them, uses ferrets and dogs, hangs the skins on the front fence and frightens my mother."

"Your mother from Uley?"

"My mother from Uley, and that fine parish church. I suppose she may have watched the kites flying across the Vale from Edge."

Tom looked up from the stone floor. "She may have, indeed. My father made box kites and they flew in the sun. I shall never forget that. They flew toward Wales, and once the string broke and my favourite kite never came back. I was inconsolable." Tom got to his feet and walked around the cell. "Memories, eh?"

"Yes," David said, watching the English soldier. "Memories."

10

Major Kim

"Well, Mr Fleetwood," Kim said, "where is Syngman Rhee?"

"Who?"

"Syngman Rhee, the corrupt President of South Korea, the criminal who started this war."

"I've got no idea," Tom said, "I've got simply no idea."

"You must know where that rascal is. You work for him." Then Kim coughed and said: "I regret the dead man, that was most unfortunate. Had we known he was going to pass away, we would have made other arrangements. Please accept my apologies." He shifted in his chair. "So you have no information about Mr Rhee?"

"None whatsoever."

"That is a pity. You do his dirty work and I thought you would know his whereabouts. He is wanted for trial by the People's Court. You will have to sign a paper to that effect." Kim sighed and rolled a cigarette. "This is a poor country and I am out of, what you call, tailor-mades. An accurate description, do you not think? Tell me, where do you get your hair cut in London?"

"Trumper's." Fleetwood wondered what on earth the Korean would ask next.

"Trumpeter's?"

"No, Trumper's."

"And in which street is that?"

"Curzon Street."

"It is a place where all young officers go?"

"Many do."

"I must have mine cut there." Kim gazed at the varnished

picture of Kim Il Sung on the far wall. "And tell me, how is your Australian colleague, Lieutenant Andersen?"

"He's in fine form."

"Is that so? I'm glad to hear of it. War can be very dispiriting. You have known him long?"

Fleetwood wondered how to answer: it would look odd if he said a week. "Two years."

"Two years? Where did you meet him? At Trumpeter's?"

"At the Staff College."

"He was there on secondment?"

"Yes."

Kim's freshly shaven face gleamed in the early morning light. "What is the present disposition of the 8th Hussars, and how many Centurions do they have?"

"I don't know."

"Mr Andersen is a member of the 3rd Royal Australian Regiment, is he not?"

"Yes."

"What was an Australian officer doing with the Gloucesters?"

"He came to see me, to spend the weekend."

"All the way from Kapyong?"

"The Americans supplied transport, I believe."

"You believe?"

"They did."

"What?"

"Supply transport."

"What was the type of helicopter?"

"I don't know, I never saw it."

"You were not there on the landing pad to meet your old friend?" Kim's chair creaked and he leaned forward across the table.

"I was the Duty Officer of the day."

"We have strong evidence that the Americans are using bacteriological warfare. Our citizens are dying of strange diseases."

"I know nothing of that."

"I think you do. You were on the staff of your brigadier at Yongyu, were you not?" Kim sat back in his chair and watched Fleetwood.

"Yes, I was, but that was many months ago." Fleetwood's mouth was full of saliva and his stomach was starting to knot. How did Kim know?

"It does not matter how many months ago it was. Your brigadier knows General Ridgway and he knows Dulles, the criminal in the pay of the Wall Street financiers."

"I know nothing of this. These are political matters. I'm a soldier of the line."

"The brigadier may have confided in you. You were his aide, he would have told you things, information for your ears only. And if you know nothing of political matters, you should make it your business to know. Our soldiers know all about political matters, they believe in what they are doing, and you running dogs do not. That is the difference between us." Kim rose and stood up behind the table. "But I think you know, I think you know many things."

Fleetwood also got to his feet. "I must use the latrine, Major."

"The latrine? Is it something you have eaten? We do our best, but I regret to say we cannot match the standards of the Naval and Military Club. You may go, Mr Fleetwood, but do not try to run off. One of my men will show you the way." Kim watched Fleetwood as he left the room.

*   *   *

"You are feeling better now, Lieutenant?" Kim said. "A little more comfortable?"

"Yes, thank you."

"We do not seem to be getting very far, do we? You know nothing about the 8th Hussars, nothing about helicopters, nothing about your brigadier and nothing about the Americans' plans for the genocide of our people. All we know is that you did *not* meet Mr Andersen at Trumpeter's. But I

205

am a patient man. Tomorrow you will sign a statement saying that you do not know the whereabouts of Syngman Rhee."

"With pleasure."

"With pleasure? You may be asked to sign other statements without pleasure, with no pleasure at all. You have a bill-fold on your person, I assume?"

"Yes, I have."

"You will kindly pass it over."

"I shall want it back."

"You will have it back when these proceedings are completed. Koreans are noted for their honesty. They do not steal, like other races." Kim opened Fleetwood's wallet. "What is this?"

"An opera ticket."

"Indeed? What was the title of the opera?"

"I'm afraid I can't remember."

"Then why have you kept the ticket?"

"It's of sentimental value."

"But you cannot remember the title? Was it *Peter and the Wolf*?"

"I don't think that's an opera."

"You do not think so? You are not sure?"

"No."

Kim held up a photograph. "This is your mother?"

"Yes."

"There is a strong family likeness. Does she love you?"

"Yes, she does."

"There is nothing like the love of a mother for her son. Alas I have no children, but I shall find a wife when the war is won. It would be sad if your mother received unwelcome news." Kim rolled another cigarette. "It is a pity you cannot remember the title of the opera. Does Mr Andersen go to the opera?"

"I don't know."

"Why?"

"We've never discussed the opera."

"But you are old friends?"

Fleetwood felt foolish and weak now. "The subject has never cropped up."

"Cropped up?"

"Arisen, come about."

"What do you discuss?"

"Football, cricket, military matters."

"What military matters?"

Fleetwood tried to laugh. "Drill sergeants we knew when we were cadets. That kind of thing."

"Mr Fleetwood," Kim said, "I find all your answers unsatisfactory. You are a liar, you come from a corrupt class, you are a mercenary, you have no cause, you work for Rhee and Dulles, you work for the Wall Street capitalists who are trying to destroy the people's democracies, you are a disloyal dog running with the pack. But I am a patient man and I have plenty of time to wait for the correct answers. You are in a small village in Korea, you and Mr Andersen, and no one knows you are here. You have stolen equipment and food from the *Imnun-Gun* and you will be brought to trial." He proffered the tobacco. "Would you care for a cigarette?"

"No thank you."

Kim stuffed Fleetwood's wallet inside his civilian jacket.

"You must excuse me, I have pressing military duties to attend to."

*   *   *

A new picture was on the wall: a caricature of General MacArthur; he was an octopus with some of the tentacles feeding Korean women and children into its mouth and bags of US dollars into it with the others.

"Tell me about the cricket, Mr Andersen," Major Kim said.

"The cricket?"

"Is it not what your race plays? Is it not your national

207

game? I have seen it played on the green pitches of Hong Kong."

"What would you like to know?" David said.

"How is Mr Bradman? Is he not the finest batsman in the world?"

"We Australians think so."

"How do the British regard Mr Bradman?"

"I think they're glad when his wicket is taken."

"So they don't like him?"

David hesitated. "I wouldn't say that. I think they're glad when he's back in the pavilion."

"The British do not like the Australians, do they? It shows in the cricket."

"It's playing the game as hard as you can. It's sportsmanship."

"Playing the game? Sportsmanship? I think the British regard Australia as a colony, as a place to be exploited. You Australians are under the heel of the imperialists."

"I think those days are over."

"I think not, I think they see you as a client race. You are on the wrong side, Mr Andersen. You should be fighting with us against the British and the Americans. You have made a grave error."

"I don't think we have."

"We?"

"The government."

"But what do the masses think?"

"Masses?"

"Your working class, those who produce the wealth by their labour."

"I'm sure they're entirely in favour of our fighting Communist aggression."

"Everyone knows that South Korea attacked us, led by that gangster Syngman Rhee and helped by the Wall Street imperialists."

"That's not what we were told."

"By whom?"

"By the government."

"Who is the leader of your government?"

"Mr Menzies."

"Who?"

"Mr Menzies."

"What is his full name?"

"Robert Gordon Menzies."

"Then Mr Menzies is a liar, in league with Mr Dulles and the other capitalists. Your government has led you astray, Mr Andersen, you have been duped. Why are you in league with Mr Fleetwood when he is your enemy?"

"He is my friend, not my enemy."

"How long have you known Mr Fleetwood?"

"Two years."

"And where did you meet him?"

"At the Staff College at Camberley."

"He told me that you had met at Trumpeter's."

"Trumpeter's?"

"A barber's shop."

"I've never heard of it."

"You have not heard of it?"

"No."

"You are a liar, Mr Andersen. Mr Fleetwood told me that you met at Trumpeter's; you were having your hair trimmed. All the young English capitalists go there. I know."

"I don't know what you're talking about."

Kim poked at the ends of his cigarette with a match. "I think you do. Do you play the cricket?"

"Cricket?"

"What?"

"Cricket."

"That is what I said, Mr Andersen. You will not correct me. I passed my Cambridge Overseas Examination. You will not correct me, I am a student of the language." Kim lit his cigarette. "I may be in a small village in North Korea, but I am an educated man."

"I'm sure you are, Major."

"You flatter me like a dog, Mr Andersen. You are a soldier, not a dog. Excuse me, I am wrong: you are a disloyal dog, like Mr Fleetwood, and you lie, and you have stolen property. You are in serious trouble. One of our gallant soldiers has been found dead by the river. What do you know of that?"

"Nothing."

"I think you do, he was killed with great cruelty, it took him many hours to die. He was wearing a black Russian greatcoat and armed with a long rifle and bayonet. Did you not have these things in your illegal possession when you were caught trespassing on *Imnun-Gun* territory?"

"Yes."

"And where did you get them?"

"We found them."

"Where?"

"In a house."

"And where was the house?"

"In the paddies."

"The house where you stole the food from our people?"

"I think so."

"But I have been informed that you were at the door of the house and that you were holding the Russian rifle, and that you attempted to murder an innocent child."

"That's not true." David was apprehensive now.

"I think it is. So we have a number of charges: trespassing, murder, stealing and attempted murder. These are serious matters, do you not agree?"

"I have done none of these things."

"Do you own a dog, Mr Andersen?"

"Yes, I do."

"Do you treat him well?"

"Yes, I do." David thought of Ben, the lost tennis balls and the summer parties.

"You would not kill him and eat him?"

"No, I would not."

"I, too, own a dog. I love my dog, he is faithful to me. You have been told that Koreans eat dogs?"

"That has been mentioned to me."

"What?"

"I've heard that."

"That is not true, it is another lie put out by the capitalists. We do not eat dogs. A dog is man's best friend, do you not agree?"

"Yes, I do."

"But dogs can be unfaithful, can they not?"

"I suppose so."

"Then they are jackals and hyenas; like the Australians, the New Zealanders, the Belgians and the Canadians. Have you noticed how many Negroid soldiers there are in the American army?"

"I can't say I have."

"The American army is full of Negroid soldiers; they have been put there by the white imperialists against their will. They, too, are on the wrong side. What do you say to that?"

"I don't know what to say."

"You don't know what to say? You are in bad need of re-education, Mr Andersen, I have a profound sorrow for you."

"You needn't worry about me, Major." David tried to smile.

Kim stood up. "How many guns have the 45th Field Regiment?"

"That's an English regiment."

"I know that, Mr Andersen. I am well informed."

"I don't know anything about the 45th."

"If you do not tell me, I will have bamboo splinters driven up your fingernails and set alight." Kim sat down. "Please forgive me, we cannot do that under the Convention. Instead, you will sign a paper saying that you are well looked after and that you have seen the error of your ways. It will be sent to *The Times*."

David was tired now; his legs were cramped and his head ached, but he said: "I won't do that."

"Why not?"

"Because it is not true."

"Why is it not true?"

"Because we're being threatened and we're half-starved."

"Half-starved? You are getting what our gallant soldiers get, no more, no less."

"It's not enough for an Australian."

"Not enough for an Australian?" Kim laughed. "You will have to learn to adjust." He got up a second time. "You will have to excuse me, it is time for me to feed my dog. I will continue tomorrow."

*   *   *

"How did you go?" Fleetwood said.

"I'm not sure, I remembered we met at the Staff College, but he said we met at some place called Trumpeter's. The man's mad."

"Trumper's. It's a barber in Mayfair. Did he say where he was sending us?"

"I didn't get a chance to ask him; he left to feed his dog."

"Feed his dog? Aren't they all eaten? Why isn't his eaten? Jesus Christ, we've fallen into the hands of a lunatic."

"It looks that way. How do you feel?"

"Bloody hungry, but the shits have stopped, thank God. Did you mention the food, or lack of it?"

"Yes."

"What did he say? Did he mention the opera ticket?"

"He said we were getting the same as his soldiers."

"Do you think he's trying to starve us out?"

David sat on the floor, his shoulders hunched: "I'm not sure, I'm not sure of anything. He's either very intelligent or starkers, but whatever the answer, his methods are having the desired effect."

"I wish they'd let us shave," Fleetwood said. "What do I look like?"

"Would you stop asking questions?" David said, "I've been at it all the bloody afternoon."

"Sorry." Fleetwood wondered about the opera. Whom had he taken?

Each looked at the other and knew they should not have left the column: there was emotional safety in numbers, no matter how hard the going got. How long would Kim keep them here? It could be months, or even years. They could rot in this cell forever; Fleetwood thought of the Count of Monte Cristo. Was it Robert Donat? He couldn't recall. Fear spread through his body like some dreadful disease, his bowels rumbled again and for a moment he found it hard to see.

"We killed that Korean soldier," David said. "Kim knows about it, and the child says I tried to kill her with the rifle. It's murder and attempted murder, plus stealing and God knows what."

"Jesus Christ, it's not true."

"Part of it is: we knocked off the soldier, stole the rifle, the greatcoat and the potatoes."

"Great Scot," Fleetwood said, "we're at war, not some boy scouts' jamboree, not some girl guides' camp run by Princess Margaret. What does he expect us to do? Play up! and play the game! There's not exactly a breathless hush in the Close tonight. This is not an expedition to the north pole where we both walk around the spinney."

David thought. Then he said: "Kim will threaten us, starve us, confuse us, but we have to be like him."

"What's that?'

"Patient and cunning, and he can't speak the English language as well as we can."

"Good for him, I can't speak one word of Korean. He speaks English damned well, I admire Kim for that."

"That's not the point: *we* wear him down; he's a snob, he's proud of his English."

"I don't know what you're talking about, he can kill us anytime."

"But he won't, he'll question and threaten, but he won't kill."

"Why not?"

"Because he wants to convert us. He's a missionary of sorts. He cares for us."

"Cares for us? He's threatening and starving us."

"Look," David said, "Major Kim is in the North Korean People's Army, he's politically motivated and he wants to win us over to his side. He's not a military man. He may threaten us, he may starve us, but he won't kill us. Killing us means he's been defeated and he doesn't want that."

"He's bound to send us on sooner or later," Fleetwood said.

"That's right: it's his way out. He can invent some story that his seniors want us for some purpose."

"And he may separate us."

"That's most likely."

"And that means solitary."

"I think we can cope with that," David said. "Why did you ask me to go with you? Surely you had plenty of pals in the Gloucesters?"

"It goes back to the show in the apple orchard," Tom said. "I thought you were a cool customer. You run like a greyhound, and escaping seemed like an adventure at the time: somebody new on the spur of the moment, and we're both soldiers in the King's army. My father once met Monash — a great soldier, he thought. I'm sure we'll survive." He smiled, despite his hunger. "The stiff upper lip. If I may be frank, you're not like an Australian at all."

"How?"

"Well, you know, the hard drinking, whoring, *Rats of Tobruk* image."

"We aren't all like that," David said, "especially from Melbourne and the Western District. We aren't all larrikins, God forbid. What's Wellington like?"

Tom sat on the floor, his back against the wall.

"I wish they'd give us something to sit on. Have you noticed that Asiatics squat? They don't sit. What I miss most, apart from decent food, is a comfortable chair. I think my back's never going to recover."

"What's Wellington like?"

"Tough, but bloody marvellous. A few too many beatings at times, but that's the system, isn't it?" He remembered the voices of the time fags, singing out the minutes for breakfast.

"Any famous old boys?"

"We call them OWs. Lots, Lord Gort, Auchinleck and fifteen Victoria Crosses. We were all proud of that. It's in beautiful, rolling country in Berkshire. The happiest days of my life." He thought of the Lent term runs to the Blackwater Meadows, with ice in the grass, the spring oaks pale green and his breath steaming in the cold, still air. "Then on to Sandhurst. I wonder what sort of dog it is."

"Dog?"

"Kim's dog."

"God knows," David said. "I didn't think there were any left in the country." He laughed. "Love me, love my dog. A bitzer, I should think."

"We all had dogs at Sandhurst," Fleetwood said. "Dogs and the army seem to go together, so even our friend Kim fits into that tradition."

David dragged himself up and walked around the cell; it was only their third evening, but already he was starting to feel black and helpless. He recalled that diet had something to do with fits of depression. It was getting dark outside, and they sat silently in the gathering gloom. The blood from the dead ROK soldier was caked on the floor and the decaying smell of the countryside drifted in through the window. All was still and nobody seemed to be about. Maybe they were forgotten? Not even a fly buzzed and Tom sat quite still on the floor. Had he fallen asleep? David thought of going across and touching him, but decided not.

215

He stood in the corner below the window and thought. The colonel would have him posted missing now and a telegram would have been sent to his parents. His mother would be distraught and wander around the garden and walk up and down the drive under the May trees. What was the season at home? Autumn, of course. Would they say: *Missing*, or *Missing, believed killed in action*? It was all a disaster: Jones, Brownlee and Kershaw killed and he locked up in a God-forsaken village in North Korea, interrogated by some kind of lunatic zealot who knew about cricket and who accused him of crimes he hadn't committed. He felt the wallets inside his tunic. He must see Jones's widow. The war was also a disaster: the Chinese were probably in Seoul now. What was even the point of trying to get there? They should have tried to get to their own lines. Another error. If the North Korean soldier was dead, Kim could quite reasonably have them on that. But weren't soldiers expected to kill each other? That was their profession. He wondered if his name would be in the paper, the Hamilton *Spectator*, probably. He was a local boy, *In Memoriam, David Kinross Andersen, AD 1951*, poppies on his headstone on Anzac Day, and the fire brigade band, the medals clinking and the old men marching under the pine trees as the galahs called and chattered. He stood in the corner, his back pressed hard against the stone wall. The rats were silent now. Had they, too, gone away? The cell grew dark. No one was alive but them.

*   *   *

Footsteps sounded outside the cell and a match was struck. The kerosene smelled and the light flickered as a guard shoved something under the door. David went over to see two bowls of fermented cabbage with boiled rice and chicken fat that smelt dreadful. His stomach heaved.

"Wake up, Tom," he called, "it's dinner time."

"What's that?"

"Dinner, and it's bloody awful."

"How odd, I was dreaming of roast beef and Yorkshire pud at Simpson's."

"Well, this is rotten cabbage and rice."

"Lord, help us, and to think the Chows win battles on it."

David passed him a bowl and they sat on the floor and ate. The guard sat on his bench, cleaning his pistol, and watched them through the bars. He put the Russian pistol down, took off his canvas boots and picked his toes. He wasn't more than eighteen.

"Do you have to do that?" Tom shouted. "God's truth, man." But the guard smiled, picked up his pistol and aimed at them. "It's like living in Old Tartary," Tom said. "We have to eat shit and the waiter picks his feet. Even the worst lorry drivers' café in Liverpool couldn't give worse service than this. Good grief, we can't go on. We've got a Marxist maniac asking us stupid questions, threatening us with torture and feeding his dog. What on earth is happening?"

David tried the cabbage and spat it back into the bowl. "Were you beaten at Wellington?"

"Of course I was."

"And what did you do?"

"What did I do? I didn't do anything, I didn't utter a sound."

"Well?"

"Well, what?"

"Isn't that the point now?"

Fleetwood looked up from his bowl and smiled. "David, you're absolutely right. Why didn't I think of that?"

"I don't know."

They shoved the bowls back under the door and the guard grinned. The night was mild and the kerosene lamp burned. Fleetwood laid his greatcoat on the floor and said: "If you don't mind, I shall kip down now. Whose turn is it with Kim tomorrow?"

"I think it's yours."

"Right then, I shall prepare for it."

David walked back and stood in the corner by the window. But there were no smells from the countryside in the dark and lonely night. He sat down in the corner of the cell and watched the young Korean clean his pistol.

*　　*　　*

"Good morning, Mr Fleetwood," Kim said. "A pleasant day, is it not?"

"I don't know, Major," Tom said, "I've not seen it."

"You have not seen it? That is a pity. Spring has come to North Korea and the country is being liberated from the imperialist yoke. We shall soon be growing vegetables again and the fruit trees will be heavy with the crop by the end of the summer. The aggressors will be gone, they will be driven into the sea and the People's Democratic Republic will triumph. The lackeys, jackals and hyenas will be destroyed and our country will prosper."

"I have a complaint to make," Tom said.

"A complaint?"

"Yes, Major."

"What is your complaint? Do you wish to see the day? Do you wish to see Tuju-ri? It is an ordinary village, but there are some burial mounds where the ancient kings of Shilla are buried. I can arrange that in exchange for certain information."

"My complaint, Major, is that Mr Andersen and I are being kept in inhuman conditions. We are forced to sleep on the floor, we have primitive toilet facilities, we cannot shave or wash, we have no exercise and the food is inadequate. All these things contravene the Geneva Convention."

"Contra-vene? Alas, Mr Fleetwood, my English is not as good as yours. You had the wealth to go to university, I did not."

"I didn't go to university, Major, I went into the army."

"Where you met Mr Andersen?"

"Some years later in the Staff College, yes."

"Not the barber's shop?"

"Jesus Christ, Major, not at the bloody barber's shop."

"You are forgetting your manners, Mr Fleetwood. I know all about manners. Have you been a guest at the Peninsula Hotel?"

"Yes, I have."

"They have Rolls Royces there for the guests, do they not?"

"Yes, they do."

"The Rolls Royce is a fine engine, is it not?"

"Yes, it is."

"The Centurions have Rolls Royce engines, do they not?"

"Yes, they do."

"How many gallons of petrol do the Centurions burn to the mile?"

"I'm an infantryman, I have no idea."

"You will tell me about the fuel reservations of the Centurion tanks."

"I have no information about tanks, I am a soldier of the line."

"So you have told me, Mr Fleetwood. I remember that, I remember everything." Kim stretched his legs and the chair creaked. "Contra-vene? What does that mean? Please forgive my ignorance." He smiled, opened the holster on his belt and placed the Beretta on the table. He flicked off the safety catch. "Do you prefer the Beretta or the Webley?"

Fleetwood watched Kim's hand resting on the revolver.

"Contravene," he said, "means breaking the rules."

"As in the cricket?"

"If you like, yes."

"And I am breaking the rules of accommodation for prisoners, is that what you are saying?"

"Yes, Major, I am."

Kim took up the Beretta and pointed it at Fleetwood's head. "These excellent pistols are made in Italy, are they not?"

Fleetwood sat quite still. "Yes, they are."

"I am in command of Tuju-ri," Kim said, "and nobody knows you and Mr Andersen are here."

"That is correct."

"And you have a list of complaints?"

"We do."

"If you tell me how many tanks the 8th Hussars have, I shall give you and Mr Andersen a table, chairs and two beds."

"I have no information about the 8th Hussars."

"Do you have a large garden at your country estate?"

Kim played with the Beretta and looked straight at Fleetwood.

"I would hardly call it a country estate."

"Do you have a gardener?"

"Yes."

"And what is he paid?"

"I can't remember."

"And a gamekeeper?"

"We have no gamekeeper."

"What does a gamekeeper do, Mr Fleetwood?"

"He keeps out the poachers."

"Poacher? What is a poacher?"

"Someone who steals the game."

"Steals the game?"

"Someone who kills the game illegally."

"You and Mr Andersen are poachers, are you not? You are trespassers and you are killing illegally. Is that not correct?"

"We are soldiers."

"You are not soldiers, you are murderers and thieves, and murderers and thieves deserve to be treated like pigs. How many times have you stayed at the Peninsula Hotel?"

"Twice."

"And there was a house-boy who looked after you?"

"Yes, there was."

"He changed the sheets and took away your dirty linen?"

"Yes, he did."

"Where is General Ridgway? You will tell me his movements."

"I don't know the movements of General Ridgway."

"Nor of that dog, MacArthur?"

"Nor of General MacArthur."

"President Truman and the Wall Street financiers have plans to use the atomic bomb on innocent Korean and Chinese people, do they not?"

"I know of no such plans."

"What is the state of health of King George?"

"King George? He's well, I should think."

"Is that so? And the two princesses?"

"The same, I should think."

"It is a shame that the King and the two princesses are in league with Truman and Dulles. Do you not agree?"

"That's absolute rubbish, the princesses probably haven't even heard of Mr Dulles."

"Margaret Rose is the more beautiful?"

"I have no opinion."

"Why do your planes bomb innocent women and children?"

"I'm in the Commonwealth Brigade, we have no aircraft here."

"But the Australians do."

"I have no knowledge of aircraft at all, and if women and children have been killed, it must have been an unfortunate mistake."

"But you admit they have been killed?" Kim said. "You will admit that in writing?"

"I will admit nothing in writing."

"You come from a corrupt class, Mr Fleetwood. I have seen your kind in Hong Kong, I have seen them at the Peninsula Hotel and being pulled around the streets in rickshaws while the beggars huddled in doorways; it was the British who sat in their comfortable clubs, drinking gin, while the masses slaved in factories. It is still going on there,

I know, but our Chinese allies will one day drive the British into the sea. It is all inevitable. Have you read the works of Marx and Engels?"

"No."

"I shall obtain a copy for you and Mr Andersen to study; it will help pass the time away as you will both be here for a long period." Kim put the Beretta back in the holster. "You will both have many hours to reconsider your positions."

"What do you intend to do about our requests?" Fleetwood said.

"We Koreans have little use for furniture; we eat, sit, and sleep and have sexual intercourse on the floor and you will have to do the same." Kim laughed. "I do not think you will have any sexual intercourse."

"Then we each want a blanket."

"Mr Fleetwood, you have given me nothing, I will give you nothing." Kim yawned and the room was silent. Then he said: "I am living on *kimchee*, you will live on *kimchee*. There is no roast beef and Yorkshire pudding here." He rose from the table and walked around the room, his measured steps ringing on the stone floor. "Comfort has corrupted your morals; the King and Queen and the two princesses live in luxury while the masses labour and toil. All that will be changed." He stopped, "If you agree to go to Pyongyang," he said, "you will have chairs, beds and better food; but you will sign a message to King George, saying that you have been duped by Truman and Dulles, that Syngman Rhee is a war criminal and that you are ashamed of your part in this unjust war."

Fleetwood thought. "I won't do that because it's not true, but I would have to ask Mr Andersen."

"He may agree to go to Pyongyang? It is a delightful city despite the bombing."

"He may, he may not. I cannot answer for him."

"If you and Mr Andersen will not go to Pyongyang, it will be necessary to separate you and the standards of accommodation are not good in Tuju-ri. The individual cells are somewhat small and uncomfortable."

"I will ask Mr Andersen," Fleetwood said.

"I think you should."

Fleetwood felt the lice in his underclothes and armpits and ran his filthy hands over his beard; his fingernails were black and his feet were swollen in his boots; his breath foul and there were nits in his hair and scalp. "Major," he said, "Mr Andersen and I have not bathed or shaved for two weeks and I'm asking you for hot water and razors."

Kim thought. "I will supply hot water and send you a barber, but you will think most seriously about the message to King George."

"I'll discuss that with Mr Andersen."

"It is a pity," Kim said, "that you cannot see the azaleas, the air is most bracing." He spoke to the guard. "You, Mr Fleetwood, will excuse me."

The door banged shut and Kim whistled to his dog.

* * *

That evening it rained: they heard the water pouring down the broken gutters and the roof chains outside. They sat in the cell and Tom told David about Pyongyang. "I think we should fox for about a week," he said, "and then tell him we're prepared to go."

He remembered the Christmas message and the slight stutter.

"To sign a statement for King George?" David laughed. He looked at Tom who was haggard: the dirt was lined in his thin face, his eyes were deep in his head and his teeth were black. David knew that he, too, looked the same. The rain poured outside and ran down the stone walls; the rats scampered in the thatch roof. David went to stand up, but felt giddy and slid to the floor. "O *Valiant Hearts*," he said.

"What?"

"I said, O *Valiant Hearts*. Did you sing it at Wellington?"

"Yes, we did."

"We sang it at Melbourne. It always brought a lump to my throat. What else did you sing?"

"When?"

"In the choir. You sang in the choir, didn't you?"

"Yes."

"Well, what did you sing?"

"*Gaudeamus Igitur, O No, John* and *The Lincolnshire Poacher.*"

"I don't know that one. How does it go?"

"I can't remember."

"When our school choir sang, the music master called it mass screeching." David laughed.

"Kim said we were poachers," Tom said.

"Did he? I suppose we are, and he's the gamekeeper."

David thought of Tom rummaging in the house and the little girl outside the door. He thought of his father with the Winchester on the Dunkeld Road and the starving cattle breaking down the fences. They were on someone else's property. He thought of the burning of the villages, the people fleeing and the refugees dying on the road to Chasan and the guns and corpses in the frozen river. "How does it go," he said.

"What?"

"*The Lincolnshire Poacher.*"

"Jesus Christ, I told you I can't remember. What do you think about going to Pyongyang?"

"It's in the opposite direction," David said. "It's north and we're going south."

"We aren't exactly going anywhere at the moment."

"What did Kim say about washing and shaving?"

"I think he half promised that. I think that's part of the deal."

"Whoopee, why didn't you tell me before?"

"And a barber as well."

"Is it part of the Pyongyang deal?"

"I don't think so, but who can tell? He's a crafty bastard."

David suddenly felt very tired now and listened to the rain outside. Was that a rat in the corner? He wasn't sure. And is there honey still for tea? It was his turn with Kim tomorrow. He would trick him, he would tie him up with Latin grammar and Greek syntax. He tried to remember parsing of verbs, the conjunctive, his lessons. *Demosthenes: It seems to me, men of Athens, that you have become absolutely apathetic, waiting there dumbly for the catastrophe that is about to fall upon you.*

"Kim threatened us with solitary," Tom said.

"If what?"

"If we didn't go to Pyongyang and send the message to the King."

David thought about King George reading a message from two captured subalterns in Korea. "I don't mind solitary, I've been there all my life."

"What do you mean?" Fleetwood looked at David as the rain poured down outside.

"Did he mention the princesses?"

"Yes," Fleetwood said, "he did."

"My mother," David said, "always said that Margaret Rose would come to no good."

"What do you mean?"

"About what?"

"Solitary and having been there all your life?"

"Just a figure of speech." David thought of his mother walking under the May trees, his time in bed and drawing maps from the atlas, the rain and the long winter nights at school. "I don't mind doing solitary for a week, then we give in and go to Pyongyang and sign the statement for King George. But we escape on the way. That's the point, isn't it?"

"Yes," Tom said, "that's the point."

"Well, okay then, that's what we'll do."

"You don't mind the prospect of solitary?" Tom said.

"I don't mean to be rude," David said, "but not particularly."

"Why?"

"I don't suppose I'd like it for too long, but I'm a solitary person. Do *you* mind the prospect?"

"Yes, I do."

"I don't think it's very convincing," David said, "if we agree to go to Pyongyang without some further show of resistance; and you've already said that you won't."

"Have you got any brothers or sisters?" Tom said.

"No, there's just me."

"The same with me. But I've got lots of cousins and uncles. We're well known in the village."

"It all sounds rather like *Country Life*," David said.

Tom laughed. "I suppose it does. We're a social mob: lots of parties and riding, a country family. I've just realized that the whole class thing bolts me together. No one knows me here, I'm disconnected; sometimes I feel like shouting, 'I'm Thomas Reginald Fleetwood, my father's a colonel in the Royal Artillery.' I've got no defences. Jesus Christ, my great-great-grandfather fought in the Peninsular War."

"Was he decorated?" David said.

"Yes he was, he got the Military Medal."

"Did he?" David said. "What do you think of Kim?"

"Kim? I keep on thinking of Rudyard Kipling."

"And so do I."

"He's clever and tricky," Fleetwood said. "I've never struck anyone like him before. He's obviously worked at the Peninsula Hotel in Hong Kong and hates the Brits. You wouldn't happen to know how King George is, would you?"

David laughed. "It's more your field than mine."

"Should soldiers be involved in politics?"

"I don't know," David said, "all I want is a good meal."

"Have you read the works of Karl Marx?"

"No."

"He's getting us a copy."

"Great, we can wipe our bums on it."

The rain was easing now and people moved outside,

laughing and talking, their sandals sloshing in the mud: it was the old men and children returning from the fields and David thought of the rural routine: the dogs in the morning, the shearing and the fencing. Tom sat in his usual place, his back against the wall and wondered if he would ever go home again. He thought of going with his mother to Bath and watching the Morris dancers on the cobbles outside the Abbey, and the memorial tablets. One of them read:

> By the death of this Gentleman,
> an Ancient and Respectable Family
> in England became extinct.

11

Solitary

In the cold morning a cuckoo called, a now familiar sound. Then a guard appeared, shoved two bowls of rice and bean-sprouts under the door and went away. The building still smelled of candle grease, and mice scampered in the straw. Somewhere mortars thudded.

"I wish that bloody bird would stop," Fleetwood said as he stretched his aching body.

"I wish the hot water and barber would come," David said. The rice and bean-sprouts tasted good and he shovelled it in with his hands and licked the bowl. He licked up every last grain and wiped his lips. He cleaned his teeth with his finger. "The best meal yet. Now where's that hot water?" He got up and peered through the bars. His joints cracked and his head ached.

Fleetwood finished his food and sat and listened to the cuckoo. "Maybe he was just raising our hopes, maybe he spoke with a forked tongue." Then he too got up, went to the window and shouted: "Shut up, you damned bird." He grabbed the bars of the window and tried to heave himself up. "What's a delightful bird like a cuckoo doing in this dreadful place? Do you have cuckoos in Australia?" His voice sounded hoarse as he let go the bars.

"Yes, we do," David said, "but I'm not sure if they're the same as yours."

"What's the poem? Cuckoo, cuckoo, jug jug?" He tried to remember.

"I'll go cuckoo if the hot water doesn't come." David continued to peer through the bars.

"Don't build up your hopes, old boy," Fleetwood said.

"We're in the hands of the most bizarre human being I've ever met."

The cuckoo stopped calling and they waited and shivered in the cold half-light. Fleetwood had grazed his knuckles on the stone and the blood dribbled down his fingers. The cuckoo called once more and they listened.

*   *   *

After an hour, two guards arrived and unlocked the door of the cell, motioning with their machine guns. They were boys, and one wore hand grenades on his trouser belt.

"Don't tell me this is bath time," Fleetwood said. "I don't believe it, and I haven't got my Wright's Coal Tar. Where's my aftershave?"

They were taken out into the prison yard, where the light was strong. They rubbed their eyes as they walked across the gravel toward two wooden tubs on a bench. The steam rose in the cold morning air as they stripped off their dirty uniforms. Some mules were tethered by the gates and an old wooden gun carriage lay upturned nearby. The yard stank of animal shit and rotting rice stalks. But the hot water felt good and they washed themselves carefully, sharing the small piece of hard soap. Lice and fleas struggled in the cloudy water. Beyond the mud walls came the sound of carts and men marching: it sounded like yet another Chinese column going south. Had the offensive been stopped? It didn't seem so. They dried themselves as best they could with a small towel, sat on the bench and washed their socks in the filthy water. David discovered he had lost two of his toenails, and his feet were now too swollen for his boots. He laced them together and struggled back into his dirty underwear. He was losing weight fast, his skin was grey, and his legs were stiff. His gums were sore and his mouth ulcerated. He looked at Fleetwood and wondered how he felt.

A tank ground by on the cobbles, the diesel heavy in the

air. "Christ," Fleetwood said as he tried to smooth his wet hair with his hands, "they've got armour. I wonder how the lads are doing?"

David did not reply. A rat scuttled across the compound and disappeared into a pile of old rice stalks. A blackness descended, and he wondered what questions Kim would ask him later in the morning. Did the Koreans advise the United Nations about prisoners they held? He didn't know, and he thought of Hart machine-gunning the two boys against the tank. *Life for life, eye for eye, tooth for tooth, hand for hand, foot for foot.*

"Are you all right?" Fleetwood said.

"Yes," David said, "I was just thinking. I'm all right." The spring sun was stronger now and they sat on the bench in their grimy underwear and eased their backs. Somewhere outside, children laughed and played, but the sound was not comforting. There was no joy in this place.

"We hold out for a week," Fleetwood said, "and then agree to go to Pyongyang. Is that it?"

"Yes," David said, "that's it."

The children had run off and the village was silent. They couldn't see the poplars and the azaleas on the mountainsides.

*   *   *

The barber was very young, about fourteen and carrying a cut-throat, a brush and a bowl of hot water. He grinned as he came up and put his gear on the bench. He opened the cut-throat and pointed at Fleetwood.

"By the good Lord," said Fleetwood, "I hope this young devil knows what he's doing. Do you remember Sweeney Todd?" He watched the boy with the razor.

"I do, indeed," David said as the boy lathered Fleetwood's dark bristly face.

"Farewell, sweet prince," Fleetwood said as the boy flourished the razor. But the Korean lad shaved them both well, bowed, smiled, and walked back across the yard.

"They're good at it, aren't they?" David said as he felt his clean, smooth chin.

"What?"

"Threats and then small comforts. You never know what way they're going to jump. Maybe we *should* have read Marx."

"Read Marx? I'm a soldier, not a philosopher."

"Well," David said, "we're in the hands of some kind of mad philosopher."

"And we're going to get *out of* his hands."

They heard the sound of aircraft and then the thud of anti-aircraft batteries. The planes were some way off, but they both stood up and tried to see. Maybe they were Gloster Meteors and Starfighters? Across the compound a door opened and Kim strode out, his boots crunching on the stones.

"It is as I said," he shouted, "United Nations aeroplanes are bombing innocent civilians, innocent women and children." He stood before them, the Beretta in the holster. "I take care that you are washed, shaved and fed according to the rules, and your colleagues break those rules. What do you have to say to that?" His riding boots were dirty.

"I have no doubt, Major," Fleetwood said, "that it's a routine bombing mission and that only military targets are involved."

"Tonight," Kim said, "I shall prove you wrong. I shall prove that you are a liar, Mr Fleetwood. I shall lay the burned bodies of little babies at your feet." He looked at them both.

"I am asking you to get dressed. There have been new developments." Kim turned as the guards moved up. They left the yard while the distant guns continued to rumble.

*   *   *

231

A slender young woman was standing in the cold room. She was wearing a long, ragged, peasant dress and standing like a fragile statue by the window. She looked fearful. The planes had gone now and the guns were silent.

Kim sat behind the table and said: "You will stand where you are. A further crime has been brought to my attention." He paused. "This woman, Mr Andersen, says you have ravished her."

David stood stock still in his bare feet. This was a nightmare. "That's not true," he said. He looked at the young woman, but her face was expressionless. He went to step toward her. "It's not true," he said. "It's simply not true."

"You will not move, Mr Andersen," Kim said, "you will stand where you are."

"This charge, Major," Tom said, "is not only ridiculous, it's foul. British soldiers do not interfere with women."

"I did not use the word interfere. I used the word ravish. The purpose of American and British soldiers in Korea is three: to take our food, to kill our civilians, and to ravish our women."

"This is a trumped-up charge," Fleetwood said.

"Trumped up? I do not understand."

"Invented, false."

"And," Kim said, "you eat our red apples."

"Your red apples?"

"Our red apples. They are the symbol of Korea." Kim looked at David. "You should learn to control your sexual lusts, Mr Andersen."

What could David say? That he had no sexual lusts? "My sexual feelings are always under control," he said.

What was happening to him? The mainstays of his life were being removed. He started to shake, and his feet were numb on the stone floor. There seemed to be no rules now.

"Ravishing women, Mr Andersen," Kim said, "is a crime punishable by death."

Ravishing women? David started to laugh and his laughter grew louder in the small room where the frightened

232

Korean woman stood. He turned and looked at her sad face, her dark eyes and thin arms.

"Lord Jesus Christ, I've never made love to anybody; or as soldiers say, fucked, let alone raped." He laughed some more and Fleetwood turned away from David in his bare feet, dirty shirt and braces.

"You are saying that this woman is a liar?" Kim said.

"No, Major," David said. He tried to control his shaking and raised his voice. "I'm saying that this innocent woman has been dragged in here by you, that she knows nothing of what's going on, that *you* are the liar, *you* are the trickster, the false accuser, the man without morals, the man with no conscience, the thief in the night. You are a man to be damned for your crimes, not me." He pulled at his braces and stood on the stone floor: he was proud now. "You are corrupt and evil," he shouted, "corrupt and evil. You twist the truth and you condemn innocent people. It is you who should be standing here accused, not I."

"You have no business here, Mr Andersen," Kim said, "not you, not Mr Fleetwood, not the Americans; you are all jackals and pariahs. But the financiers of Wall Street will not destroy the revolution of the people. Your society is corrupt and degenerate, and some of your members are coming over to our side; when this unjust war is over, some of your soldiers will stay with us, they will have seen the truth. I have personally seen the decadence of the Peninsula Hotel and the gambling dens in Macao, I have comrades who have worked for the imperialist rubber planters in Malaya, I have comrades who are fighting the French in Indo-China, and you say that it is I who should be accused of crimes. Your culture is degenerate, it is in decline."

"Why are the Chinese in Korea?" David said.

"When a neighbour sees a burglar in his neighbour's house, he drives him out." Kim stood up. "And we shall drive you out, we shall kill you as you swim and die in the sea, and we shall be victorious. You are a burglar, Mr

Andersen. You have trespassed and you will be punished. You are a trespasser."

Tom Fleetwood heard all of this, looked at the Korean woman in the corner of the room, looked at Kim and David and sat down on the floor.

"Mr Fleetwood," Kim said, "you will remain standing, it is a military custom."

"No, Major, if you can't supply chairs, I shall sit on the floor."

"You will stand up."

"No."

"Then," Kim said, "I shall place you in solitary confinement. Your food will be shortened."

"You do that, Major."

"You will be treated harshly for disobeying the lawful command of a senior officer. Those are the rules, those are the orders."

Fleetwood remained on the floor. "Do what you like, these charges against Mr Andersen are preposterous."

"I cannot understand," Kim said, "my English is poor."

"Ridiculous."

"You are saying that I am a funny man, a clown?"

Fleetwood laughed. "Yes, I am, I'm saying you're a bloody joke, I'm saying that you're an incompetent soldier, I'm saying you're a bloody fool, I'm saying that you're a soldier's bloody arsehole."

"We shall see, Mr Fleetwood. Tonight, when you are in your little cage, I shall come by and push the burnt body of a little baby through the bars, and you will have the corpse of a child for your dinner. You will pay for your sins, and so will Mr Andersen. You kill our little children, you eat our red apples, and you will both pay. I will see to that."

David, too, sat down next to Fleetwood. Where were the rules, where were the rights and wrongs? The Korean woman still stood in the corner and he looked at his swollen, blackened toes. Where were the guidelines?

234

"You, too, will get up, Mr Andersen," Kim said from the table.

"No."

"Have you considered my request concerning the statement to the King?"

"We have," Fleetwood said.

"And what is your answer?"

"We refuse."

"Very well, you will each have two weeks' solitary confinement to reconsider your position. As for the charge of ravishment, Mr Andersen, it will be continued later."

Kim spoke to the Korean woman who bowed and left the room. She did not look at David, but he watched her go. She was beautiful.

"The solitary confinements are unfortunately somewhat small and you may find them uncomfortable. You will be allowed out to stretch yourselves for half an hour each day. If you do not raise yourselves from the floor, you will be beaten."

Kim rose and turned on his heel as the guards came forward.

* * *

David watched the Korean soldiers playing basketball in the evening light. They shouted and played hard and the gravel spun from their canvas boots. The Koreans were husky, tough and fit and David wondered how good he would be at basketball; he longed to be out there with the players in the cold evening air. He thought of the young Korean woman; she was beautiful, flat-chested, with long brown arms and black eyes. What would she have been like? They were supposed to have no body hair. He wondered. He thought of her. What did Tom Fleetwood think of him? The cell measured six feet by four and was six feet high. It stank of piss and at the far end lay a pile of old rubber slippers, a small tin can, a petrol drum and a box of lime. A couple of rice bowls and a spoon lay on the mud floor. David paced it out, and then he tried to make the cell orderly: he shifted the rubber slippers, moved the petrol drum and rearranged the box of lime. He found he could lie out full length on his greatcoat and watch what was happening outside. It wasn't as bad as he expected; at least people were coming and going in the compound, and now there was basketball. The ball thudded on the gravel, the Koreans sidestepped and ran in the still evening, and David watched the players. In some ways this was better than the cell he had shared with Tom. Once the ball rolled toward the bars of the cell door and a player retrieved it, but he didn't look inside. It was as though David had ceased to exist.

He felt inside his tunic pocket and drew out Jones's wallet and dog tag. The two little girls in their print frocks were still smiling in front of the old Ford and two bottles of lager lay in the grass next to the picnic basket. Would he ever get to see Mrs Jones? And if he did, what would he say to her? That Jones hadn't died in vain? He remembered the smell of steaks and of smoke drifting through the pines and tea-tree, children playing and sand castles collapsing as the tide turned and the big sea started to run. Would he see the lighthouse and the stone walls of the river again? It seemed then that the cicadas sang all summer and the hot, dusty months would never end. He put Jones's wallet and dog tag back carefully as the Koreans left the compound, laughing and pushing each other. Then all was silent. He thought of the Korean woman. Dirt and gravel blew around the yard, and the lights from the soldiers' quarters gleamed. David lay full length on his greatcoat, and his thoughts wandered back to *Killara* and his grandfather reading Tennyson:

> *One equal temper of heroic hearts,*
> *Made weak by time and fate, but strong in will*
> *To strive, to seek, to find, and not to yield.*

He wondered how Tom Fleetwood was faring. He said to himself, *I am still alive, I am still alive.*

*   *   *

From his cell on the other side of the compound, Tom Fleetwood also watched the basketball game. His cell was small and dark and he couldn't stand up straight. He was not prepared for two weeks: it was going to be a very long time. He examined the wooden door, but it was hinged on the outside; he felt the hasp and staple and the cold metal of the big padlock. The earth by the door was hard as rock, and he had nothing to dig with except a small spoon. What was the point? He and David had agreed not to try for a break until on the way to Pyongyang. He would have to grin and bear it. What time was it? It was getting dark now and the basketballers were gone; the compound was silent and moonlight shone beyond the walls.

Fleetwood took off his battledress jacket and picked out the fleas and lice. He killed the hard-backed lice with his long, black fingernails and wondered if he and David would be fed this evening. Jesus, this was a bloody mess. Fear and uncertainty began to grow within him. No doubt, some Gloucesters must have escaped the disaster at Hill 235, and they would have reported him captured and his mother and father would have the telegram. First, his father's disgrace at Dunkirk and now this; his father would open the bottle of Gordon's, mix a double pink gin and disappear to his room upstairs while she read the telegram over and over in the garden, where the daffodils and jonquils were in bloom.

He thought about David, the Korean girl and the accusation of rape. What was the point of that? Humiliation? If it were so, Kim had succeeded. Andersen had never been to bed with a woman. How odd, but he could never ask him why. What were the colonel and the adjutant doing? They would give the Chows a run for their money, and so would he and Andersen once they got out of this hole. The night came down as black as coal and Fleetwood wrapped himself in his greatcoat; he was afraid now; the war could drag on for years and Kim could keep them locked up for ever. But that was impossible – sooner or later MacArthur would be allowed to bomb north of the Yalu, and then the show would be over.

Fleetwood thought about the Chinese. It wasn't just their numbers, it was their tenacity and their attitude. How could an Asiatic race armed with obsolete weapons from the last war, with no armour and aircraft to speak of, on a star-vation diet, beat the superior firepower of the Americans and British? Something was happening he couldn't under-stand. He thought of Klaus Fuchs betraying atomic secrets to the Russians. Why would he want to do that? He'd heard reports of the Mau Mau in Kenya, the Communist guerrillas in Malaya and the Viet Minh in Indo-China. They seemed to have the moral strength. There was something happening in all the colonial territories. Would the North Koreans and Chinese drive them into the sea as Kim said? Fleetwood thought of Kim's questions about cricket, Trumper's, the opera ticket and his mother – nothing he had learned at Wellington or Sandhurst had prepared him for them. Kim's baffling, disturbing interrogations were not those he had read of Stalag Thirteen or Colditz; they were more like arguing with a cousin who was a Jesuit. Pluck and physical courage would not necessarily win through. What would his father do? He hated to think. He thought of Biggles, Algy and Ginger and laughed. Rockfist Rogan would have no hope against Kim. Should he start praying? He hadn't done that for a long time. A few spots of rain fell upon the dust of the compound, and somewhere a dog barked. Was it Kim's? The lice crawled in his groin and armpits, his belly rumbled, his back ached and Fleetwood tried to sleep.

As he dozed, he thought of the cuckoo calling outside the cell. Fleetwood remembered the swallows which swooped in under the eaves of his parents' house every spring. When the swallows came and the cuckoos called, it was the official end of winter. He felt light-headed and wondered how he would see the next two weeks through. His was an ancient and honourable family. Why was this being done to him? It was said that the blood of the

Habsburgs flowed through his veins. His mouth was dry and his gums were sore and he thought of the party food of his childhood, of jellies in moulds, blancmange and fruit salad. He wanted to tell someone in authority who he was. God damn the Chinese and God damn this war. His thoughts wandered back to Gloucestershire, to the walls of Cotswold stone and the old cedars covered with ivy, the glades where the wild orchids grew and the grass was fine and green, grass for making love, and he missed its touch. He never dreamt he would miss home so much. What day was it? If it was Sunday, they would be at Matins, the organist would be playing a voluntary and in the afternoon they would take a walk down the winding lanes of Dursley to the Manor House where his father would have a whisky with the proprietor, who had been a major in the Royal Engineers. While they drank in the small house bar, his mother wandered in the garden and looked at the roses.

Now it was pitch black, and the cell seemed very small. He thought of the burial mounds of the ancient kings of Shilla and suddenly recalled the tumulus at Uley. There, many years ago, with the west wind blowing, the fields ploughed and starlings flying in droves, they had been told by their teacher that the tumulus was a burial place for Stone Age people that dated back to 2500 BC and that inside were the skeletons of twenty-four men and animals. It was spitting with rain as the children laughed and tumbled down the man-made hill. When they discovered that the wooden gate was locked, one of his friends was sent to the local farmer to get the key. Tom watched him run away over the ploughed field and hoped he would not come back; he crouched in the lee of the tumulus and hoped the farmer was out. The rain grew heavier and he huddled in his mackintosh, shivering with cold and fear; then he saw his friend running back with the key tied to a block of wood. When the grave was open the children rushed in, their laughter echoing through the stone gallery; but Tom hung around the entrance, fearful of the tomb and what was within.

"Come on, Tom," the teacher said, "down you go."

But he shouted: "No, no, I won't." And he ran away, across the muddy furrows, over the road and into the pine woods, where they couldn't find him.

Major Kim did not thrust the burned body of a Korean baby through the bars, but Tom slept uneasily in his cell as the rats ran and the bats flew.

* * *

The days and nights were long. They were fed twice a day on millet and rice shoved through the doors of their cells. Every morning they heard the sounds of the children and old men going to work in the fields. During the day, soldiers, animals and trucks could be heard on the streets of Tuju-ri; the bombing strikes were regular; they could tell the engines of the B17s, the Corsairs and the Lockheed Lightnings; the explosions echoed in the northern hills and the anti-aircraft guns thudded and popped. Sometimes, bugles echoed and there was small-arms fire: was it an execution? They could not tell. Would they face a firing squad? Each evening the Koreans played basketball in the compound.

The Korean guards woke them at dawn by banging rifle butts on the cell doors and shouting, and they were made to sit upright, legs crossed on their greatcoats, until mid-morning; then they were taken out to the latrines and the cells inspected; they were walked around the compound separately and could not speak or signal to each other. It was bright spring weather, but the nights were cold and during the day flies clung to their faces and clothes. There was no sign of Kim: it was as though he had forgotten them. Perhaps he had gone to Pyongyang to make arrangements? When they exercised on the first day, Tom looked at David and smiled. David was surprised to see him shuffling and bent. His stubble was streaked with grey and he looked like one of those men who lived in the shanty town in Penshurst during the Depression. The guard slapped Fleetwood on the face and he stumbled and fell on the gravel. Then he got to his feet and they both continued walking as though the other wasn't there. Each noon, they were given a bowl of boiled water either to wash themselves with or to drink. David drank it one day and rinsed his face and hands the next. Late in the afternoon, they were given more millet and waited for the basketballers; the game was the only event of the day. David tried to keep track of the teams and the games' results by scratching on the mud wall with the handle of the spoon. Which team would win the tournament? He added up the points and made bets against himself using bits of twig for money. One evening, he won five pounds. But after four days the soldiers disappeared and the games stopped. Sand and leaves blew across the vacant yard. Far away he heard the sound of artillery: the soldiers must have gone to the front. He was cast in upon himself and counted the days left, if Kim kept his word. He dare not contemplate what would happen if the Korean major did not.

Tom dreamed of food: jars of Chivers raspberry jam and marmalade bought at Fortnum & Mason, kippers and devilled kidneys; Dover soles, steamed vegetables, and hock, scones and cream and seed cake. One night he remembered the Christmas parties of his childhood, dancing *Roger de Coverley*, *Here We Go Gathering Nuts in May* and *Oranges and Lemons*; the girls wore party slippers and frocks of tulle and lace and danced in the dining room as his mother played the piano. When he was woken at dawn, Fleetwood shook the dust from his greatcoat and re-arranged it on the cell floor, and when he was made to sit cross-legged and upright for five hours, he recited passages from Virgil, Tacitus and Horace; he conjugated Latin verbs in the passive; he repeated the standing orders for the mounting of a quarter guard. He rubbed his beard and scratched his eyebrows. What did he look like? It was just as well the girls at the Cavendish couldn't see him now. The days were interminable, the flies swarmed, the fleas bit, the lice itched. His back ached, and his vision was blurred; the square was empty and even the mules were taken away. There was nothing to do except hope that Kim would keep his word.

*　　*　　*

One morning, in mid-May 1951, the guards shouted as usual, and they were stood in front of their cells, and were ordered to take their greatcoats with them. They were taken to the latrines where they washed as best they could; neither was allowed to talk to the other; they were fed sorghum and millet in the yard while the guards stood over them in the chilly morning; then they were taken into the main building, down the stone corridor and pushed together into the first cell and the iron door banged shut. The guards went away and they shook hands and regarded each other.

"How are you?" Tom said.

"I've been better. And you?"

"Not too chipper, not too chipper at all." Tom stretched his body and put his hands above his head; he walked stiffly and tried to touch his toes. Grey whiskers were growing in his beard. "I'm six foot two and the bloody cell was six foot. That makes it awkward, and I'd counted on seven days, not fourteen."

"He's kept his word," David said.

"He has, indeed. I thought he might not, in my bleaker moments. Maybe he learned something when he worked at the Peninsula Hotel."

"What's that?"

"That an Englishman's word is his bond."

David laughed. "Is it?"

"You know damned well it is."

"They're very good at it," David said.

"Good at what?"

"At keeping us uncomfortable, not ill-treating us, just keeping us uncomfortable." Fleetwood raised his hands. "I bet," David continued, "those were just about the rations the Korean and Chinese soldiers get in the field."

Fleetwood was about to ask David what he thought of the charge of rape, but decided not. "So it's Kim now?" he said.

"I expect so." After fourteen days solitary, there was very little to say and they walked up and down. David took off his boots. The soles and uppers were split and the laces broken. "Hobnails are no good in the snow."

"What?"

"It doesn't matter. Yes, it's Kim, and Donald Bradman, and the opera, and Trumper's, and germ warfare, and secret weapons, and Mr Dulles, and President Truman, and gamekeepers, and trespassing and our degenerate culture. It's the whole bang lot. It's the burnt bodies of babies," David said. He thought of the napalm and the refugees on the road to Chasan, Kershaw's brains spraying on his tunic, the guns and the bodies trapped in the river, Hart machine-gunning the two soldiers against the armour plate of the Chaffee, the man snorting his brains through his nose, the sniper trapped in his harness and his groin blossoming with blood. "It's the whole fucking lot."

They paced the cell, the place was dark and no roosters crowed and no birds sang; no cuckoos called that late spring morning.

"I was thinking," Fleetwood said, "why would that man Fuchs betray atomic secrets to the Russians?"

"Because he thought that our culture is degenerate," David said. He thought of Kim: *When they see a burglar in a neighbour's house, they drive him out.*

*   *   *

243

Kim was wearing clean khaki riding breeches and a clean shirt. He sat at his desk and wrinkled his nose as they came in. They were made to sit on a bench.

"You do not look very military," he said, as he looked them over. "Perhaps it was the conditions or perhaps it was your lack of discipline. The quarters are somewhat cramped, but you have had time to consider your position." He smiled. "The war is going well for us. We shall be in Seoul once more in two or three days. The Americans and their lackeys will be swimming for their lives in the Yellow Sea. Have you reconsidered your position? It is very grave, the People's Court shows little mercy."

"We have," David said.

"And what is your conclusion?"

"We've decided to go to Pyongyang, confess our crimes and send a message to King George."

"You have seen the error of your ways?"

"We have."

"That is good, you may be treated more leniently now. I will make arrangements; if you try to run away, you will be shot like mad dogs." Kim stared at them. "You will be shot and your bodies thrown into a pit of lime. You will disappear from the face of the earth, and your parents will never know where you lie." Kim stood up and his boots creaked as he walked around the room.

"As I said before, the news for the People's Democratic Republic of Korea is good: we are once more at the very gates of Seoul, and the trial of that vulture, Syngman Rhee, is not far away. You will leave for Pyongyang at dawn tomorrow. It is a beautiful city despite the savage bombings." He smiled. "My comrades will decide what is to be done with you." Kim looked at David. "The charge of ravishment, Mr Andersen, has been discontinued. The woman was not telling the truth."

"What happened to her?" David said.

"Happened to her? She is assisting our brave comrades at the front. You will both be ready when the cuckoo calls."

12

On the Run

Part II

The old General Motors truck was packed with people, some civilians and some military and all smelling of garlic. Two soldiers armed with Russian submachine guns sat on the tailgate and guarded them all. It was hard to tell who was free and who was prisoner. Were there deserters? Were there ROK men who might help them? No one took any notice of them: perhaps they had seen prisoners of war before? Their hands were not tied and the Koreans pushed and jostled. The morning was cold and foggy and the gentle breeze smelt of the sea; already the old men and children were going to work in the fields, their backs bent and some squatting on the tops of the bunds. The street was pitted and rutted by carts and torn up by tanks, and the North Korean flag flew from the roof of the barracks. Old bicycles lay on the wet ground. A gang of workers filled the pot-holes in the cobbles and the women carried earth and gravel in wicker baskets. They worked hard and didn't look at the truck. The engine wouldn't fire and reeked of cheap petrol; the driver kept his boot on the foot-start, but the motor kept coughing and dying and the fumes hung in the moist air. The battery went flat and the driver waved his arms and shouted and his comrade jumped down with the crank handle as they waited outside the police station. At last the engine started and the driver cheered and laughed and gunned the accelerator. The truck backfired and shook and David remembered the Negro drivers on the road to the apple orchard. After three weeks in prison, it was strange to see so many people, and it made them nervous and uncomfortable. The taste of the rice and chicken fat they had been given for breakfast was still in their mouths. When the time came, could they run as they had before? It seemed impossible, and David kept rubbing his thighs and legs as he had done before running at school; he thought of running spikes and embrocation and felt his Achilles tendons inside his boots. His feet seemed a little less swollen now and he looked at Fleetwood. Should he speak to him or not? Someone might know English and it seemed risky. Fleetwood looked a lot brighter now he was in the open: his beard was black, with a few grey whiskers, and he sat quite straight in the truck and watched the driver and the guards on the tailgate. He looked at David, grinned and winked. Minimize risks: no speaking. Cranes and seagulls were flying: the azaleas were still blooming in the hills.

Fleetwood rubbed the stubble on his chin and hummed to himself: *If I were a blackbird I'd whistle and sing, and follow the ship my true love sails in.* The long-legged birds sailed by and disappeared behind the willows and then away beyond the foothills. To Fleetwood, it seemed like the start of some unlikely bus tour to Bognor. He remembered King George V: *Bugger Bognor!* He smiled; but the two soldiers with the machine guns were watching them. One was a boy wearing an American helmet which was far too big for him, and the other was older, a veteran with his face scarred. Half his nose was burnt away: it looked like napalm. His finger was curled around the trigger of his machine gun. Fleetwood couldn't see if the safety was on or not: that man would need watching. But the water in the paddies shone and the poplars were green; he thought it would take about two hours to get to the river-crossing and the way this truck was running there could be some breakdowns: that would be to their favour. He wondered what the time was: it must be about seven and the longer they waited around here, the better. The road was crowded with workers, troops and animals and then a column of Chinese came marching through with mules and ponies. They had some light artillery pieces and heavy mortars; the ammunition carts rumbled and took some time to pass while they waited. They looked in fine condition. No one seemed in a hurry. Fleetwood hoped the river was up: that meant waiting for the ferry and that could take a very long time. It might be their salvation. Fleetwood looked at David, but he didn't smile and they waited for the truck to move. They both knew the longer it waited the better. The Chinese battalion passed on down the road, the mules' harnesses and the jinker wheels creaking. The Korean peasants moved in and once again filled up the ruts and pot-holes. The breeze stopped and the North Korean flag hung limp; the young soldier took off his American helmet and put it down on the tailgate. The scarred man wiped his mouth and worked the breech of his gun. The women walked to and fro with their baskets of dirt and the men filled them with their shovels. Why were they not at the front? Were the men the ROK, were they, too, prisoners of war? Clouds drifted and distant guns sounded. Men were fighting at the front and David wondered about Cash and Hart.

David and Fleetwood watched out for Kim in the crowd, but he was not there. Why not? Had he deserted them? They had to escape before they got to the Imjin. Why did the Koreans not look at them? Maybe there was some killing spot on the way to the river which they all knew; maybe they wouldn't even get to the river and they would be executed, their bodies thrown into the lime pits as the civilians watched. Fleetwood remembered the American troops massacred by the Germans in the last stages of the war; it was in a forest, but he couldn't recall the name. Where was Kim? What were these people doing on this truck? Then the driver gunned the engine, crashed the gears and at last they moved off down the road toward the poplars and the walnut trees where the women and children worked. The mist was lifting and the sun was warmer as they moved toward the river.

They hadn't gone very far when the truck stopped by a dike where a small waterwheel was turning. The driver left the engine running, got out and stood in the middle of the road; then he walked up and down, the dust rising from his boots, his service pistol banging against his hip. An old woman sitting opposite David in the truck delved into a straw bag and pulled out something wrapped in rice paper. Her arms and hands were nut brown and her nails long. She opened the rice paper and offered it to him: it was dried squid. Her lined face was impassive, but David smiled, broke a piece off and handed it back to her. She then offered it to Fleetwood: these were the first signs of kindliness and they were grateful. The squid was hard and brittle and tasted salty, but they got it down and wondered why the truck had stopped. Then a line of men appeared, walking over the paddy; the sun was higher in the sky. As the men got closer, they saw that they were tied together with rope like animals, prisoners of some sort, wet and muddy from their work in the rice fields, thin and dejected. They, too, were piled into the truck and once more they started for the river. The truck ground and lurched and it was very uncomfortable. Confusion in numbers, Fleetwood thought. He hoped the Imjin waters were high.

By the sun, it must have been mid-afternoon when they got to the crossing point of the Imjin. The truck stopped in front of what appeared to be another police station in a village by the river, a poor place with no more than a dozen houses, neglected gardens and a line of gnarled willows growing behind the levee. They were ordered off the truck to stand around in the street with the roped men who squatted in the dirt and ate balls of boiled rice and chilli wrapped in paper. The old woman who had given them the squid disappeared and the other civilians sat in groups under the willows where long river grass grew. The day was clear and fine and the night promised to be starry and

248

cold. The boy with the American helmet went inside the police station and the scarred man watched over them. They saw the driver walk along the road to the top of the levee and out of sight down the other side of the crossing. Fleetwood was anxious to see the height of the river. "Do you think it's safe to talk?"

"We'll soon know," David said. The guard seemed uninterested and so they sat down together, their feet in the dry gutter.

"I wish I could see that bloody river," Fleetwood said.

"From memory," David said, "there's a ford and a pontoon."

"Let's hope to Christ the river's too high for the ford. If it is, it means the pontoon and with luck we could wait all night for that."

"Surely our blokes must plaster it from time to time?"

David started to rub his calf muscles again. "One would think so."

"Maybe tonight's the night, but that would be too much to ask."

"You never know, as the actress said to the bishop. I wonder what that youngster with the helmet is doing."

"God knows," David said. "Perhaps he's getting our tea. How do you feel?"

"Much, much better. A breath of air, even in this wretched country, does wonders."

"The old woman was kind."

"Indeed, she was. Heaven knows how this mess will be untangled; they've been buggered up by the Japs, now by the Reds. It wouldn't have happened if the British had been here."

"What about India?" David said.

"The Indians at least have got a civil service and the railways. These poor devils have got nothing."

"Maybe they need people like Major Kim," David said.

"They may well do, but *we* don't."

"He'll take some forgetting."

249

"He certainly will. I can't wait to tell the chaps at the Staff College." Then Fleetwood saw the driver coming down the levee. "Our chauffeur's coming back, I wonder what news he brings from the Rialto."

The driver was joined by an officer whom they hadn't seen before and they both stood talking by the truck. The officer waved his arms in the air, shrugged and they went back to the top of the levee where they stood looking at the river.

"Something's up," Fleetwood said. "I think they've got to use the pontoon and if there's a battalion or two on the other side, we're in luck."

Several hours later, they were given some cold sorghum and shut inside the small police station compound. The sun was low in the west and they hung about the yard in their greatcoats, listening to the sounds outside. The truck started up, moved some way and stopped; a bugle blew and from one of the buildings they heard the clatter of mah-jongg tiles: that would mean Chinese troops. Darkness came down and they knew they would have to escape some time during the night.

*　　*　　*

It must have been shortly after midnight when they heard the sound of aircraft drumming from the south. They got to their feet.

"I hope those chappies are coming our way," Fleetwood said, "I hope to God they are."

The sound grew louder and some anti-aircraft batteries opened up, tracers streaking through the sky, yellow and green in the blackness.

"They're getting close," David said. "Do you think they're making for the crossing?"

"Probably, but if they're on target and bomb the north side, it's not going to help us much."

By the sound of it, the first parcel of bombs fell in the river; doors were flung open and men shouted and ran around outside. Several more explosions followed, the ground shook and then a flare lit the place up as bright as a summer's day.

"I think God is with us," Fleetwood said, as they stood by the doors, "I think he is. Can you run for it when the time comes?"

"I can run a country mile," David said. "Have no worries. But how do we get out?"

"God knows. We'll think of something. If the buildings are hit, something's bound to happen."

The aircraft seemed close now, two more flares hung in the night sky and a heavy machine gun thudded somewhere on the levee. David's hands started to sweat: the bombs would surely hit the street or the building. An incendiary struck a building and its thatched roof exploded and burned like a torch; the levee was hit again, the air was full of burning fragments; sparks flew like fireworks, the machine gun rattled, another building at the back of the police station was hit, then a bomb exploded in the street with a roar and the compound doors collapsed in the blast. Dust rose as thick as a London fog, fires burned all around, people were shouting and screaming and mud walls tumbled into pieces; another bomb fell over by the willows and the roof of the police station caught fire. David and Tom crouched by the fallen gates and saw the roped men lying at all angles on the road; two of them were on fire and rolling in the dirt.

"Right," Fleetwood shouted. "This is it."

They ran down the street, past the bodies of the roped prisoners, burning silos and flaming thatches into the darkness of the paddies. They ran until they fell in their tracks behind a bund. After about half an hour, the bombing stopped and the aircraft droned away toward the airfields in the south. When they had drawn their breath, they got up cautiously and walked away into the night south toward Seoul.

*   *   *

251

In the morning it was raining and they sat, resting their backs against a poplar tree. They were beside a small, shallow, stony river which flowed north into the Imjin. The countryside was deserted save for the gulls and pipers sitting on the shingle banks. The rain fell steadily, but it wasn't cold and it felt good to be in the open.

"Christ, I've just remembered," Fleetwood said. "That bastard Kim never returned my wallet."

"What was in it?"

"Bits and pieces, a photograph of my mother, ten quid and the opera ticket."

"The famous ticket?"

"Yes, and I've remembered what it was."

"What?"

"*Don Giovanni*. Have you seen it?"

"No, there was no opera in Penshurst."

"A pity, it's magnificent. Shall I hum you a few bars?"

David laughed in the rain. "Not at the moment, I'm trying to remember the map."

"Can you recall any of it?"

"Parts. The general thrust of it, I can."

"Capital. It's good to be out, isn't it?"

"Yes." They suddenly shook hands and smiled.

"That's the sort of stream," Fleetwood said, "where you could catch a trout, a brook trout; but you don't have rivers, do you?"

"There's a few," David said, "but they're no more than creeks: the Shaw, the Eumerella. The best was the Fitzroy, no trout, but bream. My grandfather used to take me there." He thought of the big sea running at the mouth, the weed and rushes, the gulls and the sand bar and egret on the posts. "I don't suppose it's like trout, but bream are quite hard to catch. You need light tackle and the right bait." He thought of his grandfather, drinking whisky from his silver flask as the south wind blew through the sedge and rushes. *Wait, David, wait. Unfurl your line, be quiet and patient and wait.*

"It's southwest, then?" Fleetwood said. He retied the broken laces on his boots. "Do we agree on that?"

"I think," David said, "we agree on many things."

"The rain's with us. Should we go as far as we can?"

"I'm for that."

"Does it rain in Australia?"

"Of course it does. Where I come from, it rains about three months of the year non-stop."

"It rained and it rained and it rained," Fleetwood said.

David looked at Tom Fleetwood and took his arm. "Let's get cracking."

They splashed over the stream, climbed the bund and sloshed through the paddies. They ran south as the rain came down.

The country they traversed was flat and marshy: a place of drowned gardens, canals, crumbling dikes and shingle banks. It rained all day and they saw no one. The hills and mountains stood north and south, overlooking this valley of the Imjin; the peaks were grey and misty and beautiful; and waders, pipers and gulls watched them as they marched. It was good to be walking. They walked increasingly strongly and were happy. Each helped the other through the bogs and streams, over the dikes and through the canals. It was sad, exhausted country, tilled and farmed for a millennium, the earth grey and leached, the rice stalks black, the poplars fallen and the glasshouses collapsed. Their bodies were getting strong and the going was easy.

In the afternoon, the rain was hard and straight and the breeze was gone. They came to a large lake ringed with oaks and poplars. There was an island on the lake, where a temple stood and fishtraps rose like skeletons from the water. As they stood on the beach and sheltered under the dripping willows, they saw smoke rising from a village to the south. Then lightning flashed and thunder boomed as they sat beneath the willows. David remembered a Japanese painting he had seen years ago in the Art Gallery in Melbourne. What to do? They had to find shelter for the night.

They looked at the island and the smoke rising like a pillar in the south. All was silent, but for the rain.

"What do you think the time is?" David said.

"Damned hard to tell, it's after three I should think."

"It's quite a hike to that village but I don't fancy a night in the wet," David said.

"Nor I." Fleetwood got up and gazed around, but not a building was to be seen. "It's the village, isn't it? I should say it will take about three hours. It's odd," he said, "you wouldn't think there was a war at all."

"I suppose this is what it was like before the war came," David said.

"It's a sad country, isn't it?"

"Yes," David said, "but it's also beautiful." He, too, got up and they headed along the shore of the lake.

Darkness was coming down when they saw a peasant wheeling his bicycle on the narrow lake road. He was balancing a big load of twigs and branches tied on the bicycle seat. He was wearing a straw hat and dirty white pyjamas and they couldn't see if he was young or old. They watched him carefully from the side of the road. He was by himself, walking slowly between the rows of poplars.

"Home is the hunter," Fleetwood said, "home from the hill."

"I think we should walk with him," David said, "just to see what happens. He must be going home and he might take us in." He thought of the old woman on the truck offering him the dried squid. "We've got to trust someone."

"Righto," Fleetwood said. "There's two of us if he gets nasty."

The rain was easing as they walked up close to the peasant, wheeling his bicycle. Fleetwood recognised the make: it was an old Hercules, made in Birmingham. He saw the Perry hub brake and thought of his young riding days. "It's a Hercules," he said. "How about that?"

"Yes," David said. "I know."

The Korean peasant looked in his forties and had a

thin, wispy beard; he didn't appear to see them at all and continued up the road as though they didn't exist. The three of them walked several hundred yards in complete silence. The rain had stopped now and the watery sky was turning to orange. David walked right alongside the Korean and was close enough to touch his shoulder, but dared not. He wasn't a big man and they could have overpowered him and taken the bicycle and the firewood, but what was the point of that? Then the Korean turned, crossed the road and walked along the other side. They followed him and David thought of the Pharisees. Would this man give them food and shelter? He thought not. Then Fleetwood put his hand on the Korean's shoulder and said: "Food, food?" But there was no reply as the sun sank behind the mountains and the birds flew in to sleep on the bunds in the paddies.

"What should we do?" David said.

"We are the original invisible men," Fleetwood said. "He shows no signs of hostility and we should follow him."

At last, the Korean turned off the road and walked up a track between small willows to a house where a light gleamed and smoke was rising. Suddenly, the Korean raised his hand, walked through the small corn patch at the front of the mud house, parked the Hercules, took off the bundle of firewood, opened the door and disappeared.

They waited and peered about outside in their wet great-coats, listening for voices within, but there were none.

"What's next?" David said as they stood about in the dusk.

"Damned if I know," Fleetwood said. "He can't tell anybody except his missus, if he's got one, and he can't telephone. I think we should stay put for a bit. We're dealing with the inscrutable orientals, aren't we?"

"Say he's got some kind of weapon?"

"I should think that's most unlikely."

David dragged his boots in the dirt and then squatted.

"It's a bit like waiting outside the poorhouse, isn't it?"

Fleetwood didn't answer, walked about and squinted at

the paddies. He walked toward the road and looked down the river flats, but no one was there. The evening star was rising and soon the moon would appear. Food and shelter were first in the order of things. What was the Korean farmer doing inside the house? Would he betray them? How could he? They would wait another half hour and then move on. God knows where. He walked back to David and saw the candles gleaming inside the house. The door opened and the Korean appeared; he was carrying two bowls of rice, he bowed and put them down in front of them. Then he took David's arm and led him around the back where he pointed to a small outbuilding. He bowed again and went inside.

There were bits of chilli in the boiled rice and it tasted hot and nourishing. They ate every last grain and licked the small wooden bowls. It was almost dark now and the evening was quiet and still. The poplars stood like ghosts in the dark.

"Not bad," Fleetwood said. "First the squid and now this. They're an odd people." He put the bowl on the ground. "He's probably hoping to Christ we'll go away."

"He's shown us the shed," David said.

"Indeed he has. Let's have a look, at least it's a roof over our poor heads."

The northern night gathered in; they dossed down and slept well in their greatcoats.

Before the sun woke them, a rooster crowed in the valley and smoke began to rise from the tiny farmhouses. The Korean who had fed them opened the door, mounted his Hercules bicycle and rode off down the track. He didn't look back at the outbuilding.

"Great Scot," Fleetwood said as he stretched his filthy body, "is that a rooster I hear? I can't believe it, I thought they'd all been eaten." He saw David stirring. "Now, where's my Horlicks? Do you have Horlicks in Australia?"

"What?"

"Horlicks."

"Horlicks what?"

"Never mind. It's time we took off. How did you sleep?"

"Like a top."

David rose, went outside into the cold, pissed on the ground and looked at the dawn. The sky was pink and misty and already people were working in the paddies, their backs bent pulling the wooden ploughs. He thought of the early mornings at Penshurst, repairing the fences, of Tom Quicksilver and Bert Lawless and his grandfather: they worked hard, but here the work was backbreaking and there seemed no end to it. He would be glad to be home. He watched a woman, walking and carrying a basket on her head, straight as a statue as she went under the chestnut trees. As she went away, he called to Fleetwood: "Tom, we're off."

"Right you are." They walked away from the house where the chimney smoked. "That man was no Pharisee," Fleetwood said.

"No," David said, "he was not." But he thought: how many people would walk on the other side?

*　　*　　*

On the road, they saw a man carrying a huge load of firewood on an A-frame pack, but, like the farmer, he paid them no heed. They were invisible. The hills were bare and the charcoal fires burned in the still morning as they marched in step, their boots wet and worn. There were many small farms now, wedged into the hills of the river valley, where only vegetables could grow. As they went, the countryside became more settled with barns, silos and potato fields. David reckoned the road wound south toward Seoul, and they would stay with it as long as they could. Somewhere, the rail-head lay and they would aim for that.

Women were washing clothes in the small streams this early morning and berry-gathering parties of old men and children were walking toward the hills. David and Tom were more confident now: maybe the Koreans thought they were

257

Russian soldiers in their long and ragged greatcoats? They trudged down the centre of the narrow country road. The rice was turning pale green in patches, but it seemed there was no wild food to be had in this grey country. Now and then they left the road to fossick in the fields and gardens, but all they picked up were a few potatoes the size of walnuts and some berries which tasted bitter. They looked for corn or maize, but couldn't see any; and by the middle of the afternoon, they were doubled up with cramps and hunger.

David sat under a willow tree, his stomach aching and limbs shaking and said: "I'm sorry, I've got to rest."

"As do I," Fleetwood said. "I think it's those wretched berries." His face was white and his body was sweating. "We've got to get help, somebody must take us in. What do you think the time is?"

"I've got no idea, I don't even know what day of the week it is. I'm absolutely buggered. Excuse me." David staggered up and dry-retched into the ditch. "We'll have to find some place around here to rest up. Anyway, there are too many people around and sooner or later we're going to strike police or soldiers. I think we should lie up during the day and march by night."

"Isn't that going to be harder?"

"Maybe, but safer, and with this weather we've got the stars to guide us. Let's see what we can find." They moved off the road and stumbled over the dry paddies toward the hills, their feet like lead and innards groaning with hunger. At last they found a small depression where rushes and tall weeds grew. They collapsed into the brambles and lay looking at the sky.

"What if the berry-gatherers come?" Fleetwood said.

"Let them come, I'm going to sleep in the sun."

They slept in the weedy hollow as the shadows grew long and the night came down. No one came near them.

* * *

258

They woke and saw the smudge fires gleaming and smoking across the countryside. The mosquitoes bit their faces and hands and they brushed them away.

"This place is the arsehole of the world," Tom Fleetwood said. "Why couldn't I have been sent to Cyprus or Kenya? Right now I could be having a gin and lime in the mess in Nicosia and saving the old empire, or what's left of it."

David stretched, got up and looked south at the lights dimly gleaming. The night was chilly and the moon full and clear. "We've got to chance our arm at that village," he said. "We can't go on like this. If we do, we'll collapse and there's no point in that."

They gathered themselves up and trudged toward the lights and the glow of the fires. The rest had revived them and they marched in time, their worn boots thumping on the clay road. Fleetwood hummed a tune in his head: *Soldiers of the Queen are we, the Queen are we, the Queen are we.* The lights grew nearer and they thought they could smell food cooking. Was that the smell of garlic and rice? Even a bowl of vile sorghum would do.

They passed burnt-out houses, peach orchards and old chestnut trees. The peach trees were late in bloom and the petals drifted in the moonlight. Then they saw a silo and what appeared to be stables; still, nobody was abroad.

"What do we do when we see a house?" David said.

"The way I'm feeling, we march right up and bang on the bloody door," Fleetwood said. "If we look military enough, they'll think we're Russkies or something. I'm sick of being hunted like some animal. We'll use the stand-and-deliver approach."

"Right," David said, "the peasants must have soldiers calling in all the time. Let's choose the next house with lights burning."

The night was cold and clear as they walked and searched.

* * *

They hammered at the door and waited, trying to look tall and fierce. It was opened and a small man stood before them; he squinted as Fleetwood put his boot on the threshold. What do we look like, David thought, what on earth do we look like?

"Food, food," he said and rubbed his stomach as he stood squarely in the doorway.

The house looked two-roomed: it was without furniture and the floor was of stamped mud; a fire was burning on the hearth and the room was stuffy and full of smoke. The man appeared to be alone, but was there anybody beyond the second door? The Korean looked frightened and tried to shut the door on them, but they stood their ground, David in front and Fleetwood blocking the entrance. They looked around for weapons, but all they saw was a fire on the hearth, a few pots and pans and piles of dirty straw on the earth floor. The peasant was ragged and unshaven, his feet in rubber sandals; he pushed David in the chest and was surprisingly strong. He shouted and somewhere in the house a baby started crying.

David delved into his tunic pocket, fished out Jones's wallet and flourished the library card. "Soviet, Soviet," he said. The man stopped pushing and they walked into the room. Fleetwood strode over to the other door, opened it and dragged out a woman holding the crying child. She, too, was very frightened and that was what they wanted. "I think we've got the advantage," Fleetwood said, "and I hope to God there's no one else lurking round. I'm going out the back to have a look."

David pushed the Korean and his wife and baby into a corner and looked in the pot steaming on the fire. It looked like millet, but anything would do. Some dried chilli were hanging on a string; he tore one off and threw it into the pot. That would liven it up. Then he showed the Koreans the library card again. They nodded and the woman comforted the baby who stopped crying. This was a very poor place and he started to understand what

Kim was about: people should not have to live like this.

"There's nobody about," Fleetwood said as he came back in. "What's in the pot?"

"Millet."

"Jesus Christ."

"It's hot. Any port in the storm."

Fleetwood looked at the Koreans. "They look suitably impressed; I thought the card was a stroke of brilliance. What is it?"

"A library card."

"Good Lord. Let's have the food, but we'd better make sure our Asiatic friend here doesn't bolt for it."

"If we stand by the doors," David said, "I think we're safe enough."

As the fire smoked and the Koreans stood silent, they ate the millet. This time they ate slowly and the meal took some time. Now and again one of them opened the front door and looked out into the blackness, but all was silent and not even a mouse or a rat moved. The moon was high in the sky and they guessed it must be about midnight. The Koreans said nothing and the baby fell asleep in its mother's arms: they gazed at the two strange soldiers with their unblinking brown eyes. David wiped his mouth and drank some warm, boiled water. "What do you reckon they're thinking about?" His voice sounded flat and hard like Sergeant Hart's.

"They're hoping we'll fuck off," Fleetwood said. He gazed about the wretched room. "There's nothing we can take with us, is there?"

"If the *Imnun-Gun* come, what will they say?"

"If they've got any sense, they won't say anything. They're unharmed and could be accused of harbouring war criminals." Fleetwood laughed. "That's what Kim called us." He put his bowl down by the fire. "I'm going out the back again to see what I can find. I shan't be long. Why didn't we do this before?"

David felt very weary now and sat down on the floor; he motioned the Koreans to do the same, but they kept standing. Death, trespassing and stealing, he thought, but his belly was full.

The Korean suddenly made for the front door; David sprang and caught him in a rugby tackle, but the peasant was all sinew and bone, writhing and slipping and groping as they struggled. My God, my God, David thought, I mustn't let him go; he went for the man's throat, but he turned his head away and writhed like a small steer being roped at a country show. They both hit the door, the baby woke and screamed and the woman made for the back. I'm going to have to kill this man, David thought, I'm going to have to kill him if I can. He tried for the jugular, but the Korean wrestled away and struck David on the bridge of the nose. Blood spurted from his nostrils, his head swam and he hit the Korean as hard as he could in the throat below his ear. He hit him again, the man grunted let go and David drove his knee into his groin. That should fix the bastard, he thought, that should fix him. The Korean lay on the floor groaning and David got to his knees and wiped his bloodied nose and mouth. Every limb shook as he crouched like an animal. This is it, David thought, this is the end. Then he heard the baby crying and the woman screaming as Fleetwood shoved them back into the room.

"Are you all right?" David heard him say.

"Yes, yes, I'm all right." He tasted the blood in his mouth and got to his feet. "We can't kill these people, can we? We've got nothing to do it with except our hands, so we'd best get out."

"Right," Fleetwood said.

They ran from the house into the night as the baby cried and the woman screamed. They walked as far as they could, stopping and listening from time to time for sounds of pursuit. When the dawn came, they found an abandoned gravel pit where they slept all day.

*   *   *

The next morning they left the road, the paddies, the dikes and the river flats where the little waterwheels turned and took a track into the foothills and the southern mountains beyond. There, the eagles, hawks and vultures flew and the mist wreathed around the peaks; there, the smoke rose high from the charcoal burners' fires; and there, the snow and ice still lay on the peaks. To the south lay Munsan and the railway to Seoul. Several times, they found deserted fields of barley and corn and patches of sweet potatoes; they ate the husks, the stems and the woody tubers and drank the water from small, icy streams. Once they saw a trout in a deep pool and watched it, motionless, in the clear water. They avoided the charcoal burners' huts and their fierce dogs and climbed the ranges to the south. The days were balmy and the nights cold. Nobody was seen for five days and it seemed this time that God was with them. But their boots were falling to pieces, their toes peeled and blistered, their bones cracking and their stomachs always empty. It was hard going.

*   *   *

On the fifth day they lay in a meadow: it was in the afternoon and the north wind draughted through the pines. They took their boots off and stretched their toes. David lay on the grass and thought of the pines at Penshurst.

"Where's Wellington exactly?" he said.

"In the pine woods of Berkshire. I was just thinking about that." Fleetwood turned and looked at David. "Are you sure we're going in the right direction?"

"Yes, I'm sure."

"We've come a long way since the apple orchard, haven't we?"

"We certainly have."

"If we get out of this, David," Fleetwood said, "do you want to come to England? You could stay with us and probably get a job at the Staff College. I've got a flat in Eaton

Place and we could spend the weekends there, drinking at 'The Grenadier'."

"And seducing debs?"

Fleetwood smiled. "Indeed."

"It sounds a little different from Penshurst."

"Maybe, but home is where the heart is, isn't it?"

"It is."

"It's been tougher than I expected," Fleetwood said. "Has it for you?"

"Yes, tougher and bloodier. I never thought a place could be so poor and why we're here is becoming a bit obscure."

"Ours is not to reason why, is it?"

"I suppose not."

Then they saw smoke rising black and straight into the sky.

"That looks like another charcoal burner," Fleetwood said. "I'm famished as usual. Dare we risk it this time?"

"It's their bloody dogs," David said. "They're the fiercest I've ever seen."

"Maybe he's eaten his."

"I doubt it; charcoal burners seem to be a race apart in this country."

"At least let's have a look," Fleetwood said, and they walked very slowly down the meadow.

*   *   *

It was not a charcoal burner's hut, but a small village of about a dozen houses surrounded by orchards of apple and chestnut trees and fields of maize. They looked for the flag of the *Imnun-Gun*, but could not see it.

"What do you think?" David said.

"There's nothing to think, is there?"

They sat in the grass at the top of the hill as the evening closed in and watched the hamlet for signs of life. Nothing stirred except the smoke from the mud chimneys: the breeze

264

moved through the young maize and then in the clear air they heard the sound of axes.

"Woodchoppers," David said.

"It sounds like it."

What on earth were they both doing out here, David wondered, and lay on the ground. Fleetwood's shoulders were bent, his uniform ragged, his hair long and turning grey and his boots falling to pieces. It was a long cry from the impeccable young subaltern with the brigadier at Yongyu. Life in a prison camp couldn't be as bad as this: at least there they would have the comfort of their comrades in arms. His spirits were failing him. How could they find Munsan and the railway in this wilderness? But they were still travelling south: he was sure of that. Should they simply walk down to the village and give themselves up? Then they could be shot. They had no choice and David prayed silently. *Almighty and most merciful Father; we have erred and strayed from Thy ways like lost sheep.* Fleetwood looked for a house away from the others, a shack up on the mountainside, but there was none. It was a tiny, compact village.

"This is going to be difficult," he said. "I should think there must be at least fifty people living down there."

"Maybe all the young men have gone to the front, maybe it's all old men and women and children."

"Only God knows," Fleetwood said, "and He won't tell. We've got to go down there, haven't we? We can't go another day like this." He looked at David. "Agreed?"

"There's no option."

"All right then, let's have a kip for a bit. Can you wake yourself up? I never learnt the art."

David smiled. "Yes, I can do that." The sun was setting.

"We'll try our luck in a few hours when it gets dark."

*   *   *

David pushed Fleetwood awake. He grumbled and stretched and they set off down the slope. The going was tricky with pits, holes and rocks. Lights gleamed from houses. Several times they blundered into tree stumps and cursed, and the smell of smoke drifted on the night air. David's heart started to thump and his limbs were shaking. It was like going into a minefield. Clouds drifted and it was hard to see; the maize rustled and an owl hooted in the night. Fleetwood thought of the owls in the woods of Berkshire, fell into another hole, gasped and blasphemed. He hoped Andersen was all right, but it was hard to tell. Which house would they choose? It didn't really matter.

Then a small boy saw them on the track between houses: it was like disturbing some small ferocious animal and he ran screaming through the broken trees and piles of ash; he ran like a small dog and they ran after him into the hamlet where the lights shone and the smudge fires smoked. Doors opened, people shouted, the boy screamed and they ran down the narrow street, stumbling over the stones, falling and picking themselves up in the darkness.

"Jesus Christ, Jesus Christ, the little bastard," David heard Fleetwood shout, "I'll get him, I'll get him." The boy disappeared between the buldings and the villagers ran from their doors, lanterns flashing, torches were lit: it seemed there were hundreds of people milling in the blackness. A shot was fired, then another: it sounded like a shotgun. My God, David thought as he ran, these people are armed and they are going to kill us. He couldn't see Fleetwood, heard the strange cries, the gunfire and ran into a man who fell. A rifle clattered, David grabbed it, saw the long bayonet and stabbed. The man grunted and the blood spurted up the stock of the rifle on to David's hands and wrists: he ran after Fleetwood.

"I've got a rifle, I've got a rifle," David shouted, but no one seemed to hear. He wanted to kill the boy. They ran between the stone walls and houses, the villagers ran after them; women, children, old men, young men, dogs: David

Andersen and Tom Fleetwood ran through the fields of maize, the stubble, the charcoal pits, their hearts pumping, lungs bursting and bones cracking into the hills of Korea. They ran as far as they could, and there seemed no end to it. The peasants came after them with guns, sticks and staves; they beat the brush, they prodded the holes and ditches, they beat down the maize and they pursued them up the slopes and into the trees where the birds were asleep. At last, the noise died down and they knew they were safe for the time being. David examined the rifle: it was Japanese and there were four rounds in the magazine. He wiped the blood off the stock as best he could, and washed his hands.

*   *   *

For the next three days, they lived on wild potatoes, green maize and chestnuts. The hills grew steep, but on the fourth day they came upon a stream flowing southwest and they rested beside it. They washed their feet, faces and hair in the cold, clear water as the mist cleared from the slopes.

"Munsan's on a river," David said. "I wonder if this is the start of it." He considered the stream, flowing. "I think we should follow it down; it makes sense and it's the best chance we've got."

"We'll strike paddies," Fleetwood said, "and that means people."

"At the first paddy, we'll change the routine again and walk at night. We've got the stream to go by."

The first terrace was cut into the valley and peasants were lifting water up the steps in wooden buckets. The stream was broader and about a dozen women were planting rice, squatting in the mud, their dresses hitched over their knees, while others were washing clothes by the narrow track. A kite was sitting on the top of a small temple at the edge of the brush and they waited for the sun to go down, sleeping in turns, each watching the peasants in the paddy until the daylight faded.

This time luck was with them: the nights were clear and cold, the stream became broader and the path easy to follow. They crept through the villages in the dead of night and picked up some sorghum; there were no dogs and no children, but the mosquitoes plagued them when they tried to sleep during the day. The sun was warm, the days grew longer and strength returned to their bodies. One evening they saw a young deer: it bounded across the track and ran up into the rocks above the stream and they were as startled as the animal. David raised the old Japanese rifle, but there was no point: the deer was gone and he didn't trust the weapon. It was the first game they had seen since last spring and their hearts were lifted. They saw it once again, outlined against the pale skyline, and then it disappeared. That night they went well, walking steadily down the path in the light of a full moon, hoping the stream would flow into the river at Munsan.

On the fifth night on the stream, they saw the lights of a village north of the paddies.

"It's a large village," David said. "It could be Munsan. We'll know for certain if we strike the railway. From what I can remember of the map, there's a bridge that crosses the river in the south."

"I hope to God you're right."

"In God, we trust," David said.

"You believe that?"

"Yes," David said, "I do."

"Well," Tom Fleetwood said, "all I want to see is that steam train. I don't care what kind it is." He thought of the train spotters, Euston Station, the crowds at St Pancras, his school holidays and the first time he had seen the *Flying Scotsman*, thundering north. He remembered his mother and father meeting him at Badminton Station, where geraniums hung in baskets. Fleetwood gazed at the grey, broken landscape and felt cast out.

"I wonder how the war is going," David said. "I wonder what happened at Kapyong." He remembered the regiment, the road to Chasan with the Scottish pipers playing.

"I expect we shall win," Fleetwood said. "We always do."

We are burglars in a neighbour's house, David thought, but said nothing. He thought of Mount Napier and Mount Abrupt rising from the plain, the Southern Ocean and the pine trees sculpted and driven by the wind. He wanted to be home.

They slept in the sun that day, undisturbed as the peasants worked in the paddies and the stream became a river.

When they came to it, they saw it was a large town with a line of sodium lamps; they could smell the sea and the mud flats. They lay in the brush on the slopes overlooking the buildings and heard the clattering and banging of rolling stock and the hiss of steam: it *was* Munsan. They shook hands.

"I must confess," David said, "I had my doubts, but we've made it." The trucks crashed in the marshalling yards. "What do you suggest?"

"That we stroll down right now and catch the train."

"Really?"

"Why not?" Fleetwood said. "We still look vaguely military, one of us shoulders the rifle and we walk down to the railway. By the smell of it, the place has been bombed recently so it's probably a bit of a shambles." David shouldered the rifle and they continued down the track past the moonlit paddies.

Munsan was badly bombed: many houses and buildings were destroyed and rubble lay in the streets. They kept their eyes open for the familiar high walls of police stations, but they saw none and they kept heading toward the sodium lamps. The goods sheds were wrecked, but coolies were loading the wagons as soldiers stood about. An old locomotive was steaming up on the south-bound track and they walked back behind the embankment.

"We're counting on the UN being in Seoul," Fleetwood said. "Do you remember what Kim said: 'We are at the very gates of Seoul.' It's a reasonable assumption. What's the distance from here? Can you remember?"

"About thirty miles." David glanced about for patrols. "They must be bombing the track by day."

"That's our chance," Fleetwood said, "but we're safer on the train than barging around the battlefield."

They waited in the dark by the embankment as the coolies worked.

They guessed it was about 02.00 when the old locomotive and its train started up. It was moving slowly, hissing, its wheels slipping and wagons banging, and two armed men walked alongside the track. The two soldiers were walking as fast as the train, but it gathered speed and overtook them.

"Thank Christ for that," Fleetwood said as they watched. The engine passed and they saw the driver and the fireman shovelling coal through the furnace door; the coals gleamed in the night and the pistons steamed and wheezed. The wagons ground by and they chose one covered with a ragged tarpaulin.

"Right," Fleetwood said, "this is it."

They rose from the embankment, leapt for the footplate, climbed the ladder and fell through a hole in the rotting canvas. David cut his arm on something sharp and cursed: the wagon was filled with ammunition boxes and light machine guns. They lay in the oil and grease: no one had seen them.

"So far, so good," David heard Fleetwood say. "Are you all right?"

"I've cut my arm. Nothing serious."

Fleetwood clambered up and peered out under the canvas. "There'll be lots of stops."

"We'll have to time it, we want the last one." David felt for some grease and plastered it on his arm as the train ground slowly through the night. It stopped seven times during the next several hours and they heard voices and the sound of crowbars and shovels as labour gangs cleared the line. They made themselves comfortable as best they could and took it in turns to watch. Now and again flashes lit the sky and artillery could be heard: they were getting near the front. The train stopped once more and a truck started up nearby.

"This is the end of the line. All passengers out," Fleetwood said.

David sliced a hole in the tarpaulin with the bayonet, they dropped to the ground and ran off into the dark. The sky was lightening and as they dashed through the paddies, jets flew low and strafed the train. Starfighters, David thought. God bless the Americans.

*   *   *

The valley was broad; wrecked tanks lay in the river and the hills were pockmarked with gun pits and craters. Stalled amphibians were burning on the sandbanks and howitzers flashed and thudded as the false dawn faded. The road was packed with men, mules, trucks, bicycles and porters carrying A-frames moving toward the front. Lorries and houses were burning in the night, flares exploded, machine guns rattled and more jets came over, firing tracers. David stopped and Tom said: "Keep moving, for Christ's sake, we've got to look as though we're going to the front."

Hurricane lamps flickered in the dark and men shouted: it looked like a company and they leapt into a ditch and listened to the soldiers going by. The harnesses creaked and the wheels rumbled as the column passed. The ditch was wet and foul and a dead horse lay reeking.

"How far do you think Seoul is?" Tom said.

"About ten miles south, what's left of it. It's obvious now the Chinese haven't retaken it. Maybe the Imjin show wasn't for nothing."

"I don't like this road very much," Tom said. "Do you want to cut away across the paddies?"

"Yes."

As they clambered from the ditch, something exploded near the railway line; the sky was lit, the ground shook and they ran.

*   *   *

They saw the platoon at first light; the Chinese were trudging back through the paddies away from the front. The ground was drowned and flat and there was no cover. The leading soldier brandished his burp gun in the streaky dawn as the Long Toms and the 25-pounders rumbled. There was no way out of it and they ran toward the enemy troops.

Fleetwood raised the rifle and shouted, "Sovietski, Moskova, Ivanovitch."

David, too, shouted, "Novaya Zemlya." He saw the Chinese were carrying litters of dead and wounded. It looked like a medical team. "Pravda," he shouted, "Pravda".

Fleetwood reached the leading Chinese, embraced him and kissed him on both cheeks; then he saw the dead and wounded and bowed deeply. "Seoul? Seoul?" he said, and the Chinese pointed.

"Muchas gracias," David said, "muchas gracias." And they ran south through the sodden, bloodied rice fields.

It was now daylight and David felt his back was broken; his legs shook and his lungs were bursting. My God, my God, he prayed, please help me. I can't run much more. In the battle, he tried to pick up familiar sounds: Brens, Brownings, .75s, the squeal of tank tracks, but there were none he knew. Fleetwood fell into the mud and rice stalks, raised himself, gestured at David and ran on. Where were the American lines? Where were the jeeps, the GMC trucks, the Shermans and the Chaffees? Only God knew. They saw another group of Chinese dragging a mortar and then a

272

column moving east. David and Tom crouched behind a shrine and watched as rain began to fall.

"We don't seem to be getting very far, do we?" Tom said, "and my Russian vocab's run out."

"We must meet the forward patrols soon." David squinted through the rain, saw the column of Chinese coming toward them, listened to the crackle of fire and the hammering of the artillery. It seemed hopeless now. Then a squadron of Corsairs appeared from the south, strafing and dropping napalm. The Chinese disappeared in the oily smoke and it seemed the whole valley was on fire. One last time, they gathered themselves up and ran from the shrine along a narrow path between the broken terraces and bunds. At a road junction they saw a Sherman, its .75 pumping and a jeep close by. The Browning crackled and the Sherman lumbered into the lee of a grove of broken poplars.

"Is that the Americans I see?" Tom said, and threw down the Japanese rifle. They ran forward, their hands in the air; David shouted and laughed, saw the familiar helmets and uniforms and they both fell by the side of the Sherman. It was the Americans and they were safe.

13

Elinor

"David," Charles Bryant said, "welcome back."

They shook hands and Charles put his arm around David's shoulders as they stood about in the driveway. The sky was cloudless and the noonday light blinding. A fire was burning near Mount Napier, the smoke rising from the gum trees; the lawn was brown and dead and lizards scuttled over the gravel. His mother and father stood beside the Vauxhall and greeted their old friend.

"Keith Miller's still there," his father said.

"Good," Charles Bryant said, but David was thinking of Don Bradman and Major Kim. A young woman was standing beside him. She was tall and slender and wearing a white summer dress; her hair was dark and pinned up around her neck; her eyes were large and brown and her arms and legs tanned. She was very beautiful. "David," Charles said, "this is Elinor."

She smiled and held out her hand, and he took it.

"Shouldn't we go inside, Charles?" David's mother said. "It's dreadfully hot out here."

"I'm sorry, Elizabeth," Charles said, "but this is Australia, isn't it?"

The white parakeets called and settled on the branches as they went inside. David walked alongside Elinor. She was wearing sandals and her pearl necklace gleamed around her throat. His mother walked ahead, alone, toward the front door as his father wiped his brow.

"Another day over the century," his father said.

Elinor looked at David in his grey slacks and white shirt: he looked lean and strong and was getting sunburnt.

The front room was dark and cool, some of the venetian blinds were down and the floor was of polished wood. There was an old grand piano, shelves of books, cane furniture, nests of tables and dried flowers in tall vases. David sat in an armchair by the bay window and looked out at the dry landscape. After the mountains of Korea, it was flat, endless and disturbing. He had thought that dusty plains would comfort him, but they seemed unfamiliar now and the ranges to the west were obscured by the haze. Where was Mount Abrupt? He saw Elinor Bryant disappear toward the kitchen and heard the clink of glasses. He wondered if there might be bush fires this summer and remembered the dust storms from the north. Charles turned on the radio for the cricket and stood in the centre of the front room in his white shirt, pressed moleskin trousers and brown leather boots. He was still a big, handsome man. He ran his hands through his thick grey hair and said: "Well, Miller's still there. I think the South Africans may be harder to beat than the Poms." He smiled at David's mother. "No offence, Elizabeth."

She smiled back. She had always liked Charles; he was unlike most of the other men in the district. There was gossip because Elinor was almost twenty years younger, but Charles was charming and well-bred and had been devoted to his first wife, Mary, throughout her illness, so why should he not marry Elinor as long as he was happy?

"Charles," Elizabeth Andersen said, "I don't mind at all. We all know colonials are strong men." Charles put a tray of drinks down and bowed in the centre of the large, cool room with its comfortable furniture, paintings and oriental wall hangings. "What would you all like to drink?" He turned to David who was still looking out of the window. "You're our guest of honour, David," he said. "What would you like?"

David didn't reply, then saw they were all looking at him and said, "I'll have beer, thanks."

A large black and white cat was sleeping on the cushions

in the bay window. "Whose cat is that?" he said. He'd always hated the animals; they were untrustworthy and their affection false.

"It's mine," Elinor said.

She sat on the piano stool, her white dress draped over her bare, brown legs.

David didn't reply. He thought of asking her if the cat had a name, but decided not. He wondered what the music on the grand piano was. Did Elinor play? He stared back out of the window. "Do you want a shandy or a straight beer, David?" Elinor said.

"Straight, please." He glanced at his parents: his mother had opened *Better Homes and Gardens* and his father was listening to the radio. A cool breeze was blowing through the open hall door and David considered Elinor. He had never encountered a woman as striking before. Mrs Bryant had died of cancer in 1949 when he was at Duntroon. Elinor rose from the piano stool, smoothed her dress and walked over to the table. The cat stretched and licked itself and somewhere, from the back of the house, dogs barked. David thought of the Chinese soldiers and their dogs in the paddies. Tomorrow, he would go and visit his grandfather's grave on the windswept hill where the snakes slept in the sun and the rabbits ran. *You'll soon be as strong as a bull, old son.*

"You've left the army, David?" Elinor Bryant said. "Your father's just told me."

He took the beer from her hands as she sat next to him.

Cheering and clapping came from the radio and his father turned up the volume. "Miller's out," he said. "Caught on the boundary. But there's still young Craig, there'll be no worries."

David's mother looked up from her magazine. "Where are they playing?" she said.

"It doesn't matter," her husband said. "It doesn't matter."

"You've left the army?" Elinor asked.

"Yes," he said. He drank his beer and looked at her. The beer was cold and refreshing and the glass wet on his fingers. "Do you play the piano?"

"Yes, I do."

Charles and his father were hunched by the radio listening to the cheering and the clapping. It sounded as though someone had scored a six. His mother turned the pages and sipped her lemon squash.

"Do you play?" Elinor said.

"No, I never learnt."

She looked at his spare, bony frame, his neat civilian clothes, his hard blue eyes and short-cropped blond hair. She thought he must have been a most efficient soldier. "What music do you like?"

"Elgar, Edward Elgar," David said. "*Pomp and Circumstance.*"

Elinor laughed. "That's not very good music."

"Yes," David said. "Yes it is."

She shrugged her shoulders, the pearls at her throat, her cat sleeping, and her husband opening another bottle. More cheering came from the radio: it seemed that the Australians were winning, the game was within their grasp.

"Not all soldiers are without taste," David said. He thought of Tom Fleetwood. "One I knew liked *Don Giovanni.*"

"A friend of yours?"

"Yes. He was an officer in the Gloucesters."

Elinor stood up and left him and David listened to the cricket. He listened to the north wind, blowing around the house. The roses were dead in the garden. There was nothing he wanted to do. The two men were listening to the cricket and his mother was still reading, but Elinor had left the room. How long had she been married to Charles? She was hardly more than twenty-four and Charles was in his forties. That would have scandalized the locals. What did his mother think, and his father? His grandfather would have been all in favour. He reached over to stroke Elinor's cat, but it hissed at him. He withdrew his hand. It was getting hotter now and he dozed in the armchair by the window.

Charles was intrigued by David's appearance as he lay sleeping comfortably in the armchair. He looked like an Olympic runner; and he had been mentioned in dispatches: the whole district was proud of him.

It was time for afternoon tea. Should one of his parents wake him up? But David woke on his own: he was having a bad dream about Paul Cash and Sergeant Hart; it was something to do with a rosary. The room seemed darker and his mother was saying, "Really, David, your manners, going to sleep. You're lucky you're with friends."

Elinor was back and put a cup of tea on a table by the armchair. It was like being a patient in a hospital. David drank quickly and stood up. "If no one minds, I'll go for a short walk. I've not seen the garden for ages."

"I'll come with you," Elinor said.

"Please do."

"Mind the sun," his mother said, "and don't be long. I want to be home by six."

David saluted and smiled, but did not reply. As he went down the hall into the sunlight, he heard his name mentioned. They were talking about him. He didn't care. The rose garden was a handsome, ornamental place with a bird bath, seats and winding paths. A gazebo stood on a grassy rise by the oaks and cypresses. The sun beat down and the hot wind scattered the dead leaves and twigs. Elinor came up. She was wearing a straw hat and her sandals crunched on the gravel.

"You should wear a hat too," she said. The wind blew at her white dress and she pulled it down over her legs.

David shoved his hands into his trouser pockets. "It's not that hot."

"It is, you know," Elinor said. "Let's sit in the gazebo, it's cooler there." They walked up the path through the

278

English garden, where Indian mynahs swooped and flew.

"I've never liked mynahs," Elinor said, "have you?"

"I'm afraid I've never considered them." David thought of the kites and buzzards wheeling and attacking in Korea.

"Mynahs are predatory, inquisitive birds," Elinor said. "They don't belong here." They walked on without speaking. Clouds were gathering in the south behind Mount Napier: a weather change was coming.

"When did you marry Charles?" David said. He laughed. "I used to call him Uncle Charles, but I suppose that's a bit odd now."

She laughed too. "You can hardly call me Aunt Elinor, can you?"

"No, I can't." He thought of asking her what people thought of Charles Bryant marrying someone young enough to be his daughter, but didn't. It was none of his business. They sat in the gazebo on the wooden seats, where sparrows and blackbirds pecked and poked in the dust.

"I looked after Charles's wife until she went to hospital," Elinor said. "Then I went away for a year and came back. It was all quite proper." She took off her hat and shook out her dark hair. "Some people have talked, but I don't care."

"They all talk in small country towns," David said. "There's nothing else to do." He sniffed. "The weather, wool prices and affairs."

"When did you return?" Elinor asked.

"Four months ago."

"This is a hot summer. Do you find it uncomfortable?"

David laughed. "Yes, I do. I never thought that would happen. Korea's not exactly tropical."

"Is it odd to be back?" Elinor said.

"Yes, it is."

"How?"

"So much has happened. I was a boy when I left."

"You're hardly a boy now," she said. "Who was the man who liked *Don Giovanni*?"

"Tom Fleetwood, the officer in the Gloucesters. We escaped together."

"Escaped?"

"We got captured at the battle for the Imjin and spent several weeks on the run in the mountains." He tried to make light of it. "*Boy's Own Paper* stuff."

"But it wasn't, was it?"

"No."

"What were you good at?" she said. She hadn't met a professional soldier before.

"Good at?"

"Your skills."

"I was an officer," David said. "I looked after my men, I made sure they all came back."

"From what?"

"From patrol or battle." He remembered Jones and Kershaw. "Some of them didn't, but I did my best." The wooden seat in the gazebo was uncomfortable and he twisted his body.

"Why did you join the army?"

David looked at her and considered the question. What should he say? "Soldiering's an honourable profession."

"You were mentioned in dispatches?"

"I was." It seemed a long time ago.

Elinor looked across the garden. "It's a marvellous house," she said.

"It's been in the Bryant family a long time," David said.

"No, *Killara*."

"My house?" David said.

"Yes, yours."

"Oh, yes." The house and the farm held him together now. He didn't want to work it, just own it: the house, the outbuildings, the stock and the slopes of Mount Rouse. *I am Lord of all I survey.* "I'd better be getting back," he said. "My mother will be champing at the bit. It's been nice talking to you. Charles is a good man, you're very lucky."

"Come again, David," Elinor said.

"Thank you, I will if I'm over this way." He gave her the straw hat and they went back to the house. Nothing more was said.

*　　*　　*

David stood on the top of Mount Rouse and looked west and south. The plains stretched south to the ocean and west to the mountain ranges; the townships sprawled, their low-slung buildings trailing away on each side of the highway. The lakes and dams shone in the early summer sunlight, and in the paddocks lone chimneys stood; the power poles disappeared into the horizon and the tides ran through the wheatfields, around the battered chimneys and deserted hearths. Beyond the belts of pines he could see the bluestone mansions of the wealthy graziers, flags flying from their turrets. The summer breeze blew through the sedge and flax, and terns and sea-swallows flocked by the lakes. The fire was still burning near Mount Napier, but the smoke was lighter now: it was burning itself out. This place, David thought, holds me together. Each house was self-sufficient with its cowshed and chicken pen, its vegetable patch and flowers and shrubs. And in the paddocks lay abandoned Fords, Chevrolets, trucks and threshing machines among the outbuildings that rambled across the landscape. This is my land, David thought, this is my land. He thought of the still lakes, the charcoal burners' fires and the straight rain in the paddies of Korea.

*　　*　　*

David walked down the winding track on to the gravel road, past the quarry and along the fence line where the sheep browsed among the rocks. He thought of Elinor Bryant and her questions in the rose garden. He thought of Tom Fleetwood and the helicopters moving in and the American medics running toward him across the smashed streets of Seoul. He remembered the Korean children screaming. David strode to the highway, past the stone walls of Mr Schultz's farm and then of *Killara*. He passed the mailbox, looked inside, but it was empty. No newspapers and magazines from England today; it was Sunday and his mother was at Holy Communion in Hamilton. He walked down the highway toward Penshurst, its convent, churches, pub, grocery store and Masonic Lodge. He reached the town war memorial and stood, uncertain, as the roosters crowed. A train hissed and steamed in the shunting yard, the wagons rattled and the land smelt of dry manure. Cows bellowed, the church bell rang and he paused up the street from St James's where the parishioners were gathered in their black suits and summer frocks, their prayerbooks in their hands. They looked dour and weather-beaten as they stood in the sun, the men rolling their cigarettes and the women chatting to the vicar. He remembered Mr Dickson and the Sunday afternoon lessons in the draughty parish hall: he must be retired or dead by now. One of the men was pointing at him and he crossed the street and walked around the back of Schram's garage: he didn't want to be recognized. The War Hero was back and they might hold a special function for him; he hoped to Christ, not. He could see why his mother went to church in Hamilton.

The Penshurst District School stood on the corner, built of bluestone and ugly with corrugated iron shelter sheds and rusting outbuildings. The pepper trees were scarred and the picket fence collapsing. David remembered the timetables, the strap, the carved desks, having to sit with girls, and the bullying on icy winter afternoons as he tried to run up the hill to *Killara* and his mother. He remembered the stories of bravery and valour: *Robert Bruce and the Spider, Kiss Me, Hardy, Sir Philip Sidney*, Burke and Wills and Shackleton under the upturned boat in the winter of South Georgia. He thought of the King's Royal Rifles and the 1st 28th Gloucesters, Sergeant Hart and Paul Cash.

A truck rattled up and stopped and an old man got out. He was a wood man, the truck was laden with stringy-bark and he started to hurl the logs off into the school yard. He looked at David.

"Aren't you Mr Andersen's son?"

"Yes, I am."

"The boy who's been to the war?"

"That's right."

"You got back safe and sound?"

"Yes, I did."

The man stood on the back of the truck among the piles of wood; it was mossy and peeling and for the school stove.

"Well, good luck to you. I went to the first one, so you've got me luck."

"Thanks."

The man spat and went on hurling the stringy-bark and David wandered down the street where the crows perched on the stone walls and the thistles grew. He wondered what was happening in Korea and how the armistice talks were going. He would listen to the news tonight. He must not forget to write to Tom's mother. What was her name? St James's church bell rang again. Did Elinor Bryant go to church? He thought not. Then from behind the gum trees Bert Lawless appeared with his dogs sniffing and running close to the ground. Lawless was carrying his .22 over his shoulder and his shirt and waistcoat were open as he walked through the burnt stumps and thistles. It was too late to avoid him.

"Good morning," David said.

Lawless touched the brim of his slouch hat and moved on. David counted in his head; his father had employed Lawless for sixteen years now. When jobs were scarce, men kept the ones they had.

*   *   *

It was one o'clock and the three of them sat at the luncheon table. The windows were open and the venetian blinds fluttered in the warm wind. His mother passed around the cold beef and salad and his father drank his lager. He had put on weight and was going grey. David's plate was filled with sliced meat and cold potato.

"Eat it up," his mother said. "You've grown awfully thin."

His father got up and went toward the radio.

"Where are you going, Richard?" his mother said.

"I want to listen to the cricket."

"It's Sunday and it's not on. At least I know that much."

"I'd forgotten."

"How was Hamilton?" David said.

"Hamilton?"

"Church."

"Where did you go this morning?" his father said.

"I walked to the top of Mount Rouse and then I went to the village."

"The township."

"Hamilton was just the same," his mother said. "It never changes. Nothing ever changes. What did you think of Elinor Bryant?"

"She's a very striking young woman," David said.

"Not too young for him, do you think?"

"I've got no idea."

"I'm going to have a game of golf this afternoon," his father said. "Do you want to come?"

"You know I don't play golf, Dad."

"I just thought I'd ask you. You could learn and I expect one or two of the chaps would like to talk to you."

"Not today, Dad." He picked up his cold meat. Why to Christ didn't they ask him about the war? But if they did, what would he tell them?

"Elinor nursed Mary Bryant for a year," his mother said. "She ran the place, poor Charles, he was so busy."

Richard Andersen topped up his glass. "She's a good-looker, there's no doubt about that."

"You should know, Richard."

"What's Korea like?" his father said.

"Like?"

"I must say I'm still not quite sure where it is." Richard Andersen folded a slice of meat on to his fork and put it into his mouth. He drank his beer.

"She's twenty years younger than he is," Elizabeth Andersen said. "Her father was a doctor in Hamilton."

David thought of Elinor in her white dress and sandals. "Korea's mountainous, it's a bad place for armour."

"Armour?"

"Tanks, Crusaders and Centurions. The roads are bad and there are refuelling problems." Should he tell them about the sniper caught in the harness? He put his knife and fork down on his plate.

"We've still got a very good chance," his father said.

"At what?" Elizabeth watched her son at the table.

"At the cricket," Richard Andersen said. "What else?"

David looked around at the dining room, at the ormolu clock, the Hepplewhite chairs, the firescreen, the sideboard and the *chaise longue*. Nothing had changed: the dried tea-tree still stood in the brass vase and the walls were stained from countless winters. He remembered the gulls flying and the possums scuttling in the ceiling as he lay in his bed upstairs when he was young.

"She took great care of Mary," his mother said. She passed David some more cold lamb.

"I hope they have children. It's a marvellous property and it would be a shame if it went out of the family."

David pushed his plate back and watched his father opening a fresh bottle. "Thank you, Mother, that was good. There's nothing like home-cooked food. It's much better than the army's." He thought of the cold C-rations and the men brewing up in the ice on the road to Chasan.

"You haven't eaten much."

285

"If you don't want to play golf," his father said, "what will you do?"

'I'm going for another walk. I'm going to see Grand-father's grave." It's none of your bloody business, David thought.

"It's an ugly cemetery," Elizabeth said.

"Most cemeteries are."

"But Penshurst's is particularly ugly."

"I don't think that matters," David said. "The dead are dead, and that's the end of it."

"How morbid."

"I've become used to death," David said to both to them. The venetian blinds were banging in the wind now. "Please excuse me."

*　　　*　　　*

On the road to the cemetery, David saw a rider coming up, and as the horse got closer, he recognized Elinor in a blouse, jodhpurs and riding boots. She was riding a big bay gelding and her hair was tied back. Dust rose from the horse's feet and its hooves scattered the gravel.

"Hullo," she said, "where are you going?"

He squinted up at her with surprise. "I'm taking a walk to the cemetery."

"To the cemetery? That's a long way."

"It's a long time since I could walk without being shot at or pursued."

She remained on the horse: its flanks shone and it was in fine condition. "But why the cemetery?"

"My grandfather's buried there."

"Oh," Elinor said, jumped down and stood in front of him. "He died while you were away, didn't he?"

"Yes."

"And you loved him?"

"Yes."

"And he loved you. He told me."

"You knew him then?"

"Not for long, but we became good friends. A marvellous man, always talking about you; he was proud to have a grandson as a soldier. You look very like him." She wiped her face with her silk scarf. "God, it's getting hot. Let's find some shade, and you've got no hat on."

"Neither have you."

"But I'm used to it and you're not."

They walked over to a pine tree. Elinor was dark-skinned and her hair black and shining. Was she Jewish? He thought not. Celtic perhaps? She tethered the horse to the fence, sat on a stump and grinned.

"Where are *you* going?" David said.

"I was coming to see you."

"Me?"

"Yes, you."

"Why?"

"Because I wanted to. Charles has gone to Mortlake to look at some rams, and your father's playing golf and your mother's probably having a nap. Poor old you."

"You seem to know a lot about the Andersen family."

"Do I? I'm a bit sharp, you've guessed that already, haven't you?"

"How far is it to the cemetery?" David asked.

"Have you forgotten? About three miles, I should think. Can you ride?"

"Of course."

"We could double up on Julius, he's big enough."

"Julius?"

"My horse."

"No thanks, I'd rather walk." He didn't know if he was pleased to see her or not: he had planned to be alone. He didn't want to talk and he didn't want to answer questions, but he was surprised she was coming to see him.

"Walk, why?" Elinor said.

"I need the exercise and I like walking."

"All right then, I'll walk with you, or do you want to be

by yourself?" Elinor shrugged and smiled again. "I don't mind." She sat on the stump in her blouse and jodhpurs and fiddled with her riding crop. "Really, I don't mind at all."

David looked at her sitting on the stump, her legs apart, and said: "I'd like you to come."

"All right," Elinor said. "That settles it, we can always double back if our legs give out."

David looked at his watch: it was 2.30 and they set off down the road as the birds flew and the cicadas sang in the hawthorn hedges.

* * *

They ambled up the road where the pines grew and the flies buzzed. Elinor looked at him, took off her scarf and gave it to him. "Here," she said, "put this around your neck."

"I don't need it."

"Don't be silly, you're getting like a tomato." She waved it in the breeze. "Put it around your neck, or you'll die of sunstroke."

He did as he was told. The scarf smelled of her body.

"Thanks," David said.

The weatherboard houses needed painting, their iron roofs were rusting, the gardens neglected and pigs and chickens browsed among the logs and discarded trucks and machinery. Hollyhocks and hydrangeas grew, but the wild daffodils were withering and dying. At one house an old couple were asleep on a sofa on the front veranda. The Sunday afternoon was dusty and quiet and the Jersey cows stood motionless by the tanks in the dry paddocks.

"*Tobacco Road*," Elinor said.

"What's that?"

"A novel of moral turpitude in America's Deep South. It was banned, but I read it on the sly."

David peered through the trees at the couple sleeping.

"They don't look turpitudinous to me. More like Rip and his wife, I'd say."

"Rip?"

"Van Winkle."

"Ah." Elinor walked by his side and her horse followed them.

"Isn't it hard to leave the army?" she said.

"They try to persuade you to stay, but it's not a convent."

"Well, why did you get out?"

"I didn't get out, I resigned."

"Oops, why did you resign?"

David thought. Should he try to explain it to her or not?

"If I say it myself, I was a good soldier."

"I'm sure you were; you still look like one."

"I wasn't prepared for defeat, I wasn't prepared to be hunted, I liked soldiering, but I didn't count on death."

"Surely all soldiers count on death?"

'We don't," David said. "It's always the enemy."

"But you haven't become a pacifist?"

"Christ no, I'm proud of my record. But I saw men I loved killed and I couldn't take that risk again." David kicked at the dirt and thought of Jones's wife sobbing in the kitchen. "The army considered my application favourably."

"May I ask why?"

"I was mentioned in dispatches."

"Yes, we all know. For bravery?"

"Yes, what else?"

"And were you brave?"

David stopped in the middle of the road where the sparrows fluttered. "Of course I was."

She didn't ask him what he had done and he liked her for that.

"Have you seen that hedge?" Elinor said.

"It's been there as long as I can remember." He stopped. "What's the art of hedge-cutting called?"

"Topiary."

"That's it, topiary." The fir hedge kept invaders out: he had seen it over sixteen years ago. It had turrets, arches, crenellations, towers and arrow-slit windows.

"I wonder why they grew and cut it?" David said.

"To keep trespassers out, I suppose. I must show it to Charles."

"I expect he's seen it."

"I don't think so. If he had, he would have mentioned it to me." Elinor stood in the middle of the road and looked at the sky. "There's a weather change coming."

"Where were you born?" David said. "Around here?"

"Not really, a place called Edenhope, my father was the general practitioner there. Have you been to Edenhope?"

"Yes, I have, once or twice." He thought of the Mallee dust storms and the soldier-settlers in the Depression.

"My father," Elinor said, "had the biggest practice in the whole of Victoria." She laughed. "The biggest in size, but the smallest in numbers, so we shifted to Hamilton. He was a very good doctor."

"Was?"

"He's dead."

"What was he like?"

"A bit like your grandfather: he liked pretty girls."

David wanted to ask where she met Charles Bryant, but didn't. "Where did you go to school?"

"St Catherine's, Melbourne, and I loved it. And you?"

"Melbourne Grammar."

"Did you like it?"

"Yes, finally."

"Finally?"

David kicked at a stone and wondered what he should tell her. He knotted Elinor's scarf around his neck; it felt like his now. "I didn't at first, but I was good at running and the cadets."

"Sprint or long distance?"

"The mile." He laughed. "I'm a lean and hungry man."

"Yes," Elinor said as she looked at him. "You are. And the cadets?"

"I was the Regimental Sergeant Major."

She laughed. "Really?"

"I was."

"What did you do?"

"I was very efficient, they all feared me."

"Why was that?"

"I never made a mistake."

Elinor said no more and they walked to the south as the clouds bunched up from the coast.

They walked toward the high ground, her horse following. The horizon shimmered, the stone walls stood by the side of the road, and the weatherbeaten trees grew on the boundaries of the paddocks where sheep and cattle browsed in the summer sun. The dragonflies hovered over the ponds and ditches; and the butterflies flew over the dry land, through the grass and thistles, past the barns and implement sheds where the tractors and antediluvian machinery lay in the brown grass of the long summer. An eagle hung in the clear blue, dived and disappeared; a cow bellowed and a prime Hereford bull drank at a trough. Wild flowers grew at the roadside. The ranges and Mount Abrupt rose from the plain and the locusts and cicadas sang. They walked for some time, saying nothing, and David wondered what Elinor was thinking about. She walked easily and the dust rose from her riding boots. She was strong and graceful.

The cemetery lay on high ground, facing east; the little wooden chapel was gutted, its windows vacant and doors smashed. Rabbits and bush rats ran through the grass and the white parakeets watched them from the pine trees. The gate was broken, Elinor tethered her horse and they walked down the weedy path. Many of the graves were unmarked and David wondered who the people were. Had they died during the Depression? David stopped and looked at a headstone.

L/Corp Jack Townley
Killed in Action, Messines Ridge
8 June 1917, aged 22 years

Elinor touched his arm. "I know where it is," she said. She
led him down the slope, through the weeds and cypresses,
and showed him the grave.

Alistair Kinross Andersen
Born 1879
Died 1951
Blessed are the Dead

David knelt on the gravel and Elinor stood beside him.

"If you don't mind, David," she said, "I think I'll ride
home now."

The north wind blew through the grass and he didn't
reply.

*　　*　　*

When he got up and walked toward the gate, he remembered he had her silk scarf. He looked down the shallow
landscape, but she was gone.

14

Trespass

David woke to the sound of the station bell, and looked around his room. The blowflies buzzed and the sun shone in dusty shafts through the casements. The birds called outside the window and as he lay in bed he thought of Tom Fleetwood, of the Chinese soldiers clambering up the barren slopes of Hill 235 and Major Kim. Tom had written three times since Seoul; the last letter was from Gloucestershire where he was on leave. Tom said that now David had re-signed his commission, he was free to come to London to have that long-promised drink at "The Grenadier" and to chase debs and to go rambling in Gloucestershire and Wales; but England seemed a long way away now and David knew he wouldn't ask his parents for the fare. It was nine months since their escape, but the memory of it was still very clear and he remembered the North Korean soldiers in their white smocks, the dead children on the road to Chasan and the English tank commander with his Kent cigarettes and Erwin Rommel glasses. The war was still dragging on, despite the truce talks. It was hardly reported in the papers and he had to listen to the BBC for news. Few people knew or cared what was happening in the mountains and paddies of Korea. Was Kim still in Tuju-ri, rolling his cigarettes and feeding his dog? *How is Mr Bradman, Mr Andersen?* David laughed, lay on his back and wondered about Elinor Bryant. Then he remembered he still had her silk scarf; he would have to return it to her, but how would he do that? He wanted to see her again. Could he not return the social call? But she was married. *You are a disloyal dog, Mr Andersen.* He thought about the Chinese sniper and Sergeant Hart:

thank God he didn't have to see him any more. Outside in the early summer sun, the dogs were barking and the tractor started; his father was already at work, and he should be up helping him. They seemed to have nothing to say to each other and it was all a bit awkward. What had happened between his mother and father? She seemed like a displaced person and should never have come to Australia. He thought of *Country Life* and the picture of the manor house: for her, the time and place were out of joint. The floor boards creaked and there was a knock at the door. "May I come in, David?" It was his mother's voice.

"Yes, Mother."

She was carrying a tea tray and he could smell the hot-buttered toast and marmalade. Elizabeth's face was thin and her fair hair streaked with grey; David sat up straight in bed and felt guilty: he should have been up at 0600 hours.

"You needn't have done that." She was still beautiful. Elizabeth looked at the mention in dispatches, framed in black on his bedroom wall, and said: "It's no trouble, and I wanted to have a talk." She passed him the cup of tea. "It's good to have you back, David."

"It's been four months now." Sugar was in his tea, but he swallowed it down.

Elizabeth sat on the end of his bed as she had done throughout his childhood. She tidied her hair and smoothed her dress. "There's no news from your friend, Tom Fleetwood?"

"You always get the mail, don't you? I think he may have gone to Kenya."

"Why would he have gone there?"

"The blacks are causing trouble and I read somewhere the Gloucesters were being sent to sort things out."

"How unfortunate."

David thought about the colonel addressing them on the last day of the battle for the Imjin as the men lay dying in the rocks and bloodied brambles. "War," he had said, "is generally unfortunate." The toast was cold and the marmalade dry. Once again, he thought of Elinor on her bay gelding by the pine hedge and the north wind blowing across the cemetery where his grandfather was buried. "What did you want to talk about?"

"We're both proud of you, David."

"Both?"

"Your father and I."

David swallowed the cold, sweet tea and fiddled with the fingers of toast. The dogs barked and he heard the tractor moving from the yard. There was work to do. "I should go and help Dad."

"I'm sure he can manage quite well without you."

It was like being ill again and David wanted to get out of bed and escape her questions. "If you don't mind, Mother, I want to get up."

"What are you going to do?" she said.

"You mean why did I give up a good career?"

"I didn't say that."

"But that's what you mean." David laughed. "I could have been a general, had I stayed for thirty years."

"I don't know anything about the army."

"No, you don't."

"There's no need to snap." She sniffed and took the cup.

"I wasn't snapping. All I said was that you know nothing about soldiering. Thank God you don't."

"Soldiering?"

"Soldiers, Mother, kill each other." He watched her sitting on the bed end. Her blue eyes avoided him.

"What are you going to do?"

"About what?"

"You know, getting a job."

"I could stay here and help Dad."

"You don't like farming," his mother said.

"And neither do you, at least not the Australian kind."

"Why do you say that? I'm perfectly happy here." She

295

pulled out her embroidered handkerchief. "It's the summers I don't like."

And the other three seasons, David thought, the fires, the floods, the killing and the house where possums scuttled in the roof and rotting timbers. "I wonder how Tom is?"

"Tom?"

"Fleetwood."

"You said he was in Kenya, fighting the blacks."

"I don't know that, I said I thought he might be there."

"We worry about you."

"We?" David said. He thought of Kim and the inquisition, the frightened Korean girl in the corner of the room.

"Your father and I."

David raised his knees under the sheets. "There was one man who worried about me."

"One man? Who was that?"

"A man called Major Kim. He worried about my morals."

"Major Kim? But you said he was the enemy."

"He may have been the enemy, but he worried about my morals."

"How? I don't understand."

"He said I was a trespasser." *You are a mercenary.*

Elizabeth Andersen gathered up his breakfast. "I don't understand."

"I'll tell you what I'm going to do today."

"What?"

"I'm going to drive over to the Bryants'."

"The Bryants'? Why?"

"A social call," David said. His room was getting hot now and the sun was blinding. The ash lay in the fireplace. "They inv.ted me back."

"When?"

"When we had lunch."

"When you fell asleep?"

"When I fell asleep." David thought: when I sat in the gazebo and when the roses were dying in the garden. He

296

must write to Tom's mother and find out where he was. He thought of the small boy screaming as they dashed down the main street of the village in the mountains and stabbed with the bayonet.

"Why do you want to see the Bryants?" his mother said.

Because I want to see her again, David thought. "Because they asked me back and I thought I'd go today."

"Have you phoned them? It might not be convenient."

"It's early, not yet. But I shall."

"She's very young, you know."

"Who?" David said.

"Elinor Bryant, twenty years younger than he."

"I'm sure they're happy," David said. He thought of her white dress and bare legs and her scarf around his neck as they walked the long dusty road where the trees bent. One day, maybe, he would tell Elinor about the apple orchard, the Chinese sniper, the road to Chasan and Major Kim.

"Well, you'll have to decide soon what you're going to do," his mother said. "You don't like farming and there's nothing for you in Penshurst."

David looked at her as she took up the tray. "Yes, I'll have to decide." He threw off the sheets. "I must go and help my father." Elizabeth bent and went to kiss him, but he avoided her lips. "I'm proud of my mention," he said.

"We all are, dear."

"Grandfather would have been proud too."

"I'm sure."

His mother left the room with the tray.

*   *   *

The lager was icy and the smoked salmon sweet. Somewhere in the house, music was playing. It was *Don Giovanni* and he heard Elinor singing softly in the kitchen.

"I see the Indian peace plan has failed," Charles Bryant said.

"Where did you learn that?" David hoped Elinor would return to the table.

"Tucked away on the bottom of page four. It hardly gets the headlines, does it?"

"No," David said, "it doesn't. A lot of people don't even know where the place is."

"What's it like?" Charles said.

"The country or the war?"

"Both, and I'm not asking you out of idle curiosity, I would like to know."

Elinor came in and sat down by her husband. She drank her cold beer and listened. The faint music played and the house was dark and cool.

"Mountainous and messy," David said.

"Messy in what way?"

"Militarily and morally."

"Morally? There's no doubt who started it?"

"There's no doubt at all, but it's hard to tell which is the enemy when civilians are involved. Until the Chinese came in the enemy didn't wear any regular uniforms, so it was hard to tell who was on your side."

"So the wrong people were killed?" Elinor said.

"Yes. I suppose they are in any war." David laughed. "But I hadn't fought before."

"It was hard, then?" Charles said.

"Very, at least I found it so." David thought of Paul Cash on the road to Chasan. *He didn't die in vain, sir.*

"Were you badly treated as a prisoner?" Elinor said.

David thought. "No, not really, just questioned and threatened for hours by a very intelligent Korean officer. I was lucky I had a friend with me, so we could share it for some of the time."

"The Englishman," Elinor said. "Is he the man who knew *Don Giovanni*?"

David smiled at her. "Yes."

298

"Do you miss him?"

"Yes." They had run through the misty valleys together like the wind.

"Where is he now?"

"I'm not sure, I haven't heard from him for a month. I think he may have been posted to Kenya."

"The Mau Mau," Charles said. He motioned at the bottle, but David shook his head. "The Empire's going, isn't it? But it's good for wool prices." Charles laughed.

"So my father keeps saying."

"Of course it's good to be home?"

"Yes, it is," David said.

"Who's going to win?"

"We are," David said. "Wars are about winning."

"That's what both sides say."

"We will win," David said, "because we've got superior firepower." But he thought of the Chinese clambering up the ravines at the Imjin.

"What did you think of Truman sacking MacArthur?"

"It was a mistake," David said.

"You think so?"

"Yes."

"If you were in command, you'd have let MacArthur bomb north of the Yalu?"

David laughed. "Charles, you're the first man I've met who's heard of the river."

"I follow the news, David."

"You certainly do. I've just told you: wars are about winning. What's the point of stopping short of the enemy supply depots?"

"But the Chinese could have entered the war."

David laughed. "They were there anyway. I should know, I saw them, I fought them."

"Was there thought of using the bomb?" Charles asked.

"There were rumours. I don't think anybody in the field wanted it, we were the better side." But David thought of the nut-brown Chinese laughing after Imjin, of Kim and the columns of men and the peasants who turned their backs on the UN troops.

"What about the bomb tests?" Charles said. He drank his lager.

"The enemy test, we test; we have to be as strong as they are."

David was becoming irritated, but tried to conceal it. This was another interrogation: would Charles ask him where he got his hair cut? "I was a soldier of the line, and you do what you have to do."

"I'm sorry for the questions, David," Charles said, "but some of us have doubts."

"I've got no doubts, Charles. I may have left the army, but we've got to defend ourselves. We've got to hold what we've got and let no one take it away from us."

"What are the Koreans like?" Elinor asked.

"Poor, I've never seen people so poor."

He remembered struggling with the peasant, the woman screaming and the baby crying. "There are few roads and hardly any transport. It's like the Dark Ages and the climate is abominable. The Americans got it all wrong: you can't use tanks and trucks in Korea. All they were good at was getting their casualties out. It's a new kind of war, the French are having the same trouble with the Communists in Indo-China."

"I didn't know there was a war there," Elinor said.

"Well, there is. The Communists are led by a man called Ho Chi Minh, and he'll be hard to beat."

David looked at her crossing her long legs as she sat back from the table. The three top buttons of her blouse were undone, and her black hair was drawn back into a pony tail. Her breasts were small.

"Do you have any plans?" she said.

"I'll help my father for a bit, then I thought I'd go into business."

"Have you thought what kind?"

"Finance, stockbroking. I'm not going to be around the

District all my life." David laughed. "They still help returned soldiers, don't they?" He got up from the table, tall and sinewy, and ran his hand through his fair hair. He looks like a racehorse, she thought. "Thanks for the lunch," David said, "it was most enjoyable."

Charles also got up and kissed Elinor on the nape of her neck. "I'll clear away; you two go into the front room and talk."

* * *

"Do you want some music?" Elinor said. "We've just bought a long-player."

"Yes, I would."

"What would you like? There's not a great deal, we're just starting to collect."

"Whatever you like, I'm not fussy."

"Do you like Frank Sinatra?"

"I've never really listened to him."

"David Andersen," Elinor said, "everybody listens to Frank Sinatra."

"I've heard the name somewhere, but I can't place the voice." He watched her as she bent over the shelf and riffled through the records. She returned and said: "You're kidding me, aren't you?"

He suddenly felt young and light-headed. "Yes, Elinor Bryant, I'm kidding you."

"Do you dance?"

"Not for ages. I learnt at school and it was terrible. Nobody knew what to do."

"Who were the girls?"

"Methodist Ladies."

"Especially brought in for the occasion?"

He remembered and smiled. "Yes, it was awful."

"You could have met me. St Catherine's could have been brought in."

"I suppose they could, but you wouldn't have noticed. I was ghastly: freckles, skin and bone."

"Well, you're not ghastly now."

David was flattered. "Thank you. Who did *you* have over?"

"The boys from Scotch. It was all very formal." She turned over more records. "I loved dancing, I was good at it."

Elinor was lithe. "I'm sure you were," he said.

"What did they play on the gramophone?" she asked him.

"The same as they played on yours, I expect: Joe Loss, Victor Sylvester. We jigged around wearing cotton gloves and our best school suits."

"Cotton gloves?"

"They thought our sweaty hands might stain the girls' frocks."

Elinor laughed. "Did your hands sweat?"

"Yes, they did."

"Then what did you do?"

"After what?"

"The dance."

"We all went back to the dorm. It was cold showers, then bed, and athletics training in the morning."

"For the mile?"

"For the mile. What happened at St Catherine's?"

"Much the same. We had a formal ball at the end of the year and the boys wore dinner suits. I had a ball gown, it was marvellous."

David had her silk scarf in his pocket; should he give it back to her? How could he? She hadn't mentioned the walk to the cemetery and she mightn't have told Charles. He heard his footsteps on the parquet and stared out of the window. Charles came in, sat on the sofa and stretched his legs in his moleskins.

"What will happen in Korea?"

"I told you, we shall win," David said. "We always do."

"I suppose it depends on what you mean by winning." Charles considered David once more. "If you'd known what it would be like, would you have gone?"

"Yes."

"Why?"

"Because I was a soldier: it was my profession."

"I must confess I'm not quite sure about all this," Charles said.

"When you're a soldier, you're a soldier and that's all there is to it."

"Ours not to reason why?" Charles sat up.

"You do the job as best you can."

"Don't soldiers have a code of honour?"

"Yes."

"Is it formal?"

"No, it's implied, you learn it."

"What is it?"

"Never let your men down." David thought of Kershaw and Brownlee dying in the ice. Was that his fault?

"There are rules, aren't there?" Charles Bryant asked.

David faced Charles. "In the army they're called standing orders."

"Are they written down?"

"Yes, they're written down."

"And what happens if you break a standing order?"

"You're tried; and if you're found guilty, you're punished."

"Look, you chaps," Elinor said, "I want to play a Frank Sinatra record. Does anybody mind?"

Charles laughed, rose to his feet and kissed her again on the neck. "Of course nobody minds. I still have some work to do." He bowed toward David. "This has been interesting, but may I be excused? You two can go on talking and listening to Frank Sinatra."

David, too, got to his feet. "It's about time I was going, the lunch was excellent and thanks for your hospitality."

"For God's sake, David," Charles said, "I've known you

since you were at primary school; you've no need to be so formal."

But David said, "It's the first time we've talked, isn't it?"

"It is indeed." Charles moved toward the door. "I shan't be long, Elinor." The door closed and he was gone.

David listened to Charles Bryant's boots on the front veranda. "Charles would have made a fine senior officer," he said.

Frank Sinatra sang on the LP but David didn't know the song.

"Christ, you're a bit pompous, David Andersen," Elinor said.

He flushed and looked away. "Pompous?"

"Yes, pompous. 'When you're a soldier, you're a soldier; never let your men down; Charles would have made a fine senior officer; if you're found guilty, you're punished; standing orders.' It's all shit."

David looked at her: it was like listening to Sergeant Hart. "So you don't believe in it then?"

"What?"

"Standing orders, morals."

"I believe in morals, not standing orders."

David didn't know what to say. He fished in his pocket. "I've got your scarf."

"Keep it, it's a present."

"Why?"

"Because you may get sunburnt again." Elinor got up and turned off the radiogram. "You're the first soldier I've met."

"There aren't too many of us."

She laughed and shifted her body in her dress. "No, there are not."

"Why haven't you mentioned our meeting yesterday?"

"Because I wanted to call on you, and it's nobody's business."

"Not your husband's?"

"His name is Charles. Why should he know?"

304

"Don't you tell him where you're going?"

Elinor laughed and bent to find another record. "Why should I tell him? It's none of his business; is it in standing orders?"

"No."

"Are women mentioned in standing orders?"

"Yes, they are."

"What is said about them?"

"That you should treat women as you would treat your mother."

"Jesus Christ," Elinor said, "Jesus Christ."

David thought he should leave now, but couldn't bring himself to it. He walked around the room and looked at the piano, the shotguns in the gun cupboard and the books on the shelves. H. G. Wells, *A Short History of the World*, *The Forsyte Saga*, *The Cruel Sea*, *Pride and Prejudice*. Two watercolours hung on the wall; one was of Mount Napier and the other of Mount Abrupt.

"Where did you get these?"

"They're mine."

"Yours?"

"I painted them." Elinor watched David stalking around the room. "Do you like them?"

"Yes, I do. You should have painted Korea."

"What would I have painted?"

"Mountains, rows of poplars, ruined temples, refugees. And the straight rain falling."

"Hiroshige," Elinor said.

"Who?"

"A Japanese painter."

David looked again at the books on the shelves. "What's *Kon Tiki* like?"

"It's a marvellous book, full of mysteries. Charles is reading it now, I'm sure he'll lend it to you when he's finished."

David faced her. "I like your watercolours."

"Thank you. Do you want to go for a walk?"

"I certainly would."

Elinor grinned. "Come on then." She stopped in the middle of the room. "Have you got a hat?"

"Yes."

"Where is it?"

"I put it on the hall stand."

She ran out and came back, holding his new panama. "Wow, put it on."

"What do you think?" David said.

"Very smart. Stay where you are, I'll get my parasol and we can perambulate."

The parasol was white and beneath it she looked beautiful. They stepped on to the front veranda, walked down the stone steps and strolled through the garden to the trees beyond. Charles Bryant saw them from the corner of the home paddock, went to shout a greeting, but stayed silent.

"Why *didn't* you mention our meeting yesterday?" David asked.

"I've already told you." She twirled the parasol.

"Wives usually tell their husbands where they're going."

"Well, I don't. I may be married to Charles, but I'm not his property."

"You're an unusual girl, then."

"I'm not a girl, I'm a woman."

He laughed. "Sorry."

They strolled along a narrow path as the insects sang and buzzed.

"You seem to know what's what," Elinor said.

"I don't understand."

"About the war." Her arms were bare and she was wearing no jewellery apart from her wedding ring.

"As I said to Charles, wars are about winning; make the other fellow die for his country. Is that being pompous?"

"No, don't take what I said too seriously. Who said that?"

"What?"

"Make the other fellow die."

306

"An instructor I once knew."

She stopped. "Have *you* made another fellow die for his country?"

He wondered what to say; she had asked the question. He stared straight at her. "What you are really asking, is have I killed anybody close up personally. Is that what you want to know?"

"Yes."

"The answer is, I have. Do you want me to tell you how I did it and what it was like?"

She stared back. "No, maybe later."

They stood on the path to the shearing sheds and wheat silos.

"At least you've asked me in your indirect way," David said. "It's more than anyone else has done." He kicked at the gravel with his new boots. "The second time was at night, so I couldn't see what I'd done."

"I don't want you to tell me any more," Elinor said.

The afternoon was hot and David was sweating in his shirt. The parakeets swooped and he thought of the kites and buzzards. Elinor undid her pony tail and her hair fell to her shoulders. She, too, was sweating and her shoulder blades were showing through her dress.

"You look marvellous in that panama," she said.

"And you look good under that parasol."

The sun was high and there was no shade. The dust rose and the cattle fed in the grass; the dams were half empty and the distant ranges shimmered in the heat. Old stone chimneys stood and many of the trees were dead, their stony branches pointing at the sky. Elinor walked tall and straight: she looked like an Aztec as they made for the row of pines. Sheep browsed, a bull stood alone at a dam and rabbits scuttled. There was nobody about. They reached the shade and sat down on the pine needles; she looked at David sitting cross-legged, his panama hat on the ground. Then she saw an eagle, hovering and wheeling, dropping in the down-draughts and winging away; it flew high and disappeared beyond a stand of gums. The ants ran upon the earth, the sun shone hard and bright and a truck battled down the highway.

"Did you see the eagle, David?" Elinor said.

"Yes, I did."

There was dust in her dark hair. The eagle had gone to some secret place in the Western Divide, the mountains that sprawled toward the desert where the red winds blew. Elinor lay on her back and looked up through the branches. "What was the Imjin battle like? No one knows about it here."

"No one knows about it anywhere, except the men who fought."

"What was it like, David?" Her voice was soft.

"Dreadful, many men were killed. It was a slaughter."

"What did you do?"

"I fought, I worked, it was hard work."

"Work?"

"Soldiers work like other people."

She wanted to ask him again about killing, death and dying, but could not. "Did you get hurt?"

"No, not a scratch. Very odd with all that metal flying about." David smiled. "I suppose God looked after me."

"Do you think he did?"

"Oh yes."

"Who was at the Imjin?"

"An outfit called the 1st 28th Gloucesters, a crack British regiment. I was the only Australian. I was the liaison officer and got caught. Unlucky, you might say, but there was Tom Fleetwood, a marvellous man, I'll never forget him. We made plans to meet in London, to stay in his flat and drink at a pub called 'The Grenadier'. I've got my doubts now."

"What was he like?"

"Tall, very good-looking, supposed to be somehow related to the Habsburgs, but I doubt that. He looked like Douglas Fairbanks."

"*The Khyber Rifles?*" Elinor said.

"Just like that."

"So such men exist?"

"They certainly do. You'd have fallen in love with him instantly."

"Would I? Why?"

"Tom had style, he was a thoroughbred."

"So I've got style?"

"Yes," David said, "I think you have. Tom would have gone for you."

"But David, I'm married." Elinor grinned.

"I shouldn't think that would have worried Tom."

Elinor was going to ask if it worried him, but decided against it. "Did he like you, even though you were an Australian?"

"Yes, Tom liked me. We were both public schoolboys." David looked at her lying on the pine needles with her parasol. I think my mother would have left my father for him, David thought. "There's something about the English officer class. He went to a school called Wellington. It's in the pine woods in Berkshire. A lot of them go on to Sandhurst. Major Kim was intrigued by him."

"Major Kim?"

"The North Korean officer who kept us captive in a small village. I'll tell you about him later."

"Will there be a later?"

"Yes," David said, "I hope so."

They sat in the shade of the pines and considered the plains, the cattle and the wheatfields. Elinor lay quite still and David wanted to touch her. *You are a mercenary, Mr Andersen.*

"I'm sorry I was pompous," he said.

"It doesn't matter, David," Elinor said. "It doesn't." She paused. "Why *did* you leave the army?"

"I've told you: I liked being a soldier, but I didn't like being at war."

"But you believed in what you were doing?"

"Of course. I still do." David thought of Demosthenes.

"We should be prepared to defend ourselves," he said. "The ash in the bread."

"Ash in the bread?"

"Something a master said on the first day at Grammar. He gave us a lecture about the enemy within the halls. He was a stern old bugger. I was dead scared of him."

"More than the officers in the army?"

David laughed. "I was an officer, a junior one, but an officer. I suppose some of the men were scared of me." He thought of Paul Cash crouched in the slit trench, fingering his rosary. "There was a man called Hart; he was one I was scared of."

"Why?"

"He was a veteran and a killer, he knew more than I did."

"What did he know?"

"He knew about the enemy, he knew when to move, he knew when to take them."

"I'm sorry, David, I can't understand."

He told her about the retreat to Chasan, the Chaffee tank and the two Chinese boys. "I was the killer," he said, "not Hart." *You bastards! You bastards!* "I flourished the Webley."

"I wonder where Hart is now," Elinor said.

"He's probably at Singleton Army Camp having a beer with the boys and, my God, I hope he stays there."

"Do you feel guilty?" Elinor asked.

"I'm not sure. It can't be life for life, eye for eye, it can't be as bad as that."

Elinor sat under the pine trees as the birds flew and the insects buzzed. David looked at her, fiddled with his panama hat and envied her husband: Charles was working on the property somewhere and he was sitting with Charles's wife. He leaned over gently and picked up the parasol: what was a girl like Elinor doing here? She should be in London or Paris.

"What are Korean women like?" she said.

"I don't know, I only saw one and I was accused of raping her." David watched Elinor as she sat up. "I didn't, of course."

"Who accused you?"

"Major Kim."

"Why would he do that?"

"It was part of his whole procedure: military and moral confusion. He was damned good at it. He followed the fortunes of King George and the two princesses, and Donald Bradman."

"And what did you do?"

"I laughed, sat down on the floor and made some kind of impromptu speech about lying and deceit."

"What did Tom Fleetwood do?"

"I think he sat down too."

"What happened to the Korean woman?"

"I don't know. She was sent to the front, I think. The charge was dropped."

"What was she like?" Elinor said.

"She was beautiful."

"And Major Kim?"

"He'd been a house boy at the Peninsula Hotel in Hong Kong, spoke perfect English. He was great at the moral questioning, mixed up with military matters. I admired him."

"Why?"

"He was dedicated to the cause. He said Tom and I were trespassers."

"Were you?"

"I suppose we were, I don't know." David twirled his panama, stood up, put it on and said: "I think it's about time we were getting back, don't you?"

"You're right," Elinor said, "I think you're right."

She gathered herself up, took her parasol and they left the stand of pines.

*　　*　　*

The ormolu clock ticked, the owls hooted and Elinor thought of David Andersen. She lay in bed, her arms around her husband as he slept. She thought of the school dances at St Catherine's, singing in the choir at St Paul's and shopping at George's on Saturday mornings. The ballroom, she remembered, was decorated with hyacinths and azaleas, balloons and streamers, and a small orchestra played. What were the tunes? *The Old Missouri Waltz, Tea for Two, Charmaine, My Blue Heaven*? Outside their house a dog howled and the midsummer moon shone through the blinds. What to do? The night was hot and smelt of ash: fires were burning on the rim of the plain. Elinor remembered the school rhyme:

> *St Catherine, St Catherine,*
> *Oh, lend me thine aid;*
> *And grant me that I may never die*
> *An old maid.*

Elinor shifted gently and lay under the sheets in her nightdress smiling gently. Her hair lay over her face. She stretched her legs, felt her breasts, and thought once more of the child she had never seen. She lifted her nightdress and ran her hands up her legs and thighs; she touched herself and dreamed of the rose garden at St Catherine's and secret conversations in the dark. *What did he do to you?* She kept her hands there, her fingers moving and caressing; David reminded her of the fair-headed boys at the Christmas ball, their nervous hands around her waist as she danced. *What did he do to you: was it number one, number two or number three?* She thought of David and the eagle as they sat beneath the pines. She must see him again during this long summer. At last Elinor shuddered, sighed and drifted into sleep, her hair spread upon her pillow.

*   *   *

"What do you think of David Andersen?" Charles said as they drank their tea on the veranda. The sky was cloudless: it was going to be another hot day.

"Intense, intelligent and self-opinionated."

"That's a bit hard, he's young."

"You forget, Charles, he's the same age as me."

"It's still hard."

"Well, you asked me."

"Even though he's been a soldier and fought in what I imagine is a very nasty war, he seems vulnerable."

"Vulnerable?" Elinor asked.

"Not of this world. He's an only child and his parents' marriage isn't exactly a resounding success."

She looked up. "Isn't it?"

"Richard committed an indiscretion years ago," Charles said, "and she's never forgiven him. There's no point in not forgiving, is there?"

"I'm not sure. I suppose if someone hurts you badly enough. . . . I wonder what they think of us." She wanted him to talk about their marriage.

"I'm sure Elizabeth disapproves and he casts his eye over you. Poor old Richard's a closet lecher."

"I think he's rather dull. What was the indiscretion, do you know?"

"It happened about sixteen or seventeen years ago, the local school teacher, the children found her dead in the school house."

"Dead?"

"She was pregnant by him and tried to get rid of it."

"So he abandoned her? Richard Andersen's a bastard."

"For a girl with a private school education, your language is robust. I would say that Richard's conduct was unbecoming to a gentleman."

"Rubbish, the man's a bastard, he deserted her. And you think Elizabeth disapproves? Of what?"

"Of your being nineteen years younger than me, and

your being beautiful." He wanted her and thought about David Andersen.

"The entire populace have been holding their breath since we were married. What's age got to do with it?" But Elinor knew it had something.

"Are you still happy with me?" Charles said. He knew she was not.

"Yes."

"No regrets?"

"No."

"I want to have children before long, you know that?"

"Of course I do. Just give me a little more time." One day she had to tell him about the child. "Are *you* happy with me?"

"I never thought I could be so happy."

"Even after Mary?"

"Yes. I love you."

"Despite my robust language?"

Charles laughed. "Of course. You can say whatever you like. Well, almost." He got up and put his arms around her. He kissed her neck and hair. "What are you going to do today?"

"I've got lots to do around the house, then I'm going sketching."

"You don't find life dull here? Do you want to go to Melbourne? *Kismet*'s starting soon and there's a Bergman film on."

She unwound his arms and leaned over the veranda rail. "Look, Charles, I'm perfectly happy. Please stop fussing."

She thought about having his child. Why was she different? The cicadas were already drumming and the noise was deafening: it was as though some great and dreadful energy was deep within the earth. The parakeets screamed, an eagle hovered, the fires burned on Mount Napier, the garden was dead, the fence posts were splitting and the boards of the veranda were already burning her bare feet.

314

The entire plain was a cauldron and it seemed that the ancient volcanoes might erupt.

Charles's boots creaked on the veranda and he put his arms around her again; he kissed her once more and smelt her brown body. "I love you, Elinor."

And she said: "Charles, I love you, too."

"Mind the sun."

"I shall."

"Take your parasol."

"I shall." But she knew she would find a sheltered spot beneath the gums and pines and lie naked in the grass.

Elinor watched him ride away on his big black horse. He was wearing a wide-brimmed straw hat and saluted her as he disappeared behind the outbuildings. His dogs ran alongside, barking, their tails pointed; the rooster crowed, a cow bellowed and a truck rattled down the highway, the dust rising. She went back into the cool, dark house, put a record on the player and went to get her sketching paper and pencils. She listened to the LP.

> *Time on my hands,*
> *You in my arms*
> *And love in my heart*
> *All for you.*

15

Port Victoria

David stood at the gate under the oaks and looked at the envelope. It was postmarked Gloucester and the handwriting was feminine and unfamiliar. He tore the envelope open and read the letter.

Dear Mr Andersen,

This is the first time we have corresponded and I'm sorry the occasion is such an unhappy one.

Last week, Tom died of wounds received in action against the Mau Mau terrorists in Kenya. He often spoke of you and your adventures in Korea and I thought I should give you this sad news as soon as possible.

Tom told me your mother is from Uley and perhaps we can all meet some day.

Yrs sincerely,
Veronica Fleetwood

David looked at the date: 3 February 1953. Tom had been dead for over a month. He read the letter a second time, put it in his pocket next to his wallet and walked up the drive under the hawthorns.

His mother was drinking her morning tea in the drawing room, and the blinds were down against the eastern sun. "Was there any mail?" she said.

"No, there wasn't."

"They seem to get slower and slower."

David didn't reply and looked out of the window. Elizabeth poured herself a second cup and the fine china rattled. "Do you want any tea?"

"No thanks." He sat down, picked up the paper and read the headline: 'Premier Stalin Dead'. He heard his mother stirring.

"You've been seen riding with Elinor Bryant," she said.

"Riding?"

"You've been seen riding together."

"Where?"

"I don't know, but you've been seen. You should know."

"So?" David thought of raising the venetians to let the light in.

"So you shouldn't. She may be your age, but she's a married woman."

"She's a friend."

"A friend? You can't be friendly with a married woman."

"Why not?"

"You know, David, you know. It can lead to other things." Elizabeth put down the cup. "We don't want any more trouble."

"More trouble?"

"Never mind. I want you to promise me."

"Promise you what?"

"Stop being so obtuse. I want you to promise me that you won't go gallivanting around the countryside with Elinor Bryant. Why don't you go to Melbourne and get a job? There's nothing for you here."

David threw the paper down, went outside on to the stone veranda and faced the day. He stopped under the monkey-puzzle tree, took the letter out and read it again. *Your adventures.* There was only one person he could tell. Somewhere a bull bellowed and the warm wind drifted through the branches. Where were monkey-puzzle trees from? *Every war's a soldier's war.* Who had seen them? Bert Lawless? It was like being watched by enemy snipers. Then he saw his father coming up, across the garden, carrying his BSA .22.

"Ah, there you are," Richard said. "Have you heard the news?"

"No."

"Joe Stalin's dead. What do you think?" He faced his son under the tree. He was pot-bellied now, dusty and greying.

"I suppose it's good news."

"Suppose? It's bloody marvellous. You fought the buggers, didn't you?"

"Yes, Dad," David said. "Can I borrow the car?"

"What for?"

"I want to go to Hamilton."

"Do you? Why?"

"It's about a job."

"Really?" his father said, "who with?"

"Dalgetty's."

"Jim McPherson's the man to see."

"I know."

"Aren't you pleased about Uncle Joe Stalin?"

"Yes, Dad," David said. "Very."

Richard Andersen shouldered his rifle and watched his son walk away.

*   *   *

They stood on the slopes of Mount Napier, and the plain stretched before them. Her hair was as black as coal and drifted in the wind; she touched it with her fingers to draw it away from her face.

"Hullo, David," Elinor said.

He wanted to take her hand and wondered if he should. "Tom Fleetwood's dead," he said.

"No, no." She came up and took his hand in hers. "When?"

"Over a month ago: he died of wounds, fighting the Mau Mau."

"Died of wounds?"

"That means he suffered. Men dying of wounds usually do."

318

She still kept his hand within hers. "How did you learn?"

"His mother wrote to me and the letter came this morning."

Elinor let him go, swung around and looked down the slopes. "What did she say?"

David pulled the letter out and gave it to her. "She's called Veronica," he said. "Isn't it a beautiful name?"

Elinor read the letter, folded it and gave it back. "After all he went through."

"Yes," David said, "after all he went through. He was a hero." He sat down on the grass and wished she were alongside him. "And there's other news."

"What?"

"My mother says we've been seen riding together."

"So?"

"That's what I said. She says I shouldn't be seen with you, that you're married, that it will lead to other things." David laughed. "I said you were a friend."

Elinor still stood, tall and strong. "You are a friend, but it's more than that now, isn't it?"

"Is it?"

"I think you know, David." She sat down beside him and stretched her legs. "Poor Tom Fleetwood."

"There's even more news."

"What?"

"Joe Stalin's dead."

"Should we celebrate? What about our being seen together?"

He put his hand on her back. "I'm not sure."

"What do you mean, you're not sure?"

"Why shouldn't we be together, if that's what we want? Do you want that?"

"Yes, David," Elinor said, "I do."

Their hands touched in the grass, he took her fingers and felt hers gripping his; she tickled his palm with her nails and he smelt her body. She kissed him on the lips and her hair drifted across his face: it was like a feather's touch as he put his hands on her shoulders. The breeze was warm and gentle now: he felt her arms slipping around his waist and her breasts against him: then her tongue pressed against his teeth and her hands wandered down his back. "Try not to grieve about Tom," he heard her say. She comforted him, tasted sweet and his tongue was in her mouth; he, too, felt her body with his hands, kissed her hard as they swayed a little, gripped and she felt him hard against her; then her hands were under his shirt and her nails scratched his skin; she felt his heart thudding and gripped him strongly. Then she pushed him away, kissed him again lightly and said: "You want me, don't you?"

"My God," David said.

She kissed him once more and ran her tongue along his lips. "There's nothing wrong with good, old-fashioned lust." She threw her hair back and laughed. "You've got a strong, bony body, haven't you? I can see how you and Tom survived the rigours of Korea." She took his hands and locked her fingers in his as they lay upon the grass. The breeze blew across the slopes and her dress clung. David glanced through the small pines. "What are you looking for?' Elinor said.

"People, there could be someone around." His heart was still thudding and his head swam.

"Like Charles?"

"Like Charles, like anybody."

"He doesn't own me, I've told you that."

"You're married to him, for God's sake."

"Is your conduct unbecoming to an officer and a gentleman?" Elinor laughed again. "Are you letting the side down? It's happened before, you know. It's the stuff of literature, poetry and pulp novels. It's nothing new. You want me, don't you? Say it."

"Yes, Elinor, I want you, but you're married."

"So you keep on saying. What do we do?" She was mischievous now and played with his fingers and he felt her wedding ring.

"Nothing."

"All right, we'll do nothing. But I think we will. You're an intriguing man, David Andersen."

"Intriguing?"

"You've fought at the Imjin River, been taken prisoner, escaped and lived to tell the tale."

"And killed," David said.

"And killed, and I want you, too. There, I've said it." Elinor lay beside him. "Have you ever read John Donne, the metaphysical poet, John Donne the Divine?"

"No."

"Well, you should have. What poetry have you read?"

"Rudyard Kipling and Robert W. Service."

"We all know about Kipling," Elinor said, "but who's Robert W. Service?"

"A Canadian poet of the north." He thought of his grandfather.

"Did he write love poetry?"

"Not that I know."

"John Donne did, and a poet called Andrew Marvell. Have you heard of him?"

"No."

"David Andersen, you may be a soldier, but you're also an ignoramus. Do you think poetry is for girls?"

"No."

"When next we meet, I'll give you John Donne and Andrew Marvell, and you read them. All right?"

"Yes." He was loving her all the more now. "Do you want me to write an essay on them?"

Elinor sat up. "Yes, David, I do."

"If I don't are there demerits?"

"Yes, there are demerits."

They both laughed and kissed each other: it was like a romantic film.

"Have you seen Ingrid Bergman?" Elinor said.

"No."

"Jesus Christ, what have you been doing all your life? Living in a monastery?"

David thought of school and the army. "Just about. Wasn't St Catherine's strict?"

"It was a bit like a convent, but I survived." Elinor thought of the long nights in the dormitory overlooking the rose garden, the news of the war at assemblies, and the secret talk of sex. "It was *very* like a convent, but I enjoyed it. Like you, I ran. Did you play hockey?"

"Yes, I did, I was no good at football."

"Why?"

"Look at me, Elinor."

"I am, David."

"What are we going to do?"

"We're going to go on seeing each other, if that's what you want. Is it?"

"Yes."

The sky was blue and cloudless and the starlings chattered on the powerlines. To the east, a steam train rumbled, shooting cinders, the black smoke rising straight, the rolling stock banging. She put out her hand and he gripped her fingers, her nails and gold ring. Somewhere a shot was fired: they crouched and looked, but nothing was to be seen. To David, it was like being in battle.

"Come on," Elinor said. "We can't sit here all day, let's go for a walk."

They strode down the slope toward the wheatfields.

"Do you know this all used to be timbered country?" Elinor said. "The silly buggers cut the trees down."

But for David, the plain was vast and beautiful, with windmills, rock walls and abandoned cottages of stone. No Corsairs and Starfighters swooped in the clear, southern sky.

"Why were you no good at football?" she said.

"I'm not exactly built for it."

"You're a lean and hungry man. How did you get on with the other chaps in the army?"

"All right. I had no close friends, only Fleetwood."

"Or Duntroon?"

"The same. I think they thought I was a bit of a martinet."

"Why?"

David smiled. "I was a stickler for the rules, I went by the book."

"Why?"

"There are rules," David said.

"Rules are made to be broken, and we're breaking one now, aren't we?" Elinor doffed her straw hat and walked alongside through the dry grass. "Life isn't all going by the book."

"I didn't go by the book once and ran into trouble."

"When you killed the Chinese sniper?"

"Yes."

"What about at school?"

"What about it?"

"Close friends. Did you go by the book there?"

"I tried to."

"And you won the mile three times and they made you a captain. And the most outstanding cadet?"

"I had one good friend at school right through, fellow called Jack Gage. You'd have liked him."

"As much as Tom Fleetwood?" She took his hand.

"Very few men could be compared with Tom Fleetwood."

Elinor still held his hand. "You could be."

"Why?"

"Because you both came through. You must have helped him. You must have been as strong as he."

"I take it," David said, "that you didn't go by the book."

"Where?"

"At school."

Elinor laughed and laughed. "I ignored the book, I broke every rule and they still made me a captain."

"What did you do?"

"All sorts of things, right from the very first day."

"What?"

323

"Running around the dorm after lights-out, answering back, asking awkward questions."

"What questions?"

"Questions about love, questions about sex, questions about soldiers with women in parks. I asked questions about poetry. Shall I quote you some?"

David held her hand. "If you like."

"'I wonder, by my troth what you and I
Did, till we loved? Were we not weaned till then?'"

David took her by both hands, drew her close and kissed her.

"My dear David," Elinor said as they clung, "I'm falling in love with you."

He took off her straw hat and kissed her hair and she touched his chest and felt his shoulders; they fell gently and lay on the ground where the insects ran and the lizards scuttled. The mid-day sun shone as they loved, one the other. In the grass, they lay thigh on thigh, she took his hand in hers, and pulled him laughing into the dusty fern that grew upon the hill where young pines stood tall and perpendicular; she felt his muscle in the leaves that feathered them, each gleaming in the eye of the sun that shone in its axis, pin-pointing them, her legs bare, his fingers at her tiny buttons as he fingered and touched her, she laughing and sighing, he gazing and she looking, too, as they held each other on the slopes above the endless plain. *Were we not weaned till then?*

They lay under the conifers and listened to the sounds of the summer. This secret place, with its stone walls, pines and hawthorns, was like a cathedral, the shafts of sun shining through the old branches and the locusts singing. Elinor thought once more of being at school: Sundays in the park by the river, the fours and the eights rowing, the boys' backs bending and the coxes shouting the stroke through their megaphones; she thought of the men and

324

girls lying under rugs on the grass and the soldiers stretched out, sleeping it off.

"You're not a man's man, are you?" she said.

"I suppose I'm not." David thought of his childhood days at Penshurst school, the bullying, the bloody noses, the futile tests of bravery, the smutty jokes and Rose Braddon lying in her bloodied dressing gown. "We were taught that men and boys should be tough, but it seemed I was always the victim until my last years at Grammar."

"Did you bully the younger boys then?"

"No," David said, "I just put the fear of God into them." He thought of the unexploded shell. "I taught them to save their lives. I've told you about Sergeant Hart?"

"Yes you have."

"He seems to be with me all the time." David thought yet again of the machine-gunning of the two Chinese on the road to Chasan. "Hart," he said, "was a natural killer. He's like Bert Lawless."

"I've met Mr Lawless," Elinor said.

"You've met him?" David laughed. "No one *meets* Bert Lawless."

"I've seen him twice, or rather he's seen me."

"Seen you?"

"Looked at me. Do you know what I mean, David?"

He thought of the Korean girl. "Yes, I do. Never was a man more aptly named. Why my father's employed him for sixteen years, I'll never know."

"Because, I'm told," Elinor said, "he's the best shooter in the District."

"He's also a snooper," David said. "I wouldn't be surprised if he were crouching behind that wall with his dogs." He got up. "I think I'll go and have a look."

Elinor watched him coming back, striding easily between the fallen branches and stumps. David Andersen, she thought, moved like a tiger. "Was he there?"

"No," he said, as he sat down beside her. "There was nothing."

325

"Weren't you looking out for Charles?"

"Not particularly."

"I think you were. What do you think of him?"

"Christ, what a question. I've known him for over fifteen years. I used to call him Uncle, remember?"

Elinor sat up and faced him. "We're falling in love, aren't we?"

"So you say."

"What do you think?"

"I think, Elinor Bryant, that you're the most beautiful woman I've ever met — not that I've met too many."

"And?"

"And you're married to one of my father's best friends, a good man, upright, honest, intelligent, and if we go on seeing each other, there'll be a bloody disaster."

"Do you feel guilty?" she said.

"I'm not sure."

"Not going by the book?"

"I suppose so."

"Have you wondered why I married Charles?"

"Often."

"I married him on the rebound," Elinor said.

"The rebound from what?"

"A love affair." She smiled at him. "You may be a veteran of war, David. I'm a veteran of loving."

"You're a bit young to be a veteran."

"And so are you. I fell in love when I was seventeen and had a child."

"You did?"

"Yes."

"Where is it now?"

"I've no idea," Elinor said. "They took him away from me. I wanted to keep him, but they wouldn't let me."

"Who were they?"

"My mother, the doctors, everybody. Had my father been alive, it might have been different. It seems one can't look after one's own love child."

"So you weren't married?"

"Of course not. Having a child out of wedlock is worse than murder."

"Does Charles know about this?"

"No," Elinor said, "no, he doesn't. Do you think I'm a scarlet woman?" She thought of the boys and the kissing after the dances.

"Of course not." He wanted to take her hand.

"I met Charles eighteen months later and, a year after his wife died, he asked me to marry him and I did."

"Why, if you're such an independent person?"

"I wasn't feeling very independent at the time, and he's all the things you say he is. Charles is the original good man. He's got no weaknesses or vices that I can see."

"You'd better stand by him then."

"Why stand by a man with no weaknesses?"

"There's such a thing as honour," David said.

"And there's such a thing as loving, and I don't mean screwing, I mean loving." Elinor got up and moved from the shade into the sun. "Are you falling in love with me?"

"I don't know, it's never happened to me before."

"You're in unknown territory, then?"

David thought of the paddies and brambles, the charcoal burners' fires and the old peasant woman in the truck. "Yes."

"Have you ever been to bed with a woman?"

"No," David said, "not properly."

"You're a loving man, David Andersen."

He was pleased, but said, "I think it's gone far enough, I think we should stop seeing each other."

"All right then, that's what we'll do." She stepped up and kissed him on the cheek. "Can you find your way back? I'm sure you can."

He watched her move off through the pines, now in the

sun, now in the shadows. Within an instant, she was gone. He had forgotten about Tom Fleetwood.

*   *   *

For two months, David worked with his father at *Killara*. They repaired fences, put out several dangerous fires, went to sheep sales and, when he could, he rode alone along the straight, dusty roads toward the ranges. He went to church with his mother in Hamilton, listened to the cricket on the radio, tried a round or two of golf and chatted to his father's friends in the club house. But it was no use: the summer was long; the days were hot from dawn to dusk; the dust blew in from the Mallee and he saw her in every tree, in every rock and stone, and there was nothing he could do about it.

*   *   *

It was late April and the oak leaves were starting to fall. They stood beneath the trees and Elinor picked up an acorn. "What are conkers?" she said.

"I'm not sure, some kind of English game. You can't play conkers with acorns. Tom Fleetwood could have told you."

"Charles is going away," she said.

"Going away? Where?"

"His mother's ill. She lives in Melbourne, he'll be gone a week."

"So you're alone?"

Elinor threw an acorn at a fence post. "Yes, David, I'm alone."

"When does he go?"

"Charles? In a day or two, as soon as he can get away."

"So?"

"Good God, David, I wish you'd stop saying, 'So?' We can go away together, if that's what you want."

"Where?"

"There's a house I can get in Port Victoria. Do you know anybody there?"

"No," David said, "I don't think so. I've not been to Port Victoria for ten years." He thought of the reef, the headland, the south wind and the big sea running. "I used to fish on the Fitzroy River with my grandfather. Do you know it?"

"No."

"I could show it to you."

Elinor grinned. "It'll be a great adventure."

"Like *Coral Island*?"

"Like Toad and Mole going into the wild wood."

"Didn't they have a bad time?" David said.

"They did, but they got home safely and toasted their feet in front of the fire."

"Vowing never to go there again."

"Well," she said, "do you want to go to Port Victoria or not?"

"Yes," David said, "yes, I do."

"Can you get a car?"

"I can hire one and say I'm going to Melbourne, and I can face their questions. I've been questioned before; I'm not only a veteran of war, I'm a veteran of the inquisition. I'll go to Port Victoria with you. Come here, please."

She did and he kissed her beneath the oaks where the crows swooped and the parakeets talked and flew.

*   *   *

The day was cool, but the countryside was still yellow and the sky was blue. The windows were down and Elinor sat, her dress above her knees; bushflies buzzed against the windscreen; the gravel was thick, and David banged through the gears.

"Do you want some lunch?" he said. He looked at his watch. "It's almost one o'clock." He glanced in the rear mirror, but the road was deserted. "There should be a township soon."

"I'd like something," Elinor said. She was enjoying the country: the plains, the piles of rock, the stone walls, the wheatfields and the ruined cottages. It was hers, it was within her; the clouds bunched and gathered, a million starlings sat on the power lines, the sheep stood like stones and the prime Herefords wandered; the dams gleamed in the afternoon sun, the post and rail fences staggered and the western ranges had disappeared. Now she could smell the salt of the southern ocean.

"There's nothing around here," David said. "It's all a bit primitive."

"You sound like your mother."

"My mother?"

"She hates Australia."

"It's not that she hates it: she's dislocated, there's nothing here for her. I didn't realize how she felt until I went away."

"To Korea?"

"It wasn't just that it was Korea, I had no landscape in my mind, or if I did, it bewildered me. Soldiers are not taught to look at hills or trees, Elinor. They are taught to wonder what's behind them."

A Bedford truck came up behind, followed the car for about two miles, then turned off the highway on to a side road, dust pluming. David thought of the convoys of trucks, the big GMCs, their exhausts pumping and the young soldiers laughing and drinking beer as they went into combat. The dirt road turned into tar-seal and they drove down an avenue of pines.

"Memorial Avenue," David said, "there'll be a town in a minute."

"I wonder why they always grow pines," she said, "they're gloomy trees."

At the end of Memorial Avenue they saw the shrine, the soldier with his slouch hat, his rifle upturned between his boots. Tomorrow was Anzac Day, David thought; the men would march, the bands would play, the war widows would weep, the school children would wave Union Jacks, the trumpeters would sound the Last Post and the soldiers would drink their beer and swap tales of death and derring-do. He would not be marching toward the monument, he would be loving by the southern sea. His father would be marching with the best of them down the main street of Penshurst, past St James's Church, the Convent, the Masonic Hall, the Shire Offices and the pub where Tom Quicksilver's father sat on the veranda. There was a prefabricated cross in the Western Desert for Tom Quicksilver now; and there were crosses for Kershaw and Brownlee. He thought of the colonel at the apple orchard. *A fine show, Mr Andersen.* They drew up; he stopped the car, got out and opened the door for her. David stood, his boots in the dust, and saw a shooter with his dogs in the main street. *Home is the hunter, home from the hill.* Was it Bert Lawless? A cock crowed, a chill wind blew, the dirty children laughed and ran and the old men sat on their front porches and watched them.

*   *   *

Toward the evening they saw the sea, the rows of trees, the water tower and the salt mist drifting. Elinor thought of Wordsworth:

> *It is a beauteous evening, calm and free;*
> *The holy time is quiet as a nun*
> *Breathless with adoration.*

Port Victoria was small, with one main street, rows of Norfolk pines, a few shops, narrow streets of stone cottages with their backs toward the sea. There were five pubs, a Masonic Hall, six churches, a Victorian town hall, a Mechanics' Institute and a graveyard upon the hill where the oaks and cypresses grew. Now in the dusk it was cold and threatening to rain. The main street was broad enough for bullocks' drays; the timber fences were collapsing and the railway station was deserted. Box cars and cattle trucks stood on the line and egrets crouched on the posts. No locomotives steamed by the stationmaster's house where the dim lights shone. Nobody was abroad.

The magpies caw-cawed in the old trees, chickens picked and poked among the abandoned Model Ts and wrecked General Motors trucks. Iron scrap and wire grew from the earth: it was an impoverished seaward place. The hotels were magnificent: high-pitched, rococo, with balconies of iron lace, french windows, vast public bars with stained glass, but there was no one to drink in them. Sealers and whalers had been here one hundred years ago; cast-iron pots had stewed on the beaches; the sea had run with blood, oil and sperm; there had been grog houses, whores, wild horses, teamsters and whips cracking, oaths and profanities, bottles of French champagne, brandy in casks, Holy Mass on Sundays, the chiming of church bells, crinolines and Irish music, but that had all long since gone.

They found the house easily. It was small, built of wood, in the street by the river. The front fence had fallen and the garden was neglected and bare. The path to the front door was overgrown, the grass was wet and long, tall thistles grew and starlings sat on the powerlines. No one had been here since the summer. They got out of the car and stood in the weeds.

Elinor heard the big sea running and said: "Let's not go in yet, it's still light and I want to walk with you." David looked at the small, wooden house, its blinded windows, the weeds rank and tall, the grass growing through the woodpile and said: "Should we not put our things inside?"

"No," Elinor said, "that can wait, I want to walk with you, I want to see the ocean."

The weather had changed. In that rainy afternoon they walked hand in hand down the deserted streets, past the huddled cottages, the unpainted picket fences and ruined customs shed to the wharf where the fishing trawlers lay. Nobody was about, not even a cat or a dog: the weather forbade work. The gravel crunched beneath their shoes, the curlews swooped and the ducks sheltered in the marshy estuaries. Another weather change was coming: the boats heaved on the river; the old hemp ropes rose and fell; tattered flags fluttered and the lobster pots were piled high on the wooden decks. Two mullet boats were sunk at their moorings and the weed streamed over the gunwales. David and Elinor stood arm in arm and looked over at the harbourmaster's house, half-hidden in the tea-tree and the Norfolk pines. A flock of gulls streaked through the windy sky and rain clouds gathered in the southwest, beyond the reef. The smell of salt, fish and kelp was on the breeze. Elinor gripped his hand.

"It looks as though it's going to be a bad winter, David."

Her dark hair flowed in the wind and he did not reply. What would the night bring? What would happen in the wooden house?

They walked south along the sea wall toward the causeway and the southern sea. Thunder clouds were rising: it was getting dark. Silently, they walked along the crumbling path, along the sea wall and over to the island where the seabirds lived in rookeries burrowed in the soft, black ground and the surveyor's station stood on the hill. To the east stood the lighthouse, white-stoned and red-roofed, facing the sea. The white and blue water ran and broke against the rocks, the spray flew, the birds screamed and there was no quiet. The lighthouse had been built one hundred years earlier. Over 500 wrecks lay in the bay; the *Essington*, the *Swift*, the *Pearl*, the *Cyprus* and many others: brigs, yawls, schooners, barquentines, human bones and studded chests of gold plate, wine bottles from the Loire and cheap wedding rings from Belfast, Hull and Liverpool. There was a legend that in the dunes to the north lay a mahogany ship from Spain, the first to see this coast before the French or the English, but no one had ever seen its wooden bones.

They walked the narrow path, stood on the bluestone

steps before the lighthouse, looked at its perpendicular windows, wondered about the keeper, turned back through the treacherous spiky brush, marched along the small beach and made for home. The weather, gathering dark and wet from the south now, had beaten them. They were tired and cold.

"Let's go back, David," Elinor said. "Let's go back."

She remembered a poem from school: *cliffs of fall, sheer, no-man-fathomed*. A small boat was beating up from the west: it might not make the river mouth and she dared not look. Nor could she look upon the sea.

*   *   *

Breathless and cold, they stopped at the front door. David searched his pockets for the key and couldn't find it. Elinor was close to him in the wind as it blew on the front veranda. "I've got the key, David, I've got it here."

Her hair was wet and fell around her shoulders. He touched her cold hands; they laughed and unlocked the door. The hall was dark, the house unused since the summer and all was silent. David turned on a light. Ashes blew in the grate in the small front room and spiders' webs trailed from the high, redwood ceiling. The varnished walls were bare and the floor creaked. There was a clock on the mantelpiece, a rocking-chair in the corner, a settee and a table. The house smelt of dust and damp.

"We should have a fire," David said. He dropped the bags on the threadbare carpet. "There must be some wood somewhere." He remembered the fires in his bedroom at *Killara*, his grandfather smoking his pipe and smelling of whisky and Irish tobacco and the gum logs steaming.

"I'll help you, David." Elinor stood in the centre of the dark front room.

"No, no, I'll find something."

"All right then, you find some wood and I'll see what's what." She came over and kissed him on the forehead. "Go

334

and find some firewood and make us warm. You're a soldier."

While David rummaged in the backyard, he still sensed her body in the dark. There was no moon or light to guide him and he stumbled and fell into strange objects: fence posts, trees, clothes props and the soft earth of the abandoned vegetable garden. All was ghostly and uncertain and he thought of the patrol, of the men standing on the piquet, the trees in his arc of fire, of noises and bugles in the night, of the smell of sweat and tobacco, of Paul Cash counting his rosary beads and shaking. He was very cold now and the wind blew into his bones. What was Elinor doing? Had anybody seen them? He saw a light turned on in one of the bedrooms and saw her for a moment in the window. It was a strange house. Was she in the bedroom? What was she doing there?

At last David found an upturned water tank and felt the familiar round ridges with his fingers. He knew that wood was kept there. He knelt, brushed away the cobwebs clinging to his face, found the logs and kindling and carried them to the house. He heard Elinor moving in another room, found an old newspaper, built the fire carefully, lit it and watched the flames race up the chimney. The fire burned well, he placed the logs and sat down. The fire comforted him. What if they had been seen? But no one here knew them. He fiddled with the buckles of his portmanteau and thought of Elinor. Then she was at the door.

"There's nothing to eat, David. We shall have to go to the shops in the morning. But there's this." She was holding a bottle.

"What is it?"

"Glenfiddich." She laughed. "Nice girls don't drink whisky." Elinor watched the flames. "Do you want a drink?"

"Yes, I do." He thought of the cheap Australian whisky and the men gathered around the charcoal pit.

She sat beside him near the hearth and passed him the

335

bottle and two glasses. "We shouldn't have gone for that walk."

"Yes," David said, "yes we should."

"Scouting out the ground?"

"In a way, but it was far more than that." The Glenfiddich tasted good. It warmed his gut and went to his head. He drank some more and gave her the bottle. Then he took her hand and kissed her on the neck. He felt her fingers touching his. She, too, drank and they watched the fire. The grate glowed and they drank the whisky. Then she took his hands again and kissed him. He felt the tip of her tongue and touched her breasts, just for a moment as, outside, the wind blew.

* * *

The wind blew around the small house. It rattled the old iron roof, whistled under the eaves and through the worn lattice work; it bent the struggling, salty gum trees, scattered the leaves of the dead rose bushes and raised huge breakers on the ocean. The autumn wind blew from the Antarctic where Scott and his men had died. The gannets, kittiwakes and terns huddled in the seagrass in the dunes and on the beach in the lee of the rocks: no birds were out to sea. No stars shone, the moon was gone and the night was black and cold. The fire burned and they drank the whisky. Elinor watched David as he crouched by the fire and heard the surf thumping on the beach. She stood by the fire and said: "I want to go to bed."

They lay on the bed in the dark room and she kissed him with her tongue and he kissed her with his: he ran his hands down her backbone, over her breasts, then beneath her skirt and up her thighs, her hands between his. She felt him shiver as his fingers gripped and she touched him everywhere; she was his and she smelled of sun and salt and grass, her body, hair, ears, arms and legs. They grappled and kissed each other, twisting in the half-light as the fire's shadows moved, fingering, laced and traced as the old bed

336

creaked and the watery moon rose above the small, bent trees on the sedgeland where the birds were fast asleep.

She put her arms around his neck, her breasts on his chest, her fingers in his hair as they whispered like children in the night. They undressed each other, she twisting his shirt buttons, loving him and telling him what to do; they laughed, trembled and sighed as they fingered and touched each other's limbs, as they lay upon the eiderdown, soft and cold under their bodies. There, they lay, laughing for the sheer joy of it, legs tangled, her hair in his mouth, his hands on her nipples and hers stroking and loving him. He felt her hands upon him and thought his heart would break as she held him, gently playing; then she took his hands and placed them upon her, where they, too, touched and fondled while she breathed and lay upon the bed that held them both in that loving dark.

Elinor put his hands in her mouth, bit his fingers, sat up and said: "It's cold, David, we should be under the blankets."

"We should."

She heard his voice and loved him; she raised her arms, they helped each other, touched and breathed, one the other, pulled up the blankets and whispered as the nocturnal creatures crept and the hidden spiders spun and weaved. She cupped her breasts with her hands for his mouth; he sucked them, kissed her belly, hair and cleft; and she held him tightly, her fingers stroking as she guided him. They grappled and sprang, sinewy and strong, and once they shouted, she spreadeagled and crying. When it was done, they lay quietly, each within the other: the fire gleamed, the trees beat against the windows, the rain fell and the salt spray drifted in the ruined garden.

*   *   *

"What is to be done?" David said. She was warm and tender and lay by his side. Somewhere in the house, a clock ticked. He could not remember having wound it; he was

337

puzzled and listened. He looked at her and she looked at him: *two eyes on a single thread*. She moved and brushed her hair away. He considered her throat and breasts, the wedding ring on her left hand: the long, strong fingers. Then he remembered a line from a poem he had learned at school: *When in disgrace with fortune and men's eyes, I all alone beweep my outcast state.*

"What do we do?"

Elinor didn't reply. Then she said: "All I know is, this is our time and nobody can take it away from us. This is our business, and if we can't have this, we can't have anything."

She put her legs between his. To plunge forever into the dark of her, David thought as he felt her move, her heart pumping and her blood flowing through millions of tiny veins. The mystery of it. Nothing more was said: it was colder now and they held each other like children. They would have to light the fire first thing in the morning. The rain rattled on the roof now and poured down the rusted guttering.

"Do you want a brew?" David said.

"A brew?"

"A cup of tea."

Elinor laughed out loud. "David, I think you're marvellous. We're in this pickle and you suggest a cup of tea."

"Why not? Many's the time I've had a brew when all looked finished and done."

"Are we finished and done?"

"I don't think so. Do you want a cup of tea or not?"

"Of course I do."

"Okay, I shan't be a tick."

David put his trousers on and left her. She heard him moving easily down the strange hall, and loved him. Would he find the tea and matches? No doubt he was used to the dark: that was where he had fought. The rain fell and the casements rattled as she drew the blankets around her.

Elinor was asleep when he came back with the tea. She

338

was breathing easily and looked like an angel. He put out the light and slept.

* * *

In the morning the rain had stopped, the birds were singing and a bicycle bell rang. They lay with each other, his legs between hers, her body smelling of talcum. Elinor kissed him and said: "Good-day, cobber." Then she drifted back to sleep.

David lay for a while, then got up, trying not to disturb her. He dressed hurriedly, poked the ashes of the fire, pottered around the house, then stood on the front veranda. The street was empty, then he saw the postman on his bike disappearing around the corner. He could hear the sound of the sea as it banged on the beach. They would walk there, later in the day. He opened his arms and breathed in the salty air and thought of Elinor: he had never been so happy. The day was cold and cloudless, the old pines climbed into the sky, the starlings chattered, the gulls dived and flew and an egret was watching him. David's heart lifted as he walked across the garden, saw some daisies, picked a bunch for her and went inside. He looked at Elinor sleeping: she looked like a child, she looked like Alice in Wonderland. In the kitchen, he found a jar, filled it, arranged the flowers and put them on a chair by the bed. Then he lit the fire and thought about going to the bakery to buy some bread: they could have toast and jam for breakfast. It would be a secret feast, breakfast in bed with no station bell to sound the hour and no one to disturb them.

Elinor woke and saw the flowers; she smiled and opened her arms.

"I've just remembered," David said.

"Remembered what? The flowers are beautiful and so are you."

"I *have* read poetry other than Kipling and Robert W. Service."

"Come here." She kissed him and he kissed her back.

339

"What?"

"*Other Men's Flowers* by General Wavell."

"Was he a poet too?"

"No, silly, it's an anthology by one of our most distinguished soldiers. I told you when I first met you: not all soldiers are morons."

"You're certainly not. Can you remember a poem?"

"I think I can."

"Well, go on."

"*Blow, bugle, blow, set the wild echoes flying.*"

"Is that all?" She was smiling.

"It's all I can remember."

"Anything else?" she said as she loved him.

"I think so."

"What?" She put her hands on his chest.

"Do you want a cup of morning tea? I put the kettle on."

"I want to hear the second poem."

"*Break, break, break, on thy cold grey stones, O Sea.*"

"Bravo," Elinor said as she cuddled him under the blankets. "Who was the poet?"

"Have a guess, he wrote both the lines."

"Shakespeare?"

"No."

"Elizabeth Barrett Browning?"

"No."

"Samuel Taylor Coleridge?"

"No."

"I give up. Who was it?"

"Alfred, Lord Tennyson."

"Alfred, Lord Tennyson? I'd never have guessed, what a well-read young soldier you are."

"Do you know what, Elinor?"

"You're mad and I'm not. What?"

"I want a cup of tea."

"And, David, so do I. But the problem is: who's going to get it? Tom Cobbler's cold."

"What? Who's Tom Cobbler?"

"Never mind, who's going to get the cup of tea?"

David rose and pulled the sheets around him. "I am."

"My God," she said, "you look like Cassius."

"More like Julius Caesar, or Lord Cardigan, I'd say, before the Charge of the Light Brigade." He squinted across the small room. "Where exactly *are* my men?"

Elinor laughed and laughed. "I love you, David, now where's me bloody tea."

"Coming, ma'am, coming."

"No sugar, please."

"Yes, ma'am."

The tea was strong and hot and they lay, loving, in bed until noon.

* * *

They walked up the beach toward the headland, where the salmon swam and fed in the deep blue troughs and the gannets and shags flew in the spume and the driving rain from the south. Two thousand miles away, the icebergs grumbled and muttered, whales spouted, Mount Erebus smoked and the wind blew forever. They watched the sea break on the reef where a thousand wrecks lay; bits of kelp as large as elephants' trunks were strewn on the sand; the salt water ran back to the sea between bottles, rocks, timber and encrusted artefacts. The beach was pitted by horses' hooves, dogs' paws and the fragile imprints of birds' feet. Sandpipers sat on the sandbanks, flew when they approached, settled, then flew again. The sun was in the west and the afternoon was becoming shadowy and cold.

They walked arm in arm, their feet bare, the wind and the sand in their faces; her hair flew, her dress clung and she wore her cardigan around her shoulders. David saw a fisherman on the edge of the rocks; salmon were running in those deep, mysterious troughs and he wished he were fishing too. He stopped, his heels in the sand as the water

341

ran, held her body, kissed her on the mouth and said, "Elinor, I love you."

"And I love you, David."

The water raced between their legs and they clung, the sand shifted, they almost fell, the blue water foamed around their thighs, they ran for safety toward the dunes and watched the sea.

"I never saw the sea in Korea," David said, "only the paddies, the estuaries and the mountains. And the smashed port of Inchon, where the Americans landed."

"What was it like?" She was feeling colder now and sat close to him.

"Inchon? Everything was ruined, every breakwater, every sea wall, every warehouse, every dwelling. Bodies of soldiers floated in the water and not a gull flew."

David sat on the dune and remembered the Imjin, the strange stranded boats, the herring and the Korean soldier standing on the wall. *Is this river good for fishing?* She let go his arm and then he walked down to the sea and stood in the water as it ran over his feet and trousers. The water ran out, the sand shifted, but David didn't stumble. Elinor ran down too, and stood beside him, the water running between her bare legs; her dress was wet, the big waves rolled and they laughed and clutched each other; rain started to fall, the wind turned into their faces, but they continued and walked toward the headland. The rain squalled, the sun shone and the rainbow gleamed, red, yellow and blue as they held hands, dodged the big waves and ran across the streaming channels. They held hands and ran.

*   *   *

In the afternoon, they sat on a seat by the river and watched the tide running and the pelicans dipping and diving. An old man and a boy were fishing from the wall; the air smelt of octopus and seaweed, the ocean broke upon the breakwater and beat upon the reef where the gulls swooped and hovered. A church bell rang. Married couples slept in their cars and others watched the sea. It was a quiet afternoon and nobody knew them; children laughed and played on the slides and merry-go-rounds and an old woman cycled past, uncertainly, her dress billowing. David thought of the Chinese soldiers on their Hercules. A fishing boat went up the river, its exhaust pluming and its wake lapping and foaming against the mossy stones. The church bell sounded again. What was the time? They had forgotten. Elinor put her hands between David's legs and fondled him. He was hard and he kissed her on the neck.

"What do you want to do?" she said.

"I want to be in bed with you."

"Later," she said, "it's a lovely afternoon." But her hand still stayed. "Will they catch anything?"

David looked at the old man and the boy. "No, they won't catch anything. The wind and the tide are against them."

"You are my darling," Elinor said. "Do you want to go for a walk?"

"No."

"What do you want to do?"

"I've told you."

Elinor looked at the sky. "It's going to rain and we shall have to go indoors. Do you want it to rain?"

"Yes, I want it to rain for as long as we are here."

"For as long as we are here? We should have to stay indoors all the time."

"We would."

She felt him. "Should we both pray for rain?"

"We've no need to," David said, as the first spots fell. "I think God's on my side."

The drops fell into her hair, but she still held him. "I think he is: he rewards the faithful. Are you faithful? I am."

"Forever?"

"Yes."

"Come on, darling," Elinor said, "let's go back, but put on your raincoat. I love you like that, but the locals might not."

*　　*　　*

When they got in, they pulled the blinds and stripped. She made him lie on the bed, then crouched over him, her breasts hanging; she took him with her hands, ran her tongue up his penis and kissed it. She sat on the bed, holding him tight as he lay.

"There," Elinor said, "I've got you now, haven't I?"

"I think you've always had me, right from the first day."

"This is what you wanted when we sat by the river, isn't it?"

"Yes."

She bent, kissed lightly and sucked. "When I do this," she said, "I own you. Do you want to be owned?"

"Yes."

"Only by me?"

"Yes, only by you."

"*You* own me," Elinor said. "You know that?"

"I hope so."

"You do, David, you do." She gripped him with both hands, her fingers working; she watched him close his eyes. "Do I own you?"

"Yes."

"Say it."

"You own me."

"Good." She worked quickly and hard.

"Jesus Christ," he said as he lay helpless, her fingers and hands stroking.

"Be quiet, I want to watch you." She put it in her mouth, sucked, held it up and watched him release. "My darling," she said, "my darling, you're like a fountain." His juice ran through her fingers as she leant forward and kissed him. "I

344

own you, that's good, and I shan't let you go, do you understand? I shan't let you go."

*   *   *

That night, they sat by the fire, she on the sofa and he in the rocking-chair. The house creaked and animals scuttled in the roof.

"Do you think marriage is forever?" David said.

"Of course not, loving is, for as long as you're in that state. What do you think?"

"I don't know what to think. All I know is that I'm in love with you."

"Look at your mother and father," Elinor said. "Are they in love?"

"No."

"Do you know why?"

"A mistake they have to live with, I suppose. But why my mother hates my father, I've never really understood."

"I'll tell you why. Do you remember a young woman called Rose Braddon?"

"She was my school teacher."

"Your father got her pregnant, abandoned her and she died trying to abort herself."

David stopped rocking and placed another log on the fire.

"And my mother knows?"

"Lots of people know."

"Except me."

"Except you, and your mother's never forgiven him."

"Who told you?"

"Charles."

David got up. "Is this going to be a night of True Confessions? Do you want a drink and something to eat?"

Elinor laughed. "I thought you'd never ask."

"I shan't be a moment."

She sat on the sofa and listened to his footsteps down the hall. What was he thinking?

*   *   *

"I liked Rose Braddon," David said. "She was my best teacher."

"What was she like?"

"I was only a kid then. She was tall, thin, good at her job and she tried."

"Did she like you?"

"Yes, I think she did."

"Why?"

"I'm not sure. I didn't fit in. I was an outsider, the son of the grazier who owned *Killara* on the hill." David gave Elinor the whisky. "The respectable grazier on the hill. Poor Rose Braddon."

"Poor Rose Braddon, and your poor mother."

"Isn't what we're doing to Charles the same?"

"I take it that if I were pregnant, you wouldn't abandon me and send me home?"

"You know damned well I wouldn't. But aren't we betraying him?"

"We're betraying him," Elinor said, "if we don't tell him sooner or later."

"When is sooner or later?"

"I don't know."

"I'm beginning to wish I were back in the army."

"Why?"

"Life's much simpler there."

"There are orders to go by, aren't there?" she said. "Isn't it like living in a monastery where everything's cut-and-dried?"

"Not quite."

"Don't soldiers fall in love?"

"This one has." David drank his whisky down and it burnt his throat. He coughed. "Christ, what a tangle: my

346

father and Rose Braddon, my mother, Charles, you and I."

"And my child." Elinor drank her whisky straight down and wanted him.

"And your child. I can't cope with that." David looked at his watch. "Can I go and turn the radio on?"

"Why?"

"It's nine o'clock and there might be news of the truce talks."

"If you like."

"President Eisenhower's doing his best."

"I'm sure he is."

"I won't be long."

Elinor sat by the fire and listened to him twiddling the dial in the other room. There were snatches of music, voices from a serial and a baritone. Was it Peter Dawson? A voice droned. After a while, David came back with his empty glass and sat next to her.

"They've arrested Jomo Kenyatta. Preparations for the Coronation, and a progress report on the climb on Everest. Nothing about the war. Do you want another drink?"

"Yes, David, I do. And I want you in bed."

"You do?"

"Of course I do."

"My poor, bloody father."

"What's that?"

"He made a mistake and he's been punished for it for more than sixteen years."

"The mistake your father made," Elinor said, "was abandoning Rose Braddon. He killed her."

"He didn't kill her, she killed herself." David drank the whisky and wondered where the conversation was going. "I'm trespassing," he said.

"You're what?"

"I'm trespassing. I'm on Charles's territory."

"Charles's territory? What am I? Some kind of prize mare or something?" Elinor drank. "What do you see yourself as, some kind of cattle rustler?"

347

"I don't know what I am."

"David darling, you're a good man, a soldier who's fought, who's fallen in love with a woman who loves you. That's what you are. And I want a child by you."

"A child? Why?"

"Because I love you, it's the ultimate act."

"Why don't you have a child with Charles?"

"Because I don't love him as I love you."

"Why do you love me?"

"I've told you: because you're intelligent, because you see other things most people don't see."

"Such as?"

"The fishtraps on the lake, the azaleas, the poplars, the guns in the ice, Kershaw's death, the view from Mount Napier."

"Other men must see those things."

"Not in the same way, not with passion." Elinor put her glass down. "I've already told you: this is our time, this is our business. Come to bed, I want you to make love to me."

*   *   *

For the next five days, they lived together. They made love; he helped her, she helped him; they cooked breakfast, brought in the firewood, bathed each other, walked along the beach, listened to music, heard the Matins bell chiming and explored rock pools like children. The weather remained cold and they walked the high cliffs, the middens and the dunes where the wild flowers grew. Each day it rained, the wind was cold and from the front window, they watched old men on bicycles, dogs running and women shopping. Each evening a rainbow shone over the bay.

16

Melbourne

In the dusk, Elinor sat in the gazebo and thought of Port Victoria; she thought of the Imjin, Sergeant Hart, the death of the sniper and Kim's questions. She thought of David making love to her and the big sea running. *I own you.* The sound of rifle fire echoed in the evening. She would tell Charles soon. The sky was clear and cold and Venus was rising. *I wonder, by my troth.* She shivered as the leaves fell.

"A penny for your thoughts," Charles said as he stood in the entrance. "Are you ready?"

"Yes," she said, "I'm ready."

"Aren't you cold?"

"No, I like sitting in the gazebo."

Elinor threw her cardigan around her shoulders and they walked down to the car.

"I've got two bottles of champagne," he said.

"Good, I like champagne."

They drove down the long, straight road as the evening star shone and the Southern Cross appeared in the eastern sky.

David was standing under the light on the flagstone veranda. The moths and insects fluttered and the smell of woodsmoke was in the air. He ran down the steps and opened the door for her. "Good evening," he said.

"Hullo," Elinor said. "It's nice to see you. Has it started?"

"Not really, there's lots of martial music." He smiled. "I know you'll enjoy that."

She also smiled. "I'm sure I shall."

"David," Charles said, "where have you been hiding?"

"I've been in Melbourne about a job."

"Have you? I was there myself a couple of weeks ago. You should have told me and we could have driven up together."

"Come inside, all of you," his father said. "It's colder than a brass monkey out here."

A fire was burning in the drawing room and drinks were set out on the oak table. Elinor noticed the Glenfiddich and looked at David standing by the door.

"Good evening, Elinor, good evening, Charles," Elizabeth said as she got up from the *chaise longue*.

"Stirring times," Charles said and kissed her hand. "First Everest and now the Coronation."

"What will you have to drink?" Richard said to Elinor.

"I'll have a whisky."

"A whisky?"

"With water, no ice."

Elizabeth watched her husband pour the drink and Elinor taking the glass. "Cheers," Elinor said, as she looked at them all.

David went over to the radio and fiddled with the reception, then looked at Charles Bryant as he talked with his mother. He was a big, square-shouldered man. What would he do when Elinor told him? What would they all do? He watched Elinor drinking her whisky and was proud of her. She came over and said:

"Well, David, what have you been doing?"

"This and that."

"How was Melbourne?" She grinned. "Did you meet any eligible girls?"

"Lots, I had to beat them off with a stick."

"You're a handsome man, I'm not surprised." She listened to the bands playing."I'm a secret republican, did you know that?"

"No."

"Well, I am."

"This is hardly the time to announce it."

"We'll see." She held out her glass and he touched her fingers. "Could I have another drink please?"

She looked mischievous and David wondered what was going to happen this evening. "There you are," he said. "Please excuse me, I'd better get in some more wood for the fire."

"You do that," Elinor said. "You're good at it." She watched him go and loved him.

"What did you think of Everest?" Richard Andersen said. "Good for the old prestige?" Like his father, Richard smelt of whisky, but there the resemblance ended. *Poor* Rose Braddon.

"Prestige?" Elinor said.

"The old Empire." Richard poured himself another Glenfiddich.

"Oh that."

"All this talk about moral decline," he said. "It proved there are still men around who can do it."

"Do what?"

"Climb mountains, endure hardship."

Elinor was about to say that his son had done both, but decided not. She saw Charles talking to Elizabeth: they got on very well. Maybe they should have an affair; but he was just being polite.

"There are lots of men enduring hardship right now," she said.

"Where?"

"The war."

"What war?" Richard said.

"The Korean war."

"A bit of a sideshow, don't you think?"

Elinor turned on her heel and joined David as he built up the fire. "Will the Gloucesters be marching at the Coronation?" she asked.

"No, they've been decimated and most of the poor devils are in prison camps, hoping for a truce."

She touched his arm. "Please forgive me."

He smiled at her. "There's nothing to forgive, you weren't to know. Are you enjoying yourself?"

"No, not very."

"Cheer up," David said, "there'll be lots of military music, there'll be Edward Elgar. You like him, don't you?"

"I do now." She watched his hands as he fiddled with the poker. "I keep on thinking of Edward and Mrs Simpson."

"What are you two talking about?" Elizabeth said. She put her sherry on the mantelpiece next to the German clock.

"Edward and Mrs Simpson," they both said.

"Poor Teddy, such a weak man."

"He married the woman he loved," David said. "*Amor omnia vincit.*"

Elizabeth drank her sherry. "What does that mean? I'm afraid I've forgotten."

"It means, Mother, love conquers all."

"Do you believe that, David?" Elinor said.

"Yes, Elinor, I do."

"But Mrs Simpson was twice divorced," Elizabeth said.

"I don't think that matters at all, Mrs Andersen," Elinor said.

"Well, I do."

"Don't you think people should get divorced?"

"No, Elinor, I don't. Marriage is a sacrament."

"Even when one of the partners might be very unhappy?"

"How's your glass, Elinor?" David said.

She held it out. "Glenfiddich was always the best."

"Do you often drink whisky, Elinor?" Elizabeth asked.

"Not often, Mrs Andersen. Only at coronations."

Someone turned the radio up and the Fairey Aviation Works band thundered.

"*Land of Hope and Glory,*" Richard Andersen announced. "It still sends shivers down my spine."

"Land of soap and borax," Elinor sang, but David took her arm and they sat and listened to the radio.

The bells of St Paul's, St Martin-in-the-Fields and

352

Southwark Cathedral pealed, the crowds cheered the Horse Guards and the Household Cavalry, the drums rolled and the BBC announcers intoned. Charles Bryant opened the first bottle of champagne. The glasses were passed to celebrate the great event and David and Elinor listened. David thought of her over him, her breasts hanging. *You own me.*

"I hate to say this," Elizabeth said, "but I still think Margaret Rose is the prettier of the two, though her sister has far more character."

"I think she'll make a damned fine Queen," Richard Andersen said. "It's what we want, some moral leadership, some guts to fight the enemy. We've got a crisis on our hands."

"A crisis?" Charles Bryant said.

They drank the champagne, the beer and the whisky, ate the savouries and listened to the sounds of the Coronation.

"Oh to be in England," Elizabeth said.

"Ask David," Richard said, "he's fought the buggers."

"Well, David?" Charles said, as Elinor watched him.

David looked at her downy arms, her cardigan, her legs and the buttons at her throat and thought of the sea running over her bare feet. "What are you asking me?" he said.

Elinor touched his arm. "Charles is asking you if there's a crisis."

"It seems there's a permanent crisis, but it's the puzzles that concern me." He thought of Brownlee lying in the ice. *He didn't die in vain, sir.* David drank his whisky. The military bands played, a million voices cheered and he heard the sounds of *A Trumpet Voluntary.* The fire smoked, he was getting weary and wanted to be in her arms: he wanted to be within her and he wanted to hear the birds calling through the pines.

"What kind of puzzles?" Charles said.

"Moral puzzles."

"I don't think there are moral puzzles," Richard

353

Andersen said as he raised his glass. "I think it's all bloody straightforward."

"How is it straightforward?" Elinor said.

"It's them and us, isn't it?"

The church bells pealed, the drums rolled and sounds of jubilation came from the radio.

"They're riding down the Mall, Prince Philip is with her and we'll soon have a new Queen," Elizabeth said.

"How is it straightforward, Mr Andersen?" Elinor asked.

"There's good and bad, isn't there?" David's father was drunk now and he clutched the table. "There's rules, isn't there?"

"For God's sake, Richard," his wife said, "why don't you be quiet, this is the Coronation."

"Excuse me," her husband said, "excuse me," and left the room.

The choristers sang, the Archbishop of Canterbury took the service before the lords, barons, earls and assembled dignitaries, the trumpets echoed, the Queen was crowned and Elizabeth Andersen wept. *Long live the Queen.*

"I'm sorry about Richard," she said. "Would anyone care for tea?"

"I'll make it," Elinor said.

"But you won't know where anything is."

"I'm sure I can manage."

David wondered if he should offer to help her in the kitchen, but remained by the fire. "If you want a hand," he said, "give me a call."

"I shall, David, I shall."

"Well, Elizabeth," Charles said, "it's been your day."

"It has and it hasn't." She wondered about David and Elinor: they hadn't spoken much and she was comforted.

"I suppose the whole of Australia's been up listening."

"I'm sure they have." Charles spoke to David: "Would there have been big celebrations at the military college?"

"I've no doubt. Lots of port passed to the left, speeches

and toasts." Had Tom's parents gone up to London? He supposed they had.

"I think I'll see how Elinor's coping," Elizabeth said. "Please excuse me."

Both men got to their feet and then faced each other.

"Where did you stay in Melbourne?" Charles said.

"I stayed with a friend, a school friend, the old-boy network, you know."

"What have you got in mind?"

"I think I told you: stockbroking, something in money. Would you like another drink?" David said.

"No thanks. It was an important evening for your mother – she takes these things very seriously."

David thought about Major Kim and the message for King George.

"I know she does." I'm in love with Elinor, he thought, and I'm going to take her away from you.

"I'm not sure what your grandfather would have thought of the evening," Charles said.

"In what way?"

"Well, he was a Scot and the Scots don't like the Sassenachs, do they?"

"I suppose not." When would she tell him? They were committed now: it was like running across the open ground toward the sniper's hut. Resolution, wasn't there a battleship with that name?

"Do you ever regret having fought?"

"No," David said, "not for one instant. No, I don't."

"And would you fight again?"

"Oh yes, of course."

Charles Bryant thought David Andersen was a most formidable young man and watched Elinor as she came in with the tea.

"Long live the Queen," Elinor said, "long live the Queen."

Both men laughed and Elizabeth smiled and David went to help her. She was graceful as she served and his heart leapt. *What did we until we loved?* He thought of her on the slopes of Mount Napier: there was no retreat now.

*　　*　　*

David waited for the train at Spencer Street Station. The afternoon was dull and rainy and a pall of mist and smoke lay over the city. The locomotives hissed and steamed, the gangers and fettlers worked on the lines with their picks and crowbars, the rain dripping down their grimy, broad-brimmed hats. The train was late and David walked up and down the platform in his raincoat; several people bumped into him and children ran around his legs, but no one knew him. He walked to the edge of the parapet and looked down on Spencer Street at the taxi cabs and motor trucks jammed up at the intersections, the exhaust rising. Melbourne looked formidable and uncomfortable. The Victorian buildings and church spires towered. For the third time in his life he wanted a stiff drink, but Elinor would have the Glenfiddich with her. As the trains came in, the crowds pushed and jostled and rushed to greet their loved ones. The afternoon was growing cold and the soot settled.

He felt a hand gripping his shoulder.

"Hullo," she said. She was wearing a camel coat and felt hat and dumped her attaché case down.

"I didn't see you arrive."

"You were on the wrong platform."

"I'm sorry."

"It doesn't matter. Isn't it stupid catching separate trains?"

"Necessary," David said.

"Where are we staying?"

"The Carlton."

"Well, come on then," Elinor said, "let's go to the Carlton. What's it like?"

"Three stars, quite comfortable."

"Aren't there lots of Italians?"

356

"That's why I chose it, nobody will know us there, and we can eat spaghetti," David said.

"And drink lots of red wine."

The rain gusted her coat and hair and David thought she looked beautiful. She picked up her suitcase and started for the taxi rank.

"I'll take that for you," David said.

"Don't be silly, I want to get to our room." Elinor jumped the queue and flagged a taxi down.

* * *

"David," Elinor said, "this is fine, we can see over the street, but the plastic flowers are a bit much." She pushed the vase to one side, then shoved it behind the curtains. She looked out of the window at the people hurrying in the rain and the lights gleaming. "Look," she said. "There's a restaurant we can try." Elinor threw off her coat and sat on the bed. "What did you say to the man at the desk?"

"I said we were Mr and Mrs Andersen."

"There's a small hotel with a wishing well." She lay on the bed, still wearing her hat. "Would you remove your raincoat, please?"

David did as requested and knelt by the bed. He was hard and wanted her. "Well, Elinor Bryant?" he said.

"Well, David Andersen?"

"We're in Melbourne, but I'm not quite sure why."

"You know damned well why. We're here to live together."

"For a short time."

"But a short time's better than no time at all, isn't it? We can eat out, walk in the parks and go shopping. We can do all manner of things. It's a beautiful Victorian city." She laughed. "It's the Paris of the southern hemisphere, and I want you to lie beside me."

He took off his jacket and boots, lay on the bed and they took each other in their arms. She threw her hat to the floor.

357

They heard voices outside in the corridor, a door slamming and Elinor said: "David, I want you to make love to me."

They undid each other's buttons, kissed, shrugged off their clothes until the bed was littered and both were naked. There she lay, her legs gripping, her breasts bare and her fingers within his.

"I want to kiss you," David said.

"Do you? Where?"

"On your body."

"Where on my body?"

"Your breasts."

"Where else?"

"Your belly."

"Where else?"

"Between your legs."

"You may. I'd like you to kiss me now."

Elinor opened her legs and watched him as he crouched. Then she felt his lips on her nipples and on her belly: he was very gentle, because he loved her. He kissed her breasts again, her ribs, her nipples, he kissed her mount, her thighs and she felt his lips upon her, then his tongue, his tongue again, his lips, then his teeth gripping. She opened up as he sucked the juices from her body; he was loving and patient, she arched her back, felt him pause, prayed he wouldn't stop, then felt his tongue again, his teeth; she began to cry softly, her haunches rising and falling as he took her with his tongue and teeth, his hand opening her wide for all the world to see. Christ, she bucked like a horse, cried, cried out again and closed her legs so he was trapped in her loving dark where secret tides and rivers ran. David kissed her on the mouth and comforted her.

"So that's what I taste like?" she said.

"That's what you taste like, and I love you."

She drifted into sleep and he with her, that late rainy afternoon; outside, the street lights gleamed, the traffic ran along the boulevards, the chimneys smoked, the bells tolled, the pigeons fluttered to the architraves of the grimy buildings,

and far away toward the peak of Mount Napier, the eagle
flew.

*   *   *

They walked down Collins Street as the winter sun shone.
The tram bells clanged and the traffic ran: a brewer's truck
and Clydesdales clattered past; a light breeze blew her dress
and hair and they stopped in front of the shop windows
and looked at the glittering merchandise. Starlings and
pigeons flew and flags drifted from the roof of the Parlia-
ment building. They strolled and dodged the errand boys.
Commissionaires wearing war medals stood in the ornate
doorways. Elinor and David considered the jewellery, the
bespoke suits, the walking sticks, the riding gear and the
dresses from London and Paris. Now and again, their hands
touched as they ambled in the cold sunlight. It was good
to be in Melbourne, where no one knew them.

"David Andersen," a man's voice called. "Long time, no
see."

David looked up to see Jack Gage standing with two
other men on the top step of the Melbourne Club. He was
wearing a pinstripe suit and a waistcoat. He bounded down
the steps and took David's hand.

"Hullo, Jack," David said. Jack looked at Elinor as she
stood on the flagstones, the breeze billowing her dress.
"Elinor Sheffield, Jack Gage," David said. "We were mates
at school."

Jack smiled and bowed. "My pleasure," he said.

She, too, smiled and said: "How do you do, Mr Gage."

"How's the army?" Jack said. "Are you on leave?"

"I've resigned my commission."

"Is that so? When?"

"Not long after I got back from Korea."

"Korea?"

"The war."

"Ah, of course."

359

"If you don't mind, David," Elinor said, "I want to go down to George's to collect something. May I be excused? It was nice to meet you, Mr Gage."

"As I said, it was my pleasure." Jack bowed again and watched her walk away through the shoppers. "Wow," he said, "where did you meet her? You're a sly old devil."

"She's just a friend, she lives in the District. I met her in town by chance."

"Come on," Jack said, "she's mad about you. I can tell, I'm an expert, it's in the air." He grinned. "You should pursue that, but maybe you don't need to. Lucky bugger."

David wondered how long Jack had been watching them from the top of the club steps. "What have you been doing?" he said.

"I've just finished my articles and been offered a share in a practice and put up for the Melbourne Club." Jack Gage had put on weight and looked suntanned and prosperous.

"Lucky you. Congratulations."

"Are you living in Melbourne? We must have lunch."

"I'm living in Penshurst, I don't get up here very much."

"Where are you staying then? It's been a long time, we could have a drink tonight. I know several places we can go. There's the Club, I could get you in there."

"I'm sorry, Jack," David said, "I'd like to but I'm tied up this evening with an ancient aunt of mine and I'm going back in the morning."

"I didn't know you had an aunt in Melbourne. You never mentioned her."

"Yes I have," David said. He laughed. "Your memory's going."

"How long's the train trip?"

"About five hours."

"That's too bad. Have you got a minute now to meet my new partners?"

"Don't think I'm being rude, Jack, but I'd better be going. These trips to town are pretty rushed affairs."

"That's a pity." Jack took out his wallet: it was old leather and he thumbed through it. "Here's my card, drop me a note next time you're coming and we can do the town and take in a show. Bring your friend, Elinor Sheffield, and I'll bring one of mine." He grinned. "I'm playing the field, but it doesn't look as though you need to."

David stuck out his hand. "It was good seeing you, Jack."

"Likewise." They shook hands. "Look after yourself, sport."

*   *   *

"He seemed a pleasant chap," she said as they drank their tea.

David ate his ham sandwich. "We were best friends at school. Jack was the school boxing champion and he's now a solicitor." He looked around at the people at the tables, but it seemed there was no one who knew him. "He's just been put up for the Melbourne Club."

"A handsome man, who'll go far." Elinor laughed. "For God's sake, David, don't look so serious."

"Sorry, I was a bit unnerved seeing Jack."

"There's nothing wrong in seeing old school friends." She put her cup down and touched his arm. "It's pleasurable, but we can't stay in the hotel room all the time."

"Jack was rather taken with you."

"Good, I like being admired. He's a nice man, very gallant. Do you think we could have more tea?"

David looked for the waitress but she had gone. "I wonder what Jack will say about us."

"For God's sake, David, what would he say? He'll say he's seen you in Collins Street with a pretty girl."

"He'll remember your name."

"Who did you say I was?"

"Elinor Sheffield."

"My maiden name." She took his arm and shifted her chair.

361

"Yes. He said next time I'm up we should go to a show, do the town."

"I'd like that. What's on?"

"I don't think we should go to a show."

"Why not? What's on?"

"I don't know. *Kismet*, I think."

"The negative fate." Elinor raised her hand at the waitress. "Do you believe in the negative fate?"

David thought. "Yes, I think I do."

"I love you, darling," Elinor said, "but you're a terrible pessimist."

"Can we leave?" David said. "The winter sun is shining."

"What do you want to do?"

"I want to walk with you. I want to go shopping and sit in the park; we haven't got much time."

"When this is all finished and done," Elinor said, "we may have all the time in the world."

She got up, smoothed her dress and several women looked at her. David paid the bill and they went out into the sunlight, shining through the trees. He bought a newspaper and looked for news of the Korean war, but there was none.

* * *

Suddenly, it was threatening to rain and they sat in the Treasury Gardens.

"My God," David said, "this is an incredible climate, I'll never understand it. Four seasons in one day."

He thought of *Kismet* and the negative fate: they watched the people walking home along the pavement, at the end of the day. The gardens were empty: even the pigeons were gone and the black clouds bundled from the southwest. They thought of Port Victoria and the sea rolling in on the bay.

"I want a child by you, David," Elinor said, "I've told you."

He took her hands. "We can't yet, it's impossible."

"Yes we can: it's quite possible, I stopped taking precautions. I hate the damned thing anyway, I want you in my womb, David. I want to be seen carrying your baby, I want to be big with you, I want the world to know."

A couple was walking arm in arm by the greenhouse and David watched them. "That would be insane."

"Do *you* want your baby inside me?"

"I've thought about it."

"All right then," Elinor said, "we'll go public. Bugger the lot of them."

"What about Charles?"

"He's had me for two years, he's got no rights over me. We've discussed all that."

"Charles is a good man," David said.

"You're a good man, David."

"So, one morning, you say to Charles at breakfast: 'I'm in love with David Andersen and I'm going to have his baby.'"

"Something like that."

"It would kill him."

"He'd probably kill me," Elinor said.

"Charles is not the killing type."

"I'm not sure: most men are killers if provoked hard enough."

"I've killed," David said. He looked for the loving couple through the trees, but they had gone.

"That was under duress, you were fighting for your life."

"So will Charles."

"Good-day, sir," a voice said.

David turned around and saw Sergeant Hart standing behind the seat. Two ghosts on the same day: he was being pursued now. Hart was in civvies, but his face was the same and he seemed very tall as he stood over them. David rose and faced the veteran. "Good afternoon, Hart," he said, "this is a surprise. What are you doing in Melbourne?"

He looked at Elinor huddled in her coat. "Like you, sir, I've given the army away."

"This is Miss Sheffield," David said. "Elinor, this is Sergeant Hart."

"Pleased to meet you." The big sergeant grinned as the spots of rain fell.

"So you've resigned?" David said.

"I sure have. Twelve years was a long time, so I give it away."

Hart stood there, his hands in his old overcoat pockets, and David thought of some job he could give him to do: he thought of the road to Chasan. "What brings you here?" he said.

"Aw, I thought I'd travel around a bit with me pay-off, I never been outside New South Wales, except to the islands and Korea of course." He fished into his inside pocket and dragged out his rolling tobacco. "What are you doing, sir?"

"I'm managing my father's farm."

The two men stood and talked while Elinor listened. So this was Hart. What was he doing here? She shivered in the cold and wished they could find somewhere to sit; she wanted to get away from this strange, ugly man. But Hart stood like a barren tree in the middle of the pathway.

"Is that so?" he said. "Would there be any jobs going there?"

"I'm afraid not, things are a bit difficult at the moment."

"Go on? I heard the farmers are making a fortune out of the war. I was born and raised on a farm. Remember?"

Hart looked again at Elinor, and then back to David. "What do you do, miss?"

"I'm a school teacher in the country."

"Good on you. I didn't know the holidays were on now, it must be different in Victoria." Hart lit his cigarette and blew the smoke from his nostrils into the cold air. "Funny seeing you here, sir. I said to meself, that can't be Mr Andersen."

The sun was disappearing behind the office buildings and

churches as the trains rumbled. It was getting dark and the city was becoming silent.

"Miss Sheffield and I are going to a meeting," David said.

"A meeting?"

David looked at his watch and then at Elinor. "We don't want to be late."

But Hart stood. "Are you here long? We could have a beer and talk about old times." He grinned again at Elinor. "We could go to the ladies' lounge, miss."

"I'm going back to Penshurst in the morning," David said.

"Are you? How far is it?"

"About three hundred miles."

"Aw, that's a cock's stride by New South Wales standards. I might drift down there. I reckon I've got to pick something to do. If I do, I'll call in, okay?"

"That would be fine," David said, "but things are a bit grim in the Western District."

"I think I'll survive." Hart tossed the cigarette butt into the flowerbed. "Have you heard what happened to Cashie?"

"No."

"He got a mention in Kapyong and he's now a full corporal. I never thought the little bastard had it in him. Sorry, miss."

David shifted on the pathway. "All right, Hart, it's been good seeing you. Try Gippsland, I've heard there's work over there. Good luck." He extended his hand and felt Hart's bony fingers gripping his.

"I might run into you again, sir," Hart said, "you never know, do you?"

"That's right. Well, cheerio then."

David took Elinor by the arm and they walked away to the street, leaving Hart standing in the park. The rain blew in their faces.

"So that's Hart," Elinor said as they walked down Bourke Street.

"That's Hart. My God, that's him. What on earth is he doing here? And if he turns up at Penshurst, I don't know what will happen."

"Will he turn up?"

"God knows. It's on the cards, he's a loner and he's tough. That man's bad news."

"What can he do?"

"Cause trouble, say he's seen us in Melbourne."

"They're going to know sooner or later."

"It's not only when they know," David said, "it's how they know."

"What's the time?" Elinor said.

"Half-past five."

"Let's have a drink."

"The pubs will be crowded, they close at six."

"I know that," she said. "Let's go down to the 'Australia', they've got a little bar, I went there once."

They sat in a cubicle and heard the noise from the public bar. "I never drank Scotch until I met you," David said.

"Another rule broken?"

"No, something new."

"Enjoyable?"

"With you, yes."

"Is all this madness?"

"All what?"

"Us."

"No, it's no madder than going on patrol or running across paddy fields."

"I'm not sure I like the comparison," Elinor said.

"Fear," David said.

"You're frightened, then?"

"That was the wrong word. Commitment. It's like the night Tom and I went down into that village in the mountains. There's no going back."

"I love you, David, you know that? This is not just some illicit week, nor was Port Victoria."

"I know that. Do you really want to have a child?"

"By you, yes, only by you. Do you?"

"Yes."

"Let's not go back," she said, "let's stay here."

"You know that's not on. We've both got tidying up to do. Leave with a clean slate."

"You're right. Are you hungry?"

"I could do with something, after our friend Hart."

"There's that restaurant near the hotel," Elinor said.

"Right, we'll go there."

Before they left, they bought a bottle of wine to drink in their room.

"I wonder where your child is," David said.

"He's either alive or dead, and if he's alive, I hope he's happy."

"Will you ever get over it?"

"Who knows? Probably not. It's like you and the Chinese sniper: you carry tragedy with you as long as you live."

"We're going to get married, aren't we?" David drank the wine as she lay on the bed.

"Oh yes, there's no doubt about that."

"So you tell Charles, I tell my parents and we start with a clean slate?"

"Yes. Do you want to come to bed now and hope it's never morning?"

"Yes," David said. "Yes, I do."

Jack Gage was not seen again, nor was Hart. The weather held fine: they picnicked at Brighton, strolled through the Botanical Gardens, visited the art gallery, saw Ingrid Bergman in *Spellbound* and took the train to the beaches on the peninsula. Each night they went to bed early, and at the end of the week David saw her off at the railway station. It was agreed: there would be no retreat now.

17

Mount Napier

"There's no doubt," Elinor said, "no doubt at all."

They sheltered behind the stone wall away from the wind that blew from the south. "What do you think?"

"It's what you wanted."

"I asked you what you thought."

"It's until death us do part, isn't it?"

"No, it's for as long as we last."

"We look like lasting a long time."

"If you're wondering about Charles, it happened when we made love in Melbourne."

"When are you going to tell him?"

"Tonight maybe, I'll choose my time."

"Do you want me there?"

"No, I'll do it on my own."

"Where are we going to live?"

"It's got to be Melbourne, hasn't it? You can get a job there."

"That won't be hard," David said, "there's a boom on, thanks to the war, and there's the old-boy network."

"What will the old boys think of us?"

"Some will look down their noses; others, like Jack Gage, won't give a stuff. The people around here will probably drum us out of town. I might have a sword broken over my shoulder. Charles is the one I'm worried about." David looked down the slopes at the livestock grazing. "He's been good to you, beware of the fury of a patient man."

"Charles is my problem."

"He's mine too, he might come after me with a shotgun."

"Christ," Elinor said, "this is like two farmers fighting

over a prize ewe serviced by the wrong ram. What will your father say?"

"He'll roar and bluster and worry about being president of the golf club."

"And your mother?"

"What do you think?"

"Memories of Rose Braddon, but I think she's tougher than we think. All the best country families have their scandals."

"They can't kill us," David said.

"No, they can't do that."

They walked down the track toward the pines; it was starting to rain and David took off his jacket and put it around her shoulders. He looked back and it was then that they saw a man about a hundred yards away watching them. He dashed to the spot and peered through the trees and shadows; the grass was trampled but the man had gone.

"Who was that?" Elinor said.

David kept looking and glancing, but nothing was to be seen. It was like being on patrol.

"I'm not sure," he said, "I'm not sure."

They didn't make love that cold day.

*　　*　　*

His mother was standing by the empty fireplace and the wind scattered the ashes on the carpet. It was raining hard now and the room was dark.

"There was a long-distance call for you while you were out," she said. She was white-faced and her knitting lay on the floor.

"Who was it?"

"A friend of yours called Hart. He was phoning from Melbourne."

"What did he say?"

"He said he'd seen you in Melbourne and that you had

said there might be a job here; he sounded rather rough. Apparently you were in the army together."

David stood, motionless, by the door. "He was my sergeant," he said. "He's left the army, and I met him one day in Collins Street. He was looking for work and I told him there was nothing in Penshurst."

"Mr Hart also had a message," his mother said.

"What was that?"

"He said to say good day to Miss Elinor Sheffield."

David stood silent. "I seem to remember," his mother said, "that Sheffield was Elinor Bryant's maiden name."

"Was it?"

"Yes, David, it was." She stared at him. "Elinor Bryant was with you in Melbourne, wasn't she?"

"Yes, she was, and it's none of your damned business."

"Yes it is, David, oh yes it is."

"I'm in love with her."

"In love with her? It's lust, my boy, lust: you're an adulterer and she's a harlot. My God, when Charles hears of this. . . ."

"And you intend to tell him?"

"No, David, I do not, but I take it that his unfaithful wife will. Will she not?"

"Yes."

"You've seen her today, then?"

"Yes."

"Where?"

"Mount Napier."

"Why Mount Napier?"

"We like the view."

"I think you like more than that," his mother said. "How long has this thing been going on? I warned you."

"Since February."

"Five months. You're like your father: you're furtive, dishonest, a transgressor, a thief." His mother's blue eyes gleamed. "Do you remember Rose Braddon?"

David thought. "Yes, of course."

"Do you know what happened to her?"

"She died."

"Of course she died, but do you know how?"

"No."

"She tried to abort herself, and do you know who was the culprit?"

"No.'

"Your father." His mother waited. "Well, what do you have to say?"

"Nothing."

"You're worse than your father. At least that poor girl wasn't married; you're a thief as well. Thou shalt not covet thy neighbour's wife, or have you forgotten?"

"Rose Braddon was a long time ago, Mother."

"So you think time corrects sins and transgressions? It's in the blood, young man, it's in the Andersen blood."

"What?"

"You know damned well, adultery, you're all tainted, the three generations, your grandfather, your father and now you."

"You will not talk about my grandfather," David said.

"I'll talk about whom I like. You're like both of them: sly, lascivious. You're a deep one, aren't you? The proud, young soldier with a mention, the school's most outstanding cadet: you've got no idea how proud I was, but now I find you deceiving and wallowing. I hope to God the girl's not pregnant."

"What girl?"

"Elinor. Don't be obtuse with me."

"No."

"How do you know?"

"I just know."

"Has she told you she's not?"

"Yes."

"How do you know she's not lying?"

"Elinor doesn't lie."

"Well if she is, she can go to the best to get rid of it, can't

371

she? She won't die like that other poor girl. Have you thought what this will do to Charles Bryant?"

"Of course I have, we both have."

"Oh no you haven't, you've taken your illicit pleasure and haven't thought at all. If Charles takes a gun to you, I won't blame him at all."

"Is it eye for eye, tooth for tooth, then?" David said.

"Yes," Elizabeth Andersen said, "in your case, that's it. Did anyone see you today in your loving tryst?"

"No." David paused and said: "Who told you we were riding together?"

"You've been seen, people talk."

"So I'm being watched? Who's watching me?"

"You need to be watched, David, just like your father and your grandfather."

David moved toward the sideboard and took out the bottle of whisky. "I've told you, you will not talk about my grandfather."

"Won't I?" his mother said. "You three are all the same. Look at you, reaching for the whisky. She drinks it too, she drinks like those men in hotels, I watched her that night of the Coronation."

David swallowed the Glenfiddich. "Are you going to tell my father?"

"Oh no, you'll have to tell him." Elizabeth laughed. "Two old campaigners together."

"Elinor and I are going to get married, Mother."

"Are you? Are you forgetting she's married already? Who do you think you are, the Prince of Wales?"

"Mrs Simpson was divorced."

"It's the same thing. They have brothels for soldiers, don't they? Did you vent your lust on poor Asiatic girls? I know what soldiers are like. They sleep with anything."

"Jesus bloody Christ," David said.

Elizabeth sprang across the room and slapped his face. "You will not blaspheme, go to your woman, go to your

whore, compare notes with your father. God help us all."
The door slammed and he heard her footsteps on the tiled
hall.

*   *   *

David sat in the armchair and drank the whisky. Where
was his father? He was probably getting pissed at the golf
club. He thought about lighting the fire and remembered
finding the wood at Port Victoria. He suddenly wished he
was with Tom Fleetwood, he wished he was on the banks
of the Imjin. He thought of Hart. *Christ, sir, you're a mess.*
If he met the bastard again, he would kill him. And what
was Elinor doing? What was she saying to Charles? Then
he thought of the war: a truce must be signed soon, neither
side could win. He remembered Trumper's and "The Grenadier": he and Tom could have been chasing debs now and
dining at the Café Royale. The room was cold and he drank
more whisky; the possums scuttled in the ceiling and the
rain beat on the casements. Maybe he should walk up the
winding road on Mount Rouse to the fire-spotter's hut?
But it was too late and too cold. His grandfather would
have known what to do. *I'm proud of you, old son.* Tom
Fleetwood had died of wounds. David got up with his glass
and looked at the tennis court: not even sheep grazed there
now.

"Good evening," his father said at the door. "Where's
your mother?"

"She's in bed, I think."

"In bed? It's a bit early."

"She was rather tired."

"That's no good," his father said. He looked at the bottle.
"Having a go at the whisky, eh? You don't often do that.
Do you mind if I join you?"

"By all means," David said. His father was drunk,
but his hands were steady as he poured. "How was your
day?"

373

"I had time for a round of golf and a few drinks. How was yours?"

"I rode over to Mount Napier."

"Did you? It's good country over there; they're all as rich as Croesus. Lucky devils." Richard Andersen regarded his son. "You look a bit done in."

David thought. He didn't know his father well. What should he say to him? "I'm in love with Elinor Bryant."

"You're what?"

"I'm in love with Elinor Bryant."

"Jesus bloody Christ, you've gone mad, David, bloody mad. You mean you've gone to bed with her."

"Yes."

"Where? How did you arrange it?"

"That's hardly the point, Dad."

"You've been to Melbourne twice in the last couple of months, haven't you? You're a sly young bastard." Richard Andersen sat down. "How long has this affair been going on?"

"Over the past five months."

"Since you came home. She's a good-looker. Who knows? Does anyone in the district know?"

"Mother knows."

"What did she say?" But his father knew and remembered that morning in the garden.

"She said, 'Thou shalt not covet thy neighbour's wife.'"

"That's typical. Does Charles Bryant know?"

"Not yet, but Elinor will tell him."

Why should she tell him? Richard thought. "Why did you tell me? Why did you tell your mother?"

"I didn't tell her, she knew."

"How?"

"A man I fought with saw us in Melbourne and phoned."

His father reached for the bottle. "What's she like?"

"Who?"

"Elinor Bryant."

"I don't understand you," David said.

374

"What's she like in bed?"

"It's got nothing to do with you."

"I bet she's good. I watched her at the Coronation. Your mother won't tell Charles, I'll see to that; and I won't tell anybody. We can bottle the whole thing up, but you'd better shoot off to Melbourne, you can have the pick of the women there. Elinor may be good, but she can't be that good."

"You don't understand," David said. He was starting to hate his father now. "Elinor and I are in love."

"No, you're not, you just think you are. If I can be frank, it's a fuck on the side, we've all done that." Richard laughed. "Not that I blame you, but it's a bit close to home."

"Elinor's pregnant."

Richard stood up as the memories returned. "How do you know?"

"She told me."

"Jesus Christ, David, they all say that, it's the biggest weapon in their armoury. It's probably Charles's."

"It's my child, I know."

"Look, boy, you've been taken, hook, line and sinker. If it is yours, she can get rid of it; these things can be arranged, I know."

"Elinor and I are getting married," David said.

"You've both gone fucking mad. You can't. That means an unholy mess, that means divorce, it'll kill your mother and Charles Bryant will kill you." Richard Andersen stood over his son. "Listen, you stupid young bastard, tell her to get rid of it, and piss off to Melbourne, stick your cock up some tart who's got the sense to take precautions." His father was shaking now. "We've all got our reputations and, by Christ, you won't let this family down. Let me give you some advice: make sure the bitch gets rid of it whether it's yours or not. I can arrange that and next time you fuck, make sure you're at least three hundred miles away with somebody who can take care of herself."

David got up very fast, hit his father hard in the throat,

saw him fall across the table, heard him grunt as the whisky bottle fell. "You can thank God you're not Sergeant Hart," he said.

David went upstairs to his room as the rain fell hard and the pigeons warbled under the eaves. That night he had a bad dream: he dreamt he was standing with the two Chinese soldiers by the side of the tank on the road to Chasan, that Hart was raising his Sten and was about to machine-gun him.

*　　*　　*

The morning was cold and threatening to rain; the tanks were full once more and the water in the ditches overflowing. Mist lay in the valleys of the ranges, the May trees were bare and the leaves blew around his boots as David threw on the blanket and saddled his horse. The crows called from the fence posts and the towers of the house: two magpies swooped and the noise seemed deafening. He rode around the yard, looked at the outbuildings, the flagstone veranda, the station tower and the bluestone chimneys. No smoke drifted, only birds called and everybody was asleep.

David rode down the drive through the tunnel of trees, past the mail box and the rabbit wires and the Schultzes' old farm. The homestead and caravan had gone: where was Emil now? Tall thistles were growing rank and green in the home paddock and the fences were falling. Where was the husbandry? He thought of his father, his questions, his lust and his mother falling in the rose garden. He rode down the hill, past St James's Church, the parish hall and Schram's garage where the derelict Bedford trucks and tractors lay: it looked like a military gun-park and he rode carefully. Crows and seagulls were perched on the war memorial and the wreaths were dead. *In Memoriam.* He stopped and read: *T. R. Quicksilver, Tobruk, 1941.*

Across the park and the overgrown caravan sites, the

children's slides and the merry-go-round stood: there was no childish laughter and an early freight train rumbled. David rode down the Dunkeld road, past the hedge with its towers and buttresses and then turned left on to the road to Mount Napier. It seemed only the crows and parakeets saw him go.

Elinor was waiting with her gelding tethered to the fence beneath the pines. David dismounted, stood by his horse and said: "Have you told him?"

"Yes," she said, "I've told him."

"What did he say?"

Elinor stood under the trees in her mackinaw and jodhpurs; her face was white and she brushed her hair back. "He suspected, but was still appalled."

"What did he do?"

"He was playing Bach on the radiogram, I'll always remember that."

"Does he hate me?" David asked.

"No, he doesn't hate you, nor does he hate me. I think he sees a terrible tragedy. He wasn't surprised."

"Why?"

"He said he'd seen us talking, he said he'd seen us together."

"Has he been watching us?"

"No, I don't think so. He says he knew what might happen when you came to lunch and talked about the war."

"And then?"

"I told him that I was going to have your baby; I've never seen a man so close to tears."

"Not anger?"

"No, sorrow."

"It's to do with trespassing," David said. "I once asked Major Kim why the Chinese were in Korea and he said: 'When you see a burglar in your neighbour's house, you drive him out.'"

"Burglary is about property and I'm not property, least of all Charles's."

377

"Thou shalt not commit adultery," David said.

"That's your mother speaking. What did she say?"

"She knew, she was waiting for me."

"How did she know?"

"Do you remember Sergeant Hart that afternoon in Melbourne?"

"Of course." Elinor thought of the big man standing on the path like some ugly tree.

"He phoned from Melbourne while I was with you and left a message for you."

"What was his message?"

"Just to say, good-day."

"Treachery," Elinor said, "when the cock crows twice."

"If I see that man again," David said, "I'll kill him."

"I'm sure you will. What did your mother say?"

"She said adultery ran in the blood: my grandfather, my father and me; Rose Braddon is still with us, sixteen years of fury, she hates you, she hates me."

"My God. And your father?"

"I'd rather not tell you."

"He ran true to form then?"

"He did, the whole thing was reduced to casual fucking and your having an abortion."

"I told you," Elinor said, "this is a crime worse than murder."

"I hit him," David said.

"Hard?"

"Very, I'm an expert, I've done it before."

Elinor came up to him and stood close; she smelt of the country.

"Did you hurt him?"

"Of course I did, I meant to."

Elinor stood by her gelding as the rain clouds drifted from the west.

"We're on our own now," Elinor said.

"We are."

"Where do you want to go?"

"I want to ride south," David said. "I want to smell the sea."

They swung up, nudged their horses and rode through the damp, rolling country: they rode past barns, iron sheds, rusting silos, stands of pine and untended hedges. Once or twice, David glanced back but they were alone.

*   *   *

At mid-day they came to a ruined settlement, a place of vacant bluestone buildings, fallen walls, empty cottages, a church and a graveyard. Cypresses, oaks and aspens grew among the gums; streets had been planned, trees felled and a donkey engine lay, rusting in the grass. Frogs croaked in the weedy dam and crows and parakeets watched them from the old brittle branches. The salty wind blew.

"This looks like a planned settlement," Elinor said.

David looked at the ruins. "I think it was a plan that failed."

"Do you want to stop here?" Elinor said.

"Yes, I do, I can smell the sea." David watched the gulls as they wheeled and flew. "It's the southern ocean."

He thought of the sandbanks of the South China Sea and the wreckage of boats, drifting. Elinor opened the saddle bag and he put his arms around her. She laughed. "This place is like California; it's cold and it's damp."

"What will Charles do?"

"He will listen to his music, read his books, ride with his dogs, look after his farm and grieve."

"Will he come after me?"

"No, David, he won't do that. Do you remember his questions about soldiers and the war?"

"Yes."

"Charles is against killing."

She sat between his legs and he put his hands on her breasts; he kissed her hair and ears. "My Christ," she said, "I love you, you're in my body, do you know that?"

379

"Yes, I do."

"There's nothing more I want," she said as she played with his fingers.

The horses whinnied and stamped, David froze, got up and looked through the broken buildings. "There's someone here," he said.

Elinor sat still in silence. "Are you sure?"

"I'm sure, I know the signs. You stay here while I have a look around."

"It could be a swaggie, it could be anybody."

"We'll see," David said. "Don't move, I shan't be long." She watched him move carefully across the grass toward the rock piles and stone walls. She shivered as she saw him disappear.

Keep to the high ground. But there was no high ground here. David sniffed the air: was that tobacco? The wind blew through the buildings and piles of rubble; it blew through the long grass and oak trees. He stood still, felt defenceless and wished he had his Sten. Maybe this was a bad dream, maybe he was imagining it. It could be an animal or a farmer, but then he saw a shadow move behind the stone church, his flesh crept and he knew he was not. What should he do? He could go back to Elinor and they could simply ride away; he moved a few steps toward the church and stopped again. David was in the middle of open ground and the man could be armed. He thought again of returning to Elinor: this was the Australian countryside, not the hills of Pakchon. Then a flock of pigeons fluttered from the eaves of the building and he was certain someone was there. Why wouldn't the man come into the open? He had to find out this time. *You've got to fight again tomorrow.*

David ran to the stone wall, vaulted it, crouched behind a pile of burnt and rotting timber, ran forward and stopped: he saw a man with a rifle slipping inside the church. Was it Charles Bryant? *Charles is against killing.* He stood up straight and strode over the damp turf. Everything seemed very clear: wild flowers growing in the heaps of rubble; convolvulus had smothered the remains of a bark and wattle hut; the bell tower was fallen; the roof had collapsed; the windows were vacant and the thistles grew tall in the small graveyard. He reached the threshold, saw the broken spiders' webs drifting and stepped inside. A man was standing on the flagstones at the far end of the building. It was Lawless.

* * *

Elinor heard the sound of shotgun fire: it echoed through the pines, then all was silent. She stood up; the wind had died and nothing moved. Her horse sneezed and a flock of pigeons raced across the clearing, their wings cracking. She looked out for David, but there was no sign; her horse sneezed again and flicked away a fly. David's horse seemed very calm, but she didn't know how well it knew him. The minutes passed as she waited for his tall, familiar figure, but he didn't appear. She thought of Charles, the man David had seen in the pines yesterday, and she thought of Hart. But he was 300 miles away in Melbourne. Some crows flew in and settled in the oak trees. Elinor remembered her teacher at St Catherine's: was it a *murder* of crows? At last, she walked carefully toward the stone wall and the buildings beyond.

She found David's tracks and the imprint of his riding boots and, like him, vaulted the wall and crouched by the pile of timber. All was still and she looked at the church and the headstones in the graveyard. The weeds were tall and wild flowers grew. Nobody was about. She drew in her breath and called his name three times, but no answer came. A fly settled on her face and she brushed it away; her hands were cold and her legs were shaking. Again, she called out, waited a minute, then walked between the headstones toward the church. At the door, she smelt the whiff of gunpowder, the spiders' webs clung to her hair and she

381

went inside. David was lying on the bloodied flagstones, his chest broken and his eyes like glass. Elinor vomited, sobbed, lifted his head, his blood streaking her jodhpurs; she tried to drag him outside, but he was too heavy for her. Elinor sobbed until she thought her body would break; she crouched in the church like some wounded animal, then got to her knees, ran through the wet grass and reached the clearing. She grabbed the lead rope of David's horse, swung up and rode away.

*   *   *

David was buried next to his grandfather in the Penshurst cemetery on 27 July 1953. The headstone was simple.

David Kinross Andersen
Born 1929
Died 1953
Blessed are the Dead

The morning was cold and clear and the frost was still on the ground. The congregation was small and the pall-bearers were Richard Andersen, Charles Bryant, Sergeant Hart and Jack Gage. The coroner's finding at the inquest was that David Andersen lost his life at the hands of a person or persons unknown. Police enquiries were continuing, but all they knew was that the shells found on the flagstones were from a Winchester 12-bore shotgun. The Hamilton *Spectator* published an obituary entitled *War Hero Slain*, and a memorial service was to be held in Melbourne Grammar School Chapel.

The wreaths were laid, the prayers were said, the hymns were sung and the earth was tossed. The clouds were high and the parakeets flew in droves between the gums and pines. Elinor stood apart from the congregation; once she caught Elizabeth's gaze, but David's mother turned away. The vicar said that David had been a brave and courageous soldier who had fought against the forces of darkness, that the Lord giveth and the Lord taketh away. Twice, Richard Andersen stumbled on the rough ground and Hart steadied him. Then the flowers were thrown and the earth shovelled. As she turned away Elinor saw Lawless standing in the shade of a pine beyond the graveyard, but when she looked again, he had gone.

"There was something extraordinary about him, wasn't there?" a voice said. Elinor started and turned. It was Jack Gage in his business suit, his black shoes covered with dust.

"Hullo, Jack," Elinor said. She went to take his hand, but he kissed her. "Thanks for coming." She wondered if she should tell him about Lawless, but knew he wouldn't understand.

Jack put his arm around her shoulder and felt her shaking. "It was an honour."

"I'm carrying his child."

"That's good, isn't it?"

"Yes it is," Elinor said. She saw Charles coming up by himself from the graveside. "You must meet my husband."

"Does your husband know about the child?" Jack asked.

"Yes, he knows."

Elinor introduced them and they walked back to the car.

"I've often wondered why he chose to be a soldier," Charles said.

"Right from when I first met him," Jack said, "he believed in the rules, even if it meant going alone. I'm not sure about the forces of darkness, but David was a courageous man. And, if I might say so, a moral man, too." There was no reply and Jack said, "Does anyone know what happened?"

"No," Elinor said, "no one knows. It doesn't matter, it's over now."

"Would you like to come across for a drink?" Charles asked.

"That's kind of you, but no thanks. I've got to get back to Melbourne; it's a long drive over those plains."

"We hope we'll see you again," Charles said.

"Yes, you will.'

"Perhaps you'd stay with us?" Elinor said.

"I'd be delighted." Jack Gage took both her hands. "God speed. I'm sure that's what David would have said."

Charles took Elinor by the arm as Jack saluted from the car and drove off.

* * *

The small crowd straggled up the hill past the cypresses and yew trees. Hart was rolling a cigarette and talking to Richard and Elizabeth walked alone. Elinor thought of going up to her, but there was no point. They stood by the car, no one spoke to them and soon the cemetery was empty. The winter sun was higher now and Charles faced Elinor. "I want you to stay with me."

"And I with you. There's no doubt: it's over now."

"Do you want to be by yourself for a moment?" Charles asked. He wanted to forgive her.

"No," Elinor said, "let's go home."

As they drove past the haystacks and pines, Elinor looked at the drains and irrigation ditches: they were already full and the water-weed was spreading across the paddocks. She thought of David and Tom running through the paddies of Korea, of Major Kim and the young Korean woman. *Make the other fellow die for his country.*

"Have you *any* idea?" Charles said.

"No," Elinor said.

On the road to Mount Napier, they passed a man walking through the grass and scrub: it was Bert Lawless with his shotgun and dogs. Elinor sat still as Charles raised his hand. But the hunter did not acknowledge and strode toward the hill.

DISCARD